Singing Utopia

Voice in Musical Theatre

BEN MACPHERSON

OXFORD
UNIVERSITY PRESS

OXFORD
UNIVERSITY PRESS

Oxford University Press is a department of the University of Oxford.
It furthers the University's objective of excellence in research, scholarship,
and education by publishing worldwide. Oxford is a registered trade mark of
Oxford University Press in the UK and in certain other countries.

Published in the United States of America by Oxford University Press
198 Madison Avenue, New York, NY 10016, United States of America.

Library of Congress Cataloging-in-Publication Data
Names: Macpherson, Ben, author.
Title: Singing utopia: voice in musical theatre / Ben Macpherson.
Description: New York : Oxford University Press, 2024. |
Includes bibliographical references and index.
Identifiers: LCCN 2024026013 (print) | LCCN 2024026014 (ebook) |
ISBN 9780197557648 (paperback) | ISBN 9780197557631 (hardback) |
ISBN 9780197557679 (digital-online) | ISBN 9780197557655 (updf) | ISBN 9780197557662 (epub)
Subjects: LCSH: Musicals—History and criticism. |
Musicals—Analysis, appreciation. | Voice types (Singing)
Classification: LCC ML2054 .M22 2024 (print) | LCC ML2054 (ebook) |
DDC 782.1/4—dc23/eng/20240726
LC record available at https://lccn.loc.gov/2024026013
LC ebook record available at https://lccn.loc.gov/2024026014

DOI: 10.1093/9780197557679.001.0001

Paperback printed by Marquis Book Printing, Canada
Hardback printed by Bridgeport National Bindery, Inc., United States of America

For Lauren

Contents

List of Figures ix
Acknowledgements xi

Introduction: Songs for New Worlds 1

PART I. CULTURAL CONTEXTS

1. Reaffirmation and Rupture: Why This Is Not Opera 23
2. Decadent Appropriation: The Process and Politics of Singing Musical Theatre 54

PART II. CRITICAL APPROACHES

3. Two Voiceworlds, Three Choralities: Locating the Voice 97
4. Intermediate Vocalities: Between Speech and Song 131
5. Rediscovering Nostalgia: Whose Voice Is It, Anyway? 167

Conclusion: Keep Singing, Orpheus 199

Author's Note 207
Notes 209
Bibliography 245
Index 263

Figures

1.1 English musical comedy producer George Edwardes. Photographer unknown. NPGx194421. Reproduced under academic license. © National Portrait Gallery, London, England. 47

2.1 Evie Greene, Bassono Ltd., whole-plate glass negative, February 1915. NPGx80528. Reproduced under academic license. © National Portrait Gallery, London, England. 60

2.2 Speech-inflected delivery of the first male grouping (Top) with a lower laryngeal and legato delivery of the refrain 'If I loved you . . .' (Bottom) in 'Tell Me, Pretty Maiden'. Notated by the author from the *Florodora* vocal score, 1899. 62

2.3 'Chorus of the stage production *Florodora* as published in souvenir program'. Source: Billy Rose Theatre Division, The New York Public Library. *The New York Public Library Digital Collections*. 1900. https://digitalcollections.nypl.org/items/c62a2780-074c-0135-43ad-0cfd66933d76. Public domain. 63

2.4 Vivian Blaine (Miss Adelaide) and Sam Levene (Nathan Detroit) in the original production of *Guys and Dolls*, 46th St. Theatre, New York. Reproduced courtesy of Photofest. 76

2.5 The aural 'accommodation' of the 'dolls' in 'Marry the Man Today', as Sarah and Adelaide negotiate divergent vocal aesthetics throughout, ending the song with a shared vocal character. © Ben Macpherson. 83

2.6 Bert Williams, photography by Cavendish Morton. NPGx126389. Reproduced under academic license. © National Portrait Gallery, London, England. 89

3.1 Playbill for *Oklahoma!* St. James Theatre, New York, 1943. Reproduced courtesy of Photofest. 98

3.2 Moments of vocal intensity in 'The Pipes of Pan'. Notated by the author from *The Arcadians* vocal score, 1910. 108

4.1 Rex Harrison as Henry Higgins in *My Fair Lady*, 1956. Reproduced courtesy of Photofest. 132

4.2 George List's 'Chart for Classifying Forms Intermediate to Speech and Song' (1963). Reproduced courtesy of the Society for Ethnomusicology. 135

4.3 Scene from *Hamilton* (Lin-Manuel Miranda, downstage centre). Photograph © Joan Marcus. 156

5.1 The characteristics of vocal drag. © Ben Macpherson. 176

5.2 Ariana DuBose as Disco Donna. Photograph © Joan Marcus. 183

5.3 Venn diagram of nostalgic tendencies. © Ben Macpherson. 186

5.4 'Portraying' Cher in *The Cher Show*. In common with *Summer: The Donna Summer Musical*, *The Cher Show* also featured a 'trio' of actors to depict various stages of Cher's career. Photograph © Joan Marcus. 190

5.5 Comparative sonic visualization of Tina Turner and Adrienne Warren singing the first verse and refrain from 'River Deep, Mountain High'. © Ben Macpherson. 192

5.6 Conceptual and affective inputs which comprise 'simuloquism'. © Ben Macpherson. 196

Acknowledgements

Avoiding clichés of villages and raising children, this book has nevertheless taken a community of colleagues, students, friends, and patient family members to enable its writing. My thanks and gratitude are therefore offered to the following people. For their ongoing expertise, determined support, and ever-constructive criticism, Dominic Symonds and Millie Taylor have been central in helping shepherd a dense and interdisciplinary text into a readable volume. I could not have done this without their belief in the project. They have been aided and abetted by the expertise and rigour of Norm Hirschy and the team at Oxford. I circled Norm at various conferences for several years with the idea for this book; I am thrilled it is now a reality. My thanks to him, Laura, and their colleagues for patience and support throughout the process, along with Dominic Broomfield-McHugh, David Roeser and Elizabeth Wollman for their humbling reviews of this work.

I was privileged to share this process with several colleagues at the University of Portsmouth who were working on books of their own at the same time. My thanks, therefore, go to Matt Smith for the days spent reading each other's draft chapters—in completely divergent disciplinary areas—and making the pain bearable while having a laugh along the way. Thanks to Phoebe Rumsey and Kit Danowski for their patient listening and cheerleading via a joint document in which we shared progress on our respective drafts over a 100-day period during 2022. Thanks, too, to Vincent Adams, Walid Benkhaled, George Burrows, and Erika Hughes who have likewise always been good enough to listen, challenge, and cheerlead, and Nik Wakefield—particularly for his incisive questioning as chapter 2 was in development. I am likewise grateful to colleagues in the Faculty of Creative and Cultural Industries for their support, including Trevor Keeble, Deborah Sugg Ryan, and Joni Rhodes. In 2019, I was awarded a sabbatical to kick-start the process and later I received additional support to enable its completion. In particular, the inclusion of images in this book (and the cover image) would not have been possible without the financial support of my Faculty.

During the course of writing, I was awarded a British Academy/Leverhulme Small Research Grant (SG2122\210387). Serving several purposes, this funding facilitated the historical research that enabled me to listen to early voices, particularly of African American performers, from the late nineteenth and early twentieth centuries. Accessing sound archives at the British Library and elsewhere, I am pleased to include some of the historical case studies and specific comparisons found in chapters 1–4. I therefore acknowledge the support of the British Academy/Leverhulme Trust and extend my thanks to Grace, Stephen, and colleagues at the British Library, along with Doug, Giovanna, and colleagues at the New York Public Library. Thanks, too, to Joan Marcus, Stephen Stuempfle, and Kate Brucher of the Society of Ethnomusicology, and Derek at Photofest for the assistance, and for permission to use several of the images included in this book.

Konstantinos Thomaidis, Freya Jarman, Matt Lockitt, Cerys Coppins, Alex Purser, and Phoebe Ranger have likewise engaged in conversations and offered comments on drafts, or shown patience, active interest, and support throughout Particular thanks, too, to Paul Barker in this regard. Along the way, other colleagues and postgraduate students in various networks have listened, asked questions, or tried to understand; my thanks to all who are unnamed here but valued equally. Friends and family have given me time to think and space to write, with specific thanks to my dad, for last-minute support with some of the figures in this book. Much of the spine of this study was developed on sabbatical at home, through numerous lockdown situations during the Covid-19 pandemic, and through the brain fog and confusion that stemmed from two bouts of the virus during writing. An immeasurable debt of love and gratitude must therefore be extended to my wife Lauren; friend, sounding board, reader, editor, cheerleader, and expert coffee maker. I could not have done this without her patience, encouragement, and knowing when to suggest I take a break (and when to question my choice to do so).

The somewhat prolonged gestation of this monograph means it now contains some discussions that I have previously published elsewhere in different iterations, up to and including several conference papers. Parts of chapter 2 share ideas with chapters published in *The Routledge Companion to the Contemporary American Musical* (2019) and the collection *Blockbusters of the Victorian Theater, 1850–1910: Critical Essays* (2023), while chapter 4 contains elements of the article '"Eliza, where the devil are my songs?": Negotiating Text, Voice and Performance Analysis in Rex Harrison's Henry Higgins', *Studies in Musical Theatre* 3, no. 2 (2008), and chapter 5 draws on a review of Merrie Snell's *Lipsynching* featured in the *Journal of Interdisciplinary Voice Studies* 5, no. 2 (2020), along with a section based on the article 'Baudrillard on Broadway: Bio-musicals, the Hyperreal and the Cultural Politics of *simuloquism*', also published in *Journal of Interdisciplinary Voice Studies* 5, no. 1 (2020).

Introduction

Songs for New Worlds

Erik is restless. Alone in his Coney Island hideaway, he waits. He cannot allow himself to settle or sleep, wracked with anticipation that at any moment his one true love might return, after losing her ten years earlier to a man who was everything he despised. His life is one ruled by the absence of a voice. Until Christine Daaé walks back through the door and sings once more, Erik (The Phantom) will wallow incomplete, unfinished, and unfulfilled. Without the voice of his muse, the masked protagonist of *Love Never Dies* (2010)—Andrew Lloyd Webber's sequel to *The Phantom of the Opera* (1986)—would, presumably, have little reason to go on living.

As an agent of primal longing, voice is not just the preserve of the deformed and reclusive on the musical stage. It becomes the most immediate form of communication for Clara and Fabrizio, who otherwise struggle to connect romantically and erotically across a language barrier in *The Light in the Piazza* (2005). Elsewhere, voice can place characters in mortal danger, as Ariel found out, signing her voice away in a Faustian pact with Ursula for the promise of her prince (*The Little Mermaid*, 1989), or as Floyd discovered when the echoes from his call led him one cave too far (*Floyd Collins*, 1996). Voices can be unspeakably fragile, singing of familial connections between fathers and sons too intimate for speech (*Closer than Ever*, 1989); they can joyously celebrate newfound romance, causing a simple-minded shop assistant to declare his amazement that she *does* love him, after all (*She Loves Me*, 1963); they can be outsized, giving voice to the soul of Doris Winter far beyond the constraints of her church choir (*Mama, I Want to Sing*, 1983). Voices can assert and subvert identities, or become politicized, such as when black, Hispanic, and Asian performers sing the lives of white men and women (*Hamilton*, 2015), or when voices are dragged, toying with ideas of gender and sexuality (*Betty*, 1915; *Matilda*, 2011).[1]

Romantic, erotic, dangerous, immediate, intimate, physical, familial, joyous, outsized, assertive, subversive, politicized; voice in musical theatre

Singing Utopia. Ben Macpherson, Oxford University Press. © Oxford University Press 2024.
DOI: 10.1093/9780197557679.003.0001

can be all of these things and much more as it shifts and writhes through a complex set of sonic expressions. However, despite its shared status in the trinity of musical theatre disciplines (singing, acting, and dancing), and its primacy as an agent of meaning, emotion, and aesthetic value, most considerations of the singing voice in musical theatre have tended to focus on aspects of pedagogy and practice, examining the *how* and taking the *why*, *when*, and even at times the *what*, for granted.[2] There are exceptions, but these could almost be counted on the fingers of one hand. For example, a special issue of the journal *Studies in Musical Theatre* was published in 2012. Guest edited by Millie Taylor, it offered a rich and varied set of lenses through which voice and vocal excess were conceptualized on the musical stage. Jake Johnson's monograph *Mormons, Musical Theater, and Belonging in America* (2019) considers voice and religious identity in the American musical, while several doctoral theses have examined key aspects of musical theatre voice.[3] Scholars including Stacy Wolf, Mitchell Morris, and Raymond Knapp have further considered vocal registers and characterization, while these discussions have tended to be implicit in their reading of something else or occupy only a chapter in more broadly themed publications.[4] Elsewhere, Taylor and Johnson have considered how musical theatre voice 'encodes' meaning through the various facets of which it is composed, while Dominic Symonds has explored how musical theatre voices can be fetishized on recordings.[5] Alongside the occasional article, however, these are but three further chapters in a large and international body of musical theatre scholarship that has been cautious to explore voice beyond discrete ideas in larger collections, musicological taxonomies of voice type and character, or general discussion. This book aims to fill that void, to render present that absence, and to ask *why*, *when*, and *what* in a meaningful and provocative way. (After all, Christine *did* eventually return to Erik.)

Asking questions forms the foundation of this book. This introduction will ask several, to make sense of the ones that follow in the subsequent chapters. As we will see, the answers to each question are not definite; they exist in spaces or states between, the reasons for which will become clear throughout. First, acknowledging the lack of sustained scholarship on voice in musical theatre, it seems appropriate to ask *why*. Why has there yet been no previous attempt to write a critical or conçeptual study of voice in musical theatre?

'Betwixt and between': The State and Status of Musical Theatre

One answer might relate to the difficult status of musical theatre in popular culture, something Stacy Wolf sees as a 'paradox'. As a global phenomenon, musical theatre is 'dominant' in the cultural landscape yet 'contested' as to its legitimacy.[6] It is a cultural magpie—a chameleon—borrowing freely from a range of high, low, and contemporary forms, styles, and genres in pursuit of its commercial aims. Variously, such borrowing involves theatre genres and forms including opera, operetta, music hall, vaudeville, burlesque, minstrelsy, and melodrama, along with musical styles including jazz, blues, folk, rock, pop, gospel and liturgical music, and hip hop. Neither fully at one with the opera house nor completely at home in the music hall, it is the 'Fabulous Invalid' of popular musical entertainment. Occupying a space between the 'Great Divide' of 'high culture' and 'low culture', musical theatre might therefore be understood as 'middlebrow'.[7] This positioning relates to the fact that while musical theatre is a commercial form, its stories address many serious social issues from domestic abuse (*Carousel*, 1945) to mental health (*Next to Normal*, 2008). For David Savran, understanding musical theatre in this way offers an opportunity both to 'study the circulation of the artwork-as-commodity' and the 'sophisticated' musical and theatrical devices present in the form.[8] As chapter 2 considers in detail, this combination characterizes the ways in which we might listen to musical theatre vocality. Here, however, a more direct literary rendering of the 'middlebrow' helps articulate the complex status of musical theatre.

In a posthumous essay entitled 'Middlebrow' (1942), Virginia Woolf defined middlebrow culture as existing 'betwixt and between' in a cultural area that was 'in pursuit of no single object, neither of Art itself nor life itself'; a space where efficacy and entertainment are 'mixed indistinguishably, and rather nastily, with money, fame, power, or prestige'.[9] Early in the essay, Woolf claims that highbrow art is concerned with beauty, value, form, and integrity, while lowbrow work may not be intellectual but is modest in its aims and knows its audience, for which it is worthy of equal regard. When thinking about musical theatre, the notion of a form which exists 'betwixt and between' offers a succinct and acute description. Musical theatre is not opera, but at times it displays operatic aspirations.[10] It is not a form composed solely of American popular idioms but, along with a range of European influences, it is nevertheless characterized by influences from jazz, blues, and gospel styles, derived from African and African American musical forms, whether openly or indirectly. It is a form that once fed the popular music charts but is now inspired by (and borrows from) them, as seen in the proliferation of jukebox musicals, particularly from the late twentieth century to the present. In other words, the status of musical theatre as 'betwixt and between' highbrow and lowbrow culture has also been the paradoxical source of its (contested) success.

Stacy Wolf goes further, suggesting that this in-between character can be identified in the structures and aesthetic influences of musical theatre alongside its cultural status. Engineering the coherence of disparate textual elements (book, music, lyrics, and choreography) and requiring real-time negotiation of the divergent and conflicting demands of music, movement, and speech in performance, musical theatre often borrows from, transgresses, repurposes, or reimagines boundaries between a range of art forms and disciplines. Such conflation, circulation, and borrowing across various structures and aesthetic practices was also noted by the director Peter Brook when reflecting on the popular impulse of what he termed 'Rough Theatre'. Brook observed that: 'Brecht was rooted in the cabaret: Joan Littlewood longs for a funfair [and it is] to Broadway that American poets, choreographers and composers turn. A choreographer like Jerome Robbins is an interesting example, moving from the pure and abstract theatres of Balanchine and Martha Graham towards the roughness of the popular show'. Such a blurring of boundaries evidences the pitfalls of analysing generic conventions through a discrete or bifurcated approach.[11] As a consequence, musical theatre occupies a paradoxical space 'betwixt and between' various analytical paradigms, something which both sustains and reflects its complex cultural status. It is neither wholly the preserve of musicology, nor a discipline entirely suited to dance studies, and only temporarily resident in the realm of traditional theatre and performance studies (which, at times, have more closely aligned with literature).

Since the late 1990s, however, studies in musical theatre have flourished, examining the complex place of the form in popular culture, and critiquing its status and function as art. These studies have explored its use of intertextuality, analysed its disciplinary complexities, engaged with its cultural history and international circulation, and interrogated its capacity for performing issues including politics, identity, and nationhood, while recently re-evaluating the systemic whiteness of the form—particularly in North America. Returning to the question above, why has this not yet included an extensive study that seeks to articulate the cultural significance of musical theatre voice? One reason may be that in its liberal borrowing from musical idioms, styles, forms and cultures, any discussion of voice in the musical, by necessity, becomes a discussion of—and between—multiple *vocal* idioms, styles, forms, and cultures. It is therefore fraught with difficulty and complexity, given the breadth of vocal properties inherent within, and contingent upon, musical theatre performance. The traversing of disciplinary boundaries in the form itself also extends any consideration beyond discussions of popular music (song) or straight theatre (speech) and into the realm of multi-modal analysis. Such difficulties have long posed a challenge to the scholarly study of voice at large.

'The most beautiful sound . . .': The Voice Problem

Reflecting on what he calls the '*problem*' of voice, Konstantinos Thomaidis has observed that, until recently, there has been a 'paucity of critical writing' on voice in theatre and performance studies.[12] Beyond speech and actor training, such work remains somewhat disparate, and on this basis, Thomaidis notes the historical tendency for 'voice studies' to come from the realm of philosophy.[13] Taken together, some foundational texts in this area help to establish why voice is a '*problem*' and at the same time demonstrate why it is a rich and fruitful area of study. Drawing upon the contentious status of voice-as-sound, philosopher Adriana Cavarero's *For More than One Voice* (2005) challenges the *logocentrism* in Western critical traditions, arguing that to privilege written and semantic discourses 'devocalizes' what is said, constructing a patriarchal history of understanding and marginalizing *who* it is that speaks. In many ways, her desire to reconfigure the relationship between patriarchy, politics, and sound—a 'politics of the voice', as she proposes—is sympathetic to (while at times a critique of) theorist Jacques Derrida's work in *Of Grammatology* (1967) and *Voice and Phenomenon* (1967). Derrida took issue with the privileging of voice and speech as the bearer of meaning. Contending that an overemphasis on *phōnḗ* (what is heard) demotes writing (*logos*) to a secondary position, Derrida suggests that the sonorous and the semantic should be understood in interplay.[14]

Such a complex and equitable relationship between *phōnḗ* and *logos* is not to be found in the structural theories of linguist Ferdinand de Saussure, however, arguing as he did that sound was simply the carrier of semantic signs and symbols. It was, for him, an agent without agency—something with which Roland Barthes seemed to struggle. In 'The Death of the Author' (1967), Barthes betrays logocentrism when he suggests that readers re-author texts at the expense of authorial intention. To this extent, Barthes's thinking echoes that of Derrida, sharing a concern for how readers engage with words. In another essay, 'The Grain of the Voice' (1972), Barthes also argues for the uniqueness of individual voices, noting that any song performed always betrays the material presence of the vocalist as it reveals 'the body speaking its mother tongue'. Cavarero is sympathetic to this position, focussing as it does on the individual singer, yet critiques Barthes for reducing voice to a mere mediating function between body and language. Echoing this hierarchy or intersectionality between voice, language, and the body, philosopher and psychoanalyst Mladen Dolar's *A Voice and Nothing More* (2006) develops Jacques Lacan's notion that alongside its sonorous properties and capacity to convey meaning, voice embodies thought and desire, while Steven Connor's work has suggested that when a voice leaves a body it becomes a 'vocalic body' of its own. Elsewhere, Michel Chion has considered the body/voice split from the perspective of what can be seen and what can be heard in cinema, developing the idea of *acousmêtre* (a voice without origin) that has been employed by scholars such as Jennifer Fleeger and Brian Kane in their considerations of voice, sound, and technology.[15]

Examining the gendered and racialized politics of voice, its presence and/or absence, the psychology and biology of the voice in production, the relationship between *logos* and *phōnḗ*, the nature of vocal sound when mediated by technology, and its configuration via cultural spaces of listening therefore offers rich and complex possibilities in theatre and performance studies, something Thomaidis has called for more purposefully in his recent work. Taken together, the works mentioned might also form the basis of thinking that constitutes the growing field of voice studies—a trans-, cross-, and interdisciplinary area that has been developing as a specific concern since the mid-2010s in Western scholarship and beyond.

Interdisciplinary approaches to the study of voice have been codified as a field of inquiry through the establishment of the *Journal of Interdisciplinary Voice Studies* (2014–) and the Routledge Voice Studies monograph series, which launched in 2015 with the edited collection *Voice Studies: Critical Approaches to Process, Performance and Experience*. In the introduction to that edited volume, a critical perspective on voice is offered, understanding its sonic space as an 'in-between': 'the junction point for multiple encodings of experience to be negotiated and understood'.[16] Such experience may relate to the foregoing concerns of gender, technology, language, or presence, or they might include aspects of eroticism, intimacy, family dynamics, unabashed joy, or political subversion, mentioned at the outset. As an in-between space, musical theatre voice is also complicated by *what* and *who* is singing, and indeed, the very act of making a sound. Seeking to codify voice in popular music, Simon Frith tells us that a voice can be all-at-once a musical instrument, a body, a person, and a character.[17] In other words, any voice that sings can be heard as a sound, a vocal presence, as the person singing, and the persona determined by the lyric. Each of these layers encodes the voice, as it occupies an in-between space in which embodied presence, technological mediation, outsize expression, emotional solitude, vectors of gender or race, character or performer, sound, and word freely negotiate, play, coexist, or vie for dominance.

As chapter 1 explores in detail, these concerns—and the philosophical tenets that underpin them—are already to be found in the large body of writing on voice in opera. For example, Mary Ann Smart, Catherine Clément, and Carolyn Abbate have explored complex notions of the female voice in opera and its relationship to presence, patriarchy, and politics, while Wayne Koestenbaum has considered operatic vocality with regard to queerness and sexuality. In each case, the materiality of the voice as a sonic object or point of focus serves as a departure or complication, something also seen in works by Michel Poizat and Gary Tomlinson, as they listen to vocal presence and absence in opera, considering notions of transcendence and metaphysical sonority.[18] Such ideas have, at times, found their way into musical theatre scholarship, the uses of which are considered in the following chapter. However, as mentioned above, beyond pedagogy or practice, a sustained exploration of the cultural, philosophical, or conceptual properties of musical theatre vocality analogous to the work of Tomlinson, Poizat, Abbate, and other opera scholars mentioned above has yet to be forthcoming. There are several reasons for this.

First, opera studies focus on an older and more assuredly 'highbrow' cultural form with closer ideological links to the philosophical concerns seen in the writing of Cavarero or Dolar, for example. Second, musical theatre occupies an in-between space in popular culture and is paradoxical in its structural conceits, expressive qualities, and formal conventions. Third, the recent concept of studying voice as an interdisciplinary in-between brings with it a peculiar challenge. It asks us to move beyond ideas or analyses of register, range, character, or the conventions of style or stereotypes. It requires that we allow all of those things free rein in a sonic space that is plural and fluid. Instead of listening *to*, it needs us to listen *in*, *through*, *across,* and *between* 'multiple encodings', a position developed later in this introduction, and which exceeds current analytical parameters in musical theatre scholarship.[19] In this context, the study of voice in musical theatre becomes the study of a vocal in-between in a form that already exists 'betwixt and between'. The challenge of how to approach this is therefore significant and fraught with possible complications, blind alleys, contradictions, and unknowns. To begin mapping a path, we need to return to first principles and ask another question: why *do* musicals sing?

'The song that goes like this': Why Musicals Sing

Received wisdom says that characters, and any choruses to which they may belong or might attach themselves, must have a *reason* to sing. This reason cannot be simply that 'musical theatre has music and songs' (even if that statement says more about the cultural value of the form than its cynical naiveté might suggest). Musical theatre lore tells us that the primary reason song (and dance) occurs in a musical is because a character's emotional state has *outgrown* the expressive potential of speech. This focus on emotional expressivity is seen in Scott McMillin's 2006 book, *The Musical as Drama.* He argued that the ideal of integration so beloved of Rodgers and Hammerstein was an impossibility. Suggesting that the unavoidable tension in the gear changes between book, music, lyrics, and dance in performance provides musical theatre with its distinct thrill, McMillin proposed that musical theatre operates through two 'orders of time'. First, 'book time' concerns the narrative, exposition, and dramatic action, while in 'lyric time' songs stop the action to *enlarge* on thoughts and feelings, as characters uncover what Carey Wall calls their 'full self' in performance.[20]

Whether focussing on conventional book musicals, so-called concept musicals that toy with linearity and the nature of storytelling, through-sung works such as the megamusicals of the 1980s and 1990s, or more challenging pieces that play with accepted conventions of melody, shape, and form (such as *London Road*, 2011; or, *A Strange Loop*, 2022), the gospel of heightened emotion or realism is still perpetuated as the rationale for musical theatre's reliance on singing (and dancing). As recently as 2019, a panel of musical theatre and popular music scholars continued to agree that 'the voice is where musical theater places its truest meaning'.[21] While this is a central tenet of the form, and while emotions—such as those offered at the outset—are many and varied, might there be more to it?

In his seminal essay 'Entertainment and Utopia' (1977), Richard Dyer suggests that through sustained melodic expressivity, singing enables performers (and the characters they create) to communicate with emotional 'intensity' and 'transparency'. For Dyer, this allows musical films to offer an image of utopia—defined as 'something better' than lived reality and, here, transposed to live musical theatre performance.[22] Through the outsized emotional 'energy' inherent in song and dance, in its many variations, musical theatre configures human relationships and stories not as they are, but as they *could be*, with a directness that suggests resolutions can be easy and complexities reduced to their simplest, essential, or discrete components.[23] For example, while Erik is wracked with self-doubt, anxiety, loss, confusion, and unresolved bitterness, the opening moments of *Love Never Dies* hear the Phantom reach fever pitch in a soaring tenor torch song, ''Till I Hear You Sing'. Complex though his emotions may be, they are distilled into a moment of full expression as his dream of Christine's return is given voice. Dyer says that the utopia evoked from this transparency of emotion, facilitated by the intensity and energy of performance, is something for audiences 'to escape into, or something we want deeply that our day-to-day lives don't provide'.[24]

Therefore, beyond giving a character an emotional outlet they would be denied in reality, singing in musical theatre serves an ideological function. McMillin once wrote that as a performer moves from speech to song (or dance) in live performance, they enter a 'space of vulnerability' in which the voice could crack, or strain, or break, and in which minds can blank and lyrics or choreography could be forgotten. The act of witnessing someone overcome this vulnerability, facing down the 'danger of failure' through the intensity and emotional expressivity of song and dance, is, in itself, an image of something beyond the mundane—something outside the lived reality of audiences.[25] On this basis, as Dyer further reasons, utopia is experienced 'at the level of sensibility' or feeling—not in *where*, *how*, or *why* songs occur—but in the experience of their *performance*. Utopia is therefore an affective rather than structural ideal.[26] This position is echoed by Jill Dolan, who considers the liveness of performance essential to the experience of utopia. Since live performance is transient, any intensity experienced in musical theatre song is also transient. This means that any glimpse of utopia can never be fixed. Dolan suggests it is 'not a world in being' but merely an 'index of the possible'—a *feeling* of 'something better'. In this context, song and dance function as 'never finished gestures toward a potentially better future', categorized as what Dolan might term 'utopian performatives'.[27] Some moments proffer what theorist Ernst Bloch understood to be an 'abstract utopia' of compensation; a state that is wishful rather than wilful; expressing a desire for change rather than an anticipation of material difference.[28] At the 'level of sensibility', the abstract 'utopian performatives' of the musical stage are not *song* and *dance* as structural, textual, or narrative entities. Rather, they are *singing* and *dancing*—non-representational gestures of 'something better' that are never fully actualized, even if their sonic intensity suggests emotions can be overt, direct, tangible, and uncomplicated.[29] Borrowing a term from sound studies scholar Salomé Voegelin, we might say that the utopian performative of the sung voice in musical theatre offers audiences a 'sonic *possible* world' through voice, a vocal utopia.[30]

The term 'vocal utopia' might sound tempting as a way to talk about the quality of voice in musical theatre through the lens of Dyer's essay. Yet, if voice—and the sonic space it creates—is in itself a messy in-between full of 'multiple encodings', then might this destabilize Dyer's claim to the transparency and intensity of *singing* in musical theatre?[31] Does it challenge the emotional directness that is key to Dyer's idea of 'something better'? Developing this question further, if vocal sonority is always plural and fluid, then a 'vocal utopia' must also be plural and fluid. Is this what Dyer meant? To answer these questions, a closer look at the nature of utopia will demonstrate that, in many ways, it is similarly complex, fluid, and plural—a fact that both enhances and complicates the ways in which we might listen to voice in musical theatre.

'Singing the world into tune': Vocal Utopia(s)

In Western thought, the idea of utopia can first be found in Plato's *Republic*—a manifesto for a political and social ideal. Among Plato's policies, there would be a rigid set of social hierarchies, fairly distributed wealth and resources, the promotion of law and order (but few laws and no lawyers), and the removal of theatrical performance to ensure citizens were protected from succumbing to craven (or rebellious) desires. A similar form of social utopia was also found in England in 1516, with the publication of Thomas More's *Utopia*.[32] While More's text has variously been seen as a representation of an ideal society and a secular satire, at its heart is a dilemma over the meaning of 'utopia'. Derived from the original Greek, 'utopia' might mean either 'no place' (*ou topos*) or 'good place' (*eu topos*), which are homophonic in the original language. Paradoxically, it might mean both of these at the same time: a good place which does not exist. As theorist Edward Rothstein puts it, this 'good place' is an 'ideal toward which the mundane world must reach'.[33] Through the intensity of its performance structures and aesthetic, musical theatre does indeed elevate the mundane to the utopian, as audiences listen to and thrill at bank clerks, barbers, bakers, cavers, coves, children, politicians, princesses and preachers, or witches, wives, and widows achieve the intensity of voice that might reach towards 'something better' in their emotional fulfilment or social relationships. In such moments, Dolan suggests that 'audiences feel themselves allied with each other [as] social discourse articulates the possible, rather than insurmountable obstacles of human potential'.[34] However, as the best place never to have existed, utopia also has several additional characteristics not considered in Dyer's essay which may challenge a singular view of utopia and its possibilities.

As a human concept borne of 'the conviction that humanity is perfectible', utopia is a future realm of 'impossible perfection'.[35] In other words, the nature of utopia is rooted in paradox and contradiction. In his essay 'Utopia and Its Discontents' (2003), Rothstein observes that 'one man's utopia is another man's dystopia'. Turning to literature to demonstrate his point, Rothstein considers the fact that both Aldous Huxley's *Brave New World* and George Orwell's *1984* depict societies 'specifically designed by their rulers to be *utopias*'. He notes that neither 'show societies designed to create unhappiness', and yet—because of the oppressive, authoritarian, and inhumane effects on the central characters—Huxley's and Orwell's novels are paradigmatic works of *dystopian* fiction.[36] In a broader social example, the mythological ideal of the American Dream—celebrating economic success and individual achievement—may be vaunted as a capitalist utopia, yet as geo-political and global economic shifts have taken place across the last fifty years, the American Dream is viewed increasingly as a 'nightmare' world of 'joyless materialism and brutal exploitation'.[37] In short, as Rothstein concludes, the greatest contradiction in utopia is that 'all of these paradises are really varieties of hell'.[38]

This foundational contradiction may be because while 'something better' is an idealized future state, it is built upon versions of present (or past) social structures.[39] As utopian scholar Lyman Tower Sargent suggests, these may include ideals which are 'socialist, capitalist, monarchical, democratic, anarchist, ecological, feminist, patriarchal, egalitarian, hierarchical, racist, left-wing, right-wing, reformist'. For Sargent, these ideals also embrace everything from 'Naturism/Nude Christians [and] free love' to the whole spectrum of nuclear, extended, and blended families.[40] Yet such contradictions may be negotiable, surmountable, or even desirable, as a way of achieving utopia. Demonstrating Sargent's argument, political sociologist Luke Martell considers the complexities of economic capital in an illustrative utopia founded on 'collective ownership of the economy and of work'. Acknowledging that some in that society may not conform entirely to such an ideal, that particular utopia may 'accept pluralism and diversity, including a minority role for private enterprise. To not do so would require authoritarian imposition on those who wish to do something different'.[41] For Martell, '[t]his does not mean utopia is a variety of utopias but a utopia to which alternatives are permitted'.[42] Far from being a homogeneous state of 'escape' and wish-fulfilment, and notwithstanding the internal contradictions at play, utopia may therefore be characterized by plurality and accommodation.[43] This sense of accommodation is also understood as indicative of utopia's malleability and openness to change to reflect shifting cultural or social ideals. For example, republics overthrow monarchies, Judeo-Christian governance cedes place to secular politics over time, and civil rights or social justice is championed, reckoned with, or achieved. As Martell notes, '[w]hat is utopian now or at the time it is achieved may not continue to be ideal because of developments, intended or unforeseen, such as in technology or human nature . . . and so will need change'.[44]

To speak of a vocal utopia in musical theatre, then, is to invoke a contradictory, plural, and changeable ideal of a flawed but good place that does not exist. In many ways, this echoes the idea of voice as a plural in-between seeking to negotiate multiple ideas and experiences which, over time, may change in their nature or value. While the vocal utopia of musical theatre might not explicitly engage or encode some of the political ideals Sargent outlines (even if many narratives of musical theatre do), the plurality of styles and aesthetics inherent in musical theatre vocality gives evidence of complexity, changeability, and lack of homogeneity, considered in chapter 2. Of course, if voice is all-at-once an index of intense expressivity and yet so multi-faceted that it performs a range of cultures, styles, emotions, ideals, intentions, and situations, questions arise in light of the complex nature of utopia identified above.

Do all voices in musical theatre sing utopia? Do different voices give space for 'alternatives' in a sonic demonstration of utopian plurality? If the ideal of 'something better' changes over time (and is always flawed), does the sonic quality of voice change with it, betraying imperfections as it does so? Can the singing voice in musical theatre ever really capture a sense of emotional intensity or transparency if utopia is always a negotiation founded upon a contradiction? What happens when musical theatre rejects such imperatives from Dyer, when characters appear to resist the urge to sing, or when the entire musical is characterized by a style or idiom such as hip hop which places voice on a continuum somewhere closer to speech than song (*In the Heights*, 2008; *Hamilton*, 2015)? Can these voices also be understood as utopian? If any definition of utopia also implies its opposite, are there communities for whom certain voices may be heard or experienced as dystopian; communities excluded or silenced from the dream of 'something better' such as those from whom certain musical or vocal styles have been appropriated at the service of white privilege and culture? Elsewhere, how are we to understand voices that sound like other voices, in tribute or imitation? Do they perhaps epitomize a utopia defined as 'nowhere'?[45]

Such questions give pause for thought and demonstrate the complexity of examining voice as a utopian property or ideal in musical theatre. This book, then, will seek to examine the ways in which the plural, contradictory in-between of voice—in a form that is paradoxical, and occupies a 'betwixt and between' space amidst various spheres of popular culture—reflects, critiques, negotiates, denies, or reaches towards 'something better'; the paradoxical, changeable, plural, imperfectly perfect utopian. How might such an undertaking be approached?[46]

'Someone's gonna listen . . .': Approaches to the In-between

Conceiving of voice as an in-between means it is no longer possible only to listen *to* a fixed idea of vocal utterance. Rather, we need to find other ways of listening to help identify the 'multiple encodings' and negotiations taking place. As a first step, we might borrow an approach from Thomaidis and engage in an act of 'listening across' the sonic (and plural) qualities of vocality as they play out within, between, and across time, space, culture, and race.[47] Thomaidis observes that '[n]ot only is voice multiple [in its sonic, semantic, and cultural properties], it is also heard plurally' by those who listen. Such listening may be complicated, however, because 'listening is also a culturally and historically situated practice' offering the listener agency in constructing the affective characteristics of the voices that are heard from a given position.[48] Exploring vocal utopia therefore entails a reflective understanding of *how* we listen to what is sung and asks us to situate our own listening practices in relation to the world.

A further way to listen is once more found in the work of Salomé Voegelin, who has argued that as material, sound (and, by extension, vocal sonority) exists in an experiential space 'anterior' to the tyranny of speech and the predominance of visual culture (a duo which have jointly 'muted' sound in Western culture and philosophical thought since Plato). Freed from seeing the world through the 'signs and symbols' with which 'language and culture assert their superiority' and determine boundaries of analysis, this consideration of vocal utopia in musical theatre therefore rejects what Voegelin has termed the 'chronological and patrimonial ancestrality' of traditional Western analysis.[49] Instead, it focuses on the sound and uses the complex interplay and multi-faceted intersectionality of sonic properties, form, style, and texture as a way of listening to popular culture across, between, and within eras, races, genders, politics, and thought.[50]

Beyond such an approach to listening, the cultural and historical situatedness of the listener has informed recent thinking about the relationship between voice and race. Building on established paradigms from voice studies outlined above, Nina Sun Eidsheim frames notions of 'hearing race' as 'the acousmatic question'. She suggests that the very enquiry 'who is speaking?' invites the listener into an acousmatic search for identity and meaning beyond the body of the voicer. Building from the position that 'voice is not innate; it is cultural', Eidsheim interrogates at times problematic or stereotypical assumptions made about the relationship between voice and racial identity.[51] As a complementary study which precedes Eidsheim's work, Jennifer Lynn Stoever develops the concept of 'the sonic color line' using W. E. B. Du Bois's original term 'the color line' to listen for the ways (white American) culture 'racially codes sonic phenomena such as vocal timbre, accents, and musical tones'.[52] Both Stoever and Eidsheim are acknowledged in the work of music scholar Matthew D. Morrison, whose concept of 'Blacksound' offers tools for listening to and 'uncovering the political implications of embodying, making, and commercializing popular music [and forms of popular entertainment such as the musical] in the United States, from its origins in blackface to the present'.[53]

As seen throughout this book, the relationship between race, voice, and utopia in musical theatre is a complex one, particularly in light of the (mis) appropriation of African vocal styles and practices, along with those from other communities and cultures, in developing an artform often understood as white and middle-class. Engaging with these complexities, my own cultural and historical 'listening ear' (to borrow a further phrase from Stoever) has inevitably informed this book.[54] As a Caucasian male, born and raised in the UK, my ability to listen to 'Blacksound' or (have the right to) speak with authority about cultural sensitivities regarding African American vocal practice and its appropriation into musical theatre on Broadway is accordingly limited.[55] Yet, recognizing the centrality of such issues to the properties, potentials, and problems of a 'vocal utopia' in musical theatre as a form, where such issues are raised, I use the listening experience as a means of questioning assumptions or exploring what may be inaudible, relying on scholars (some of whom are listed above) to enable my 'listening ear' in this and other areas, to be as informed and attuned as possible.

'Raise your voice': How to Read *Singing Utopia*

Drawing together the above positions on listening, voice, sound, culture, and identity, *Singing Utopia* comprises five chapters in two parts and features fifteen wide-ranging case studies from musicals produced between 1900 and 2019, informed and expanded with reference to many more. The voices these works contain are heard as sonic pluralities anterior to the fixedness of traditions, politics, or culture, while nevertheless imbricated within and between them. *Singing Utopia* therefore uses the complex interplay and multi-faceted intersectionality of sonic properties, form, style, and texture as a way of listening to popular culture across, between, and within eras, races, genders, politics, and thought. On this basis, Yiddish comic vocality will be listened to in the same space as crooning; the queer spectrality of a disfigured musical genius will be heard to occupy the same vocal sphere as a Kentucky spelunker; and the ambivalent solitude of a man on the outside engages in a provocation with the chaotic cacophony of his married friends. Each relationship demands that we listen 'across' and 'between' rather than *to* the voices, treating them as sound beyond the confines of their time, place, or character, but always imbricated with these facets.

Part I ('Cultural Contexts') sets a foundation for how musical theatre voice might be explored on its own terms. Chapter 1 begins by distinguishing the metaphysical vocality of opera and the vernacular properties of musical theatre (and its progenitor musical comedy) as a middlebrow form. With specific reference to the work of utopian theorist Paul Ricoeur, the chapter explores the limitations of reliance on psychoanalytical or phenomenal paradigms often transposed from opera studies to listen across voices in musical theatre. Centred at a point of divergence in the late nineteenth century, it finds that while the high cultural status of opera can often be heard to give voice to otherworldly grandeur at the service of implied cultural capital or dissimulated power structures, the development of musical theatre might be understood as a form of utopian 'rupture' whose voices sing of possibilities beyond the status quo.

Building from this position, chapter 2 examines musical theatre as a middlebrow form drawing liberally from a smorgasbord of lowbrow and popular vocal styles while retaining some of the aesthetics heard in its progenitors of opera and operetta. As an in-between space, voice in musical theatre is therefore heard as a plurality configured by means of recrafting other styles within conventions of the form. Listening closely to five works of the musical stage, from the British fin de siècle to a twenty-first-century African American rock musical, the chapter borrows from musicologist John Potter and Marxist theorist Antonio Gramsci to construct a theory of vocal style. Doing so, the chapter considers the complex stylistic properties of musical theatre voices, hearing in them what Paul Ricoeur has called an 'exploration of the possible' through which 'various alternatives are permitted', but not without challenge, provocation, and the occasional threat.[56]

Part II ('Critical Approaches') progresses to develop new approaches for listening to voice in musical theatre, examining how some of its complexities might be understood taxonomically. Chapter 3 turns its attention to the dramaturgical structures of different vocal groupings in a further three case studies. Listening across the intersection and interaction of generalized choral declamation and the particularity of solo songs, duets, trios, quartets, and quintets, the chapter combines neurobiological research and discourses from the social sciences to consider the utopian properties of 'community', drawing on ideas from Lyman Tower Sargent, Victor Turner, and Zygmunt Bauman. Borrowing from musical theatre scholar Bethany Hughes, the chapter asks how musical theatre might give voice to a 'manifestation of community' across its various vocal groupings, and how in turn, these reveal different characteristics of utopia (or, in some instances, challenge them).[57] What, for example, is shared—and what differs—between the choral aesthetic of the Arcadians before James Smith arrives (*The Arcadians*, 1909) and the foundry workers of *Hadestown* (2019)? They are worlds apart. Can they both sing utopia? What might have changed; the voice, or the definition of utopia? Chapter 3 also listens to the ambivalent speech-inflection heard in Stephen Sondheim and George Furth's *Company* (1970)—an aesthetic which expands in focus in the following chapter.

What else might be revealed about the complexity of musical theatre performance and its ideals of 'something better' when musicals feature performers or characters who appear to resist the shift from speech to song?[58] Engaging phonetic, ethnomusicological, and linguistic analysis, chapter 4 asks what happens when characters eschew the seeming transparency or immediacy of melody. Placing an American revolutionary in dialogue with the ringleader of Victorian pickpockets, and a bandleading con artist side by side with Milky White's best friend, the chapter invites us to listen beyond our current understanding of utopia, hearing in such voices inaudible aspects of what it might mean to 'sing' utopia, including the emerging spectre of what Malcolm Chase and Christopher Shaw called the 'counterpart' of exploring the utopia: nostalgia.[59]

Before the conclusion, chapter 5 borrows from cultural theorist Svetlana Boym to further listen to two competing tendencies of nostalgia, listening across them through the imitative vocal representation in bio-musical performances. Drawing from three twenty-first-century examples of voices that sound like other voices, a close listening to the vocal space in-between utopia and nostalgia is developed through the application of three theoretical audio filters: sonic drag, responding to ideas from José Esteban Muñoz; ventriloquism, using the work of Steven Connor; and simulacrum, after Jean Baudrillard. The chapter concludes by introducing a new way of articulating the binary interactions of past and present with real-life voices and theatrical imitations. Together, these interactions reveal further tensions, complexities, and limitations in the relationship between nostalgia and utopia.

Each chapter informs its listening using key philosophical or theoretical approaches including linguistics, narratology, sound studies, musicology, dramaturgy, literary studies, sociology, anthropology, and more, applied at liberty across a range of discussions and ideas. While some readers might wish for a more consistent set of tools, this approach aims to demonstrate the rich potential in listening across both the numerous kinds of musical theatre voices and the diverse range of analytical approaches that can be used to do so. This interdisciplinary approach will be most rewarding when the book is taken as a whole and its analytical approaches are understood in context. However, chapters may also be read discretely should a reader want to take other possible routes through the discussion. For example, readers interested in musicological analyses may wish to focus on chapters 1, 2, and 3, with the third of these also including dramaturgical and sociological concerns. Chapters 2 and 5 foreground sonority or aurality in particular, while chapter 4 employs a synthesis of ethnographic and linguistic analysis.

At certain points, the book considers what voices are heard and what voices are silenced; when they are present, and how often they appear. At other points, it explores aesthetic properties, the vocal qualities or production of musical theatre vocality, or offers a sense of what it means to listen as well as to sing. In some cases, this involves focussing on specific performances of a song or character by a particular artist or a specific cast recording; in others, the analysis listens to a general iteration of the character as written or usually performed—details of which will be evident in each example. Where case studies rely on particular recordings to inform the analysis, these are—where possible—the original cast recordings in due recognition of the impact this has on the history of the musical. It is, of course, recognized that cast recordings are not representative of the entire history or sound of a given musical, with cast changes or cultural shifts offering new ways of listening across. In such cases, the analyses are indicative of the approach taken or the possibilities of listening across musical theatre vocality, rather than assuming a prescriptive or definitive position.

While raising an abundance of questions (many of which act as rhetorical provocations), this book repeatedly returns to one predominant concern: what kind of voice is this? Of course, it is foolhardy to suggest that—individually or collectively—the examples here are in any way paradigmatic or universal in their content or what they reveal about voice in musical theatre. What this book offers, then, is a starting point—an invitation or provocation for each reader to find other examples to which they might listen across, and which may yield parallel or surprising results. The contradictions, impossibilities, dangers, and pitfalls may already seem clear as the volume listens to a paradoxical ideal, voiced as a plural in-between, that evokes the romantic, erotic, dangerous, immediate, intimate, physical, familial, joyous, outsized, assertive, subversive, and politicized within a cultural 'betwixt and between'. Against such a background, perhaps it is understandable that no book on this subject has yet been written. It is also my explicit motivation for writing *Singing Utopia*. As musical theatre scholarship and sound studies thrive, and interdisciplinary approaches to voice flourish, the time seems right to tackle the 'problem' of voice in a form which can scale the heights and plumb the depths of human emotion with a universal appeal and intensity that no other form of theatre has. As such, this book—with exciting finds, contentious claims, unresolved loose ends, and thorny contradictions—is a beginning, and it starts with the complicated 'problem' of middlebrow vocality.

PART I
CULTURAL CONTEXTS

1
Reaffirmation and Rupture
Why This Is Not Opera

In a cosy scene from *The Sound of Music* (1959), the nun-turned-governess Maria is trying to teach the seven von Trapp children to be more musical. Strumming her guitar, she suggests that they start the lesson at the very beginning because it is, after all, a very good place to start. This chapter also starts at the beginning, reiterating the common lore of musical theatre history which begins in Florence in 1600, encompasses the development of monody and its historical aspiration, moves forward through *opera seria*, *opera buffa*, and *opéra comique*, and traverses Europe through to the nineteenth century. Arriving in New York by way of London, it picks up a strand of the narrative involving a mediated or diluted operatic form—operetta (or comic opera)—from the pens of W. S. Gilbert and Arthur Sullivan, Franz Lehár, or Jacques Offenbach, moving through the musical comedies produced by George Edwardes, Charles Frohman, and others, the musical plays of Rodgers and Hammerstein, the work of Stephen Sondheim, Andrew Lloyd Webber, their contemporaries, and those who followed in their footsteps. This history is easily compartmentalized. It has a clear beginning, with what Pietro Bardi once called the 'birth' of opera in Jacopo Peri's *L'Euridice* in the early seventeenth century. This implies that, notwithstanding geopolitical shifts and cultural changes, there is a genetic link between Peri's *L'Euridice* and Anaïs Mitchell's *Hadestown* (2019), even if it also acknowledges the influence of other forms on the popular musical.[1] Of course, no history can be so linear, unbroken, or entirely accurate, so this chapter begins more readily with a less idealized statement:

Musical theatre is not opera.

To the casual theatregoer, the differences between the two may seem obvious. They might notice differences in ticket prices, venue expectations, and audience demographics.[2] Aesthetically, they might perceive differences in

Singing Utopia. Ben Macpherson, Oxford University Press. © Oxford University Press 2024.
DOI: 10.1093/9780197557679.003.0002

the grandiosity and overt earnestness of through-composed operas in comparison with the lighter-hearted frivolity of book musicals, full of jazz hands and kick-lines. Some of these differences may be (partially) accurate, and there are some to which we will return. What happens, though, if the differentiation becomes more specific?

Musical theatre voice is not operatic voice.[3]

This is a bold claim. Beyond the perceived differences above, opera and musical theatre are both musical-dramatic forms and share certain structural and generic conventions. For example, in common with the book musical, numerous operas feature spoken dialogue between the formal musical numbers, including *The Magic Flute* (1791), *Carmen* (1875), and *Hansel and Gretel* (1893). Likewise, the use of declamatory vocal writing is a feature of both operatic recitative and through-sung musicals like *Porgy and Bess* (1935) and *Les Misérables*. According to Carolyn Abbate and Roger Parker, recitative in opera serves an expository and plot-driven function, while arias (and other set numbers) are 'static', illuminating a moment or emotion. This description parallels Scott McMillin's distinction between 'book time' and 'lyric time' in the musical.[4] However, while these two forms may have such structural and dramaturgical conceits in common, a close consideration of the aesthetic qualities and cultural lode of the voices that sing in opera and musical theatre offers some clear distinctions.

In opera, vocal control, beauty, and virtuosity are often 'desired, worshipped and fetishized' by audiences and scholars, many of whom 'locate [opera's] aesthetic foundation in the singing', and through which the genre 'marks its own singularity'.[5] In the most dramatic or emotional arias, 'the literary text melts away . . . or even completely loses its meaning' as the text cedes dominance to the virtuosic, exaggerated, and cultivated sound of the 'trained operatic voice'. Achieving this requires a specific emphasis on diaphragmatic control and a strong command of vocal tract resonance to affect vocal timbre. On this basis, as Lawrence Kramer puts it, '[v]irtually everyone can sing; very few people can sing opera'.[6]

Musical theatre also fetishizes the singing voice (otherwise, there would be no need for this book). In contrast with opera, it does so by giving primary emphasis to lyrical intelligibility, focussing on characters and stories. Often written with a lower tessitura and more limited range, musical theatre also places less emphasis on legato delivery and emphasizes straighter tone phonation (especially since the 1940s). In combination, these aspects produce a more speech-like quality in all aspects of vocal performance, from moments of declamatory vocal delivery to comedic patter songs and even soaring ballads. As Ana Flavia Zuim has argued, musical theatre 'requires a different muscular demand' from opera: it *sounds* different.[7] The expectation for a different sound is perhaps exemplified in the experience of actor Celeste Holm when she auditioned for the comedic supporting role of Ado Annie in *Oklahoma!* (1943). Composer Richard Rodgers asked her to sing 'as if you've never had a lesson in your life'. Shocked, Holm exclaimed: 'You mean I've studied three years for that?' Rodgers replied: 'Oh, you have to know how to in order to know how not to'.[8] In other words, technique is vital to both forms, while the primary concern of musical theatre tends towards a more vernacular, rather than virtuosic, sound.

Classical singing pedagogy from the nineteenth century onwards has placed great emphasis on the singer's formant. With a resonant frequency between 2500 and 3200 Hz, this allows opera singers to be heard over an orchestra without the need for amplification. The acoustic ring is produced by the narrowing of the laryngeal resonator and is independent of the vowels being sung. Referred to as *squillo*, the timbral aesthetic of this common operatic vocal sound is concentrated in the vocal tract, augmented by an increased presence of vibrato to carry the sound further. Yet, while opera performance remains largely acoustic, with performers appearing two or three times a week, contemporary musical theatre voices are amplified by throat or head microphones, allowing performers to sing in a more 'intimate, conversational manner' than their operatic counterparts and performing six to eight times each week.[9] The embrace of microphone technology also allowed musical theatre to incorporate popular genres in the form, such as rock and hip hop, which rely on amplification as part of their aesthetic. Before amplification, the necessary presence of classical singing techniques in early twentieth-century musical comedy was a result of the 'practicalities of projection' across the orchestra and into the auditorium: '[T]o be heard at the back . . . required a fuller tone that is a consequence of lowering the larynx. This inevitably made popular singers in both operetta and musical comedy closer in timbre to classical singers than they would be after amplification'.[10]

The technical requirements of a vocal style 'closer in timbre' to the classical or operatic was therefore part of early musical comedy as it emerged from operetta, and it can still be heard in the style commonly referred to as 'legitimate' (often abbreviated to 'legit'). It is the 'cultured' and 'trained' sound heard in voices ranging from Emile in *South Pacific* (1949) to Maria in *West*

Side Story (1957) or Clara and Fabrizio in *The Light in the Piazza* (2005). A common assumption equates the 'legit' voice with the operatic or classical, and it is perhaps revealing that such a 'cultured' voice quality is attributed as 'legitimate' in its designation, perhaps reinforcing the 'divide' between high and low cultural practices considered in the introduction. Yet, while it derives from classical singing, 'legit' is different, emphasizing speech inflection in a way not found in opera and with a predominance in the high-middle range. The delivery is therefore brighter, with 'twangier' vowel formants than those in classical singing.[11]

While opera has *squillo*, musical theatre has the 'belt' sound typified by Ethel Merman holding a C5 for sixteen bars at the close of 'I've Got Rhythm' in George and Ira Gershwin's *Girl Crazy* (1930). Performed without amplification, Merman's singing prompted the composer to tell her never to take a proper vocal lesson for fear of becoming 'diaphragm conscious' and losing the 'natural quality' of her instrument.[12] Yet, belting is produced—and 'rings' differently—to *squillo*. While opera singers of the nineteenth century may have projected their voices across the rich orchestral music of Puccini or Wagner, the musical theatre orchestra (and latterly the pit band) often produces a harsher, more contemporary or urban sound for the singer to negotiate with brass, reeds, drums, and in later work, electronic synthesizers and guitars. Because of this, when belt voice is used it may be more 'aggressive, visceral and intense', imbued with a 'twang' quality in its character.[13] It comes from the chest rather than laryngeal or pharyngeal resonators, and as voice teacher Jeanette LoVetri puts it, belting is 'just chest register . . . carried up above normal speaking range, and at high volume'.[14] Such examples are not exhaustive but demonstrate contrasts in vocal production and sound quality between these two forms.

The technical, mechanical, or artistic production of musical theatre voice is not, however, the focus here. While giving attention to the means of vocal production is inherent in any act of close listening, a further level of contrast between the vocal aesthetics of opera and musical theatre concerns the distinct cultural meanings attributed to, or encoded within, the sung voices of these two forms. A bold claim has already been made in the Introduction, and in the very title of this book: musical theatre sings utopia, offering a cultural meaning that dreams forwards through a sonic exploration of the possible. Given that these two forms 'sing' differently, what distinct cultural meanings might be heard, produced, or encoded in operatic vocality in contrast, divergence, or similitude with musical theatre?

In his essay 'The Creativity of Language', utopian theorist Paul Ricoeur considers the 'ensemble of symbolic discourses' that comprise the 'socio-political imaginaire' of a given society. This 'imaginaire' operates as either a 'rupture' or a 'reaffirmation' in the production of cultural meanings. Ricoeur assigns the quality of rupture to 'utopian' ideals as they serve to *critique* the present and configure a 'symbolic opening towards the future'. By contrast, the imaginaire of reaffirmation functions via the notion of 'ideology', using the 'foundational symbols' of a given society to enact a 'symbolic confirmation of the past' to justify the present.[15] Ricoeur therefore constructs a contrast between two cultural discourses, articulating a temporal pull between 'cultures [which] create themselves by telling stories of their past' via ideology, and a utopian exploration of the possible.[16] If musical theatre 'sings' utopia, it seems logical to infer that opera can be heard to 'sing' ideology. What 'stories of the past' might opera use to create a culture and how might it do so? What social imaginaire is justified or reaffirmed in the moment of performance? To answer these questions, we will revisit the 'birth' of opera in the sixteenth century and progress through its cultural development to arrive at what Ricoeur might call the 'turning point' of the nineteenth century—the period in which ideology and utopia become distinguishable in their function, and the development of popular musical theatre begins.[17] Only after considering this history can the assertion that voice in opera is ideological be understood, and a distinction drawn with the cultural imperatives of voice in musical theatre.

'Stories of the past': Opera and the (Re)creation of (High) Culture

The story goes that opera had its beginning in seventeenth-century Italy, where the Florentine Camerata—an informal group of scholars, composers, musicians, and philosophers including Vincenzo Galilei and Jacopo Peri—would meet to discuss art, literature, and science. Often credited with early innovations in opera, these men were supported by the patronage of the wealthy Count Giovanni Bardi who, it is believed, sponsored Vincenzo Galilei's musical studies as early as 1560.[18] The Camerata and their patron were among 'the most refined and intelligent' noblemen in Italy.[19] Italian opera would continue to be sponsored by wealthy aristocratic patrons through the early decades of its history. The Medici family commissioned

Peri to write a proto-operatic spectacle (*La Pellegrina*) for a dynastic wedding in 1589, while Claudio Monteverdi's *L'Orfeo* (1607) was commissioned by the Gonzaga family at the Court of Mantua. In the courtly surroundings of Italian palaces, proto-operatic and early operatic spectacles were apt to recreate 'stories of the past', featuring fantastical and mythological themes blended with the pastoral.[20] Renaissance Florence saw musical-dramatic 'stories about nymphs, shepherds and half-gods, living in marvellous gardens or fantastic country paradises [with] characters so exceptional that they might plausibly be imagined to converse in music'. Such characters thus acted as fitting 'foundation symbols' for the social imaginaire of the rich and powerful among the audiences, reaffirming their exceptional status.[21]

While this elite culture fostered the development of opera in Europe, it did not remain exclusive. Teatro San Cassiano—the first Venetian opera house—opened in 1637, and welcomed an audience of 'all social classes' from 'the general public'.[22] In the 1600s, the public may have attended an '*attione in musica* or a *festa teatrale*, a *drama musicale* or a *favola regia*, a *tragedia musicale* or an *opera scenica*', while the *New Grove Dictionary of Music and Musicians* helps to further define the form by directing readers to no fewer than eighty-nine other subject categories as part of its entry on 'opera'.[23] For much of the seventeenth and eighteenth centuries, opera was a popular and accessible form, characterized by a broad audience demographic enjoying a 'messy variety of musical drama'.[24] It was not until the nineteenth century that this variety was more formally brought under the nominal umbrella of a single term, and—with a focus on the United States and Great Britain from the 1860s onwards—it is at this point that the familiar social imaginaire of elitism re-emerges and, in this context, gives credence to an ideological understanding of voice in opera.

In 1865, the American Civil War was coming to its bitter end. Following surrender by the Confederacy, the release of over four million African American slaves as nominally 'free' men and women would begin to reorient the social fabric of America. Across the Atlantic, that same year saw the birth of the future King George V, as Queen Victoria reigned over a nation and Empire being reshaped in real-time as the consequences of the Industrial Revolution were felt. In 1866, the SS *Great Eastern* would sail from Sheerness to commence laying the first durable transatlantic telegraph cable in the 'first age of globalisation'.[25] By the early 1880s, North American free-market capitalism had recovered from the war, and 'urban, urbane' centres including New York and Boston were coming to exert influence in both a national and increasingly transnational economy, creating a nouveau riche borne of industry (those now known by their surnames: Vanderbilt, Rockefeller, Carnegie, and others). This coincided with unprecedented migration to America from Germany, Italy, and Scandinavia, as migrants sought to improve their lives beyond European struggles with war, drought, and economic instability.[26] In the United Kingdom, the mid-to-late nineteenth century saw similar growth in industrial and metropolitan centres, migration from towns to cities, and the parallel establishment of a similarly industrialized middle class borne of new money.[27]

Along with social, technological, and political change, increased migratory networks and economic change led to a concomitant reorientation of cultural structures, values, and ideals. For example, the stratifying concepts of 'high culture', 'mass culture', and latterly, 'popular culture' became consolidated. While these terms have been debated and examined elsewhere, one specific consequence is that this period saw opera once again occupy the echelons of 'high culture' in the United States, a status also reinforced in the cultural landscape of Great Britain.[28] The reasons for the return of the form to its Renaissance status of patronage and elitism offer a fascinating insight into the way opera may sing ideology, becoming its own 'story of the past'.

Reflecting on the ascent of new money in New York and other American urban centres, Daniel Snowman suggests that once 'the Frontier was closed' in the years following the Civil War, a new American identity was needed. The mythologized 'winning of the West', complete with cowboys, caravans, and prairie homesteads, had to be replaced by something more sympathetic to modernity, more metropolitan, and, in a word, more 'cultured'. Rather than capitalize on the potential for 'rupture' and engage in a utopian exploration of the possible now the war was won, the nouveau riche that emerged in its aftermath sought to assuage the vulgarity of their parvenu status through a process of 'reaffirmation', perpetuating 'symbolic discourses of the past' by transposing established, historical forms and claiming them as American 'high culture' in an act of 'invented tradition'.[29] They turned to the art and culture of Europe—imbued with the very values of hierarchy the United States was established to reject—lionizing classical music, the work of Shakespeare, and notably, opera.

These forms were not new to American audiences, but their political elevation to high culture imbued them with an elite, 'civilising agency' that served an affirmatory function, conferring immense cultural capital on the nouveau riche and acting as a bulwark against criticism from the older antebellum aristocracy regarding their 'vulgar acquisitiveness'.[30] To 'reaffirm' their sense of status, 'upper-class New Yorkers increasingly insisted that only foreign-language opera could meet their standards of excellence . . . employing foreign words and specialized language impenetrable to all but the cognoscenti'.[31] After two centuries during which it had been 'enjoyed and understood by a broad cross-section of urban Europeans and Americans . . . of all social classes', audiences at foreign-language operas were reported to be 'the most refined and intelligent of our citizens' as the nineteenth century drew to a close.[32] Italian and German opera thrived in purpose-built opera houses replete with strict standards of audience etiquette and dress codes.[33] The historical and cultural elitism of opera therefore became subjected to an organizing narrative spanning three centuries, beginning with the Florentine Camerata and extending to Wagner and Puccini.

This 'story of the past' created a culture which was afforded a conservative, respectable, and 'historically closed' status privileging a specific and narrow repertoire of 'celebrated classics' that would have been equally at home in the courtly surroundings of Renaissance palaces, as fantastical and mythological themes blended with the pastoral.[34] Such 'active appropriation' of opera to the realms of North American high culture served as an ideological 'reaffirmation' of a social imaginaire that drew on the past in order to perpetuate what Ricoeur elsewhere called 'the duration of a system of authority'. Doing so, it dissimulated structures of the status quo in order to 'preserve the power' of the new upper-middle classes during a time of social change.[35]

Given its extant social structures, things were somewhat different in Victorian Britain, as class and status were made 'visible [in an] imminent and actual' sense, with the monarchy at the top and the humblest agricultural labourer just above an underclass of villains, prostitutes, and immigrants.[36] Complex, stringent, and shaped by the imperial and insular worldview of the British, these hierarchies also conditioned responses to cultural engagement, including the socio-political function of certain art forms. British opera houses had long been a forum for 'conspicuous display' by the aristocracy and 'fashionable upper crust' wealthy enough to enjoy patronage.[37] The Georgian elite of the late eighteenth century often indulged in social hobnobbing and business dealings between themselves, supported by subscriptions to opera house seasons and reservations in private boxes. In this sense, opera was systemically high culture in the United Kingdom and supported an ideological reaffirmation of a fixed class system.

However, the nineteenth century wrought changes to the nature of such 'conspicuous display'. During her reign, Queen Victoria attended more opera than any British monarch before or since. In a nation founded on hierarchy, the cultural change that resulted from such royal patronage further embedded opera in the sphere of high culture. Victoria's particular passion was for Italian opera of the kind that subsequently predominated in London seasons at the Royal Italian Opera House in Covent Garden, built in 1847.[38] The prevalence of continental opera during this period has even led some historians to suggest that mid-century London rivalled Paris as the operatic and cultural epicentre of Europe because its proximity to the French capital allowed easy commuting between opera houses for a whole community of composers, conductors, and performers at this time. In any case, when essayist Hermann Klein saw fit to claim that 'the richest and most productive period *in the history of opera* coincided in date and length with what is known as the Victorian Era [and] is a fact that must be generally conceded', this related primarily to a romanticized view of the 'Grand' Italian operas that dominated Covent Garden and elsewhere in the West End. In other words, opera in Britain—or rather, a particular *kind* of European opera in London—was associated with high culture and royalty.[39]

Royal patronage and fashionable Italian work aside, the second half of the nineteenth century saw the British class system become more complicated and polarized. Industrial power and the concomitant shift from an agricultural economy to a mechanized industry brought with it an expanded labour class benefitting from enhanced union strength. At the same time, the newly moneyed middle classes comprising factory owners, import entrepreneurs, accountants, and tradesmen, embraced all things commercial, material, and aspirational.[40] Desperate to shore up a dividing line between themselves and their workers, this social shift led to an increase of 'conspicuous display', as the new middle class sought to affirm or perform their economic and cultural capital, not just between themselves, but to those above and below them in the hierarchy. Gradually, the opulence of opera attendance became about such 'fashionable acts': *being seen* by the right patron or sponsor from the aristocracy.[41] While the regnal aspect differentiated the British landscape from the scene in America, attendance at Italian opera and a display of cultural capital paralleled the American landscape mentioned above, as operatic culture in London became an index of taste and refinement, an ideological justification for the perpetuation of 'an elitist audience more interested in protecting its own exclusivity than in culture itself'.[42]

On both sides of the Atlantic, then, opera became an *ideologically* elite form in mid-to-late nineteenth-century culture. It transformed into an institution that would help perpetuate 'the duration of a system of authority', dissimulating power structures of the status quo in both the United States and Great Britain, as a nouveau riche borne variously of civil war or industrial development used 'stories of the past' to construct a particular 'socio-political imaginaire'.[43] However, the ideological parallels of power and prestige between seventeenth- and nineteenth-century Western operatic culture go beyond the elitism of patronage, thematic content, language of performance, or country of origin. In a very specific way, opera in the nineteenth century can be understood to sing ideology in its relationship to conceptions of voice throughout the history of the form.

'These warbling throats . . . ': Operatic Vocality and Metaphysical Ideology

Reflecting on the word setting for *L'Euridice* in 1601, Jacopo Peri wrote that:

> seeing that it was a question of dramatic poetry, and that therefore it was necessary by means of song to imitate speech (and there is no doubt that no one ever spoke singing), I judged that the ancient Greeks and Romans (whose tragedies, in the opinion of many, were sung throughout upon the stage) used a harmony which, transcending that of ordinary speech, was yet somewhat below the melody of song and took an intermediate form.[44]

Beyond the 'extraordinary' and mythological themes of operatic performance befitting aristocratic patronage, ancient theories of music and drama exerted a strong influence in the sixteenth and seventeenth centuries, including 'the opinion of many' which held that ancient Greek and Roman tragedy was 'sung throughout' in an 'intermediate form' of vocal expression (something Peri suggested would be captured in the monodic aesthetic of *stile rappresentativo* and would develop through versions of operatic recitative across the centuries).[45] Opera was therefore viewed as bringing ancient aesthetics into the Renaissance age.[46] Yet, beyond even the dramatic theories of Greek and Roman tragedians, this supposed reclamation of ancient performance practice was influenced by a more deep-seated fascination with antique philosophical thought. During the Renaissance, works including

Natale Comitis' *Mythologiae, sive explicationis fabularim libri decem (Ten Books of Mythology of Explanations of Fables)* (1551) depicted the universal order on a descending scale from the divine to the damned, with gods at the top, angelic realms at their service in the planetary sphere, the middling world of the mundane and earthly plain, and the underworld of fire and fury.

From Pythagoras through Plato, early Western philosophy had conceived of the universe as just such an 'unbroken' web of substantial and supersensible realms, even if various antique philosophers conceived of this in different ways. The Renaissance view of the world was not dualistic but holistic, and it placed humankind as both a bridge and 'borderline between material and immaterial worlds'.[47] With a fleshly, material body and an immortal, immaterial soul, the meeting point that connected these realms in humankind was their 'spirit', defined in the writings of early Renaissance theologian and humanist Marsilio Ficino. For Ficino, the 'spirit' was an airy and ethereal substance that was not quite body and not quite soul. This ineffability, as Gary Tomlinson has observed, meant that the 'spirit' had a special correspondence to voice, song, and music in Ficinian thinking. This is because the combination of music, with its 'rational harmonic motions' that paralleled the cosmological harmony of the universe, and song, with its 'airy and mimetic motions' that marked out a 'liminal place' of 'gesture, affect' and emotion rather than materiality, were, in Ficino's words, 'almost nothing other than another spirit'.[48] On this basis, Peri's reference to harmony, transcendence, and intermediate forms of vocal expression in his word settings of *L'Euridice* take on a metaphysical quality. Early experiments in operatic writing, then, not only offered convenient political resonances with grand ideals of mythology and ancient gods but imbued the voices that sang of these myths with an otherworldly sonority, connecting the elite culture of Renaissance Florence with the mysteries and power of the metaphysical realm by vocal and musical means.

As scholars including Tomlinson and Carolyn Abbate have suggested, this is one primary reason for the popularity of Orpheus as a figure in opera. In Greek mythology, Orpheus was a demigod and a musician—a useful diegetic tool in early operatic experiments to overcome the evident artifice of the form. Orpheus' 'powers of singing' were such that his voice persuaded Apollo to let him descend into hell and rescue his beloved Eurydice; allowed him to appeal to Hades for her release; and overwhelmed (but did not overpower) the Bacchantes—frenzied women who eventually took his life by severing his head in a Dionysian orgy. Orpheus therefore embodied the

Renaissance fascination with voice as something otherworldly. He acted as 'an encrypted [acoustic] image of opera's power to move its listeners' by putting audience members 'in touch with invisible, supersensory realms'.[49] This power is displayed in the many operas that re-tell the Orphic myth when the musical demigod, grief-stricken from losing Eurydice through his own weakness (looking back), retreats to the hills of Thrace and sings in lamentation, in moments such as Monteverdi and Striggio's 'Tu se Morta' (*L'Orfeo*, 1607, SV 318, act two). His voice—and the emotional excess it displays—moves the trees and birds to come and listen, joining him in his pain. In other words, Orpheus' voice leads to a change of nature and 'humoral disharmony'; his voice unbalances the universe. Little wonder that in *L'Orfeo* (1607), Orpheus' father arrives as a deux ex machina to restore Apollonian harmony to the cosmos and the universe. Understood as 'another spirit' in neo-Platonic Renaissance thought, then, voice became central to the ideological workings of a genre that has acted as 'the chief staging ground in elite Western culture for a belief in the existence of two worlds'—one material and one immaterial—since antiquity.[50] In received wisdom, voice has 'almost always been at the centre of operatic experience', inspiring 'feelings of devotion' in those who love the form and a sense of irritated confusion in those who do not, as it adapts, reflects, or gives voice to shifting cultural conceptions of the physical and metaphysical.[51]

While Renaissance thinking placed the human subject at the centre of the universe and the free flow of correspondences between the material and immaterial realms, Enlightenment thinkers such as René Descartes reconfigured this relationship. Descartes' phrase *cogito ergo sum* ('I think, therefore I am') encapsulated a cultural reorientation towards dualism rather than monism (such as the interconnectedness of the universe) in the mid-to-late seventeenth century. In his *Meditations of First Philosophy* (1641), Descartes argued that aside from the supernatural realm, the *mind* itself was immaterial; a person's ability to think, doubt, believe, and be self-aware of such was what made him or her a 'thinking thing' or 'soul'.[52]

The body, however, was material—separate from the immaterial soul of the mind. In this duality, the notion of 'spirits' with which voice had long been associated was understood as a material, bodily concept. '[W]hat I here name spirits', said Descartes, 'are nothing but material bodies and their one peculiarity is that they are bodies of extreme minuteness and that they move very quickly'.[53] Derived from pneumatology, these were chiefly physical and medical spirits, held to vibrate through the physical being, yet Descartes offers a further conception of their function in Article 27 of *Passions of the Soul* (1649): 'the perceptions, feelings, or emotions of the [immaterial] soul . . . are caused, maintained, and fortified by some movement of the spirits'. Separate from the semantics of words, voice—as an agent of feeling and emotion—is therefore rendered *material*, aligned with spirits that move through the body. The correspondences between the body and mind were now 'beyond the grasp of the intellect' and transcendent, and the power of the voice to arouse passions in the soul was therefore only experienced at the behest of an all-knowing, beneficent God. By this time, voice in opera had become a 'cipher' of the 'troubling separation' between physical and metaphysical realms.[54]

These currents of thought had discernible ramifications on operatic aesthetics from the mid-seventeenth century onwards. By 1670, French literary critic and essayist Charles de Saint-Évremond bemoaned that Italian opera had become 'contrary to Nature' because of all the singing.[55] In large part, this irritation related to the change in thought regarding matters of the supernatural realm. While the emotional excess of Orpheus' lament could change the universe through song, the intensity of such emotion—caused by matter and apprehended only by the unknowns of 'supersensible correspondence' between body and soul—had now become superfluous.[56] After all, in his *Compendium Musicae* (1618), Descartes asserted that while the bodily spirits cause and maintain passions in the soul, 'a proportion of some kind between the object and the sense itself is required' in order for it to be balanced and pleasurable, concluding that this logic meant 'the racket of guns or thunder is not apt for music, because it would evidently hurt the ears'. As Aristotle considered in his writing on sense perception, 'excess [of sound], whether high or low pitch, destroys hearing'.[57] In other words, the excessive vocality of Italian opera was becoming 'contrary to Nature' in the dualistic, scientific and 'rational' world of the Enlightenment. The 'juxtaposition of metaphysics with the material unleashes huge energies in certain librettists and opera composers' across the following century manifest through the development of national styles of opera in Italy and France and resulted in many operatic conventions that persist to this day.[58] For example, the style of Venetian opera that irritated de Saint-Évremond featured expositional recitative and '[a]rias in which virtuosity triumphed over recitative-like clarity'; a phono-centric aesthetic that prioritized sensation over reason, 'diminishing the signifying role of words' in the process.[59]

Such a focus on virtuosity rather than intelligibility has become a stereotype of the genre to the present day, seen here in work that would develop into the style of *opera seria.* As Tim Carter observes: 'For many, these warbling throats are indeed what opera is all about'.[60] Notwithstanding the dramatic and narrative agency of music within opera, or the historical changes of musical style, compositional approach, instrumentation, and orchestration across four centuries (subjects about which others have written), the so-called operatic voice has now become 'positioned above all other constituents as . . . essential to [the genre]'. In all of their 'artificial, stylized, eccentric, extreme, extravagant, exaggerated, excessive, grotesque, irrational and absurd' glory, voices in opera are 'hyper-real, seductive, irresistible, desired, worshipped and fetishized' by audiences and by scholars.[61]

In response to the Italianate excess popular with mass audiences in Vienna, the likes of which had so annoyed de Saint-Évremond, the work of composer Jean-Baptiste Lully came to exemplify French Baroque opera and the development of a French style, *tragédie en musique.* Perhaps as a direct reclamation of earlier operatic culture—and certainly as a reaction to the growing populism of decorous Venetian opera—Lullian opera was courtly and championed by King Louis XIV, who had commissioned the composer to establish the Royal Academy of Music in Paris in 1672.[62] French opera was therefore also an elite cultural form, with a reliance on classical tales befitting royal patronage in its growing canon of national work. For example, Lully's earlier works included *Alceste* (1674) based on Euripides' *Alcestis*, and *Isis* (1677) which was inspired by Ovid's *Metamorphoses.* Where Lullian operas did not concern themselves with the supernatural world of myths and demigods, these were nevertheless found in the Prologue, a brief opening section that was often designed as a nationalistic 'dedication to its royal patron and ideal(ised) spectator'.[63]

Functioning as propaganda to 'preserve the power' of the monarchy at the time, French opera was also ideologically elite, featuring antique gods and heroes in a way that perpetuated ancient notions in French culture. In short, it likewise told stories of the past in a way that paralleled, but differed from, the emotional excess of its sixteenth-century Italian counterpart or its American and British manifestation two centuries later.[64] Through the development of *tragédie en musique*, Lully and his contemporaries shifted the focus from elaborate Italian alternations of recitative and aria to a more integrated compositional approach, enhancing the clarity of words and limiting the presence of coloratura or vocalise in performance practice. In addition, French opera tended towards other forms of musical-poetic and theatrical expression, including the use of ballet and extended instrumental sections.

In a world that separated matter (vocal sound) from nonmatter (subsequent affect or experience), music and language 'grew more and more distinct from one another', operating through difference rather than the similitude of Renaissance thought.[65] Beyond the narratives of *tragédie en musique,* the richness of musical variations in French opera and its employment of dance as a dramatic form meant that, in increasing fashion, 'music and action [were] presumed to stand in for the speech', a notion that has come to typify many contemporary views of the genre.[66] After all, writing about the effect of music in performance, the composer Jean-Philippe Rameau (a defender of Lully's work and successor to his dominance of French theatrical art in the early eighteenth century) wrote that to enjoy music fully 'calls for a sheer abandonment of oneself'. Rameau went further, considering the nature of vocal performance itself: 'It is necessary first to sing . . . with the motion the words require, without adding to them and without concerning oneself with any other feeling but that which the melody is able to give rise to of itself'.[67] In other words, while correspondences between the body and mind were supernatural, Rameau abandoned Aristotelian proportion. Instead, vocal *affect*—the result of correspondence, if not convergence, between the material and metaphysical realms—became the focus, even in French opera.

The relationship between voice, materiality, and metaphysics continued to be explored through the eighteenth century, with Mozart offering echoes of the approaches discussed above. Like the recurring figure of Orpheus, Mozart's operas have been much discussed, but any consideration of opera such as this would seem incomplete without some reference to his work and, in particular, to the ways in which voice type became associated formally with character during the Classical period in which Mozart was writing. In 1788, *Don Giovanni* first graced the stage of the National Theatre of Bohemia (in what is now Prague). Mozart's opera tells the story of the unrepentant titular libertine, murderer, and seducer who meets his fate in the finale, at the hands of Don Pedro (Il Commendatore)—his victim from early in act one, killed by Don Juan while protecting his daughter's honour. First performed by Luigi Bassi, the protagonist's voice is written for a baritone, and in its tessitura, with angular rhythms and rapid changes of pace, Tomlinson suggests it is a voice of 'sensuous immediacy'.[68] As K. Mitchells has noted, from the Classical period onwards, 'the baritone voice is invested with a particular meaning, owing to its middle position between the "eccentric" voice types of tenor and bass. The baritone is well placed to represent normal man' with all his imperfections and fatal flaws.[69] Much like Don Juan in Mozart and Da

Ponte's opera, baritone characters 'often . . . fail and sometimes . . . die' as a result of their flaws.[70]

It is notable that while Don Juan is a baritone role, this voice type did not become a standard designation until the nineteenth century. The formal relationships between voice type and stock character traits in opera became established between the Classical period and the early nineteenth century, following developments in the *opera buffa* and dialogue opera traditions in which stock comic characters were voiced using an early *Fach* system. Before this, virtuosity was valued more than range or type, with castrati frequently voicing the roles of female protagonists in the Italian tradition. The Classical period, however, saw the arrival of the 'heroic tenor' and led to the recognizable voice types of bass, mezzo-soprano, and baritone.[71]

These voice types—largely unchanged since the early nineteenth century—are summarized by opera scholar Catherine Clément.[72] While she does not consider directly the baritone voice, a young soprano often sings a naïve heroine or a victim, someone perhaps given to a descent into madness. Older soprano and mezzo-soprano voices are often associated with a female character who resists, who is worldly-wise, contentious, perhaps at times even malevolent. The tenor is a young, love-struck hero—a courageous masculine figure who, in many operas, meets a less-than-ideal demise along with his soprano lover. The bass and contralto (the lowest male and female voice types) are more specific in their designation, representing maturity and wisdom as 'voices from beyond the human world'.[73]

It is revealing that Don Pedro, and Don Juan's long-suffering servant Leporello, are both performed by bass voices. Throughout the opera, Leporello is the voice of reason—with richer, legato vocal lines, contrasted with Don Juan's hurried, harried vocality. In this, Leporello is wise and authoritative. If a bass voice sings of something otherworldly, metaphysical, then it must also be appropriate for Don Pedro—whose statue in act three starts magically to sing, interrupting a conversation between Don Juan and Leporello, and banishing Don Juan to hell among the demons when he proves unrepentant of his ways. A statue that sings—much like Orpheus' head on the lyre—performs a metaphysical voice that contrasts with the protagonist in a performance of mutual 'exclusion', rendering them inextricably bound. In other words, in Mozart's writing, contrasting voice types offered a sonic performance of the distinction and simultaneous co-dependence of the material and immaterial worlds. To understand the one required the de facto presence of the other.[74]

Just as low voices sing of wisdom and otherworldliness, at the other extreme, the coloratura soprano of the Queen of the Night (*Die Zauberflöte*, 1791) offers another example of metaphysical vocality in Mozart's writing.[75] The ways in which Mozart and Da Ponte use 'acoustic symbolism' to characterize the Queen of the Night do more than offer another voice type.[76] Desiring to rescue her daughter Pamina from the evil demon Sarastro, the Queen implores the handsome prince Tamino for his help in her first aria, 'O zittre nicht, mein lieber Sohn' ('Oh, tremble not, my beloved son'). Later, handing Pamina a dagger, the Queen commands her daughter to exact revenge upon her captor in the aria, 'Der Hölle Rache kocht in meinem Herzen' ('Hell's vengeance rages in my heart'). Both moments see the Queen display intense emotion akin to Orpheus' grief for the loss of Eurydice. While vocal extremity is employed in both arias, with the soprano originally expected to reach F6 (F above high C), Mozart's royal protagonist does this during virtuosic displays of voice beyond words.

While Saint-Évremond had earlier bemoaned Venetian opera because it prioritized sensation over reason through a focus on voice over text, the Queen's use of vocalise may be heard as maternal anger. Jason D'Aoust has argued that operatic vocality often acts as a 'historically expanding portal to the unconscious desires that lie beyond linguistic representation'.[77] In this case, such desires are for revenge that cannot be expressed through words. As Mladen Dolar puts it when language dissolves into mere sound, 'the voice becomes senseless and threatening, all the more so because of its seductive and intoxicating powers'.[78] The Queen's voice, then, at times offers 'pure music as a transcendent utterance' in a metaphysical demonstration of emotional excess that, like its Renaissance antecedent, seems otherworldly.[79] Considering the Queen's emotional turmoil, Michel Poizat has even suggested that in these moments, the 'scansion of the vocalise' drives towards a purer and more transcendent voice than Renaissance participation in supernatural realms or access to the metaphysical plane in the theosophical dualities of the early modern period: the 'vocal cry'.[80] This 'cry'—an untenable emotion divorced entirely from words—has become a well-known aspect of operatic performance.

If voices in opera act as a 'portal' to 'unconscious desires', how might moments of vocal cry be understood? How do these moments relate to the recurring presence of metaphysical vocality in opera? While the Renaissance world understood itself in relation to Platonic and Pythagorean philosophies of the universe, and the Enlightenment reconfigured metaphysical ideals through Cartesian dualities, the world of the late eighteenth and nineteenth centuries was conditioned by the transcendent idealism of Kantian philosophy. Echoing Cartesian distinctions between the material and immaterial, Immanuel Kant's *Critique of Pure Reason* (1781) sought to distinguish between the *phenomenal* world perceived by conscious awareness and its *noumenal* counterpart—the world as it was behind the mask of the phenomenal. Unlike Descartes, however, Kantian thinking (and, later, that of Arthur Schopenhauer) relocated the correspondences between knowable *phenomenon* and the unknowable *noumenon* within the mind of individual subjects. The negotiation between sensible apprehension and its supersensible properties, therefore, became an internal experience as a means of constituting subjective knowledge, rather than metaphysical negotiation at the behest of a beneficent deity.

This new subjectivity, now implicit, has often been identified in operatic vocality of the nineteenth century and the recurring feature of vocal cry. Present in the Queen of the Night's arias, we might also hear this cry in Isolde's transfiguration during Wagner's *Tristan and Isolde* (1865), in the death scene of Berg's *Lulu* (1937), or the 'Bell Song' from Delibes' *Lakmé* (1883), which contains a rare moment of a cappella vocalise that arouses the 'suspicious power of music and its capacity to move us without rational speech'.[81] Vocal cry has often been inflected with a psychoanalytical quality, as something 'mythical', 'an unattainable but always desired vocal object hidden somewhere behind and beyond the signifying voice'.[82] In other words, the vocal cry is *noumenal*—behind the materiality of the singing voice. For Dolar, the wordless excesses of this voice represent a Lacanian *objet petit a*—the unattainable object that is always trying to be found.[83] Carlo Zuccarini has likewise suggested that vocal cry represents a 'lost object', a primal voice *before* language. In Zuccarini's analysis, this relates to an infant's cry, a pre-linguistic form of direct and intense expressivity. The anthropology of Steven Mithen takes this one step further, suggesting that the primal quality of this cry signifies the very origins of human communicative capacity; before language, there was only voice.[84] Whether from the noumenal perspective of Kantian thought, the Lacanian view of the unattainable *objet petit a*, or the anthropological position of prelinguistic primal utterance, vocal cry has been understood as a phonic evocation of a metaphysical origin beyond and before linguistic understanding or reason throughout its history in opera. From the metaphysical song of Orpheus to the *Singspiel* by Mozart about a magical flute, or the Norse mythologies and sorcery of Wagner's Ring Cycle, vocal cry—along with the metaphysical properties of voice types, and an emphasis on virtuosity—continued to render voice in opera richly fetishized, through to the nineteenth century.

By the early twentieth century, however, Dolar and Žižek wryly claim that the social imaginaire of cultural elitism meant that opera houses were effectively museums, producing a programme of 'about fifty operas from Gluck to Puccini'.[85] Carter also agrees that '[d]espite periodic attempts to remove opera from the pantheons of high art and into more experimental theatrical (and even non-theatrical) performance spaces, it remains a highly specialized activity limited to specific performance environments'.[86] The result is that while opera began as an elite form in Western Renaissance culture, and for much of the seventeenth, eighteenth and early nineteenth centuries formed part of a 'shared' culture, the 'socio-political imaginaire' of the nineteenth-century Anglo-American world reclaimed opera as a high art form. It acted as a dissimulated 'reaffirmation' of power structures, legitimizing the authority of the new establishment through an ideological (and vocal) connection to the universal, otherworldly qualities of early civilization and the wealth and cultural prestige of Renaissance Europe. Yet, as opera ascended to the echelons of high culture in America and continued as a forum for 'conspicuous display' in the social hierarchies of Great Britain, a combination of renewed national energy, metropolitan and industrial expansion, and rapidly changing geo-political dynamics made space for a 'tangled, chaotic mess' of popular cultural forms to occupy the lower spheres of entertainment.[87] Much like the 'messy variety' of artistic currents and narratives that converged to create what we now call opera, popular musical theatre would likewise be borne of a 'myriad different types of musical theatrical forms', in parallel developments between New York and London.[88] In what ways would musical theatre eschew ideological ideals, enacting a 'rupture' in the socio-political imaginaire?

'A myriad different types . . . ': From Fracture to Rupture and the Emergence of Musical Theatre

In the same way that the 'birth' of opera cannot be agreed upon with certainty—cited variously as Peri's *L'Euridice* (1600) or Monteverdi's *L'Orfeo* (1607)—the precise moment of 'rupture' that produced what is now known as musical theatre is difficult to define. In 1984, American musicologist Edith

Borroff wrote that '[t]he history of musical comedy begins in confusion', and this confusion arises when we survey the variety of forms and formats which characterized the theatrical landscape in the United States and Great Britain during the nineteenth century.[89] Beyond the highbrow elitism of opera, North America was a world of stock repertory companies saturated with the trend for *melodrama*—a form that often alternated scenes with songs, but which, by this time, was employing music to heighten emotionally intense moments.[90] In the early nineteenth century, there was a fashion for famous singers from home and abroad to tour numerous *repertory circuits* and perform at *concert* halls, ensuring the centrality of music and vocal performance in popular cultural life.[91] Elsewhere, *extravaganzas* offered visual spectacle and featured acrobatics, circus performers, and special stage effects along with music and dance.[92] Other forms would later grow in popularity, including the social absurdism of *farce* and the more 'respectable' *French revue* and *vaudeville*—a form which would come to supersede *minstrelsy* as a dominating force in American culture.[93]

Beginning in the 1820s, minstrelsy originated with working-class white men of Anglo-Irish descent using blackface to codify their whiteness '"vis-à-vis" their collective and subjective perceptions of blackness'.[94] Borrowing from European carnival, pantomime, and using British folk melodies, minstrelsy came to be characterized by the performance of racist stereotypes, depicting black slaves through exaggerated dialect, mocking physicality, and the use of burnt cork. As 'the first original form of "popular" entertainment in the nation', minstrelsy offered 'a secondhand vision of black life created by white performers', developing to become the predominant popular art form in America.[95] As African American performers also began to form minstrel troupes while 'saddled with the stage conventions', artists including Bert Williams, Bessie Smith, and Ernest Hogan ended up perpetuating derogatory stereotypes while establishing careers that reached beyond the burlesque houses where minstrel shows commonly played.[96] For example, Hogan composed the number 'All Coons Look Alike to Me' in 1890, starting a trend for what became known as 'coon songs' (a derogatory term which is used here only for historical context).[97] Allen Woll suggests that the development of these songs in minstrelsy was responsible for the incorporation of minstrel numbers in early musical comedy. Their popularity was such that the actress May Irwin, who was blonde-haired and blue-eyed, even negotiated the contract for any musical variety and early musical comedy in which she appeared on Broadway to feature her popular success with 'Bully

Song' in 1895. The number featured a syncopated rhythm associated with African American minstrelsy, syncopation which featured in jazz, ragtime, blues, and other popular forms. As African American popular music scholar Matthew D. Morrison concludes, in this way blackface minstrelsy 'laid the foundation for the birth of American popular music', including musical theatre; a claim developed further in chapter 2.[98]

In Britain, a smorgasbord of popular forms likewise offered accessible fare attended by a large cross section of society. In particular, burlesque acts were popular, often engaging in a broad parody of an opera or ballet, satirizing or mocking the cultural pretensions and theatrical conventions of the original work. As early as 1831 in London, the burlesque *Olympic Revels* featured the grand gods of Greek mythology betting on a game of cards in a drinking den, upending the cultural reference point of early Western civilization upon which much elite art still based itself. The varied programme of music hall performances also included popular songs, dance, sketches, comedy, and humorous responses to topical news of the day.[99] In common with minstrel shows in the United States, music hall acts would likewise showcase excerpts from the latest opera in a less satirical manner than burlesque—but without the virtuosity or pomposity of the opera house. Reflecting on one such performance at the Canterbury Music Hall in Lambeth, London, in 1867, one patron wrote that the operatic excerpts were 'somewhat coarse', 'badly sung and vulgarly accompanied', but programmed for audiences who enjoyed the subversion of highbrow pretensions at the halls.[100]

While African American performers were subject to oppressive US race laws and had to work within the system, 'participating in discourses of imperialism' as a way of enacting resistance and empowerment, they nonetheless also contributed to the rich fabric of entertainment in nineteenth-century Britain.[101] The African American bandleader Frank Johnson brought his band to London in 1837, even playing by Royal command at Buckingham Palace, while Horace Weston was lauded for his virtuosic banjo playing in Henry C. Jarrett and Harry Palmer's touring production of *Uncle Tom's Cabin*, which played at the Princess Theatre, London, in September 1878.[102] The same year, the black American variety show *Oriental America* transferred to England from New York. Created by John W. Isham (an American of African descent), the show, Woll notes, was a serious effort which included sketches, buck and wing dancing, and the cakewalk. Nevertheless, its inclusion of 'selections from *Faust*, *Rigoletto*, *Carmen* and *Il Trovatore*' in the finale 'demonstrated that blacks could also perform material hitherto reserved for whites'.[103] One reviewer, in Liverpool, was particularly impressed by the vocals of Sidney Woodward, William C. Elkins, and Maggie Scott, noting the 'great musical talent . . . displayed by the principals'.[104] As Sarah Whitfield, Sean Mayes, Thomas L. Riis, and other scholars have shown, the influence of African musical styles and culture on the British musical stage cannot therefore be overlooked, with one notable example appearing in the following chapter.[105]

Somewhere between the opera house and the music hall, European operetta and its English sibling comic opera also proved popular on both sides of the Atlantic. These were forms which drew on operatic conventions such as recitative and aria while trading in high romance and sentiment (operetta) or light-hearted satire (comic opera). Richard Traubner once described operetta as 'opera that literally takes itself lightly', noting that in many instances, operetta and comic opera are treated as one form.[106] Contrasted with the grandeur or solemnity of opera as a highbrow entertainment in the nineteenth century, both of these forms were more socially respectable than burlesque or minstrelsy. A 'simplified' vocal set-up (including straighter tones in the higher registers) distinguished operetta and comic opera from grand opera, allowing for a clearer focus on the words.[107] European operetta and English comic opera therefore mediated the metaphysical encoding of operatic vocality through its more popular or light-hearted delivery. While they employed knowing topicality, romantic sentiment or light satire redolent of more popular fare, works by Gilbert and Sullivan, Lehár, Victor Herbert, or Reginald de Koven were still careful not to shock a middle-class conservative audience. For example, in the realm of English comic opera, any 'topsy-turvydom' that had taken place through the evening was always reconciled by the finale, enacting a 'reaffirmation' of existing ideals while nevertheless performing a sense of upended-ness that would resonate with a new middle-class audience yet to find their place as social aspirants.[108] Notwithstanding the ideological reaffirmation of the *dénouement*, the mere act of burlesquing, subverting, or challenging existing social structures saw comic opera begin to facilitate a subtle critique of the present. It may even be (proto)utopian, because at times 'what is at stake in utopia is the *apparent givenness* of every system of authority' rather than the authority itself.[109] The *possibility* of subversion and a charmingly melodic 'unmasking' of power structures can therefore lead to a kind of critical 'rupture'. That rupture facilitates an exploration of the possible and a consideration of what *might* happen when existing ideological structures are challenged or 'radically rethought' towards 'a different future . . . full of hope'.[110]

Through the currency of topical references and popular song, mockery of the status quo, exposure of ideological conventions, and the unmasking of power structures, the vocal delivery of operetta and comic opera, melodrama, extravaganza, minstrelsy, revue, burlesque, farce, variety, vaudeville, and music hall therefore engaged in critiques of the present, enacting moments of response or challenge to the social imaginaire of the nineteenth century on both sides of the Atlantic. Yet, as discrete forms or practices, no single genre, style, or form could entirely constitute a 'rupture'. Rather, we might think of these individual moments as 'fractures'. When a critical mass of these fractures coalesced, and the morass of attitudes, practices, conventions, and aesthetics above were drawn together in one moment, the 'rupture' that gave way to early musical theatre (in the form of musical comedy) occurred. Echoing Borroff's earlier assertion, identifying when this happened is a confusing task. As Katherine K. Preston has noted, 'disagreement on the "first" musical become[s] readily apparent as soon as one attempts to sort out the myriad different types of musical theatrical forms' that cross-fertilized during the latter stages of the nineteenth century.[111] Rather than approach this moment through an overt focus on formal or aesthetic properties, however, what happens when the question becomes one of shifting cultural meaning towards utopian performance? At what moment might a shift away from metaphysical ideologies of 'reaffirmation' occur in aesthetic encoding or performance style?

Musical theatre lore attributes the title of 'the first musical' (or 'protomusical' or 'forerunner') to works such as *The Black Crook* (1866) and *Evangeline* (1874), both produced in New York. In what ways might these two works have enacted utopian forms of 'rupture' leading to the emergence of early musical comedy? Produced by Henry C. Jarrett and Henry Palmer, *The Black Crook* opened at Niblo's Garden, New York, on 12 September 1866. A re-telling of Goethe's *Faust* by Charles M. Barras, it combined traditional and contemporary music and song interpolated into the production and arranged by Thomas Baker. These elements were augmented by the inclusion of circus and, prominently, a *corps de ballet*. Its heady combination of burlesque, dance, music, spectacle, and story earned it the moniker of the first musical. However, in its mixture of forms and styles, albeit threaded loosely together by a thin plot, the original production of *The Black Crook* was never a coherent whole, apt to change with each new production. By the time it arrived in London in December 1872, it had an entirely new score and resembled an *opéra bouffe* more than a proto-musical comedy, containing 'almost none of the vernacular attributes of books, lyrics, music and dancing which [later] distinguish musical comedy'.[112] While it appealed to 'lowly sensibilities' with scantily clad female dancers and contemporary songs, its use of *Faust* as source material hardly focused on the vernacular. Even if presented 'with a rather broad wink' through its use of circus and comedy, it more closely resembled an artfully contrived performance of a now-high cultural myth, with magic and metaphysics throughout.[113]

Likewise, *Evangeline, or The Belle of Acadia* was a musical comedy of the burlesque form. It was written by J. Cheever Goodwin and Ned Rice and was first performed on 27 July 1874, also at Niblo's Garden in New York. It differed from *The Black Crook* in its inclusion of an original score to accompany the story, while the libretto is based on Henry Wadsworth Longfellow's serious epic poem *Evangeline: A Tale of Acadia* (1847) and is written in rhyming couplets, leading to an emphasis on the *sound* rather than the *sense* of the story. Notwithstanding its use of an original score, its source material is high-minded and, in its emphasis on rhyme and rhythm rather than dialogue and prose, may even recall some of the philosophical debates to be had regarding Italian opera in the eighteenth century. On this basis, while the inclusion of popular musical forms appealed to contemporary taste beyond the 'high culture' of the opera house, both *The Black Crook* and *Evangeline* more reasonably represent stages (albeit significant ones) on the path towards a more totalizing 'rupture' of musical theatre.

If opera sings ideology through its perpetuation of metaphysical ideals and high-minded subject matter, the reliance on these in the above two works does little to suggest a departure sufficient to give rise to a new form in which voice might be heard differently. Perhaps the most decisive break might be located in England during the final decade of the century, and across the works of English producer George Edwardes (see Figure 1.1).

Edwardes was a producer with a wealth of experience across popular forms of entertainment. In 1875, at twenty years of age, Edwardes was a theatre manager for the comic opera producer Richard D'Oyly Carte. Becoming managing director of the Savoy Theatre, in 1881 he assisted in the production of Gilbert and Sullivan comic operas. Four years later, he became joint manager of the Gaiety Theatre and turned to producing the burlesques for which the Gaiety was known. Through the dual combination of operetta and burlesque, along with elements of music hall and American variety,

Figure 1.1 English musical comedy producer George Edwardes. Photographer unknown. NPGx194421. Reproduced under academic license. © National Portrait Gallery, London, England.

Edwardes facilitated the 'rupture' of musical comedy in works beginning with *In Town*.[114] Subtitled a musical farce, *In Town* opened at the Prince of Wales Theatre, London, on 15 October 1892, transferring to the Gaiety Theatre on Boxing Day, 1892. It would run for 292 performances. Opening on Broadway in September 1897, it ran for a less-successful 40 performances but still helped initiate a new form of musical comedy show on Broadway and in London. Produced by Edwardes, it was written by Adrian Ross and James T. Tanner, with an original score by F. Osmond Carr.

Unlike either *The Black Crook* or *Evangeline*, *In Town* was topical, urbane, and whimsical.[115] It told the frivolous tale of Captain Coddington, a penniless man about town who gives his upper-class friend a taste of London nightlife, from aristocratic establishments to seedy drinking dens. Constructed in episodes familiar to audiences from other popular variety forms, Ross and Tanner nevertheless told the story in a way that was more coherent than burlesque or music hall. Likewise, Osmond Carr's score (before any popular musical interpolations were added during the run) combined popular song styles such as the waltz, with operetta and speciality numbers for star performers sung with the 'simplified' vocal set-up of operetta and with elements of the speech-inflections found in music hall. As a popular work, it also featured a scene in which actresses—viewed as little more than prostitutes in Victorian England—lunched with the upper set, challenging the 'apparent givenness' of ideologically constrained social attitudes in a manner reminiscent of comic opera.[116] In other words, *In Town* was also utopian. True to form, however, the finale saw Coddington win the heart of the *prima donna* as she became ennobled, much in the same way that future Edwardes productions would perform rags-to-riches tales of shop girls and runaway girls marrying into the aristocracy. Yet, when such challenges were combined with a decisive shift away from the metaphysical and an overt celebration of modernity was given voice through more vernacular or popular singing styles derived from operetta and burlesque, musical comedy (and later, musical theatre on both sides of the Atlantic) enacted a 'rupture' in the social imaginaire.

This is not to suggest that one work, in 1892, birthed an entirely new form. *In Town* was not even called a 'musical comedy' by Edwardes and, for several decades, the creative teams, producers, musicians, and performers who made names for themselves in musical comedy were equally at home in operetta, comic opera, music hall, and even serious opera. In contrast with the pastoral concerns of *Evangeline* or the metaphysical qualities of *The Black Crook*, the urban modernity and topicality of *In Town* offered a foundation from which musical comedy (and later, musical theatre) would develop. By explicitly rejecting an ideological 'reaffirmation' of the past, it relocated its ideals away from the sanctity of high culture and towards something more utopian.

In its liberal combination of high and low cultural reference points and styles, *In Town*—and the works that followed—drew together a wealth of 'fractures' into a 'rupture', and came to occupy a realm of popular culture described in the introduction as 'middlebrow' with respect to the potential production of cultural meanings.[117] Sufficiently distanced from lowbrow sensibilities through knowing parody, while owing its 'charm' to the fact it lovingly references the high culture to which it aspires, middlebrow fare has elsewhere been characterized as 'parasitical'.[118] In this sense, it is 'dependent on the existence of both a high and a low brow for its identity', while assuming the role of cultural critic by 'reworking their structures and aping their insights' as a predominantly middle-class form, the politics of which is explored further in the next chapter.[119]

The middlebrow blend of high and low vocal aesthetics is also heard in the 'parasitical' plurality of musical and vocal styles across musical theatre. While the vocal aesthetics of *In Town* would have been shared with operetta by virtue of the technique needed to project and the performers involved, the combination of straighter tones of operetta, presence of interpolated speciality songs, burlesque parody, and popular musical styles to tell an urban, topical story nevertheless served to 'rework' these references in a new and modern way. Indeed, musical theatre at large has grown unafraid to borrow musical and vocal styles from anywhere, including the opera house and the music hall, drawing on white European operetta, the 'Blacksound' of American popular music, and other cultural influences at will.[120] With the arrival of amplification in auditoria and the frequent use of microphones from the mid-twentieth century onwards, voice in musical theatre experienced a technological revolution—perhaps even a further 'rupture'. This facilitated an even greater stylistic palette in performance, shifting musical theatre vocal aesthetics ever further away from the operatic properties of early musical comedy.

For example, *Bye Bye Birdie* (1960) features rock and roll sounds, *Hair* (1968) is styled using folk-rock, and *Spring Awakening* (2008) uses rock music, while *Dear Evan Hansen* (2016) features pop sounds, *Dreamgirls* (1981) bears influences of R&B and soul music, and *In the Heights* (2008) blends hip hop and rap with Latino rhythms. Unlike the relatively ossified codification of operatic voices, musical theatre has been able to adjust, adapt, and adopt as required, a process and characteristic of the musical stage explored in chapter 2.[121] The result is a sound-world that has become 'unique among musical genres involving vocal performance in that it draws upon whatever musical styles suit its purpose, especially popular music'.[122] Musical theatre vocality, then, is the perpetual in-between—a heady mix of cultures, ideals, and styles encoded with diverse and divergent cultural meanings, while rooted in the vernacular rather than metaphysical.

'Better than an opera': Easy Transpositions?

Given the marked differences between a form which sings utopia and one which gives voice to metaphysical ideologies, it may seem surprising that analyses of voice in musical theatre often rely on paradigms and parameters from opera studies. However, this borrowing is understandable as it allows for useful comparisons and transpositions using established reference points. For example, the foregoing trope of voice type as an index of characterization in Mozart's opera is alive and well in musical theatre scholarship of the twenty-first century. In *Changed for Good* (2008) Stacy Wolf used reference to classical voice types in constructing a feminist reading of voice, exploring how stereotypical associations of voice and character are both used *and* challenged in the musical. Wolf notes that even in the mid-twentieth century, voice types still adhered to operatic characterizations.[123] In *West Side Story* (1957), 'Maria, the soprano [is] the naive "virgin"-in-love who can see beyond skin color [and] persuades Anita, the mezzo and sexually experienced woman bound to her ethnicity, that love conquers all'.[124]

By the early twenty-first century, however, Wolf listens to the voices of G(a)linda and Elphaba in *Wicked* (2003) and hears more nuanced and subversive characterization than other iterations of female leads. With a particular focus on the duets between the two witches (one bad, one good, both much misunderstood), Wolf suggests that while these characters seem at odds with each other in a narrative that conspires to separate them, their voices bring them together. Considering the closing number 'For Good', Wolf notes that:

> their voices [are] in the same register, as if the music insists on putting them in the same place. Emotionally and musically, the two are intertwined, as they switch between alto and soprano parts, each taking her turn to sing higher than the other. They share the melody and the harmony, and each woman's voice crosses over the others [then they] sing the last line in unison, ending together on the same, mid-range note.[125]

Wolf—incisive, detailed, and provocative throughout her analysis—builds an argument with explicit reference to classical voice types and characterizations, noting the peculiarity that both are witches and yet both transgress the vocal boundaries between the soprano-heroine and the more familiar mezzo voice type. Yet, this reading replicates Tomlinson's in the consideration of Don Pedro and Don Juan above. The vocal relationship between G(a)linda and Elphaba is a variation of the mutual 'exclusion' which renders them bound together forever.[126] Wolf's argument requires the de facto presence of opposing phonic ideals: good and bad. Put another way, the analytical constraints in Wolf's analysis reinforce a construction of binary opposites which echo those heard in ideological properties of operatic vocality: material and immaterial, matter and nonmatter, *noumenal* and *phenomenal*.[127]

This is not to dismiss Wolf's analysis. Such paradigms allow for useful and engaging positions to be taken and developed. Yet, might such an inclusion imply that an operatic reference point—perpetuating a 'reaffirmation' of metaphysical ideologies—is a necessary precondition to legitimate the way we read, listen to, talk about, or understand the utopian potential of musical theatre voice(s)? After all, in the introduction to *Changed for Good*, Wolf herself cites opera scholar Carolyn Abbate to note that 'in opera, although some female roles are narrow, demeaning, passive, or long-suffering and convey weakness, the performer sings with incredible strength'.[128] Notwithstanding the richness of Wolf's study, this invocation of the female *in opera* acts as a catalyst for the entire consideration. Operatic paradigms, then, serve to validate musical theatre scholarship, a situation repeated in discussions of effect and reception.

At times, the idea of vocal cry (or 'money notes', as Millie Taylor more colloquially puts it in the 'commercial jargon' of contemporary musical theatre) offers a palatable and transposable reference point for analysis.[129] At such extreme moments, the human voice seems at its most devastating and otherworldly through a pure sonority which becomes the sole object of a listener's attention. The emotional intent is often so great that the voice seems to transcend the need for words or even the body.[130] This phonic disembodiment is an affective precondition for audience members or listeners to experience the 'power' of the voice as a 'becoming' rather than a 'being' object; active, powerful, moving, apt to 'strike us without our being able to foresee or control' its impact.[131] Small wonder, then, that at such moments in musical theatre, the transcendent ideal that characterized the Queen of the Night, Lulu's death scene, or Isolde's transfiguration seems apt. Using Abbate and Poizat, Alison L. McKee (2012) has considered the fetishizing and function of disembodied voice in opera as an agent of erotic desire for Christine by the Phantom in Lloyd Webber's musical.[132]

Elsewhere, moments of vocal cry are heard in *Jesus Christ Superstar* (1971). Using falsetto, both Jesus Christ and his betrayer Judas Iscariot—one divine, one dissident—employ vocal cry at moments of extreme dramatic tension or emotion. Jesus accesses his falsetto cry during the song 'Gethsemane', while Judas does likewise in the anguished 'Damned for All Time', and in the mocking title song. While the Messiah may easily be heard to access supernatural realms through his voice—what about Judas? The parity of vocal cry between these characters could suggest that either Judas has access to the divine or Jesus is imperfect, flawed, or fallen. These two sonic possibilities fracture the idea of the metaphysical realm in one instance or the other. Lloyd Webber's use of a rock aesthetic might further complicate things. First, the tenor voices of both characters are more closely associated with 'urban rebellion' in their textural nod to rock music—a form that is often held to be 'of undisputed origin', borne from the grit of human experience, and considered in depth in chapter 2 in relation to the appropriation of African vocal styles into the realms of (white) popular music. If this voice can in any way access the primal, it is closer to Mithen's anthropological origins than divine or metaphysical transcendence. Second, in the original 1971 production, all principal vocalists sang using hand-held microphones, an aesthetic that Peter Wicke and Rachel Fogg note mediated any expressivity through technology.[133] Compared with the unamplified acoustic shock of the operatic cry (the 'angel's cry', as Poizat puts it), can the earthy effect of this rock aesthetic be understood in the same way?

As a form of vocal cry, the presence of belt in musical theatre as a paradigm of the 'Broadway sound' offers an additional challenge to the assumption that such vocal excess is always transcendent or ethereal.[134] The pained humanity of Fantine's cry in *Les Misérables* (1985), Molly's grief in *Ghost* (2011), and Kathy's frustrated despair in 'See, I'm Smiling' (*The Last Five Years,* 2001) exist on a continuum of belted voices that connect them to Ethel Merman's C5 virtuosity. Beyond the technical and mechanical production of belting noted earlier in this chapter, Tracy Bourne, Maeve Garnier, and Diana Kenny have listened closely to this aesthetics, locating its origins in the lowbrow culture of early twentieth-century vaudeville, where white performers including Stella Mayhew and Sophie Tucker parodied African American vocal styles.[135] Lyricist and scholar Masi Asare has also traced the 'lineage of Broadway belters' to blues singers such as Gertrude 'Ma' Rainey, Bessie Smith, and Ethel Walters, noting that this particular connection is 'profoundly underacknowledged' in the history of Broadway voices.[136] Drawing playfully on Richard Schechner's notion that performance is twice-behaved, Asare suggests that the Broadway belt often associated with white performers such as Merman or Bernadette Peters is a 'twice-heard' voice which exists 'across racial lines', arguing against 'listenings that would filter out the frequencies of and impact of black blues singers on the musical theatre belt sound, attending to the specific bodies through which its shouted tones resounded in historical context'.[137] If the belt voice has been co-opted from black musical aesthetics in an act of erasure, the application of Western operatic paradigms in its analysis becomes limited. How, then, are we to understand the cultural politics of the belt voice beyond emotional excess and transcendence?

It is not simply through a focus on voice types or the transcendent ideals of 'vocal cry' that analyses of musical theatre demonstrate a reliance on models or ideas borrowed from opera scholarship. Derek Miller's (2012) consideration of the pleasure of singing along to a cast recording draws explicitly on a queer reading of operatic voices from Wayne Koestenbaum.[138] Dominic Symonds's use of Abbate and Poizat sees him develop a discussion of voice, corporeality, and actor-musicianship, along with Matthew Lockitt's (2014) use of Abbate to consider the relationship between diegetic song, the world of the musical and the self-awareness of characters in Michael John LaChiusa's *Bernarda Alba* (2006).[139] In this case, Lockitt draws on Abbate's distinction between the phenomenal and noumenal in music to consider how diegetic moments can transform into something more, when the self-aware singing character is joined by those who—in the world of the musical—are not. Once again, this invocation of operatic paradigms introduces a metaphysical realm into a consideration of musical theatre voice, a realm that may seem at odds with the diegetic, earthy folk singing of LaChiusa's musical.[140] Analytical hermeneutics using voice type or vocal cry have no doubt heralded some fascinating and provocative readings. Yet, is it right to analyse musical theatre vocality through lenses more traditionally employed in considering vocal transcendence and the metaphysics of opera? In short, how useful are the tools of 'reaffirmation' in understanding the voices of 'rupture'?

If the nineteenth-century imaginaire of opera operated as a 'reaffirmation' of dissimulated power structures, with voices encoded with metaphysical ideals of the past and the grandeur of Renaissance or antique civilizations, then what values are produced by, or inscribed in, the 'rupture' of musical theatre? Specifically, how are we to understand its blend of high and low vocal aesthetics as it critiques the present? If musical theatre sings utopia, then what is revealed as it embraces (or appropriates) styles as diverse as rock, jazz, pop, folk, and—at the same time—operatic and classical aesthetics? Beyond differences in technical or anatomical production, at the level of cultural meaning, what kind of voice is this? The following chapter will begin to answer these questions.

2
Decadent Appropriation
The Process and Politics of Singing Musical Theatre

On 23 March 1939, *The Hot Mikado* opened at the Broadhurst Theater on West 44th Street, New York. Under the direction of Hassard Short, with orchestrations by Charles L. Cooke, it was a jazzy rendition of the Gilbert and Sullivan English comic opera *The Mikado* (1885). In performance, the vamped-up version was said to be '95 per cent hotcapated' by Billy Rowe, theatre critic for the *Pittsburgh Courier*. Featuring much of the original dialogue and score, and still set in Japan, the production featured an African American cast, including blues singer Rosa Brown and Bill 'Bojangles' Robinson in the title role. Less than two weeks later, *The Swing Mikado* transferred to the 44th Street Theater, having played previously at the New Yorker Theater (now Studio 54). With musical arrangements by Gentry Warden, this version moved the action from Japan to a tropical island. It also featured an all-black company and used a swing style with some dialogue rewritten and some popular dance styles interpolated into the performance, including the cakewalk. Writing in the *New York Times*, reviewer Brooks Atkinson reported that in a well-known number from the operetta, three little maids sing '"Za-zu-za-zu" . . . huskily, breaking down into a smoking caper'.[1] Thirty-six years later, Janos Bajtala, George Larnyoh, and Eddie Quansah would introduce *The Black Mikado* to London audiences. Premiering at the Cambridge Theatre on 24 April 1975, it updated the original material as a mainly black British cast sang in a mixture of rock, reggae, blues, and calypso styles. In 1986, David Bell and Rob Bowman likewise adapted *The Mikado*, calling it simply *Hot Mikado* (without the definite article). Repurposing the score through orchestration to sound like popular music of the 1940s, including jazz, gospel, swing, blues, and even some nascent rock 'n' roll, it was English comic opera in a Zoot suit.

In addition to potential insights into the relationship between race and performance, the multiple versions of Gilbert and Sullivan's work act as a synecdoche for the 'rupture' of the late nineteenth century as musical theatre

Singing Utopia. Ben Macpherson, Oxford University Press. © Oxford University Press 2024.
DOI: 10.1093/9780197557679.003.0003

borrowed liberally from vernacular and popular styles. Such versioning demonstrates how middlebrow musical theatre operates. At the same time, it also poses a question: beyond (but including) *The Mikado* and its variations, is there a means by which we can account for the various cultural meanings produced through such aesthetic shifts and styles across the full repertoire of musical theatre? How might the music hall quality heard in works such as *Florodora* (1899) and the rock sensibility of *Passing Strange* (2008) be understood as part of the same vocal history? Can these likewise be considered at the same time as the Appalachian fusion heard in *Floyd Collins* (1996), the operatic pastiche of *The Phantom of the Opera* (1986), or the crooning of *Guys and Dolls* (1950)? How does such a broad church of stylistic influences help to define, expand, or challenge the notion of utopian vocality? Do they produce a monolithic or multifaceted cultural meaning? To answer these questions, we first need to consider how such a plurality arises and then progress to consider the various cultural meanings and politics it encompasses.

'Putting it together': Vocal Plurality and the Politics of Appropriation

Defining the term as 'the process of borrowing, reworking, and combining from other sources . . . to form new cultural forms and spaces', music scholar Roy Shuker argues that all popular music evolves by means of 'appropriation'.[2] While the associated practice of adaptation tends to acknowledge its source directly, literary theorist Julie Sanders echoes Shuker in defining appropriation as a process of 'recrafting' to create 'complex, intricate and sometimes embedded' intertexts.[3] In the case of *The Mikado,* while subsequent versions acknowledge their source material, the presence of revised musical styles through voices that encoded African American, Caribbean, or Black British sounds into the world of the musical facilitated a 'recrafting' of aesthetics that transcended narrative or setting, producing new, complex, cultural meanings. As acknowledged in the introduction, musical theatre is unique in popular culture in its willingness to borrow, combine, rework, and recraft styles as diverse as opera, operetta, jazz, blues, gospel, soul, folk, Latin music, Yiddish and cantorial song, Eastern European traditions, Asian modes, vaudevillian patter, music hall, Sprechstimme, pop, rock, hip hop, and rap. The concept of appropriation may therefore help articulate the *process* by which plural vocality develops in a way that differs markedly from the ossified strictures of operatic vocality.

It also burnishes the middlebrow credentials of the form; as one musical trend establishes itself, so musical theatre seeks to 'borrow' and then 'rework' it within its own parameters. To talk about musical theatre voice at the level of cultural meaning is to be talking in the plural. The cultural 'rupture' that occurred in the late nineteenth century was not discrete or limited but can be understood as a catalyst that facilitated an ongoing process of appropriation. How, though, might we consider the various cultural meanings and politics produced by such appropriation? After all, the borrowing of music hall patter in the nineteenth century cannot reasonably be considered to produce the same cultural meaning as the assimilation of pop voice in the 1960s, the recrafting of the rock aesthetic in the 1970s, or the inclusion of folksy earnestness in the 2000s, even while each can be understood within the parameters of stylistic or aesthetic appropriation.

'The sweetest sounds . . .': Appropriative Cycles and the Politics of Decadence

In his book *Vocal Authority* (1998), John Potter proposes a theory of vocal style using a range of discussions concerning the cultural development of classical and popular voices. Echoing the notion that appropriation in musical theatre is dynamic and responsive to changing styles or trends, Potter suggests that the construction of vocal style might be understood through a tripartite cycle of *development*, *decadence*, and *renewal*. Detailing these three stages, Potter draws on the operation of hegemony in the work of Marxist theorist Antonio Gramsci. Defined with reference to the social or cultural exercise of power, Gramsci understood hegemony to comprise two facets: 'dominating' and 'leading'. In any given society, one class might 'lead' its 'allies' and 'dominate' its 'enemies'. A governing party may be 'dominant', but if they are out of touch with cultural trends or the needs of the populace, then another class or community (a party of political opposition) may be afforded the hegemonic role of 'leading' but not yet dominating.[4]

In application to popular singing, Potter conceives of hegemony in the above cycle with regard to the changing relationship between voice, text, and audience. It can be transposed equally to a consideration of stylistic hegemony. As considered in chapter 1, classical singing technique was dominant in Western stage performance in the nineteenth and early twentieth centuries, including in operetta and musical comedy, shaped through conventions of vocal type and the practicalities of projection. Yet, the knowingness of operetta and musical comedy performance, in combination with straighter tones, higher registers, and a focus on text in a way that differed from grand opera, represented 'changes to a performance practice' and enabled a diluted or mediated vocal style to 'achieve a (Gramscian) hegemonic position'. On this basis, operetta might feasibly represent the *development* phase that would lead to musical comedy and, later, musical theatre.[5]

Beyond the early years in which operetta and musical comedy were interchangeable terms for a similar kind of production, 'various alternative possibilities emerge' in the *decadent* phase, characterized by what Potter terms 'stylistic pluralism'. Here, while one style may 'dominate' in a Gramscian sense, the proliferation of alternatives means it cannot 'lead' over others.[6] This pluralism developed in musical theatre voice, as jazz-inflected vocal practices, crooning, and speech-inflection influenced musical comedy on both sides of the Atlantic, while the development of what is now referred to as 'legit' voice production became an index of musical dramas such as *Show Boat* (1928) and, later, *Oklahoma!* (1943). After the decadent phase, Potter suggests, the whole process enters a *renewal* phase, as new performance practices or varieties emerge to challenge the eventual dominance of any given style. In the case of musical theatre, the arrival of microphone amplification eventually paved the way for a range of styles to assert hegemony in line with the whims of popular culture.

For Potter, this cycle of development, decadence, and renewal is constant, and he asserts that 'it is not possible to locate the present at an exact point in a cycle of stylistic development'.[7] Considering the middlebrow responsiveness and constant aesthetic appropriation noted above, it seems reasonable to suggest that if musical theatre voice is always undergoing both development and renewal, it may be in a perpetual state of decadence. The sheer plurality of styles employed in musical theatre contributes to an opulent and excessive range of aesthetic choices in performance. Yet there are at least three further reasons to suggest that musical theatre voice might be characterized by decadence, and the possibility of singing utopia becomes evident in each case.

First, while the styles in play are numerous, they are never static or discrete. Decadence is 'dynamic' and it is often the middlebrow combination of 'new' and 'old' vocal styles that enables a critique of the present and its values.[8] Utopia is likewise dynamic and malleable and enables the production of new cultural meanings in its exploration of the possible. Beyond such a straightforward comparison, however, a second facet of decadence is its aesthetic of resistance through what performance studies scholar Adam Alston sees as 'subversive opposition' to the conservative status quo. This resistance, as part of its production of cultural meaning, happens in areas of 'taste, appearance, gender, sexuality, desire and behaviour', a further 'rupture' of dissimulated social structures which are often held to be encoded in musical theatre at large. Alston notes that as a practice of subversion, decadence 'finds refuge in marginality . . . in ways that shine a light on the exclusionary parameters and contingencies' of life.[9] Decadence can at times be understood to give voice to those outside or underneath the dissimulated power structures of ideology, and as such, offers a way of critiquing the present and identifying the parameters of what else might be imagined. Might this kind of decadent subversion or resistance therefore help map the boundaries of utopian vocality in musical theatre?

Third, literary scholar David Weir notes that decadence 'is attached to so many different ideas, attitudes, orientations, movements, histories, arts, artists, and so on'. On this basis, as Alston observes, '[d]ecadence can refer to different practices in a variety of time periods and continents, not least performance practices'.[10] The dynamic pluralities and subversive possibilities inherent in the notion of decadence, then, might offer a means by which we can listen across the stylistic plurality of musical theatre voice through various time periods and locales—from the 'legit' vocality of *Oklahoma!* (1943) to the shameless radio-friendly pop of *Dear Evan Hansen* (2017)—and understand them as belonging to the same musical-dramatic form. The quality or notion of decadence in this respect may reflect the ways in which utopia can, at times, mean different things to different people.

Introducing the first of several neologisms in this book, we might distil the underlying complexities of the foregoing positions to suggest that musical theatre sings utopia through, and can be characterized by, what we will call *decadent appropriation*. In short, decadence offers a way for us to listen to the cultural meanings produced via aesthetic appropriation and the contingent complexities of stylistic pluralities at play in musical theatre. As highlighted in the introduction, the middlebrow nature of the form means that it is 'dependent on the existence of both a high and a low brow for its identity, reworking their structures and aping their insights'.[11] In what ways, then, does musical theatre evidence dependence on highbrow and lowbrow vocal styles? What does its structural reworking and 'aping' of these aesthetics through appropriation reveal about the decadent characteristic of the form in relation to utopia? Developing responses to these questions, this chapter listens closely to five musicals that draw from both highbrow and lowbrow vocal styles and aesthetics. First, listening across what we might call the 'voiceworld' of three musicals that embrace aspects of highbrow operatic style, the ways in which metaphysical ideals are reworked through combination or subversion will reveal further characteristics of utopian vocality in musical theatre.[12]

'We're both on the stage, we two . . .': *Florodora* (1899) and the Development of a Rupture

Opening on 11 November 1899, *Florodora* became an early transatlantic phenomenon, playing 455 performances at the Lyric Theatre in London, with its Broadway production in 1900 running for 552 performances.[13] Its narrative concerns the exploitative business dealings of American entrepreneur Cyrus W. Gilfain, who owns the Philippine island of Florodora, and has stolen the factory which makes its eponymous perfume from the Spanish family of Dolores, a young woman who works on the island. Amid much farcical irrelevance, Dolores inherits a large fortune, marries the Welsh Lord Abercoed and through the theatrical antics of Tweedlepunch, a magician and travelling showman (who is an undercover investigator), is restored to her rightful place as the owner of the perfume factory and estates on Florodora. Written by Owen Hall, with lyrics by Edward Boyd-Jones, George Arthurs, and Paul Rubens, and music by Leslie Stuart with additional songs by Rubens, *Florodora* was also the first musical comedy to be committed extensively to record in 1900.[14] It is therefore representative of the development phase during which musical comedy was at first synonymous with, and gradually emerged from, operetta.

Sonically and semantically, listening across the vocal styles at play in *Florodora* may provide an insight into an early example of decadent appropriation and, as such, demonstrates both continuity and uncertainty in the vocal style that was emerging during the 'rupture' of the *fin de siècle*. For example, actor Evie Greene's vocal performances were recognizably operetta (see Figure 2.1). Having originated the role of Dolores in London, Greene featured in the chorus on the first recordings in 1900 but would later record a solo version of 'Queen of the Philippine Islands'. With a mezzo-soprano

Figure 2.1 Evie Greene, Bassono Ltd., whole-plate glass negative, February 1915. NPGx80528. Reproduced under academic license. © National Portrait Gallery, London, England.

range, full rounded vowels, emphatic plosives, and a vibrato present enough to support her voice while recording with an orchestra, Greene nonetheless avoids the decorous coloratura more readily associated with formal opera singing.[15] The influence of operetta, then, is heard as part of the development phase, albeit this still represented a diluted invocation of metaphysical ideology.

Elsewhere, *Florodora* gave voice to a more defined aspect of 'rupture'. In line with Potter's consideration of decadence as dynamic, the vocal continuity from the 'old' (or established) form of operetta heard in Greene's vocal coexisted with vernacular idioms and popular performance styles. In the song 'Phrenology', Tweedlepunch saves the day and exposes Gilfain's greed in the final scene. Originated by Willie Edouin in London, the role was covered at various points by actor W. Louis Bradfield, who first recorded the song in 1900. Bradfield's vocal range is limited and the tessitura of the song is reflective of this. Expressive and rhythmic, Bradfield's performance of this patter song relies on declamatory speech-inflection, appropriated from the delivery style of music hall.[16] Yet, in an explicit performance of dependence on both high and low cultural styles, the male chorus accompanying Bradfield sing more formally. While chapter 3 explores the relationship between solo and choral voices, and notwithstanding that anachronism and juxtaposition have long worked as comic devices, the contrast between music hall patter and formal choral voices is careful and unironic here. Appropriating or recrafting aesthetics from music hall within a performance that also encoded continuity through operetta, Bradfield's performance helps create a middlebrow voiceworld in which 'alternatives are permitted' to freely co-exist and to be negotiated.[17] It might even be suggested that Bradfield's vocal performance acts as a kind of 'subversive opposition' to the conservative conventions of continuity in operetta, 'rupturing' structures of taste and expectation as musical comedy began to develop.[18] Operetta may have already mediated the metaphysical ideologies of serious opera, but here, Bradfield's performance serves to further disrupt the ideological tenets of operatic vocal style in the burgeoning form.

A final example from *Florodora* further suggests that, beyond a performance of continuity or appropriated alternatives that might have the capacity to subvert or oppose, musical comedy was beginning to 'rework' structures from other cultural forms towards a new style of performance practice even during the development phase. The 1902 Columbia recording *Excerpts from Florodora* features the famous double-sextet 'Tell Me, Pretty Maiden (Are There Any More at Home like You?)'.[19] With a musical composition 'oblivious to the conventional structures' of concerted pieces, the song contains 'quaint, irregular' features such as polyrhythms and syncopation over an oom-pah accompaniment.[20] The chorus of six men and six women (baritones and mezzo-sopranos) switch between verses delivered in a conversational style appropriated from lowbrow forms such as music hall, and a refrain sung with rounded vowels and emphatic plosives redolent of operetta, while exhibiting straighter tones and more controlled vibrato than even Greene's solo (see Figure 2.2).

This recrafting of elements appropriated from operetta and music hall demonstrates the discrete combination of both highbrow and lowbrow cultural influences in one song, giving voice to a kind of stylistic uncertainty or negotiation as the 'rupture' of musical theatre took hold and shifted away from the conventions of operetta.

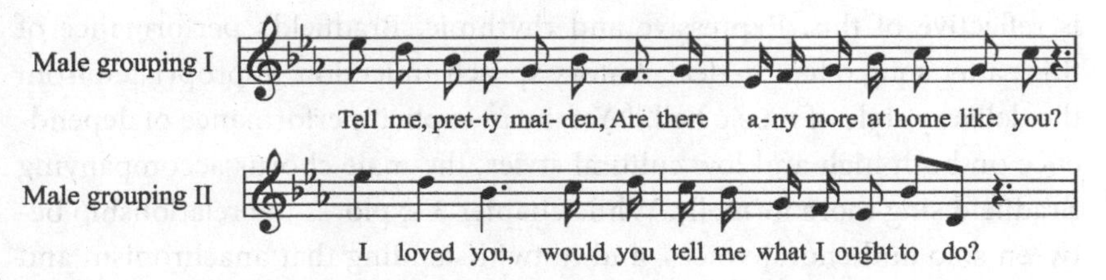

Figure 2.2 Speech-inflected delivery of the first male grouping (Top) with a lower laryngeal and legato delivery of the refrain 'If I loved you . . .' (Bottom) in 'Tell Me, Pretty Maiden'. Notated by the author from the *Florodora* vocal score, 1899.

Leslie Stuart et al., *Florodora: A Musical Comedy (Vocal Score)* (London: Francis, Day & Hunter, 1899), 145, 149.

The appropriation and 'reworking' of existing cultural forms goes even further in this song. Described by an unnamed reviewer in *The Times* as 'a little scene of courtship . . . by six couples at once', the original staging featured a walking dance with the chorines and their suitors—all white—which borrowed from lowbrow American dance forms such as the cakewalk, common in minstrel shows and vaudeville, and associated with racist stereotypes of African Americans (see Figure 2.3).[21]

From the vantage point of the twenty-first century, such implied appropriation suggests that while stylistic plurality might offer a decadent exploration of the possible through the production of various cultural meanings, these are not always as utopian as might be imagined. With respect to racial politics, they may even be contentious or offensive. The association of musical theatre voice with utopia—whether through the transparency of emotion, directness of expression, the victory over vulnerability, or the opportunity to reimagine worlds through the decadent appropriation of various styles—therefore requires a consideration of its inverse. In short, we cannot talk about utopia without also exploring dystopia, a discussion to which we will return through the rest of this book.[22]

Of course, such voices must be heard in context. Greene, Bradfield, and the other performers heard above were recorded using early acoustic technologies, huddled around a recording horn while more used to projecting in the theatre without any amplification. In short, the above analyses of the vocal performance must be understood to offer a historically contingent means of listening to the 'rupture' of musical theatre in this era, even if the speech-inflections of Bradfield's Tweedlepunch and the layered

Figure 2.3 'Chorus of the stage production *Florodora* as published in souvenir program'. Source: Billy Rose Theatre Division, The New York Public Library. *The New York Public Library Digital Collections*. 1900. https://digitalcollections.nypl.org/items/c62a2780-074c-0135-43ad-0cfd66933d76. Public domain.

complexion of the double-sextet still provide a glimpse of dilution from the operatic ideals heard in the predominantly operetta-like delivery elsewhere. What happens, then, when we consider a musical which draws on operatic aesthetics, but exists at the apex of electronic amplification and technology? What might this reveal about the possibility of utopian cultural meanings produced through decadent appropriation?

'What do we mean by opera, anyway?': *The Phantom of the Opera* (1986) as Decadent Subversion

Nearly a century after *Florodora*, a different kind of operatic mediation offers another way of listening for utopia as encoded in the decadence of musical theatre. First opening on 9 October 1986 at Her Majesty's Theatre, London, *The Phantom of the Opera* was adapted from Gaston Leroux's nineteenth-century gothic French novel of the same name. With book and music by Andrew Lloyd Webber, lyrics by Charles Hart and Richard Stilgoe, and directed by Harold Prince, it tells the tale of a disfigured musical genius who haunts the Paris Opera House, has an erotically charged obsession with chorine Christine Daaé, and stops at nothing in his attempts at seduction, despite the minor inconveniences of incumbent prima donna Carlotta and the amorous affections of Christine's childhood friend Raoul, the Vicomte de Chagny. With an indulgent aesthetic, *Phantom* exuded the opulence of nineteenth-century opera in its production values, complete with theatrical illusions and technological wizardry. The visual richness of the production was matched in the score. With its varied tonality and complex musical borrowing, Lloyd Webber revelled in the opportunity to pastiche various styles, appropriating forms and orchestral textures from opera, operetta, comic opera, and musical theatre along with some elements of pop-rock, as he consciously 'reworked' and 'aped' highbrow aesthetics.

Described as a 'popular opera' and a 'musical lovers' dream opera', *Phantom* trades on its romanticized and nostalgic allusions to historical musical forms.[23] Capturing the zeitgeist of its original production, *Phantom* was a work of 'high pop', repackaging high art as pop culture (or vice versa) in an opulent display of decadent appropriation.[24] It relied on a sung-through aesthetic often understood as indicative of operatic aspirations through a mix of recitative, arias, duets, and set choral numbers. Yet it is not an opera, best described as a 'poperetta'—the portmanteau of 'pop' and 'operetta' favoured by US journalists.[25] Despite its titular implications, *Phantom* consigned highbrow culture to the margins, rendering it inert in a manner which distinguishes it from the operetta conventions of early musical comedies beyond the trappings of acoustic technologies. While the entire plot hinges on whether Christine will sing in the Phantom's magnum opus, the world of nineteenth-century opera becomes the comedic subplot to the high romance of the love triangle between Phantom, Christine, and Raoul. In this context, then, what might the voiceworld of *Phantom* reveal about the appropriation of operatic aesthetics in the middlebrow megamusical? In what way does it set about 'aping' the culture it pastiches, and how does this relate to notions of decadent, utopian vocality?

It is notable that the first scene, set at an auction long after the events of the story, is predominantly spoken.[26] The first sung voice is that of an aged Raoul, *sotto voce*, an introspective musing rather than a declamatory expression. This is hardly the stuff operas are made of, much less the synthesized organ and drum machine that sound out as the chandelier comes to life and rises above the auditorium. With an abrupt end, the synth-heavy overture stops, and we are transported back to a rehearsal of *Hannibal*, the first of three fictional operas in *Phantom*. A cappella, the first voice heard is Carlotta, the diva of the Paris Opera House. The vocal delivery is extreme and stylized, indulgent in its coloratura and 'flowery cadenza'.[27] This is a 'cartoon world' of nineteenth-century opera, written as a generic grand opera in the style of composers such as Meyerbeer. Along with Carlotta's vocal excess, the large Italian tenor, Piangi, reaches a high C in this scene, and both perform an exchange in recitative, the artificial 'musicalized speech' so often associated with the stereotypical image of opera.[28]

Having been introduced to this musical through speech and *sotto voce* introspection, the change in vocal characteristics here is excessive. Carlotta's and Piangi's exaggerated style here serves to burlesque grand opera, caricaturing them—and the form—as outmoded, bumbling, foolish.[29] One implication of this approach is that a contrast is offered between the comedic artifice of opera and the 'genuine' music of Lloyd Webber's love story.[30] *Phantom*, therefore, performs an inversion of stylistic norms. No longer does a highbrow cultural form (or even its pastiche) exert unchallenged dominance; listeners and audience members are asked to connect with the more contemporary voices of modern musical theatre. Aping the operatic, highbrow vocality becomes a facsimile devoid of any metaphysical value.[31] The cultural meaning produced is the subversion of hackneyed stereotypes in a voiceworld that is expressly material, rupturing conventions rather than reaffirming them through charming pastiche. In this case, we might understand the voiceworld of this musical to be decadent in its resistant and subversive reworking of operatic vocality. *Phantom* might therefore be heard to perform a vocal 'rupture' of dissimulated social structures encoded in musical theatre and, as Jessica Sternfeld has noted, of the peculiar and particular conventions associated with the cultural capital of megamusical consumption in the 1980s.[32]

Such challenges to convention are on stark display when Carlotta attempts to sing the aria 'Think of Me'. The musical style represents a step change, with a gentle, unaffected accompaniment and less decorous melody, a parlour song in the style of Balfe or Schubert. Exuding artifice with indulgent alveolar trills, and the overt vowel formant modification symptomatic of certain operatic soprano conventions, Carlotta is interrupted suddenly by a huge backcloth falling from the flies, accompanied by the solo scream of a young ballerina. In this one moment, the fetishized *object voice* of operatic ideals is cut across by an extraordinary vocalization which, in Brandon LaBelle's words, proceeds to 'shatter the lyrical space' through 'voluminous expression . . . at the edge of the sounded voice'.[33] The most expressive voice in this scene is no longer the diva whose excess has been diminished, but an unnamed ballerina reacting to an unseen character. In a direct 'rupture', this scream is heard only through the use of electronic amplification in a further demarcation between the worlds of opera, operetta, and musical theatre.

Carlotta storms off, spooked by the suggestion that the 'Opera Ghost' is playing such games. With the balance of power disrupted and the dominant hegemony disturbed, a chorus girl is plucked from obscurity to cover Carlotta's performance. With 'almost folklike' simplicity, and with the song transposed down a major third in a move away from decorous excess, this moment is often characterized by Christine Daaé's 'clearer, flatter English vowels', straighter tones than Carlotta's artificial Italianate delivery, and with less reverb in the sound design.[34] In a stage picture which transitions swiftly from the rehearsal room to opening night, Christine finishes the aria with a light and unassuming cadenza which is much less indulgent than anything from Carlotta. *This* is the 'new sound' of the opera, 'purer than a conventional soprano', lighter, plainer, and clearer.[35] Overt and artificial ideals of voice in opera are here replaced by an emphasis on a more direct and popular musical theatre sound, albeit with enough 'high-status' inflections to convince as 'high pop', mediated through amplification.[36] Throughout the musical, Christine's vocal confidence grows and becomes more evidently informed by the colours and textures of a lyric soprano, notably in her final duet with the Phantom, 'The Point of No Return'. Nonetheless, at no time do the vocal indices of the so-called operatic voice—artificial, excessive, even comedic—return to dominance as they were in the development phase associated with operetta a century earlier. They have been subverted, resisted, and rendered inert.

This not-quite-operatic vocality is also mirrored in both Raoul and the Phantom. Raoul, written for a high-baritone, is 'not operatic but not pop-style either', performed by actors with 'cleaner, straightforward theatre voices with [a] light operatic flavour'.[37] In this sense, Christine's and Raoul's voices are stylistically sympathetic—giving a vocal foil for their developing relationship. In the world of the Paris Opera House, then, it is the musical theatre voice—with its capacity for utopia—that becomes hegemonic. The same is also true for the Phantom. While written for a high-baritone or tenor in an ironic (if not deliberate) mirroring of Raoul, those who perform this role are not often known for their operatic vocal qualities.

Yet, while the Phantom and Raoul share a similar voice type, one specific vocal quality distinguishes them: much of the Phantom's music is so high as to necessitate an overt use of the countertenor (falsetto) range. The highest-pitched male voice (typically D4 and above), the countertenor voice is often associated with the castrati of early opera and the metaphysical vocality of early Church music. Viewed as ethereal, tender, unnatural, deviant, vulnerable, and feminine, its predominance in the Phantom's vocal character suggests that beyond the comedic caricaturing of nineteenth-century opera, Lloyd Webber appears to offer one vocalic index from the voiceworld of opera history as a potential marker of the Phantom's otherworldliness. This is heard numerous times in the musical, but most notably on the final note of 'The Music of the Night'; held for twelve counts on C5, while a five-chord phrase shimmers, *pianissimo*, beneath the word 'night'. With the ideals of opera rendered inert through subversion and inversion in this musical, however, how might we understand the presence of the countertenor's voice? Read against the understanding of falsetto in popular music, and enabled by what Symonds has called the 'acoustic dramaturgy' facilitated through technological amplification, the use of the countertenor range might not suggest an ethereality but rather a queering of the voice, characterizing the Phantom as 'unstable and always on the edge'.[38]

At first, such instability hardly seems the stuff of a vocal utopia. Yet, once more returning to Alston's consideration of resistance through 'subversive opposition', we might listen across the falsetto character of the Phantom and the conservative vocality of Raoul. The resistance encoded in the Phantom's countertenor is a space in which the decadent critique of 'gender, sexuality, [and] desire . . . finds refuge'.[39] His character, then, gives voice to those outside or underneath the dissimulated power structures of ideology, exposing much of the heteropatriarchal history of voice in opera, operetta, and even musical theatre. As such, the Phantom gives voice to an exploration of the possible through a particular vocal 'rupture'. In this, both he—and the musical itself—might be imbued with a sense of utopian idealism—for good or ill. Of course, the finale sees Christine choose to escape the tortured and subversive world of the Phantom and the cartoon and old-fashioned world of the Opera House. Leaving with Raoul, Christine chooses the conventional musical theatre hero over the 'unstable' decadence of the Phantom in a telling endorsement of the 'new music' that had come to characterize the 'poperetta' in this era, and the utopian promise to which it gave voice. As Lloyd Webber once said: 'What do we mean by opera, anyway?'[40]

If operatic vocality has transmogrified from hegemonic dominant or technical necessity to an aesthetic which is parodied, subverted, and resisted, employed in acoustic dramaturgy through technology and then ultimately supplanted by the 'new', its loss of metaphysical associations must surely reach a natural conclusion, perhaps as part of Potter's renewal phase. What characteristics—utopian or otherwise—might *this* voice have?

'Often they fail and sometimes they die': *Floyd Collins* (1996) and the Materiality of the Metaphysical Voice

Based on the untimely death of the eponymous Kentucky caver in 1925, *Floyd Collins* first opened Off-Broadway on 9 February 1996 after a try-out in Philadelphia in 1994. Written and directed by Tina Landau with music and lyrics by Adam Guettel, it told the true story of an ill-fated rescue effort to reach Collins, trapped beneath the ground in Sand Cave, Kentucky, by a small rock that blocked his egress. With a mission headed by journalist William Burke 'Skeets' Miller from Louisville, the efforts to save Collins became one of the most covered media stories in interwar America. Seventeen days after Floyd had become trapped, a shaft was created to raise him from the ground. He was already dead.

With a score that evoked the era and location of the narrative, the sound of banjos, harmonicas, and mandolins playing pastiche bluegrass and Appalachian music evokes the rural, 'idyllic [or idealized] self-sufficient life' associated with a nostalgic and 'overwhelmingly white' Americana. Yet, signifiers of Appalachian folk music such as 'the fiddle–banjo combination, hambone percussion, the ballad tradition, and call-and-response singing' were not white European imports.[41] Instead, Appalachian music was a cultural hybrid influenced by the sounds of African Americans, European settlers from Germanic territories and the Anglo-Scottish borderlands of Britain, and some Native American traditions.[42] Appalachian music therefore exists at the 'creative intersection' of multiple traditions. It is a decadent aesthetic comprising 'so many different ideas [and] attitudes' from 'a variety of time periods and continents'.[43] Despite this rich heritage and complex network of cultural influences, reviewer David Spencer suggested that 'the score has something much more serious in mind: the bluegrass and western motifs are merely punctuation or stylistic springboards for more complex musical forms and techniques that have their antecedents in the likes of Bartók, Janáçek and Stravinsky'.[44] Notwithstanding Spencer's implied hierarchical (and hegemonic) deference to (white) European influences, how is this influence manifest in the voiceworld of this musical?

By the end of the twentieth century, popular musical theatre embraced operatic vocality by 'reworking' metaphysical ideologies on its own, confident, utopian terms, rather than through hegemonic influence (*Florodora*) or aping them through subversive resistance (*Phantom*). For example, employing established voice types in his writing, Guettel's work subverts some of the conventional relationships with which they are associated. The protagonist Floyd is a baritone who adheres to Clemént's description of baritone characterization: 'often they fail and sometimes they die'.[45] Likewise, as in *Phantom* and many other works, *Floyd Collins* features a soprano configured as helpless and repressed, with an agency determined primarily by the males in her life. Unlike Christine Daaé, however, Nellie Collins is neither a romantic ingenue nor an overly tragic figure; she is Floyd's sister. Described by one of the journalists reporting on the family's tragedy as 'a colorful example of the folkways and eccentricities of the hillbilly life' after having returned from Green Haven Mental Institution, it is Nellie's voice that is most notably operatic in this work, in a manner reminiscent of Joanna in *Sweeney Todd*.[46]

Performed by Theresa McCarthy in the original production and on the cast recording, a resonant dramatic soprano quality is heard in relation to specific ideas in the text, rather than as a generic vocal quality. In particular, when reassuring the Collins's step-mother (Miss Jane) that Floyd has 'the luck' (a quasi-spectral or supernatural force that will bring him success), Nellie imbues the song 'Lucky' with a ringing operatic quality as she sings, 'Good news, 'round the bend, trouble days is gonna end'.[47] Pleading with the lead reporter Skeets Miller to let her go into the cave to help her brother, Nellie's dramatic soprano voice veers towards a loss of intelligibility as she questions why she cannot help, blaming the men for 'running things' and asking desperately, 'what's wrong with me?'[48] When the rescue team reach Floyd, Nellie's interactions with her brother are the most operatic of the entire musical. Imagined in the mind of her now-deceased brother, in a realm beyond the material, Nellie's dramatic soprano and Floyd's countertenor drift through the air in vocalise; wordless call-and-response, as they try to locate each other. As in other works by Guettel, vocalise is prominent in *Floyd*

Collins and another index of operatic vocality.[49] Here, then, with a dramatic soprano giving voice to Nellie's dreaming, personal helplessness, and apparently supernatural or imaginary interactions with her brother, is this not an explicit return to the ideological and metaphysical realms of the operatic considered in chapter 1?

While this may appear true, the presence of lowbrow and folk aesthetics challenges such easy conclusions. Throughout the musical, the operatic quality of Nellie's voice is both interrupted by and inflected with the sounds of the Appalachian yodel. Characterized by 'a long-held natural tone [which] is followed by (or occasionally preceded by) a very brief yodelled tag' (*yodeleme*) on an individual grace note, the musical at large employs a particular kind of yodel known as 'feathering', prevalent in rockabilly music in the mid-twentieth century.[50] Heard as an 'unhidden crack in the voice' created by a glottal leap, this particular effect is associated with folk singing and acts as a 'sonic correlative' of culture, time, and place—in this case, of Kentucky in the 1920s.[51] Yet, given the diverse influences that combine to forge Appalachian folk music, what function does this 'sonic correlative' serve?

As a near-universal vocal practice, yodelling is present in most cultures around the world.[52] In particular, its presence in Appalachian folk singing is likely the confluence of the vocal pulsing and countertenor of Native American melodies, the vocal leaps of West African traditional song, the mountain songs of Central Europe, and the plaintive inflections of Celtic balladry.[53] In each case, the yodel acts as a culturally specific 'sonic correlative' of something earthbound and vernacular. Its recurrent presence in Nellie's voice therefore frustrates and reworks any evocation of the metaphysical, evoking the decadent hybridity of Appalachian folk music. The negotiations between the metaphysical associations of Nellie's operatic vocality and the vernacular qualities of the yodeleme render her voice as another in-between; the sonic space in which the binary oppositions at play in this musical are encoded: above and below ground; dreaming and reality; freedom and confinement; life and death; present and future. Her vocal character therefore facilitates an engagement with, and critique of, universal themes.

'Feathering' is also a signature inflection of Floyd's earthy baritone from his first song to the final scene. With a melodic line characterized by voice-breaks and grace notes, Floyd's intimate material relationship with the caves of Kentucky is heard in his voice. Here, in a further performance of decadence, Guettel employs a second vocal element: echo. While the yodel acts as a vocal index of character, class, and culture, the presence of echo gives voice to the specific circumstances of the narrative. As Floyd uses his voice to call out through the passageways, squeezes, and bends underground, he listens to the echo—the 'sound [which] continues after the cessation of its emission'—to negotiate surfaces, and traverse corridors and voids.[54] For centuries, from the Greek myth of Echo and Narcissus to the possibilities of digital sound design, the paradoxical properties of the disembodied echoic voice have proved fascinating, often understood as a sound which is 'not-from-this-world', imbued with metaphysical properties even as it returns to its original voicer.[55] In *Floyd Collins*, the caver's voice echoes around the space (via digital delay) and dissolves into a sonic voicescape of extended vocalise at key moments of the musical. Its echoic presence may therefore seem uncanny or metaphysical in a way that is reminiscent of its use in opera. For example, in 1600, Emilio de Cavalieri's *Rappresentazione di anima e di corpo* contained an echo-duet between Soul and Heaven, while Monteverdi's *L'Orfeo* is paradigmatic in its use of echo as such instances 'allude to noumenal [or, metaphysical] singing'.[56] Is Guettel appropriating a four-century-old noumenal vocality, albeit achieved through digital delay? What kind of voice is this?

As part of the early modern fascination with sound, echo formed the basis for many debates, with ideas proposed that countered the prevailing metaphysical doctrines in the seventeenth century. Dutch scholar Isaac Beeckman and Royal Society Fellow Walter Charleton understood echo to be corporeal particles delivered through air, ideas that find sympathy and analogues in recent thinking.[57] Conceiving of voicing and listening as somatic, Steven Connor has suggested that voice is also a corporeal entity: a 'vocalic body'.[58] Whether heard immediately or through the disorienting (or digitized) *acousmêtre* of echo, voice may still be experienced in its 'fleshness' as material rather than metaphysical.[59] This materiality has specific consequences.

Echoes are produced by sounds hitting a hard surface and being bounced back to their voicer (and heard by others). Beyond the realms of the metaphysical or material, echoes must therefore be understood in relation to the spaces in which they occur. In the dramatic space of Floyd's story, the echoes relate directly to his bodily presence underground. The acoustic dramaturgy of *Floyd Collins* is therefore predicated upon the 'fleshness' of the voice, its echo, and its relationship to material space. The same is true in the moment of performance. Lynne Kendrick has noted that because of their corporeal presence, vocal acts can 'become the co-ordinates by which we understand space' while in the realm of architectural acoustics, Barry Blesser and

Linda-Ruth Salter observe that when we are aware of a sound source 'we experience a distinct echo as bound to the original sound'.[60] Seeing Floyd onstage and hearing the echoes which follow, audience members negotiate both the dramatic and performance spaces using a particular set of coordinates. First, the echoes are 'bound' to the original sound—the 'fleshness' of the performer onstage. Second, the echo is heard as a locational index, giving voice to the claustrophobia or the unseen underground rather than a metaphysical or ethereal otherworldliness. These two coordinates are triangulated by the sense of earthy locatedness encoded in the feathering of voice-breaks which punctuate Floyd's calling and the subsequent echoes.

Having been trapped for so long, the final song of the show sees Floyd conversing with God about what heaven (or, more broadly, a generic afterlife) might be like. The song 'How Glory Goes' ends the musical with a minute of vocalise in a four-part canon of echoes which, gradually, repeat to fade. In this song, Floyd is deceased. While the performance space may remain broadly similar, the dramatic space has changed. Is this a kind of duet between Soul and Heaven, à la Cavalieri's opera? Is this an inversion of an inversion: transforming vocalic 'fleshness' back into something metaphysical? Listening to the coordinates helps us understand the dramatic space of this final song.[61] Moments before, the nature of the echo changes. In 'The Dream', Floyd hallucinates both Nellie and Homer, coming to tell him of the success of the Great Sand Cave, and the three of them sing in canon.[62] Here, Homer and Nellie assume the role of the echo, in a moment which shares striking similarities to the structure of a mid-nineteenth century song, 'The Mountain Echo'.[63] Performed by the Hutchinson Family, an American yodelling troupe, each verse of this song was 'followed by an eight-bar yodel refrain with an echo effect, likely performed with alternative voices and changes in dynamics'.[64] This sibling troupe, in canon, reinforces the sonic correlatives of character, class, and culture, but does so by intensifying the 'fleshness' of the echo in a new way. The echo is no longer residual; rather, it is corporeal in its continuing spatial immediacy. In *Floyd Collins*, 'The Dream' builds further to a final 'call' from Floyd, followed in the score with one devastating musical direction for Nellie and Homer: 'no echo'.[65] Beyond this point, the only echoes are those from Floyd's voice. The coordinates have changed as the dramatic scenario has shifted. The echoes have become a residue rather than a continuation. What is now heard? A disembodied voice from a deceased Kentucky caver—metaphysical, spectral, even Orphic? Something more material, 'reworked' from tradition or convention?

A consideration of the original Ovidian myth of Echo, along with two more recent readings, offers a useful perspective.

The nymph Echo is cursed only to speak through imitation, repeating the words that others have spoken to her, rather than using her own. Noting that Echo's words are 'forced' and 'unintentional', Adriana Cavarero states that 'Echo's is not a singing or narrating voice, but rather . . . a mere residual material'. Echo is not imbued with metaphysical agency. While drawing her love Narcissus to her, Echo may use only his words. At best imitative and at worst inert, Echo's voice is at the service of (and reliant upon) other voices: 'a sonorous substance to a semantic that is not organized according to her intentions', but only to what has already been.[66] Understanding contemporary notions of the sonic echo in light of Cavarero's reading of the original myth comes with certain consequences. Simultaneously, the echo is dislocated from its source while its imitative repetition achieves 'revocalization' through 'desemanticization'. For Cavarero, such 'revocalization' is a rediscovery of the vocal purity heard in an infant's cry or the burbling imitations of a vocal exchange between mother and child in which the '*physicality* of the vocal exchange' constitutes a clear 'acoustic relationality'.[67] In the case of Floyd's postmortem echoes, there is no mother-child relationality, and the echoes are not those of another's words. Rather, this final moment reworks indices of the operatic, giving voice to an 'acoustic relationality' in which the intense, solo 'physicality'—rather than metaphysicality—is heard in Floyd's voice.[68] In what way might this be utopian?

Along with Cavarero, Jacques Derrida had a repeated fascination with the myth of Echo. Ostensibly doomed to repetition, Derrida hears in Echo's imitation something more than the pastness of Narcissus' words. In *Rogues* (2005), Derrida focuses on the moment in Ovid's text when Narcissus begs Echo to come to him ('Come! Come!') and—crucially—her repeating of the invocation. While on one level this is inert mimicry, for Derrida it also constitutes an open invitation; a call to action. For him, Echo is finding playful possibility in the 'revocalization' of her new situation. Derrida hears in Echo's repetition a certain 'initiative' and 'responsibility'. While she cannot express herself through semantic agency, her response indicates a preparedness and anticipation for what might come next.[69] Her words are unintentional and 'residual' and yet anticipatory and inviting. In a slight departure from Cavarero's recourse to pure vocal materiality, the 'acoustic relationality' that Echo configures is one between the pastness of the sound and its future, or utopian, possibilities.[70]

Put another way, *Floyd Collins* appropriates and reworks historical structures of echo and, more broadly, the operatic aesthetics of the musical. In this sense, its decadence can be found—not in hegemony or subversion, but in its temporal and cultural contraction. Incorporating 'so many different ideas [and] attitudes' from 'a variety of time periods and continents', the 'creative intersection' of Appalachian folk music challenges the metaphysical while giving voice to the complexities of cultural hybridity and a politics of place rooted firmly on (and below) the land.[71] In its corporeal sonority and decadent disruption through voice-breaks and yodelemes which configure class, culture, and character, the contrapuntal vocal fade which ends the musical as the lights dim is, like Echo's call, a sonic summons to go further; a Derridean call into the unknown—a response from the past which embraces the possibilities of the future. This voice, too, is bound to the utopian in a way which suggests that by the end of the twentieth century, the presence of operatic vocality in musical theatre was no longer metaphysical but material, vernacular, mundane.

Having considered the operatic voice and its transition from metaphysical sonority in opera, through operetta, and then its material or mundane cultural meaning, what can be revealed by listening for, through, and across, popular vocal styles as part of the decadent sonority of the musical stage?

'You're gonna be popular': Appropriating the Popular Singing Voice and Utopian Vocality in Musical Theatre

In parallel with musical theatre, popular song has developed from a variety of lowbrow and folk music to celebrate the mundane, urbane, and vernacular in ways that contrast with the dominant concerns of highbrow culture. As such, listening to the ways in which musical theatre 'reworks' or 'apes' lowbrow (or popular) vocality as part of its utopian voiceworld seems a particularly provocative consideration. As with the so-called operatic voice, this is a huge undertaking. While musical theatre vocality might be characterized by decadence, the 'popular singing voice' is an umbrella term which similarly encompasses a broad church of styles. One taxonomy of the popular voice identified no fewer than sixteen genre categories, each with numerous and discrete stylistic subsets.[72] Considering the appropriation of the popular voice in musical theatre therefore involves listening to more than a century of stylistic pluralities, a marked contrast to the relative ossification of the high-status 'operatic voice' as a 'historically closed [and] enormous anachronism' which has not altered for over a century.[73]

In this case, what specific elements of the popular singing voice recur most frequently in musical theatre? Listening across two further examples—one from the mid-twentieth century as jazz and easy-listening music gave way to rock and roll, and another from the early twenty-first century with influences from rock, hip hop, and pop—many moments occur in which markers of popular singing are audible in the in-between space of musical theatre vocality. What do these moments reveal about the ways in which musical theatre appropriates and reworks lowbrow singing styles in pursuit of utopia?

'Call it hell, call it heaven': Accommodating Utopias in *Guys and Dolls* (1950)

First conceived by producers Cy Feuer and Ernest Martin, the musical comedy *Guys and Dolls* was written by Jo Swerling and Abe Burrows, with music and lyrics by Frank Loesser and directed by George S. Kaufman. It premiered on Broadway at the 46th Street Theater on 24 November 1950 and ran for 1,200 performances. Adapted from Damon Runyon's sharp-witted short stories about the criminal underworld of New York in the 1920s, the narrative concerns the loves and losses of Nathan Detroit, a likeable hustler down on his luck, with a fiancée (Adelaide) who is hounding him to commit to marriage after a fourteen-year engagement. Nathan, meanwhile, is determined to find $1,000 to host an underground crap game. In order to raise the money, he challenges the smooth-talking high-stakes gambler Sky Masterson to a bet, claiming that Sky will not be able to take the Salvation Army 'Mission Doll', Sister Sarah Brown, on a date. Sky accepts the wager, and sets out to secure a date with Sarah, falling in love with her in the process. The story culminates with a double wedding between Sarah and Sky, and Nathan and Adelaide.

By 1950, musical theatre vocality had developed beyond the simplistic concatenations of highbrow and lowbrow aesthetics heard in works such as *Florodora* and was beginning to diverge from standard vocal characterization. The rich mélange of popular vocal aesthetics evident in *Guys and Dolls* is evocative of the Manhattan melting pot at the time the story is set, offering a rich voiceworld across which to listen. This is evident to varying degrees in both the approach to melodic composition taken by Loesser and the subsequent vocal performances of the original cast.[74] Originated by, and written for, 'tone-deaf' comedian and actor Sam Levene, Nathan Detroit 'sang with more grits than gravy' in the tradition of Yiddish comics as one half of the long-betrothed couple.[75] His fiancée Adelaide (originally performed by Vivian Blaine) was also suitably coarse in her vocal delivery, with a characterization that 'comes from vaudeville and is rough and "noisy"' (see Figure 2.4).[76] Loesser also configured the conservative and religious Sarah Brown (originated by Isabel Bigley) as a light soprano who, nevertheless, sings with a notably lower tessitura than may more commonly have been heard. Her love interest Sky Masterson (played by Robert Alda) was a baritone like Floyd Collins, Raoul, or the Phantom.

This combination of 'tone-deaf' Jewish comic, 'noisy' vaudeville turn, religious soprano, and streetwise baritone establishes the quartet using popular vocal markers which on one level adhere to normative gender conventions. Ostensibly, the Jewish comic gambler and baritone gangster are archetypical variations of 'guys', while the worldly-wise vaudevillian broad and innocent

Figure 2.4 Vivian Blaine (Miss Adelaide) and Sam Levene (Nathan Detroit) in the original production of *Guys and Dolls*, 46th St. Theatre, New York. Reproduced courtesy of Photofest.

soprano constitute a version of the ubiquitous Madonna/whore trope as 'dolls': what Raymond Knapp sees as a parallel between 'display' and 'religion'.[77] Listening to the ways in which popular vocal markers are appropriated and 'reworked' in this musical, a subversive decadence emerges, offering a differing understanding of the musical and its vocal encoding of utopia.[78]

At 4.00 a.m. one morning, having just returned from their tequila-fuelled Cuban date in act one, Sky tells Sarah that this is 'My Time of Day'. This moment of song characterizes the smooth gambler through a decadent blend of two popular vocal markers which together produce a complex configuration of this character.[79] First, speech-inflected delivery lends Sky a casual and streetwise air. Citing Cavarero's consideration of voice and gender, Victoria Malawey observes that speech-like delivery is often coded as masculine in popular music: 'expressive' but not necessarily emotive, controlled yet *laissez-faire*, much like Sky.[80]

Yet, as with the yodel in *Floyd Collins*, the provenance of speech-inflection in musical theatre is a plural, decadent hybrid. Listening across its influences and their cultural contexts using Matthew D. Morrison's concept of 'Blacksound' may offer a more complex reading of this seemingly confident 'guy'.[81] For example, listening to English music hall patter songs and early musical comedy, such as W. Louis Bradfield's recording of 'Phrenology' from *Florodora* (discussed above), speech-inflected delivery is vernacular and often working-class. Further, its presence in musical comedies of the 1910s and 1920s confirms its 'recrafting' from early African American vocal performance, via minstrelsy, through vaudeville, and into the songs of Tin Pan Alley. Composers including Irving Berlin, Cole Porter, and Richard Rodgers wrote songs with 'repeated quarter notes or eighth notes, and if such songs were to be performed exactly as written they would sound very rigid'. As Ana Flavia Zuim notes, '[i]t was expected that the interpreter would make the song flow by allowing flexible rhythmic nuances', a strategy related to African American aesthetics and practices including 'bent notes', 'off-beat melodic phrases', and 'musical individuality'.[82] In other words, speech-inflection would help to emphasize words and meaning rather than rhythmic or melodic precision, an appropriate strategy for performing Loesser's conversational songs, given his regular use of 'extra words' in dense lyrical lines.[83]

The relationship between speech-inflection and African American music is further seen in the use of 'speech-like shaping of syllables, words and phrases' as a marker of black jazz performance, popularized in the swing music of Louis Armstrong in the early twentieth century, with an emphasis on consonants in delivery. With this aesthetic, Armstrong 'removed any residual "classical" tendencies from popular singing', further evidencing the centrality of black music in the development of Broadway singing styles in the early-to-mid-twentieth century.[84] The flexibility in delivery, relaxed rhythmic performance, and emphasis on the consonants added to the air of casual diffidence shot through with working-class masculinity, while nonetheless appropriated (and, as Morrison notes, commodified) from black sounds into a white American form.[85]

In addition, a second—and contrasting—vocal marker is also present in Alda's vocal characterization of Sky: crooning. As a style of singing, crooning acted as a 'bridge' between earlier mass entertainment forms of minstrelsy, vaudeville, or Tin Pan Alley, and 'new technically enabled forms of romantic and intimate expression' through microphone amplification. It was characterized by the 'conversational manner' of speech-inflection while emphasizing longer vowels in phrasing, with a more aspirate tone and intimate vulnerability in performance.[86] As a result, and invariably because of the slightly higher pitch or frequency with which crooning was often delivered, male crooners of the 1930s were coded as transgressive or homosexual.[87] The intimate style was heard as feminine, associated with women and mothers and, during its early development in the United States, connected with the maternal singing of black slaves as 'natural, nurturing, emotionally driven'. By the 1950s, the style was even considered adolescent, 'weak [and] immature'.[88]

Given that voice is an in-between space, it is fascinating to listen across Alda's delivery of the first verse of 'My Time of Day'. Considering the decadent negotiation of casual but cautious masculinity using speech-inflected consonant-heavy delivery (represented in the excerpt below as underlined text), and the more languid—possibly effeminate—style, emphasizing the vowels and elongating notes (denoted by bold and italicized text), offers a particular way of thinking about the vocal character of Sky:

SKY: MY TIME OF ***DAY*** | IS THE | DARK ***TIME***
A | COUPLE OF DEALS BEFORE | ***DAWN.***
WHEN THE ***STREET*** BELONGS | TO THE COP
...
WHEN THE ***SMELL*** OF | THE **RAINWASHED** PAVEMENT[89]

While masculine, expressive, calculating, and controlled in his use of speech-inflection, Alda imbues Sky with an emotional vulnerability and—if we accept the association of crooning with effeminacy—even the potential for gender transgression.

Far from the confident hustler he appears, Sky is therefore configured as anxious, vacillating between assured and fragile masculinity, with Alda's performance suggesting a complication of normative definitions of a 'guy'. As Allison McCracken further observes: 'While the highbrow entertainment of opera had rejected the gender ambiguities of the castrato stars and instituted gendered vocalizing by the nineteenth century, popular entertainments had not'.[90] Even before Sky's voice softens and simplifies in his duets with Sarah, this suggests that the encoding of musical theatre vocality forged a space where 'alternatives may be permitted' and in which the normative masculinity associated with 'guys' was not necessarily a given.[91] Even in 1950, and in large part due to the impact of recording and sound technologies on vocal performance, the decadent appropriation of popular styles encoded a challenge to the world as it *was* or was perceived to be, giving voice to a complex plurality of masculine ideals. Gangsters could be vulnerable, even transgressive.

This vulnerability was at times coded beneath a display of Alston's 'subversive opposition'. Given Sam Levene's limited vocal capabilities, Nathan Detroit features in only two musical numbers: 'The Oldest Established', in which he is introduced, and the duet 'Sue Me', where he is chastised by an angry Adelaide for continuing to gamble rather than plan for their wedding. Contrasting with Adelaide's patter-filled outburst, Nathan's responses in 'Sue Me' are resigned and plaintive. Yet, while Frank Sinatra offers a vulnerable croon as Nathan in the film version of the musical, Levene's original performance is more character-driven and abrasive, with approximations of pitch and phrasing that give voice to the 'grits' rather than the 'gravy'.[92] Levene's Nathan is not vulnerable in the same way as Alda's Sky Masterson or Sinatra's voicing of the character on screen; he is a different kind of 'guy'. Placating Adelaide with plaintive and comedic speech-inflection, the world-weary and raspy laconism in Levene's delivery is indicative of the cultural influences of vaudeville on musical comedy in America during the first half of the twentieth century. In this case, Levene exhibited what Josh Kun might describe as 'Yidditude'. Considering a contemporary comedian of Levene, Mickey Katz, Kun notes that at a time of American nativism and narratives of assimilation, performers whose Jewishness was overt were perceived as a threat to 'the melting pot's harmonious broth'.[93] In the case of Katz, his performances often included Yiddish-English parodies of well-known songs. For Levene, the 'Yidditude' heard in vocal cadence and timbre suggests this 'guy' was less vulnerable, less open to change (or, American assimilation) than even Sky.

While Nathan and Adelaide still marry, Levene's resistance remains and is heard at the very end of the musical as the title song reprise draws to a close in the finale. Taking their vows, Nathan sneezes. Beyond the specificity of Levene's performance, this is a knowing reference to Adelaide's earlier lament that through the frustration of marital hopes postponed she had developed the psychosomatic symptoms of a cold. As an extra-vocal act which occurs 'without being able to originate or oversee the process', the acoustic resonance of a sneeze is simultaneously 'violent and pleasurable' in its vibratory fleshiness.[94] Analogous in this moment to the ballerina's scream in *Phantom*, it supersedes the musical scene, fracturing the illusion of marital harmony by interrupting the choral unity of the title song. While Sky Masterson's anxious or ambiguous masculinity parallels the vulnerability of Sarah Brown, Nathan's character appears to react psychosomatically to domestic commitment. This moment of 'reconciliation' may not, therefore, be as unified as the image of a double wedding might suggest. As a result, '*Guys and Dolls* thus loads its dice in favor of reconciling the opposites it presents at the opening, so that, when reconciliation comes, it entails no significant compromise on either side, only accommodation and maturity'.[95] Nathan's sneeze—and Levene's struggle to assimilate in the original voiceworld of this musical—may suggest resistance to compromise, with a vocal presence that 'ruptures' the dissimulated structures of American integration and the mythology of the American Dream. Given the cultural and social history of Jewish émigrés in America, such vocal decadence helps 'shine a light on the exclusionary parameters and contingencies' of life, to reimagine them through 'accommodation' rather than integration.[96] After all, utopia is a plural ideal where many alternatives can be negotiated and permitted, from the complex gendering of Sky to the complicated cultural politics of Nathan.

Yet, such utopian complexities were not only the preserve of the 'guys'. They are also heard in the voices of Adelaide and Sarah Brown. Throughout the musical, Adelaide's mezzo-soprano vocality has been characterized by an affected twang, with shrillness and nasality. Returning to Masi Asare's invocation of Richard Schechner considered in the previous chapter, this vocal character is once again 'twice heard'. It evokes vaudevillian brashness and, in doing so, 'cites the vocal acts' that influence that sound—namely, the cries and uninhibited loudness of African American blues singers, and the early appropriation of Yiddish comic song into American popular music.[97] While Adelaide's nasal delivery implies a parallel with Nathan, such shrillness can also be heard to convey 'youthful tirelessness' and an energetic exuberance.[98] On this basis, no matter the age or gender of the character or performer, it is unsurprising that the brightness of twang has come to characterize the utopian vocal aesthetics of so many musicals. It is, itself, an aesthetic of determination, giving voice to a glimpse of the utopian. For Adelaide, of course, this is marriage.

The paradox of hope and frustration heard in Adelaide's lowbrow nasality is positioned as the 'perfect opposite' of Sarah Brown's reserved soprano religiosity, reinforced by the melodic constraint of her musical lines.[99] Towards the end of the musical, just before the wedding, Adelaide and Sarah sing the duet 'Marry the Man Today'. With a lyric that indicates that reconciliation through matrimony may be an ongoing project, Loesser's melodic structures of call-and-response, comprising shared and alternating lines that develop into moments of unison and harmony, offer a further narrative challenge to the heteronormative conventions and expectations of the 'dolls' in this musical.[100] Textually, both the Mission Doll and the showgirl sing of their desire to assert themselves within their respective relationships. Texturally, Stacy Wolf suggests that on the original cast recording it is only the 'flat nasal belt' of Vivian Blaine's Adelaide and the 'head voice with some vibrato' of Isabel Bigley's Sarah Brown that distinguish the women.[101] However, while a textural contrast is audible, it becomes inconsistent and alternating, a further performance of aural 'accommodation'.

Likening the process of changing the men in their life to altering clothes, Adelaide begins the song with characteristic speech-inflection and twang, while Sarah—whose lyric is an uncharacteristic innuendo—still exhibits a straight tone but with the popular aesthetic of mixed voice rather than *bel canto* sonority. While there are still notable vocal distinctions, Sarah has moved closer to Adelaide's timbre than has otherwise been suggested. This textural alternation continues until midway through the song, at which point a 'striking moment of vocal unity occurs when on the original recording they laugh on the syllable "laugh"'. In unison, Sarah and Adelaide suggest that men should be treated to 'girlish laughter'.[102] This is no innocent affectation from two naïve 'dolls'. As LaBelle has considered in an extended discussion of the political relationship between femininity and laughter:

> The laugh literally *affords* the individual a potent means for transgressing the limits that are always surrounding, either in the form of social etiquette or something greater, as an unbearable circumstance against which the laugh may provide a sudden release or route. An escape by which we may also find another form of community.[103]

Following the invocation of 'girlish laughter' with the suggestion that after marriage, men should get 'the fist', this vocal act sees both women transgress in a moment of 'escape' in which they find 'another form of community' with each other—something Wolf has elsewhere suggested concerning the structural architecture of the song. Whether this is a performance of homosocial female empowerment or encoded homosexuality remains a matter for the listener. Either way, a sense of accommodation between the conservative religiosity of Sarah and the gangster-enabling showgirl is evident as they engage in a moment of decadent 'subversive opposition' to social expectations.[104]

Notably, when the women suggest that men need educating in 'domestic life' and fidelity, Sarah employs twang in mixed voice that echoes Adelaide's coarseness and frustration heard throughout the musical. Likewise, Adelaide employs vibrato and a straighter tone when—in agreement with Sarah—she concludes that they will change his ways, but likely tomorrow, at the end of the song. By this time, both women are heard to employ different vocal aesthetics to those that have characterized them throughout the musical. While Adelaide has softened (a little) and Sarah has become (slightly) coarser, there is no sustained evidence that a sense of 'community' and 'accommodation' between these two women offers anything more than an agreement that relationships—between guys and dolls—are complex and require consistent negotiation (see Figure 2.5).

In the decadent voiceworld of this musical, such negotiations do not necessarily entail any 'significant compromise' but a recognition that the 'urban melting pot' is constituted of a 'tolerant accommodation of difference' or, in Martell's terms, may be configured as a 'utopia to which alternatives are permitted'.[105]

Encoded using popular singing styles, Sky Masterson is an anxious 'guy', forever negotiating a speech-inflected masculinity with a more vulnerable, even ambiguously gendered emotionalism. By contrast, Nathan Detroit's unrepentant vocality, drawn from Yiddish comic traditions, configures him as resistant to 'the melting pot's harmonious broth', a resistance further heard

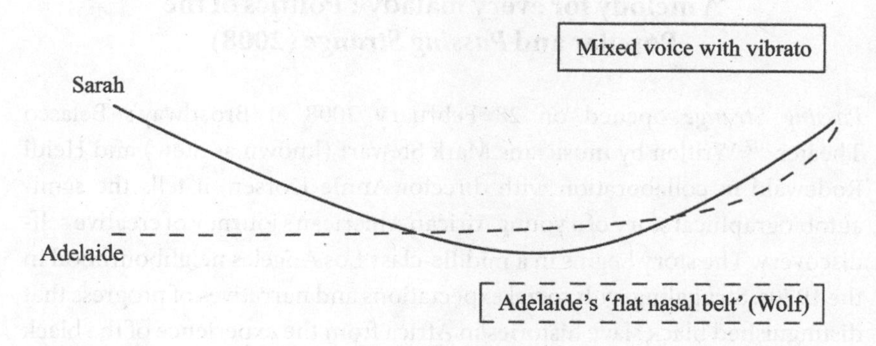

Figure 2.5 The aural 'accommodation' of the 'dolls' in 'Marry the Man Today', as Sarah and Adelaide negotiate divergent vocal aesthetics throughout, ending the song with a shared vocal character. © Ben Macpherson.

through the extra-vocal disruption of a sneeze during the wedding vows.[106] Sarah Brown is a conservative and religious doll who draws from classical European singing traditions when attempting to remain socially acceptable, but whose voice moves toward the vernacular, employing mixed voice with jazz inflections and twang. Adelaide's shrill and nasal mezzo voice evokes vaudevillian coarseness, 'twice-heard' from minstrelsy and blues singing, along with the popular appropriation of Yiddish song into American culture. Appropriate for an ageing showgirl, Adelaide's shrillness has also been associated with the 'youthful tirelessness' of popular song, a utopian energy that does not give up hope.

Guys and Dolls therefore gives voice to more than a binary, normative configuration of post-war American marital respectability. This New York melting pot is a place where anxious masculinity is freely displayed, unassimilated cultural identity is negotiated, Christian conservatism moves towards secularization, and the youthful tirelessness of hope seems to win. Not only do these concerns co-exist but they reconcile through the permanent commitment to live side-by-side. In other words, the use of lowbrow and popular aesthetics in *Guys and Dolls* performs a utopian vocality that may even go beyond Martell's accommodation of alternatives. Having considered the utopian properties of several lowbrow singing varieties, what other 'varieties' of popular vocal aesthetics are present in the decadent voiceworld of musical theatre?

'A melody for every malady': Politics of the Popular and *Passing Strange* (2008)

Passing Strange opened on 28 February 2008 at Broadway's Belasco Theater.[107] Written by musicians Mark Stewart (known as Stew) and Heidi Rodewald in collaboration with director Annie Dorsen, it tells the semi-autobiographical story of a young African American's journey of creative self-discovery. The story begins in a middle-class Los Angeles neighbourhood in the 1970s. Struggling with social expectations and narratives of progress that distinguished black slave histories in Africa from the experience of the black middle-class in America, the protagonist known as Youth is angry at the way blackness has become commodified as part of the (white) American bourgeois. He lives in a society where young black couples get married, move into a large brownstone house, and fill it with African trinketry to signify a heritage from which they are disconnected, while they venerate Malcolm X. As Youth says, he is fed up with the double consciousness at play in social conformity to a white ideal of black respectability, a world where he sees black folks 'passing for black folks' in a social imaginary which perpetuates the 'as if equal' notion of liberal social discourse while undermining it.[108]

Within this context, Youth becomes preoccupied with finding The Real—a sense of genuine identity beyond the 'phoniness of black people who have "made it" in Reagan-era America'—and runs away to indulge in a drug and sex-fuelled musical sojourn of self-discovery through Europe.[109] Youth's story therefore becomes a *bildungsroman* that challenges diasporic narratives in an exploration of the possible beyond the world he has come to mistrust. Borrowing from Ernst Bloch's utopian thinking—and perhaps with resonances of Afrofuturism—race theorist Paul Gilroy might call this 'dreaming forward', as Youth imagines a different world for himself.[110] As he does so, the presence of popular styles in the decadent voiceworld of *Passing Strange* becomes revealing as they encode utopian moments (and their limitations) in performances of recognition, re-evaluation, and reconciliation.

The musical begins with Youth (played by Daniel Breaker) being taken to church, reluctantly, by his mother. In the song 'Baptist Fashion Show', the Narrator describes a place in which piety is a performance, with services becoming a catwalk for the hypocritical exhibition of socially acceptable Christian living. With a speech-inflected delivery that borders on a chant or incantation, the Narrator berates the ladies who wave fans and the old men who snore their way through services in a church where '[t]he Holy Ghost ain't been . . . since 1972'.[111] Related genetically to the jazz phrasing of Louis Armstrong, this delivery is only possible through electronic amplification while, like Robert Alda's Sky Masterson or Sam Levene's Nathan Detroit, it imbues the Narrator with a sense of anxious ambivalence, distanced from the situation of his younger self. Delivered in short phrases, the Narrator's words cut across the congregants (and the white pit band), who answer in a controlled and monotonic *mezzo piano* chorus, performing a stylized version of the 'genre-specific prosodic marker' of call-and-response commonly associated with R&B, soul, and gospel music.[112] As the scene moves on from the Narrator's critique, two subsequent songs ('Church Blues Revelation' and 'Freight Train') see the congregation feel the spirit descend as they worship. Exhibiting a mix of speech-inflection, cries, shouts, hollers, declamations, and the heightened intensity of belt often associated with both gospel singing and musical theatre, the voices build to a frenzy beyond the controlled *mezzo piano* of the earlier call-and-response.[113] Reverend Jones asks the congregation: 'Now is God real?' to which they respond: 'Oh yes, he's real!'[114]

On this 'freight train' of religious experience, Youth gets baptized and has a spiritual revelation: God might be The Real he has been searching for. Realizing that the voices giving praise in church and the voices of African American popular music have much in common, Youth turns to his mother and exclaims: 'church ain't nothing but rock and roll!'.[115] The vocal markers to which Youth has responded derive from performance practices originating in Central and Western African culture, mediated through harmonic languages and formal structures of Euro-American song.[116] Understanding voice as 'a collective expression of a cultural fabric', Youth first hears The Real in this vocal 'fabric' composed of African folk and American popular vocal practices, negotiating 'the dialectic of identity formation by moving incessantly between its poles'; embracing the aural in-between of black and white, sacred and secular, indigenous and encultured, past and present, 'African' and 'American', in a parallel negotiation to that encoded in Nellie's voice in *Floyd Collins*.[117] Resisting the double consciousness of a world where African Americans attain respectability only by achieving a white ideal, Youth's experience of The Real is utopian in its celebration of betweenness and hybridity; 'dreaming forward' to a world that embraces a 'fundamental interconnection among supposedly disparate elements' without eliding those which are painful or troublesome.[118] This 'Real' is a world where 'alternatives' are not only 'permitted to exist', but where difference is embraced rather than commodified.

Despite the vocal utopia that Youth believes he has experienced in church, blues, rock and roll, and European harmonic sensibilities are subject to an act of 'conscious forgetting' and cultural 'denial'.[119] His mother's shock at her son identifying such complexities sees her reach out and slap him across the face, as the music stops sharply. She asks: 'Don't you know the difference between the sacred and the profane?' Uncertain how to respond, Youth simply replies: 'I can't hear the difference'.[120] The vocal practices of indigenous African culture—cries, growls, rasps, and shouts—were those associated with slavery, practices which Euro-American slave masters configured as 'noise', 'unruly', and 'primitive', and which had become subject to commodification and containment in American culture. Here, in the African American middle-class suburbia of Los Angeles in the 1970s, such sonic subjugation is once more alive and well.[121] These people are meticulous in presenting themselves neither as slaves nor as Europeans, but as successful, respectable, middle-class African Americans. In this moment, Youth's small exploration of the possible is greeted with a refusal to engage by his mother in an act which exposes both 'the complexity and radical potential of black American culture, as well as the danger of a strictly African American musical tradition [or] a strictly African-American-equals-black authenticity'.[122] In *Passing Strange*, the complex decadence of utopian vocality can be heard in momentary glimpses of recognition, using recognizable vocal markers from popular song or culturally specific aesthetics. Yet, as his mother's response indicates, utopia may also come with limitations or may be an inconvenience to privilege.[123]

This privilege later becomes a vehicle for further exploration(s) of the possible. After his mother chastises him, Youth joins the church choir, befriending the pastor's closeted son who introduces him to marijuana and European philosophy. Leaving the choir to form a punk band, Youth then travels to Europe to continue his search for The Real. Tiring of the pleasures on offer in Amsterdam, he journeys to Berlin, befriends a group of German radicals (known as the 'Nowhaus'), and engages in a series of 'masquerades' that explore the plural process of identity formation beyond the bounds of his mother's complicated double consciousness. First, Youth embraces durational avant-garde performance art, but it is in the second 'episode of masquerade' that the notion of identity fetishism and popular vocal aesthetics coalesce in a further exploration of the possible.[124] Eager to be accepted by the community of (white) German artists, thinkers, and radicals, Youth conceals his middle-class African American roots and, in the song 'The Black

One', adopts tropes from blackface minstrelsy. Without donning burnt cork, these include excess physical movements such as 'body-warping', along with 'rolling eyes', 'askance glances', and more contemporary variations of dance such as the Moonwalk, Running Man, and breakdancing—black styles often appropriated by white performers in mainstream entertainment.[125] In doing this, has Youth become the very thing he rebelled against—an African American 'passing as' an African American in order for his new white friends to feel more comfortable?

Reflecting on the problems of double consciousness, Jennifer Lynn Stoever has developed the notion of the white 'listening ear' which compels 'people of color to police themselves' through their voice as much as their actions, 'in order to gain entry to white spaces'.[126] Beyond physical stylization, Youth also appears to 'police' his vocality in the manner Stoever describes, adopting stereotypical affectations further derived from minstrelsy. Accompanied by a syncopated rag which evokes numerous moments from the history of both American musical theatre and popular song, Breaker's vocal performance exhibits three characteristics from minstrelsy that have entered the world of American popular vocal performance: 'pointedly pedantic English', 'mugging', and 'vocal exaggerations'.[127] Youth first joins the song with a proper and well-enunciated declamation: 'An artist creates surfaces', before declaring 'I call the surface me!', applying melisma and twang to the final word in a stylistic flourish recognizable from the world of musical comedy (and one which may share a genetic relationship with Adelaide's nasality in *Guys and Dolls*). This shift to a musical comedy aesthetic is further heard through the exaggeration and mugging of lyrics like 'Hot-Cha-Cha-Cha-Cha-Cha-Cha-Cha-Cha-Cha-Cha-Cha-Cha-Cha-Cha-Cha!' and the racially inflected exclamation: 'Yowzers!'[128] If Youth is policing himself to fit in with his European companions, this is hardly the sound of utopia. Heard through Stoever's 'listening ear', his appropriation of stereotypical vocal aesthetics from a difficult history of American popular song might seem to once again impose limits on the utopian, signposting a point beyond which the dystopian is heard. However, is there another way of hearing this voice?

In common with much of *Passing Strange*, 'The Black One' is framed by the Narrator who stands apart from his own history and sings with smooth tones and simple phrasing, augmented with worldly-wise speech-inflection. Towards the middle of the number, the Narrator cynically exclaims that, in Europe, Youth is held to embody an entire diasporic community as 'the real voice of America'.[129] Youth questions this assertion in vocal counterpoint, asking, 'Am I real now?' in a smooth voice, with straight tones and with no trappings of theatrical excess. Youth's adoption of minstrel vocal aesthetics may be more self-conscious, an act of vocal burlesque that enacts a 'subversive opposition', calling attention to the prejudices of the white 'listening ear' by shining a light on the 'exclusionary parameters' it configures, rather than consenting or acquiescing to them.[130] This is persuasive given that it is only *after* Youth asks this question that he mugs and exaggerates in the ways mentioned above.

Youth's decadent appropriation of minstrel aesthetics therefore configures the voiceworld of this specific number as a performance of 'Blacksound', to understand how 'the sonic and material histories of race continue to resonate through the practices embedded in the development of popular music, style, and entertainment at large'.[131] Borrowing from minstrelsy, such vocal *passing* becomes 'an exploitative act, a mode of conscious manipulation' and 'a regression back to a past that Stew is working to problematize [because] Youth cannot fully escape blackness as a filter through which he is seen [and heard]'.[132] It offers a moment of reworking or re-evaluation through a vocal in-between which interrogates notions of burlesque, subversion, exploitation, manipulation, and regression, a 'productive tension' that Brandon Woolf suggests is 'more real than any singular interpretation'.[133]

Youth's performance gives voice to the pluralistic relationship between race, history, popular culture, and the boundaries between subjective identity formation and the resultant objectification by others through fetishism. Heard as just such a re-evaluative critique, 'The Black One' offers a moment of resistance to dissimulated social and racial structures through what Louis Chude-Sokei calls a 'double minstrelsy' reminiscent of political resistance encoded in performances by early twentieth-century African American artists such as Bert Williams (see Figure 2.6). As Chude-Sokei suggests, Williams's use of burnt cork in performances enacted a visual and embodied 'double minstrelsy' because 'Williams was black but his mask was African American'. Such subversion and re-evaluation were also heard in Williams's employment of 'Blacksound'.[134] In his signature song, 'Nobody' (1905), his use of an overt Southern accent, laconic drawl, and melancholic half-spoken delivery weaponized common stereotypes of black slaves by adopting them as a mode of resistance.[135] With echoes of this practice in the vocal performance by 'Youth', 'The Black One' might be heard as a utopian exploration of what is possible when, in the words of Fred Moten, those who are objectified—from Williams to Youth—'can and do resist'.[136]

Figure 2.6 Bert Williams, photography by Cavendish Morton. NPGx126389. Reproduced under academic license. © National Portrait Gallery, London, England.

Passing Strange therefore draws on a range of popular vocal styles to perform moments of recognition, re-evaluation, and resistance, giving voice to fragments and explorations that 'dream forward' or re-evaluate the complex pluralities that may comprise the possibility of utopia. However, beyond gospel music, the blues, speech-inflected chant, call-and-response, or the 'Blacksound' of parodic minstrel vocality, and beyond the jazz crooning, vaudeville exuberance, and Yiddish comic vocality heard in *Guys and Dolls*, this musical is defined by a much broader popular style.[137] In a final, and overarching example of popular voice and its relationship to utopian vocality, the qualities associated with rock music are worth listening to more closely.

Returning to the Baptist church service in the first scene, the Narrator's straight tones and ambivalent speech-inflection become augmented with a range of what might be called 'frictive' vocalizations. These range from small instances of vocal fry through to the pressed phonation of rasps and growls, as he declares that the tensions in church, and between Youth and his mother, constitute a 'Holy war on Sunday morning.'[138] Frictive vocalizations imbue the Narrator's delivery (and later, that of others) with a vocal aesthetic that might be understood broadly as the 'Rock Voice', reinforced by distorted electric guitars, pulsating bass rhythms, a band visible on stage, and the volume of the performance.[139] In popular music, the Rock Voice is 'rougher, less controlled, and less practised' than other vocal styles.[140] Because of this, it is held to be more 'real', 'authentic', 'of undisputed [primal] origin', offering a variety of 'encodings' as the Narrator comments on the tensions felt by Youth throughout the musical.[141] The presumed 'authenticity' of the Rock Voice might be heard as an evocation of Youth's assertiveness in rebelling against his mother in the early part of the narrative.[142] It could encode his anger or sadness at the perceived hypocrisy or delusional double consciousness in his community, or it might signify 'blackness, class, masculinity'.[143]

Whichever encoding is heard by an audience member or listener, it is revealing that the Narrator—not Youth—is the one who sings using Rock Voice in the opening scenes. Contrasting vividly with the metaphysical properties of opera, the presence of the Rock Voice in the context of a narrative critique of the 'Baptist Fashion Show' undermines the pretence of piety from a distance, in a way that is more dispassionate than the conventions of 'rock operas' such as *Jesus Christ Superstar* (1971). Here, it is the absence of frictive vocality for Youth that reveals the repression driving him to search for The Real. If the Rock Voice is emblematic of authenticity or sincerity then as the older version of Youth, the Narrator's vocal aesthetic in this song and throughout the show gives a phonic indication that Youth may eventually find what he seeks.[144] In other words, The Real of the Narrator's Rock Voice sings of Youth's hoped-for utopian self-actualization.

Yet, the Rock Voice is another complicated and in-between space. As an outgrowth of rock 'n' roll, with its roots in African American cultural practice, from the 1960s onwards, rock music was appropriated and repackaged as white by music producers working within the commercial context of an institutionally segregated United States, while soul and R&B became coded as the music of black urban culture.[145] A full investigation of the complex circumstances that led to this delineation is beyond the scope of this discussion, but its consequence is that the Rock Voice is, in many ways, a racially contested space that requires the negotiation of difficult ideas.[146] If it is heard as 'rougher' and 'less practised', does this imply a subconscious value judgement or endemic racism on the part of white consumers who associate rock with something 'primitive'?[147] What consequences might this have for the way we listen to Jesus and Judas, as considered in the preceding chapter? If these 'rougher' vocal qualities are held to the 'real' or 'authentic', to whose 'authenticity' do they give voice when they have been appropriated from one cultural group by another? Does the presence of the Rock Voice in *Passing Strange* imply that beyond the middle-class double-consciousness Youth rails against, the only 'real' available is white culture in America?

As with all other thematic considerations in the musical, the voiceworld suggests that the answer to these questions is likely found in the indeterminate in-between, as it explores the possibilities of 'a Real—with a capital "R"—that is necessarily multiply defined, multiply located, unstable, in motion'.[148] Youth's search for The Real was, therefore, an act of 'dreaming forward' in which the presence of the Rock Voice, with its complex intercultural heritage, was an act of reclaiming an African American aesthetic from white commodification, and a means of reconciling the 'fundamental interconnection among supposedly disparate elements' of a complicated transcultural heritage.[149] The Real is therefore another form of Martell's pluralistic utopia, subject to 'developments, intended and unforeseen . . . and so will need to change'.[150] As such, perhaps the 'real' of the Rock Voice may also be a place where utopia can begin.

'Hear my song': Appropriated Voiceworlds, Decadent Utopias

To reframe or augment established modes of thinking about musical theatre voice, this chapter has developed the concept of decadent appropriation as a way to listen across the complex and pluralistic voices of the genre. As developed here, the term acknowledges the multiple aesthetic styles heard across the broad repertoire, encompasses the process through which highbrow and lowbrow styles are appropriated, and allows for a nuanced understanding of the cultural politics that result. Decadent appropriation is dynamic, by necessity responsive and political in its encoding of vocal tropes and styles at the service of the musical as an exploration of the possible. At times, it engages in a critique of the present through 'subversive opposition', giving voice to the dissimulation of power structures in search of something better. It is, therefore, utopian.

Listening across the decadent appropriation of both operatic and popular styles has yielded rich insights into the nature of utopian voiceworlds of the musical stage. Listening to *Florodora*, *The Phantom of the Opera*, or *Floyd Collins*, the decadent appropriation of operatic vocality enables the popular stage to examine and interrogate notions of the metaphysical, placing limits, challenging ideologies, subverting conventions, or reframing the relationship between the phenomenal and its other. Through the co-presence of operatic aesthetics and vernacular speech-inflections, yodelling, screams, or other non-linguistic vocalizations, the voiceworlds of these works offer 'space for pluralism and change but [always] with a design for an alternative', performing the beginnings of complex and unfinished utopias.[151] The same might be heard in any other musical that reframes or engages with operatic aesthetics, such as *Little Mary Sunshine* (1959) or even *Les Misérables* (1985).

The appropriation of popular styles, always through the medium of technical advances in amplification or recording, likewise revealed further complex facets of utopian vocality that are altogether more political and personal. While already vernacular, the presence of music hall speak-singing, crooning, jazz phrasing, Yiddish comedy, and the Rock Voice offers a decadence that allows us to rethink notions of gender normativity while accommodating resistance to integration in a voiceworld where 'alternatives are permitted'.[152] Elsewhere, the musical stage sings of masculine vulnerability and female empowerment exposing social delusion and disillusionment and giving voice to a 'subversive opposition' that invites a re-evaluation of narratives regarding race, ethnicity, space, and identity heard through approaches such as 'Blacksound'.[153] Responsive to the changing aesthetics of popular singing styles across the last 130 years, the musical stage therefore configures voiceworlds that are 'multiply defined, multiply located, unstable, in motion' and utopian—even if moments of definition or locatedness expose at the limitations of the utopian or its opposite.[154]

This chapter has explored the broader implications of listening across the decadent appropriation of operatic and popular vocal aesthetics as they comprise the broad voiceworlds of these works. However, beyond stylistic aesthetics or ideological considerations, what might be revealed by listening across common vocal formations or combinations on the musical stage?

How does the sonic uniformity of a chorus sing utopia, and how might this differ from the more plural characteristics of an ensemble? If a chorus gives voice to a utopian community—who is included? Who is excluded? In trios, duets, and solo performances, how are utopias defined, located, or created? We will listen to these voices in the following chapter, as the second part of this book begins to develop critical approaches to voice in musical theatre.

PART II
CRITICAL APPROACHES

3

Two Voiceworlds, Three Choralities

Locating the Voice

Act one has begun. The overture has ended. The stage is empty. From the wings, a single cowman's voice tells the audience that the haze on the meadow is bright and golden. In the finale of the same show, the entire company of farmers, cowmen, and townsfolk boldly sing in unison that they belong to the land. While hardly unique in doing so, *Oklahoma!* (1943, see Figure 3.1) therefore utilizes a wide range of different vocal groupings or categorizations in performance, groupings which form what might be called the 'vocal dramaturgy' of a musical—the structuring of a voiceworld for dramatic and affective means.[1]

This 'vocal dramaturgy' comes with certain conventions and properties. For example, the traditional musical theatre chorus of the kind heard in the finale of *Oklahoma!* is often understood to function as what Bethany Hughes has called a 'manifestation of community'.[2] To paraphrase Scott McMillin, the chorus is the voiceworld of the musical *at large*. This 'voice' is not that of individual characters but one through which they may merge with other unnamed characters in precise, synchronized, euphonious anonymity, to sing of universal ideas beyond their individual circumstances. Often spectacular because of their scale, choruses are paradigmatic of the utopian sensibilities of musical theatre in the popular imagination, configured through the directness and energy of numerous voices (and bodies) joining together as one, creating a sonic immensity; a chorus of voices.[3]

Scientific studies suggest that part of the thrill of chorus numbers may be due to a kind of affective experience which has specific consequences *in*, as well as on, the body of the listener. As heard in the case of Floyd's echo in chapter 2, the phonic/sonic properties of voices 'physically take hold of the listener', evoking a biological or corporeal response.[4] This reaction relates to the perceptual presence of the body in the voice and resultant atmospheric changes from singing such as reverberations, echoes, or waveforms that connect *physically* with the listener or audience through transmission.[5] In other

Singing Utopia. Ben Macpherson, Oxford University Press. © Oxford University Press 2024.
DOI: 10.1093/9780197557679.003.0004

Figure 3.1 Playbill for *Oklahoma!* St. James Theatre, New York, 1943. Reproduced courtesy of Photofest.

words, voices are haptic, reaching out and touching the audience (even when communicated via technological mediation or amplification).[6] On this basis, when an entire community sings together, audience members may experience a vicarious sense of joining in. This phenomenon has been considered in dance studies as an experience of 'inner mimicry', 'vicarious enactment', or 'kinaesthetic entrainment'.[7] According to neurobiologist Antonio Damasio, such an experience of community by proxy relates directly to corporeal mirroring:

> [A]s we witness an action in another, our body-sensing brain adopts the body state we would assume were we ourselves moving, and it does this . . . by a pre-activation of the motor structures ready for action . . . in some cases by motor simulation.[8]

Perhaps *this* is why, as McMillin suggests, 'the build-up of a number to a simultaneous [choral] performance is often a dramatic event in itself': the more voices that are heard, the more intense the physical, embodied, inner response to the performance.[9] Likewise, when a large chorus dissipates or suddenly halts to throw focus onto just one solo voice—'To be continued', as the Narrator interjects at the close of act one in *Into the Woods* (1987)—the physical push and pull of the voices operate together to provide audiences with the physical sensation of both 'community' and individual characters.

Distinct from the 'anonymous mass' of the chorus, the ensemble is composed of a 'community of individuals' who may each contribute discrete musical or vocal lines in moments of polyvocality. As with the chorus, they are still understood to 'work together for the good of the whole'.[10] While less direct in their energy or alleged universality than a chorus, they nevertheless build to an intensity that—according to Richard Dyer at least—may still be considered utopian. In the case of ensemble song, the intelligibility afforded by the chorus gives way to an experience of intensity and energy which may once more be considered as having utopian potential.

These larger groupings then serve as the broad phonic backdrop against (and within) which individual characters sing their thoughts and feelings through moments of more individualized address. For example, trios may be comic or celebratory ('Good Mornin'', *Singin' in the Rain*, 1985) and—along with quartets, quintets, and other smaller categories of character-led moments—explore one narrative highpoint from multiple perspectives ('I Saw Three Ships', *Caroline, or Change*, 2004). Duets may offer moments of intimate exchange ('As Long as You're Mine', *Wicked*, 2004) or express conflict ('We Do Not Belong Together', *Sunday in the Park with George*, 1984). Finally, solo songs may be thought of as musical monologues, as characters express a stream of consciousness ('Boundaries', *A Strange Loop*, 2022), converse with an imaginary, metaphorical, or even metaphysical Other ('Somebody Gonna Love You', *The Color Purple*, 2005), talk with family, friends, or others—present or absent ('Grandma's Song', *Billy Elliot*, 2005), or disclose something to the audience ('Soon as I Get Home', *The Wiz*, 1975). Even in these smaller groupings or solo numbers, because individual voices are also haptic, a sense of intensity may be experienced in performance.

Given all the above, listening across such plural, decadent groupings in performance represents an enormous analytical challenge. After all, if choruses and ensembles both have the potential to sing utopia and facilitate vicarious community through corporeal engagement by the audience, along with solo voices that enter a 'space of vulnerability' to express emotional directness and intensity, how might we best approach these varying scales of vocality?[11] One way might be to categorize the various vocal groupings into just two dramaturgical classes: those which manifest community, and those which manifest character. Extending the neologism proposed in chapter 2, we might call these *macro-* and *micro- voiceworlds.* Within this framework, macro-voiceworlds bring full chorus and ensemble numbers together as manifestations of community, while micro-voiceworlds focus on individual characters in solo performances or more discrete, limited interactions.[12] From the foundation of voice as affective and haptic, this approach allows for a focused consideration of the textural shapes, dynamic interactions, and degrees of haptic intensity between communities and characters in the configuration or encoding of utopia.

To explore how this might work in practice, this chapter listens across the macro- and micro-voiceworlds present in three examples, considering what is revealed about the nature of utopian vocality in the vocal dramaturgy of each production. Each of the works selected utilizes a broad range of vocal groupings from both voiceworlds and—while not paradigmatic of all musical theatre—combines to offer specific ways of thinking about and listening to vocal dramaturgies more broadly. As a first consideration, then, we might return to Bethany Hughes's suggestion that the chorus acts as a 'manifestation of community'.[13] What kind of 'community' is manifest? What might this sound like? In what ways may it be heard as utopian?

'To all and each': Manifestations of Community and Utopia in *The Arcadians* (1909)

Opening on 28 April 1909 at the Shaftesbury Theatre, London, *The Arcadians* was a successful three-act British Edwardian musical comedy in the development phase considered in the previous chapter. Written by Mark Ambient, A. M. Thompson, and Robert Courtneidge, with lyrics by Arthur Wimperis and music by Lionel Monckton and Howard Talbot, the musical dealt with the contrast between the beautiful, truthful, and pastoral world of Arcady and the corrupt greed of industrialized London.[14] After an airship crashes suddenly, and disturbs the tranquillity of the Arcadians, its pilot (James Smith) tries to seduce the nymph Sombra by telling her a lie. In response, he is immersed in the Arcadian Well of Truth and becomes an ageless honorary

Arcadian called Simplicitas. If he remains honest from that point, he will never grow old. Simplicitas, Sombra, and her sister Chrysea are then sent to the greedy and dishonest heart of London, on a mission to rid the metropolis of lies and ugliness. No recording was made of the full score with the original company. However, a 1913 medley by the Edison Light Opera Company, along with several solo recordings from members of the original cast, and a 1968 studio recording performance faithful to the musical directions in the original published score provide an informed sense of the aesthetic heard in the voiceworld(s) of *The Arcadians.*[15]

After a brief instrumental introduction, the first act opens in the pastoral idyll of Arcady, with a chorus composed by Howard Talbot, in which nymphs and shepherds introduce themselves ('Arcadians Are We'). A group of soprano and contralto nymphs sing the opening lines: 'Arcadians are we / Dame Nature blest our birth'. This is sung *piano*, in unison, with the second line embellished by a contralto harmony a third below the melody. Following a stanza in this style, the tenors and basses introduce themselves, celebrating their 'freedom of the weald' and 'shelter of the wood', once more in unison, moving from *piano* to *pianissimo* between the two statements.[16] The final cadence of this stanza brings all voices together, *mezzo forte*, in a harmonic sequence including moments of unison and one brief suspension in the contralto line before a resolution on the tonic (doubled in the bass) and major third. In a choral style reminiscent of pastoral operas and with more than a passing resemblance to moments in Gilbert and Sullivan's *Iolanthe* (1882), the simplicity of this vocal arrangement is complemented on the 1913 recording (and the 1968 version) by a clear choral quality in performance. In tone and timbre, the Arcadians' voices blend well, create a uniform dynamic that relates clearly to the performance markings in the published score, and demonstrate marked synchronicity in breath placement, with a consistency of vibrato, phrasing, and an evenness in the use of coordinated onset and offset.[17] As with the finale to *Oklahoma!*, what might this vocal uniformity in the chorus reveal about its 'manifestation of community'?[18]

Early twentieth-century sociological theory about the nature of 'community' derived largely from feudal and pre-modern notions of collectiveness and cohesion. Mid-century American sociologist Robert E. Nisbet (1953, 1967) developed the notion of community as social *wholeness*, arguing for 'community' in terms of a cooperative unit that was bigger than individual members but in which they might thrive through belonging and participation. In a direct way, this is echoed in McMillin's notion that the chorus is the 'voice of the musical'.[19] A community has often been conceived as a social group bound by (1) a shared place (neighbourhood or nation); (2) a personal identity (race and gender); and (3) an ideological value or belief system (religion or political persuasion).[20] Nisbet argued that this form of community 'achieves its fulfilment in a submergence of individual will' to attain social completeness.[21] Through vocal blending, dynamic balance, uniform breath placement, and even phonation, the 'manifestation of community' encoded in the macro-voiceworld of *The Arcadians* is, therefore, one of social collectiveness.[22] The opening number gives voice to the sublimation of individual will for collective identity both in lyric ('Arcadians are *we*') *and* vocal character. Working on the not-unreasonable assumption that the six main choral numbers sung by the Arcadians each display such a balance and blend, this voiceworld therefore elicits a manifestation of what utopian theorist Lyman Tower Sargent would call an 'intentional community', bound by place (Arcady), personal identity (as Arcadians) and ideology (pastoral resistance to industrial progress).[23]

This community both opens and closes the show and is a prominent feature throughout. It is the same manifestation that blended black and white voices in *Show Boat* (1928). As Scott McMillin has observed, 'the black chorus and the white chorus (the two ensembles are distinctly identified and usually hold apart) sing the same number, "Cotton Blossom"'. By singing the same melody, Kern and Hammerstein's work seems to perform an idealized comment on segregation as it 'pretends that the racial difference can be overcome in the spirit of exuberant singing' (an idea which is examined later in this chapter).[24] Likewise, the same chorus gave voice to a united community in 'Oklahoma!'; to a generation of disaffected youth who look forward to social progress beyond their parents' conservatism ('The Song of Purple Summer', *Spring Awakening*, 2008); allowed a group of revolutionaries to dream of social justice ('Do You Hear the People Sing?', *Les Misérables*, 1985); and helped a group of shipbuilders to work together ('We Got Nowt Else', *The Last Ship*, 2015). In each case, individuals become anonymized, subsumed, and submerged within a macro-voiceworld related to shared place, personal identity, and/or ideology, all encoded through blend, balance, and breath. This is the case even when individual characters may have solo vocal lines, such as Curly, who begins the rallying cry for state-wide unity at the end of *Oklahoma!*

What does this chorus—with its manifestation of 'intentional community'—reveal about the capacity of musical theatre to sing utopia? Echoing utopian theorists and philosophers including More, Locke, and Hobbes, Krishan Kumar observes that one characteristic of utopia is its conviction that man is infinitely malleable; that 'humanity is perfectible'.[25] In these choruses, the very idea of perfection may be encoded in the well-mannered and disciplined blending, balance, harmony, and synchronized breathing of the chorus. From the Arcadians to the farmers and cowmen, and French student revolutionaries, it may be that community is manifest through the chorus when it acts as a transparent and direct 'vehicle of social or political speculation', creating a macro-voiceworld moulded to sing community as it *could* or *should* be.[26] However, such a discrete understanding of 'intentional community' through the chorus (and any causal equation with a 'perfectible' vision of utopia) presents several challenges.

First, while understanding community in relation to a shared sense of place, personal identity, or ideology might be logical, it serves to reduce a complex and contradictory term to one fixed reading.[27] To define community in the singular—as a totality which 'encompasses all forms of relationship . . . personal intimacy, emotional depth, moral commitment, social cohesion, and continuity in time'—is at best inaccurate, and at worst, prejudicial.[28] This is because the notion of community based on mutual identification operates to *exclude* as much as it does to include. Returning to the first example in this chapter, the chorus in *Oklahoma!*–set in a territory around 880 miles away from the Kentucky caves of Floyd Collins's spelunking–likewise sings as white America. In the vocal dramaturgy of *Oklahoma!* Native American inhabitants of the region are nowhere to be seen or heard. While the final chorus declares: 'We know we belong to the land!', it seems this version of utopia is not available to everyone, a claim revisited later in this book.

Likewise, as Andrea Most has considered, the immigrant peddler Ali Hakim is also no longer present in the finale. An émigré from Persia, Hakim served as a 'thinly veiled representation of the Jewish immigrant' in his attempt to assimilate into American life.[29] Notably, in the first production of *Oklahoma!* the role of Hakim was played by Joseph Buloff, a Jewish comedian. As with Sam Levene's performance as Nathan Detroit in *Guys and Dolls* (1950), Buloff was reported to have such pronounced 'Yidditude' (to borrow again from Josh Kun) that 'the character was generally assumed to be Jewish'.[30] Absent from the finale, the intentional community of *Oklahoma!* has not included everyone. In a final example of such exclusion, the character of Jud Fry—characterized as deviant, dark, and with threatening sexuality—is removed from the finale when he falls on his knife in a fight with Curly. While not played by a black actor in the original production, Most also codes Jud as a cipher for the African American. Along with Native Americans and Jewish immigrants, he likewise had to be 'submerged' before the chorus could achieve its sense of community through song.[31]

Perhaps the subsuming, intentional community in the macro-voiceworld of blend, balance, and breath control was appropriate for the imperial, hierarchical, and colonial world of early British musical comedy. Perhaps it was appropriate in *My Fair Lady* (1956), to distinguish between a homogenized elite at Ascot (an intentional community) and the disruptive presence of the outsider (Eliza). Perhaps its exclusionary presence in *Oklahoma!* is unsurprising (while not excusable) given the politics of the time. Its continuing presence in more recent work, however, may indicate a theatrical tradition that does not align with the individualized and inclusive values of contemporary society. For example, the same principles of choral discipline and anonymized togetherness are heard in the contrapuntal textures of *Dear Evan Hansen* (2017), yet the idealized and totalizing formality of this kind of chorus seems at odds with the mantra of self-love and individual worth.

A second challenge to the totalizing ideal of an intentional community comes from the fact that utopia is, by definition, not irreducible; it is not, and can never be homogeneous, even when liminal. Utopias are societies in which 'alternatives are permitted to exist'.[32] Therefore, any macro-voiceworld that seeks to elicit a feeling of totalizing uniformity through the sublimation of individual experience or identity exposes an inherent flaw in the ideal of such a community. As Lyman Tower Sargent observes, utopian societies are of an 'inherently contradictory nature', exploring the possibility of perfectible homogeneity while never being able to achieve it.[33] There is, then, a paradox at the heart of a traditional chorus. It seeks to offer 'moments in which audiences feel themselves allied with each other' and the performers via vicarious entrainment, while at the same time never being able to realize the ideal.[34] Its performance of sublimation and homogeneity seems idealistic in one sense and exclusionary in another; subjugating rather than sublimating. As noted above, Jud and Ali Hakim were not simply 'submerged' in *Oklahoma!*, they were removed or absent entirely. This 'fundamental opposition' between collective homogeneity and the individual underpins much classical and modern utopian thought and always suggests that the transparency or directness of a chorus which manifests intentional community is simultaneously shot through with something contradictory—even *dystopian*.

These tensions revolve around whether personal happiness and will should be ignored in pursuit of communal homogeneity, and whether individuals have agency to leave or change the community they inhabit. Returning to Arcady, this manifestation may be evident, but because *The Arcadians* enacts an explicit contrast between a perfectible, pastoral idyll and the profane corruption of the industrialized metropolis, how might a sense of 'community' be manifest when the action moves to London? Opening at the Askwood Races, act two sees Sombra, Chrysea, and Simplicitas (James Smith) engage in their mission to restore truth and beauty to the sinful and corrupt city. At the opening of the act, Bobbie—a man-about-town—leads a chorus of punters in a paean to horse racing called 'Back Your Fancy', a song in which the assembled race day attendees manifest an altogether different kind of togetherness. Composed by Lionel Monckton, 'Back Your Fancy' had a more popular style of melody than the pastorale of 'Arcadians Are We'. An upbeat number, the choral refrain simply repeats a lyric sung by Bobbie at the end of two verses. The entire chorus is again in unison, employing straight-tone phonation and less dynamic variation than the chorus of the Arcadians. With blend and synchronized breath placement still in evidence, the lyrical repetition and unison in the melody may in some ways appear to be even more homogenized than the pastoral chorus, while at the same time offering a sense of directness, transparency, and even spontaneity. Anyone could sing along with Bobbie at the race day. This index of spontaneity is important because events such as a racing fixture offer only a temporary or liminal sense of community rather than something intentional or binding. In its temporality, it is reminiscent of the anthropological notion of *communitas* discussed by Victor Turner: a fluid experience of togetherness outside of fixed social structures and only operating with the consent of those involved. Turner considers this kind of community event in relation to specific participatory rituals or rites of passage such as religious ceremonies; discrete moments that are created, exist, and then dissipate in a way that is markedly less fixed than the place-bound 'perfectible' and intentional community of the Arcadians.[35]

The simplicity of the vocal arrangements and aesthetic, albeit performed with a sense of homogeneity, therefore becomes a phonic marker of a community that is only temporary. In this case, the race day attendees do not subscribe automatically to a shared place, identity, or ideology. Their sense of community is therefore contingent, a temporary togetherness forged through individual rather than collective will, a characteristic heard in many other moments of musical theatre chorus and manifestations of ensemble performance. Of course, there are refined exceptions to this (the 'Ascot Gavotte' in *My Fair Lady* being one such example). Still, here, the contrast between the modern community and the twee pastoral idyll of Arcadia is evoked through timbral and textural changes in the macro-voiceworld. At the Races, the chorus is modern and metropolitan, configuring a sense of belonging to what might be called a contingent community.[36]

In the macro-voiceworld of *The Arcadians*, then, the chorus appears to manifest two kinds of community in its narrative context, and in the vocal textures and complexities of performance. In one case, it is contingent and supported by individuals who agree to join the community. Yet, in another, it is imbued with a contradictory and even exclusionary dystopian character, presenting a challenge to Dyer's notion of what a chorus might be in the musical. The consequences of this might have a significant impact on the way choruses in other voiceworlds are heard or analysed, as it suggests that camp, excessive, and utopian moments in musical theatre might give voice to a very different sensibility than is often imagined. Arcadia might sing in unison at the exclusion of progress, while in a more complex and difficult reading, white America sings of its 'belonging to the land' at the exclusion of the indigene and the immigrant.

It also presents a further challenge to the make-up of the macro-voiceworld. No longer must we listen to two large vocal groupings (chorus and ensemble) but three: the intentional chorus, the contingent chorus, and the ensemble (heard later in this chapter). The distinctions are necessary, but the terminology seems awkward and inconsistent. Is there a more unified or coherent way of talking about, and listening to, the three iterations of larger vocal groupings in the macro-voiceworlds of musical theatre? One approach might be found in Steven Connor's concept of 'choralities'. While acknowledging 'a rich literature within musical history concerning the aesthetics and pedagogy of choral singing', Connor observes that 'there has been little study of collective voicing . . . across the broad range of its manifestations'. Variously, such 'acts of joint vocalisation' include:

> prayer, children's games, formalised learning processes and statements of fealty ('I pledge allegiance to the flag'), along with the chants of protest, demand or celebration found in political and sporting circumstances.[37]

It is appropriate, then, to conceive of the different kinds of chorus above as distinct choralities, a designation which will serve as a more coherent organizing principle when the nature of the ensemble is also considered in the next case study.

Connor's observation that choralities can take 'involuntary' and 'voluntary' forms gives further credence to rethinking intentional and contingent choruses in this way.[38] A chorality that is involuntary may more readily manifest an exclusionary, subjugating, or dystopian idea of community. It is one which, as Connor observes, 'is almost always concerned with the establishment of solidarity'.[39] On the other hand, a voluntary chorality may be altogether more utopian, with its focus on individual agreement and agency. On this basis, we might think of group numbers such as 'Arcadians Are We' or 'Oklahoma!' as moments of *intentional chorality*, while 'Back Your Fancy' might be heard as a moment of *contingent chorality*. Before listening to the ensemble as a further kind of chorality, however, what might be revealed about utopia and even the nature of choralities, when we listen to the micro-voiceworld of *The Arcadians*?

After introducing the Arcadian community through intentional chorality early in act one, the first character-led number is a quartet, 'The Joy of Life', sung by Sombra, Chrysea, Astrophel, and Strephon. Reaffirming an idyllic view of life and nature, this song does little to advance the narrative. However, it brings into focus Sombra's and Chrysea's Arcadian identities, neither of whom was featured as a soloist in the preceding choral numbers. Retaining the blend, balance, tone, and timbre of both intentional and contingent choralities, this micro-voiceworld of principal characters shares a kind of symbiotic relationship with contingent chorality, configuring a voluntary or conditional relationship between individual agency and communal wholeness. The focus on individual agency intensifies when James Smith crashes in on the Arcadians. Answering Smith's question as to who leads them, Sombra's solo ('The Pipes of Pan') follows 'The Joy of Life' and adheres to the conventions of a soprano aria from operetta. How might this solo voice be understood?

The intensity of solo songs contrasts with the various 'manifestations of community' heard in the two choralities above. While the macro-voiceworld may be a space which 'lies beyond' individual characters and 'exceeds their awareness', solo numbers present characters with specific moments of individual agency not expressed by a larger social group (even including a quartet), and provide a sustained focus on one voice as it inhabits the 'space of vulnerability'.[40] In this space, a wrong note, missed lyric, or vocal break is heard easily; something covered over or compensated for in moments of intentional or contingent chorality. A solo vocal performance offers individuals an opportunity to achieve an emotional transparency and intensity that exceeds mundane expressivity, assuming a utopian quality in the moment of vocal performance.

However, several other facets are at play. First, in the original cast of *The Arcadians*, 'The Pipes of Pan' was sung by soprano Florence Smithson, originating the role of Sombra. Smithson was a well-known opera singer who was cast due to the acclaimed purity of her voice; *The Times* would later report in her obituary of 13 February 1936 that audiences waited expectantly for her trademark *pianissimo* high notes, such as those composed for the character by Monckton in this song. Employing the higher end of her vocal range, this song offered listeners a vocal intensity and, through her virtuosity, even included what Cavarero terms 'extreme vocal moments' (see Figure 3.2).[41]

As considered in earlier chapters, a common analytical approach to this kind of vocal performance might render it metaphysical or transcendent; given the mythical location of Arcady, this may also make sense here. Yet, remembering that this musical comedy captures the push and pull between pastoral ideal and metropolitan progress, the work gives voice to a transition during the development phase of musical comedy. In this context, how might Sombra's solo voice be understood? Sombra's call to 'follow the pipes of Pan' is offered to the mortal, Smith, in direct response to his disruption of Arcadia. In other words, unlike the unselfconscious intentional chorality which opened act one, this solo is much more self-aware.[42] For Nancy L. Nester, such self-awareness by individuals is a vital constituent of any

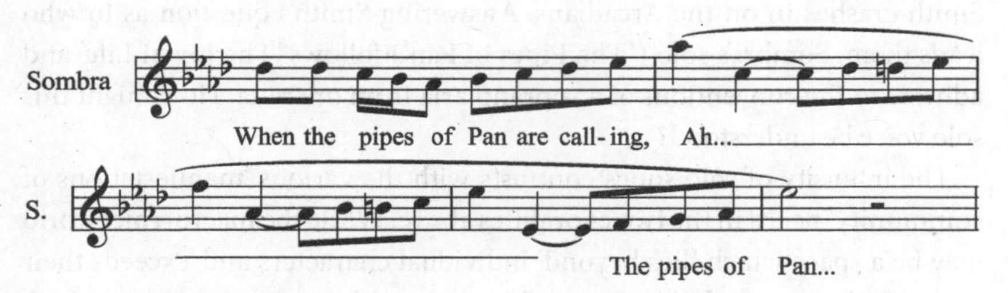

Figure 3.2 Moments of vocal intensity in 'The Pipes of Pan'. Notated by the author from *The Arcadians* vocal score, 1910.
Monckton, Talbot, and Wimperis, *The Arcadians (Vocal Score)*, 85.

society with utopian aspirations and may offer a way to understand Sombra's solo in relation to the macro-voiceworld established in the preceding songs.

Considering the relationship between the individual and community, Nester suggests that empathy—the self-awareness of recognizing another's feelings—is a precursor to the binding relationships that offer the basis for utopia.[43] She writes that '[e]mpathy assists people as they navigate relationships with others and formulate a utopian vision':

> the individual must appreciate the level of threat or enhancement to human flourishing a set of conditions presents; one must recognize the suffering or gain someone differently situated might experience. The resulting understanding may involve a visceral reaction in the beholder.[44]

If the industrial capitalism of modernity represents a threat to the Arcadians (symbolized by Smith's airship), and if Sombra believes that Smith may gain from 'following the pipes of Pan' instead of his entrepreneurial and dishonest ways, then her 'visceral reaction' here is to sing. Giving way to the intensity and transparency of the emotional opportunity song provides, this allows Sombra to navigate her relationship with the stranger from London while formulating a utopian vision beyond the disruption to her idyllic existence. In this sense, Sombra's solo voice—and the celebrated virtuosity of Smithson's original performance—may be encoded with pastoral utopianism rather than metaphysical transcendence. Elsewhere, such empathetic self-awareness, leading to relationship-building and opportunities for utopian dreaming, is heard in *Oklahoma!* when Curly promises Laurey that she will sit behind a team of snow-white horses in a romantic surrey on the way to the box social. It is the same visceral reaction that prompts Akaash to sing 'The Journey Home' (*Bombay Dreams*, 2002) as he realizes that sometimes a utopian vision begins with where you came from, and is heard when Miss Honey realizes the potential of 'This Little Girl' in *Matilda* (2011).[45]

Such moments are utopian, and as chapter 2 explored, also challenge any sense of metaphysicality in the larger voiceworld of musical theatre. Notwithstanding the mythical idyll they inhabit, this remains true in *The Arcadians.* The disrupted (or dismantled) metaphysicality of the micro-voiceworld is perpetuated further in act three when Chrysea, Sombra's cousin, declares that 'I Like London' when given a tour of the city by Bobbie. Once more, the debunking of metaphysical vocality is heard in a musical from this period, just a decade after *Florodora* was first performed. Yet, it is the solo voice which features next that proves especially noteworthy. After she tours London, Chrysea is at the Arcadian Restaurant run by Simplicitas and is seen rejecting advances from the unsuccessful jockey, Doody. As a comedically gloomy character throughout, Doody sings 'My Motter' (a mispronunciation of 'motto'), in which he concludes that it must be his upbeat manner which has disinclined Chrysea, and resolves to become more serious-minded. In the original production, Doody was played by music hall comedian Alfred Lester, whose speak-singing and affected cockney accent on a 1915 recording offers a solo borne of rejection and presented as comedic melancholy and self-delusion.[46] In *The Times* review of *The Arcadians*, the editor noted that Lester's performance as Doody was 'more hilariously melancholy than ever: the audience rocked to hear him sing that his motto was "always merry and bright" '.[47]

Lester's performance style was honed in melodrama, with one obituary commenting that 'the melancholy he had thus learnt to bathe in never quite dried off him; he used to let it drip on the musical comedy and revue stages'.[48] Along with the optimistic empathy heard in Smithson's song, comedic or wry melancholia—a bittersweet undertone in musical content, dramatic function, and vocal delivery—is also a recurring emotion in solo songs. It is the feeling that pervades the speak-singing of Astaire's 'The Half of It Dearie Blues' (*Lady, Be Good*, 1924) and its more tragic parody 'The God-Why-Don't-You-Love-Me Blues' (*Follies*, 1971). It is the emotion that characterizes Kathy's nonchalant reflection on her friends' relationships, as she concludes 'I Can Do Better than That' (*The Last Five Years*, 2001), and the sardonic bitterness of Diana, who feels 'nothing' at her old acting tutor's passing (*A Chorus Line*, 1975).

Beyond empathy, then, can melancholy—with or without comedic overtones—be heard as utopian? Often arising from a 'perceived or real sense of a loss', melancholy is an emotion of displacement, 'an awareness of not being where one wants to be . . . of a visceral discomfort, of not being at home in the world'. Melancholy may be a 'temporal dislocation' between what has been and what is to come, with a sense that what *is* in the present is unsatisfactory.[49] While empathy may prompt individuals to give voice as a means of negotiating relationships and reappraising ideals, the voicing of melancholy—whether inflected with comedy or not—offers individuals the 'space of vulnerability' to process the present and determine a means to move forward.[50] Just as Sombra's invocation to Smith arose as a 'visceral reaction' to the disruption of Arcady, Doody's song, and the other examples above, are the result of a 'visceral discomfort' with the present: the very conditions which foster an exploration of the possible.[51] Such moments of melancholic voice, then, may be *proto*-utopian in their intensity and directness. This may even be the case for Nomax, melancholy in his loneliness without Lorraine ('Early in the Morning', *Five Guys Named Moe*, 1990); for Caroline, as she reflects on the outcomes of earthly desires on the way to church ('Lot's Wife', *Caroline, or Change*, 2004); or, for Shylock, as he laments his situation as a 'Jonah Man' (*In Dahomey*, 1903).[52] In each case, melancholia is heard as an aesthetic of African American music, such as blues. How, then, might this specific cultural association, be heard as utopian?

Drawing on Sigmund Freud's 1917 essay 'Mourning and Melancholia', Jermaine Singleton has described a state of 'cultural melancholy'—in which a sense of loss is internalized to negotiate or reckon with—as a means of exploring the social and political complexities of African American art, literature, and performance, as it embodies, processes, or responds to histories of racialization.[53] In other words, the melancholy evident in popular song styles such as the blues may be indexical of an internalized loss, but only since it offers the potential for a reckoning; dissatisfied with the present. Citing Anne Anlin Cheng, Singleton highlights 'the importance of exploring the presence of the ghost of imperial and colonial past in everyday political, social, and psychical life', drawing attention to 'the central role of such insights and reflection in broadening the quality of civic life in our current multiculture "at ease with grievances but not with grief" '.[54] In other words, vocal melancholy may sing not only of dystopian oppression and subjugation but of a utopian sensibility of resistance and reckoning.

In the development phase of early musical comedy and elsewhere, it is fascinating to listen across voiceworlds and hear in various manifestations of chorality and individual voices potential limitations or possibilities. In an era which understood society through the collective rather than the individual, the intentional chorality of the chorus in *The Arcadians* can be heard as exclusionary and paradoxical: utopian in its ideal and yet somewhat dystopian in its manifestation. Community may also be contingent, and the chorality through which this might be heard offers a way of thinking about the relationship between individual intensity and the directness of group vocality. The sense of individuality to a contingent chorality in the micro-voiceworld, however, still creates a plural space where 'alternatives are permitted', encoded with empathy and even melancholy as part of its utopian potential through solo voices.[55]

In other words, the decadence of choralities and individual voices can be understood, in Potter's and Alston's terms, as dynamic and subversive. After all, in an era when community was the primary ideological marker of a functioning society, contingent chorality exposed the mechanisms of subjugation, deconstructing dissimulated power structures by enacting a vocal 'rupture' rather than 'reaffirmation'. What happens, however, when society shifts from a foundation of collectivity to individualism after World War Two? In what way was this reflected in the voiceworlds of musical theatre, and how did this impact the form and its capacity to sing utopia? A paradigmatic example from Broadway in the latter half of the twentieth century is instructive in listening for an answer to this question.

'A city of strangers': Liquid Chorality and the Dystopian Utopianism of *Company* (1970)

Forty years after *The Arcadians* arrived on Broadway, mid-twentieth-century America was gripped by something of an identity crisis. From the end of World War Two through the early years of the Cold War, individual crises and personal stress came together in the American 'age of anxiety', seen as a consequence of the rampant corporatization of society and the breakdown of the nuclear family in American life. This 'age of anxiety' ushered in a culture that reoriented social structures away from community and placed an emphasis on individualism, in what sociologist Christopher Lasch would come to call 'the culture of narcissism'.[56] Lasch contended that the rapid growth of commodity consumerism, developments in technology, and the cult of celebrity in everyday life enabled a fragmentation of society and led to an anxious citizenry trying to acclimate to a new sense of being. For Lasch, the very idea of 'society' from the 1950s onwards underwent a profound shift from an emphasis on the kind of intentional community heard in Arcady to a contingent assemblage of narcissistic and anxious individuals whose sense of society existed outside of themselves.

In much the same way that *The Arcadians* performed a transition from rurality to modernity in imperial Britain, the shifting relationship between the community and the individual during this period in America was reflected in popular culture, including musical theatre, and seen in the success of what John Bush Jones called the 'fragmented musicals' of the 1970s and 1980s. Dramaturgically, these works sought to mirror a 'fragmented society' governed by 'the "Me" mentality' through a rejection of conventional narrative structures or the hermetic aestheticism of Golden Age realism.[57] Presented through a series of episodes in which musical numbers 'are either self-encapsulated entities or Brechtian comments on what is happening', the musical *Company* is paradigmatic of the 'fragmented musical'.[58] Written by George Furth, with music and lyrics by Stephen Sondheim, the musical centres on the emotional and romantic ambivalence (or paralysis) of Robert (Bobby), a thirty-five-year-old bachelor living in New York City, whom Michael Ratcliffe describes as 'a large question-mark and an empty space: a hero who is too indecisive to move'.[59] Through a series of temporally non-specific vignettes, it is Bobby's ambiguity regarding commitment and relationships—heterosexual or otherwise—that provides the catalyst for the succession of conflicting, meandering, and often humorous discussions, during which Bobby's married friends try and give advice or match-make from their own discrete, dysfunctional perspectives.

In a variety of scenes, Bobby finds himself advised by Larry and his impetuous and cynical wife Joanne, the newly divorced Peter and Susan who nonetheless still co-habit, and the passive-aggressive parents David and Jenny, who experiment with marijuana and are not quite sure who they are. Bobby also maintains friendships with Harry and Sarah, who both struggle with addictive personalities, and Paul and Amy—one constantly optimistic, the other neurotic and insecure. In addition to this circle of dysfunctional marital bliss, Bobby is romantically (if ambiguously) involved with three girlfriends: Kathy, who suddenly announces she is to marry someone else during a romantic stroll in Central Park; April, the conservative air-stewardess with whom Bobby has a one-night stand; and Marta, the ebullient bohemian.

Within or between each vignette, moments of song arrive suddenly or without any chronological or narrative impulse, exposing the internal contradictions and paradoxes inherent in the themes of marriage, relationships, commitment, anxiety, and narcissism that the work explores.[60] What, then, might the fragmented and episodic dramaturgy of disjunction and interpolation reveal about the 'manifestation of community' in the macro-voiceworld Bobby and his friends inhabit?[61] How might the multiplicity of 'self-encapsulated [vocal] entities' alter the relationship between the individual and the group by listening to the micro-voiceworld of *Company*?[62] How does the alleged cultural shift from the community to the individual affect what utopia may (or may not) be heard in this musical?

Beginning at his thirty-fifth birthday party (which may or may not be an imagined scenario), Bobby's friends surprise him with gifts, jibes, and well-wishes, building to repeat the nominal refrain: 'Bobby . . . Bobby . . . Bobby baby . . . Bobby bubi . . . Robby'.[63] With dynamic balance, uniform breath placement and even phonation, the macro-voiceworld, therefore, begins with the sounds of an intentional chorality or, at the very least, a contingent ensemble, before it develops through small, individual, melodic units to a complex counterpoint 'made up of soloists who have to nail their lines rhythmically and melodically'.[64] This, then, is not an intentional community, even while this motif recurs throughout the piece as if to make the point.

After calling his name repeatedly, Bobby's friends variously explain that they tried to call but he did not answer his phone; ask if they can get together for drinks; check if he is free on a certain day; and ask him to do them a favour or join them on a trip. The frantic polyphonic texture that results reorients the macro-voiceworld of the musical: a fragmented song, with fragmented vocal delivery, in a fragmented musical, mirroring a fragmented society. It is a song in which speech quality dominates, and which lacks the kind of sustained vocal blend, uniformity, or synchronicity heard in any intentional or contingent chorus in *The Arcadians* or even *Oklahoma!* The macro-voiceworld of *Company*, then, offers a 'manifestation of community' in which characters 'perform their individuality . . . but who are also required to work together for the good of the whole'.[65] In vocal performance, this 'community of individuals' performs multiple melodic lines in 'self-encapsulated [vocal] entities', exhibiting the aesthetic properties of ensemble chorality rather than a chorus.[66] As John Bush Jones highlights, Sondheim's musical focuses on isolated individuals within a collective rather than community.[67] This collective may be heard as its own utopian performative, one 'that gesture[s] toward a future in which people build alliances through their common humanity, facilitated, rather than hampered, by differences'.[68] How, then, might this voiceworld of individuals allied through difference be understood?

The fragmented chorality of the contrapuntal ensemble resists the social *wholeness* of the kind considered by Nisbet. All characters live in New York, yet the musical's sense of place positions each of them in an ambivalent or transient relationship to their city.[69] As mentioned above, moments of temporary togetherness—such as when all characters exclaim 'in comes company!' at the end of the title song—may offer a glimpse of *contingent* community, but the retention of individual characteristics configure this contingence as culturally distinct from the chorality of the Askwood Races in *The Arcadians*, for example. In other words, the ensemble in *Company* gives voice to a particular form of contingence, one which requires a different definition from the choralities identified above.

First coined by Polish theorist Zygmunt Bauman in 1999, the notion of 'liquid modernity' as a means to articulate the fragmentary nature of modern life can be summarized as 'the growing conviction that change is the only permanence, and uncertainty *the* only certainty'.[70] Bauman further developed the notion of a 'liquid life', in which constant mobility and change characterize the everyday anxieties of society.[71] Living in what Bauman later called 'pointillist time', Tony Blackshaw summarizes 'liquid modernity' as a climate in which individuals 'are both forced and choose to live their lives on the hoof, with social relations experienced as speedy, fleeting and transitory . . . in episodes'.[72] To an extent, the properties of 'liquid' society may describe the characteristics of 'fragmented musicals' at large. For the macro-voiceworld of *Company*, however, liquid modernity is performed through shifting, transitory counterpoints, and the numerous vocal formations in the ensemble numbers. In short, while *The Arcadians* gave voice to a contingent chorality characterized by a sonic (if temporary) homogeneity through blend, balance, and uniform phonation, the fragmented, contrapuntal, and incidental nature of the contingent ensemble in *Company*, voiced by a 'community of individuals' who resist phonic homogeneity, may be understood as a kind of *liquid chorality*.[73] What might the presence of such liquid vocality reveal about this musical's ability to sing utopia?

If the liquid chorality of *Company* performs the macro-voiceworld of a fragmented contemporary society (at least, 'contemporary upper-middle-class New Yorkers' of the 1970s), this may indicate a potential limit to its function as a utopian performative.[74] After all, this is not a voiceworld that imagines 'sonic possible worlds' through vocal 'explorations of the possible'; it appears disillusioned with these ideals (even if it does not tilt entirely into dystopia).[75] Liquid chorality of this kind, then, may voice ambivalence towards (or anxiety about) the potential for anything beyond the present as it negotiates constant change instead of progress. If this is the case, it is particularly devastating that both acts are framed by such a utopian-limiting macro-voiceworld. After a moment of apparently intentional chorality (which returns at given moments, seemingly to perpetuate the uncertainties of liquid modernity), act one opens with the contrapuntal title song, while act two starts with an awkward celebration of friendship between Bobby, his married friends, and his three transitory girlfriends ('Side by Side by Side/What Would We Do without You?'). The fact that both acts end with a solo voice, outside of the ensemble, might further suggest the configuration of *Company* is at best ambivalent towards the utopian, and at worst dystopian. While a limit to utopianism may be the case in the macro-voiceworld of the ensemble, what might listening across the micro-voiceworld reveal?[76]

Along with two ensemble numbers, one duet, and five solo songs, there is a predominance of smaller vocal groupings in *Company*. If liquid chorality is characterized by mobility, constant change, and a sense of episodic, transitory social relations, then the restive vocal textures which run through quintets and trios, in particular, might suggest that the disillusionment of the ensemble numbers can also be heard in the micro-voiceworld of these characters.[77] If none of Bobby's friends knows each other, then moments such as the two quintets represent transitory and incidental chorality of the kind typified by the notion of liquid modernity. In the first quintet—'Have I Got a Girl for You'—the five husbands try to match-make Bobby with various single girls and wish they were also single again. Its parallel number—'Poor Baby'—sees the five wives worry about Bobby being alone, criticizing his choice of girlfriends while being jealous that they are not with him themselves.

Both songs follow the same shape and build from individual solo lines to a contrapuntal middle section and a concluding quintet in unison. This structure does not, then, begin with even liquid chorality. It begins—as with the two ensemble numbers—with solo voices, expanding as others join momentarily but asynchronously in counterpoint. Even if all the husbands end up asking the same question ('Whaddaya wanna get married for?!') or the wives wistfully sympathize ('We're the only tenderness he's ever known'), the eventual moments of contingent unison are temporary, fleeting and framed through the accretion of individual or contrapuntal voices.[78] In other words, as with the ensemble numbers, contingent chorality is not the focus of these small-group performances. Rather, it is the individuality of each character, unknown to the others, but joining their voices together 'on the hoof . . . in episodes.'[79] In contrast to 'The Joy of Life' quartet in *The Arcadians* which saw individuals work to contribute a sense of intentional community built on individual will, even in the micro-voiceworld of *Company*, these quintets may be heard as ambivalent, paradoxical, and occupying a space that is not entirely utopic.

Is there any part of the overall voiceworld of this musical that offers a potential glimpse of utopian futurity or possibility? In act one, scene five, Bobby has conversations with each of his girlfriends (Kathy, April, and Marta). Opening the scene, performed in fragments, and then acting as a transitionary space between each discrete conversation, Marta sings 'Another Hundred People', a self-encapsulated commentary on life in New York, a city full of people who are only passing through. With its 'simultaneous stimulating, exciting intensity and its alienating, lonely anonymity', the song encapsulates an anxious, disconnected, and metropolitan liquid life through its busily rhythmic accompaniment and persistent metric drive.[80] In contrast to the complex bombardment of counterpoint in the larger ensemble numbers, it is sung by a lone female. What kind of voice is this?

The literary theory of 'socially empty space' may offer an answer.[81] Drawn from Walter Benjamin's description of an old woman, excluded from the gated parks of Paris, who sits alone in a public garden and watches the sunset, 'socially empty space' may have referred to areas in a metropolis that excluded its inhabitants. Developing this notion through a study of lonely outsiders and empty spaces in nineteenth-century metropolitan novels, Matthew Beaumont suggests that the term might more specifically mean 'a species of space in which, because one expects it to be filled, densely populated . . . the absence of people is perceived almost as a presence. It is urban space that vibrates with a sense of absence'.[82] Such an intensity of absence in an empty metropolitan or urban space has clear parallels with Marta's single voice representing the last, and next, one hundred people to populate Manhattan. Whether sung by Pamela Myers in the original Broadway production, or by George Blagden as the renamed PJ in the gender-switched 2018 revival, a solo voice singing *about* the transience of liquid community provides the song with a kind of inverted immensity and intensity in performance.

Adapting Beaumont's phrase, Marta's solo becomes a vocally empty space, infused with what Beaumont would call a 'dystopian utopianism'. It is dystopian in its capacity to encapsulate a sense of 'alienating, lonely anonymity'; at the same time, the noise and bustle of the song's vocal delivery is 'stimulating [and] exciting' by virtue of its singular intensity: within the city's anonymous energy, there lay possibility beyond oneself.[83] Here, then, while the liquid chorality of the ensemble and smaller vocal groupings sings of an ambivalent or anxious disillusionment with utopia, the estranged disconnection of the solo voice enables the 'space of vulnerability' inhabited by a single character who negotiates the paradoxes of modern life in the metropolis.

The immensity of doing so is 'a sign both of the city's damnation and its redemption' and gives voice to the paradoxical possibility of both outcomes for its anxious, narcissistic, liquid inhabitants as well.[84] In the case of Marta, an energized and individual utopian space is shot through with a sense of dystopian disconnection, perhaps not in the voice which sings, but in the actual *act* of singing solo, suggesting that utopian vocality is still present but is now individualized rather than intentional or contingent (if, indeed, it was ever truly utopian in either of these instances).[85]

Listening across the interaction between Bobby and the 'hundred people' he interacts with in the liquid community of his friendship group, it is possible to hear the same dystopian utopianism in his vocally empty space. While his friends move freely in and out of the 'ironic . . . jarring . . . anticathartic' ensemble in both the macro- and micro-voiceworlds, through liquid chorality, quintets, and trios, Bobby remains separate vocally throughout the musical.[86] Even after a one-night stand with April, the melodic lines of the duet 'Barcelona' are discrete; Bobby and April take turns, singing *to*, rather than *with*, each other. His attempts to integrate or connect are frustrated. As Scott McMillin once put it, Bobby is a character who 'cannot fit into the ensemble. This is a sign of the limit he would like to overcome' but which he is denied.[87] In an ironic inversion of *Oklahoma!*, both acts of *Company* begin with the chorality of a (liquid) community only to conclude with the solo voice of Bobby. In both moments, there is an emotional ambivalence in Bobby's words. At the end of act one, Bobby wishes for a best friend who will not be exclusive, not look too deep, and not require him to change ('Marry Me a Little'). Act two reaches its *dénouement* as he longs to have a relationship with 'someone', while initially rejecting the idea because someone knowing you too well is too much of a commitment ('Being Alive'). Once more, it may be less about the voice that is singing and more about the expressive act of giving voice to one's individual vulnerabilities and ambivalences amid a liquid community with which one has a paradoxical relationship.

Further considering the relationship between the individual and community, Bauman writes that:

> In so far as they need to be defended to survive and they need to appeal to their own members to secure that survival by their individual choices . . . all communities are *postulated*; projects rather than realities, something that comes *after*, not *before* the individual choice. . . . This is the inner paradox of communitarianism.[88]

The ambivalence of examining individual choices in an age of anxiety is given voice by Bobby and Marta in this musical, in solo songs which examine the right to choose, or not choose, a certain course. On this basis, Bobby's perceived exclusion from the liquid community of his friends may not be about a vocally empty space that is alienated or disconnected. Rather, it may reframe the way we listen. If the reality of a community follows the choices made by individuals, then in focusing on Bobby's decision-making, *Company* gives voice to an exploration of the possible that is the preserve of the individual whose choices will help determine what community might be. If the idea of the 'individual in utopia revolves around whether or not individuals are . . . free to change the community from the inside', Bobby's choice not to choose offers a redefinition of his relationship with his community.[89] In the final moments of the show, with his married friends each wondering why Bobby has not shown up for his (surprise) birthday party, Joanne simply suggests: 'Maybe the surprise is on us'.[90]

As a paradigmatic example of a 'fragmented musical', listening across the ensemble vocality of *Company* reveals that, alongside the paradoxical and transient utopianism of intentional and contingent choralities, the complex and individualized liquid chorality of its macro-voiceworld yet again presents a challenge to Dyer's assertion about the utopian potential of choral transparency and community in musical theatre. Whether intentional, contingent, or liquid, the claim that the choralities of chorus and ensemble constitute the 'voice of the musical making itself heard' seems alarming in this context, because in the above examples, that overarching 'voice' becomes one of paradoxical exclusion, temporary togetherness, and frustrated alienation.[91] In this case, perhaps this book might be more correctly retitled *Singing Dystopia*, a designation which may also render visible the politics of 'Blacksound' and the appropriation of African American musical styles in the voiceworld of Broadway.[92]

However, from the empathetic and melancholic to the vocally empty space of solo voices, individuals are heard to push through the paradox of chorality and towards what utopia might be possible for them. The ways in which small solo groupings operate in *Company* suggests this was nascent in the early 'fragmented' (or, concept) musicals, but a more recent example demonstrates how plural, decadent, and individualized vocality, heard in relief against various choralities, might offer a further glimpse of what it means to sing utopia.

'Sing it again': Paradoxical Chorality and the Phonic Decadence of *Hadestown* (2019)

At the end of Anaïs Mitchell's 2019 musical *Hadestown*, the god Hermes starts over. Having narrated a retelling of the ancient Greek stories of Orpheus and Eurydice, and Hades and Persephone, during the course of the musical, its fateful ending prompts the messenger god to 'sing it again' in the hope of a different outcome. Scholar Nia Wilson suggests that this structure configures the musical as a 'repeated act of hope', a utopian dramaturgy for a musical concerned with themes of climate change, worker exploitation, inequality and immigration, and social change.[93] The reality is very different, yet to what extent might the voiceworld(s) of this musical sing utopia?

After a long gestation from a DIY performance in Vermont, to a folk album, concept album, and numerous workshop developments, a full production of *Hadestown* opened at London's National Theatre (Olivier) on 2 November 2018, directed by Rachel Chavkin, and later began previews on Broadway on 22 March 2019.[94] Set in a music club reminiscent of places like New Orleans' Preservation Hall, the musical contains a decadent blend of American popular music forms including blues, jazz, folk, gospel, and musical theatre.[95] Therefore, while it was an 'object of study' when listening across *Passing Strange*, the plurality of song styles derived from African American music means that listening across the macro- and micro-voiceworlds of *Hadestown* demands the use of 'Blacksound' as a 'methodology', reinforced by consideration of the diverse casting practices it has employed.[96] Vocally, *Hadestown* also utilizes a plural, texturally varied, and—at times—innovative approach to performance, offering a twenty-first-century example of how musical theatre voices can configure, complicate, or uncover what it might (or might not) mean to sing utopia.

The macro-voiceworld dominates *Hadestown* in a manner akin to both *The Arcadians* and *Company*. In all, 50 per cent of the musical numbers are enriched with variations of intentional, contingent, and liquid choralities.[97] In the opening song ('Road to Hell'), Hermes—narrator, emissary of the gods, and one able to move freely between worlds—introduces the scenario and each of the main characters. In a musical structure similar to 'Baptist Fashion Show' in *Passing Strange* (2008), Hermes leads the song in short, declamatory phrases imbued with speech quality, and his introductions to each character are confirmed by the company responding on the voiced bilabial nasal 'Mmmm'. This form of vocalization is common in popular song, often as a form of vocal agreement with either oneself or another singer after a lyrical statement. As with the call-and-response refrain, the voiced bilabial nasal was appropriated into American popular music from the 'hums' and 'vocables' of Central and West African song by means of African American performance practice in both sacred and secular contexts from gospel songs to slave songs, a paradoxical reference point which becomes more pertinent as the show progresses.[98]

As a sound, it may also be indicative of an intimate relationship or emotional response.[99] Distinctive through its 'indistinctness and lack of clear location', it acts as a kind of vocal 'spread', displaced and energized through the mouth, nose, chest, throat, and skull, all at once 'expressive' and yet 'impersonal'.[100] This sense of indistinctness and impersonal voicing encodes the choral response with appropriate anonymity during the introductions in the opening song. This anonymous, displaced, expressivity is imbued with an anticipatory quality because Connor further asserts that a hum is 'a song that never quite bursts into song . . . the song of the songs, the average and aggregation of all the tunes that lie latent within the voice'.[101]

While it is unlikely that Mitchell made an aesthetic choice with such a notion in mind, it is nonetheless ironic dramaturgically that a musical whose central theme concerns a song that is so beautiful it will reset and heal the earth's ills should begin with all characters joining in a song that 'never quite' becomes one. The hum of the macro-voiceworld in this first song, imbued with the politics of ritual and labour, is all-at-once expressive and anonymous, anticipatory and displaced, encoding the musical with a sense of being everywhere and nowhere, offering utopian potential while frustrating its realization. Voicing a bilabial nasal, with blend, straight tone phonation, controlled harmony, uniform dynamics, and synchronicity, the musical therefore begins with contingent chorality, a temporary togetherness at the music club for the characters of earth and the underworld. Yet, this togetherness does not hold as the paradoxical potential of the macro-voiceworld becomes clearer.

As Hades' wife and the goddess of spring, Persephone's journeying between the underworld and earth heralds the changing of the seasons. Returning below ground midway through act one, the song 'Chant' sees tensions arise between the two couples at the centre of the musical: Orpheus and his new wife Eurydice, and the older married couple of the underworld. With Persephone's departure, winter has arrived on earth, leading to Eurydice's frustration that while her musician husband idealistically and obsessively works on his magical song, they are struggling for food and shelter. Down in Hadestown, Persephone is similarly angered by Hades' rampant greed and industrialism which she says is unnatural, and immoral, and is leading to climate change on earth. Neither the 'neon-necropolis' of Hadestown nor the wintry conditions above ground seem to offer much exploration of the possible. Meanwhile, the workers repeat their mantra in unison ('Keep your head low / If you wanna keep your head') with robotic synchronicity and uniform phonation, discussed further below.[102] Yet the macro-voiceworld of this number cannot be heard as either intentional or contingent. Rather, even without the frenetic counterpoint of songs like 'Company', the plurality and decadence of voice types and styles evoke a sense of individualistic endeavour through anxious and uncertain liquid chorality, with characters separate and discrete, interrupting and interacting in episodes, or—in the case of Hermes and the Fates—commenting from a place of placelessness as they inhabit spaces beyond heaven, earth, and hades. This, then, is a song of dystopian disconnectedness.

While the workers sing in their faux-unity, and the Fates sing in close three-part harmonies or unison with other characters from either the earth or below ground, 'Chant' performs snatches of the desperate conversations between the two couples. The nasality and twang-infused mezzo-soprano of Eurydice is contrasted with the idealism of Orpheus' tenor and countertenor. The higher male vocal range may have configured the Phantom as 'unstable and always on the edge' in chapter 2, yet here it may be heard as ethereal, sensitive, powerful but tender in its youthful expressivity, and set against the increasing emotionalism of Eurydice's vocal belt.[103] Below ground, the older, husky vocal of Persephone's mezzo (placed in a lower register with a darker timbre) contrasts with Eurydice's voice and also with her husband's. Hades sings with a deep *basso profundo* associated in Western classical performance traditions with wisdom and otherworldliness.[104] Here, however, the bass voice subverts notions of wisdom, turning into an index of corruption and untrustworthiness.

These four voices therefore inhabit separate vocal spaces, along with the workers and Fates, and are joined by Hermes, who comments though speak-singing—a voice quality considered in depth in the following chapter—but which serves to place him beyond the diegesis. The emotional and situational distances between the characters are therefore given voice through liquid chorality, characterizing this moment in the macro-voiceworld as one of restlessness, uncertainty, and disconnection, rather than the anticipatory vocalizations of the contingent chorality heard in the opening number. The change from potential anticipation to anxiety is, however, challenged by the presence of intentional chorality in two moments of the musical, offering a specific contrast with both contingent and liquid choralities, and with each other.

Concerned about Persephone's criticisms, Hades goes in search of others who will appreciate Hadestown. Convinced to join him to ensure her survival, Eurydice follows Hades to the factory hoping for food, shelter, and subsistence. She arrives to find Hades leading the workers in a song: 'Why We Build the Wall'. Once again structured as a call-and-response and suggestive of an African American spiritual, the song is repetitive and rhythmically precise, with 'subtle references to the assembly line that is essential to the construction of Hades' wall'.[105] Commanding the space through confident physicality and with richness of tone, Hades poses questions to his workers: 'Why do we build the wall?'; 'Who do we call the enemy?'[106]

The workers respond in unison: the wall is built to keep them free from the enemy of poverty and from those who wish to threaten their security. Having all been employed by Hades, and giving voice to the perceived benefits of labour, this song seems to manifest another form of intentional chorality, voicing a community bound by shared ideological and political values and united against a common enemy. With synchronized onset, vocal blend, consistency of phonation, and uniformity of dynamic expression, the intentional chorality appears audible, achieved through the evident 'submergence of individual will' to build the wall and stay free.[107] Of course, as with *The Arcadians*, this form of chorality is reductive, giving voice to a mirage of a 'perfectible' community that is impossible to achieve and designed to exclude. Hades is conditioning his workers through the false hope of such a community, exploiting them for his own industrial gain, oppressing them, and keeping them from the freedoms they may have enjoyed if his greed and lust for power had not ruined the earth.[108] In other words, as in earlier examples, intentional chorality might be heard as one thing while giving voice to something else. It may sing utopia while hiding dystopian ideals of exclusion, exploitation, and oppression in plain sight.

Listening across the macro-voiceworld of act one, *Hadestown* gives voice to a dismantling of utopian potential in favour of false consciousness. It begins with contingent chorality, humming with anticipation for songs not yet sung. Disrupted by the onset of winter, the anxious and fragmented liquid chorality midway presaged a disaster heard in the intentional chorality of *Hadestown*, a performance which offers a dystopia of exclusion and oppression at the hand of a protective father figure who exploits and oppresses. What, though, might a second example of intentional chorality reveal?

At the end of act two, in keeping with the original myth, Orpheus has lost Eurydice through an act of doubt. Having looked back to check she was still with him as he made his way out of hell, he broke the agreement with Hades and condemned Eurydice to a life of oppression and exploitation with the workers in the factory. At this point, the first song is reprised as the stage is reset to the club of the opening scene. Persephone arrives once more as Hermes exclaims: 'it's an old song . . . and we're gonna sing it again'.[109] According to Nia Wilson, this act of telling and retelling is utopian: '*Hadestown* wants to persuade audiences that storytelling in itself can give us the strength to overcome differences, love each other, and fight for a better future. That even when we fail, we can, we must, start over'.[110] While this may sound idealistic, an additional moment of chorality after the bows offers evidence to underpin Wilson's assertion.

With the dramatic space having been ruptured, rendered inert by audience applause and cast bows, the curtain call of *Hadestown* takes the form of a song ('We Raise Our Cups'). Led by the actors playing Persephone and Eurydice, the cast—with all hierarchies of earth, hell, named character, or nameless swing having collapsed—stand downstage and face the audience directly. They join their voices with blend, harmony, synchronicity, and uniform dynamics as they take a moment to 'honour' those who 'sing in the dead of night' and 'bloom in the bitter snow'.[111] In doing so, they manifest an intentional community, celebrating those who, like Orpheus, fight against oppression or hopelessness, even if they fail. If voices are haptic, and audience members can experience empathetic contagion through entrainment in witnessing a live performance, then this moment—singing directly to the audience—invites them to join the community as well. As such, a paradoxical intentional chorality gives way to a contingent one, and momentarily offers a glimpse of what *might* be possible.[112] The macro-voiceworld of *Hadestown*, then, exploits a plurality of choral communities to explore the nature of hope, the possibility and ultimate fallacy of utopia, and the way narratives are constructed, adapted, and reformed. What, though, of its micro-voiceworld?

While the various choralities of the macro-voiceworld comprise 50 per cent of the musical, the micro-voiceworld is likewise rich with variety. Like *The Arcadians*, the textures of even smaller vocal numbers mean that solo voices or duets become poignant for their sparseness. Likewise, as with *Company*, the number of songs that feature small vocal groupings and perform a sense of porousness between macro- and micro-voiceworlds is evident in this musical, largely through the character of Hermes and the presence of the three Fates, who are 'always singing in the back of your mind'.[113] A close-harmony trio, the Fates watch the action unfold without direct intervention or interaction, and offer commentary and information to the audience, inviting them to reflect on the issues and moral quandaries at play in the musical. For example, assuming no specific position on Eurydice's dilemma as to whether she should accept Hades' invitation to the underworld in her desire for food and shelter, the Fates ask, 'What you gonna do when the chips are down?'[114] Later, they lament that 'nothing changes' when Hades confronts Orpheus about questions of property ownership, trespass, and employment rights.[115] These are not particularized expressions, but universal commentary from voices outside of the action. How, then, might we listen to the Fates in the micro-voiceworld of *Hadestown*?

As a cultural aesthetic, close-harmony female vocal groups—and in particular those composed of African American performers—are omnipresent in American popular music.[116] Configurations may vary to include quintets, quartets, and duos along with trios such as the Fates, but in most cases, this vocal configuration once again has its roots in African American song, with harmony groups an 'early part of modern gospel music, beginning in the 1920s'.[117] Its appropriation into American popular music took place through the first half of the twentieth century, leading to the ubiquity of African American backing singers for white rock musicians from the 1950s onwards, such as the popular 1960s vocal trio the Blossoms who supported singers including Paul Anka and Elvis Presley.[118] By the end of the decade, 'the gospel voice had become *the* authentic black female voice in pop music and musical theater, turning up in Broadway and West End musicals such as *Hair* and *Jesus Christ Superstar* (with background vocalists P. P. Arnold and Madeline Bell on the cast album)'. As backing singer Venetta Fields further recalls, the 1970s 'was the time when every act had to have three black American singers in the band. They wanted to feel and hear the blackness'.[119]

With the exception of 'When the Chips Are Down' and 'Nothing Changes', the Fates offer support to Eurydice but have little dramatic agency. They therefore share similarities with such singing groups: a constant vocal presence 'always singing in the back'.[120] Inviting memories of, and associations with, such backing trios in the micro-voiceworld of the musical, does

Hadestown perpetuate an instrumental fetishizing of black female voices? Does it replicate the notion of 'authentic blackness' through a vocal configuration which became a cultural commodity along 'the sonic color line', the 'socially constructed boundary that racially codes sonic phenomena' in American culture?[121] Listening across further characteristics of the close-harmony black backing trio and considering the dramaturgical function of the Fates in *Hadestown*, a possible answer to this question begins to emerge—one that reveals the presence of 'Blacksound' in popular culture and the possibility of utopia in this musical.[122]

Returning to Masi Asare's notion of the 'twice-heard' voice, the Fates might seem to embody the 'frequencies of and impact of' black female backing singers on popular music at large.[123] Yet, while black female backing singers of the mid-to-late twentieth century were fetishized in white popular music because listeners wanted to 'hear their blackness' (or, in the words of Susan Fast, 'their *otherness*'),[124] what constituted such 'blackness' was also 'twice-heard'. As Maureen Mahon notes: 'Through church-based music training, [black female backing singers] developed knowledge of solo and ensemble singing, arranging vocals, and singing harmony. They learned a large repertoire of songs and internalized a performance style that they carried into the rock and roll arena'.[125] This performance style was often marked by a 'departure from the standard text' characteristic of gospel singing. '[A]dding ascending or descending notes at the end of a musical line; it can also mean improvising with the slurs, slides, and scoops of melisma' as these African American women 'transported these vocal tropes from the sacred realm of gospel to the worldly context of rock and roll'.[126]

In other words, the Fates offer a duality of twice-heard African American influences on the musical stage: from popular music and the 'sacred realm of gospel' singing.[127] As beings that exist between the worlds of gods and men, the 'otherness' that is heard may therefore be indicative of the characters' liminality, employing a pair of 'twice-heard' vocal histories to characterize these women. Dependent on the listener's subject position, an invitation to 'hear their otherness' in this way may appear to inadvertently perpetuate a fetishized othering from popular music, or—as Asare might suggest—it might reveal an 'indebtedness' to pop music on the musical stage and to the gospel singer across the history American popular music as a whole.[128] In either case, the Fates' configuration as a liminal, otherworldly close-harmony backing trio is pertinent given their dramaturgical function. Throughout *Hadestown*, the Fates act as a Greek chorus—a dramatic device sympathetic to the narrative of the musical.[129] Watching the action unfold without direct intervention or interaction, offering support to a main character and commentary to the audience, the Fates' 'otherness' operates both in the liminal space of the drama (between the spiritual and earthly realms) and as a bridge between the drama and the audience.

While at times singing as individuals, the persistent use of close three-part harmonies suggests that the Fates may give voice to one thought from three different angles. Without assuming a specific moral or political position, their 'otherness' allows the commentary they offer to remain open and pluralistic. When 'the chips are down', Eurydice could stay on earth and take her chances, travel to Hadestown and risk losing Orpheus, or find another solution entirely. Likewise, the triangulation of property ownership, social mobility, and the value or exploitation of labour, is a perennial concern in Western society, given voice by the Fates at the moment Hades confronts Orpheus. To paraphrase musician Yehudi Menuhin, if harmony serves to make the incongruous compatible, then the presence of a vocal trio may perform an exploration of the possible in the micro-voiceworld of the musical. Sounding out incongruous positions in a compatible way, the audience is invited to think through various outcomes, solutions, or consequences. Beyond the cultural associations of three-part female vocal harmony, then, the Fates might also be heard to offer brief glimpses of utopian vocality as they configure a plural space for imagining the world as it could be, much like Tevye's daughters in *Fiddler on the Roof* (1964), or Charlie, Frank, and Mary in *Merrily We Roll Along* (1981).

This sense of plurality is further heard in the vocality of Orpheus. As the musician whose song will 'bring the world back into tune',[130] Orpheus' tender and innocent countertenor is augmented throughout the musical by at least five of the factory workers, who echo his melodies and certain words in rippling harmonies enriched with counterpoint and warm tonal suspensions in the melody lines. These voices are blended, balanced, and synchronized in a way that parallels the qualities heard in intentional and contingent chorality. How, then, might these echoes be heard and understood as part of the micro-voiceworld? Like Floyd Collins, the source of the original sound is visible on stage, constructing a particular relationship between the voicer and the echo(es).[131] Floyd's solo voicing elicited the echoes in the Great Sand Cave through an immediacy and materiality of the self. For Orpheus, however, the immediacy is dispersed, fragmentary, and expanded through the voices of the workers in an intense, pluralized, phonic materiality. As with the quintets in *Company*, does Orpheus' vocality indicate a porous relationship between the macro- and micro-voiceworlds of *Hadestown*? While this idea may seem logical, the 'acoustic relationality' of Orpheus' voice and its expansion through the echoes and repetitions of other performers offers a different possibility.[132] Through his song and youthful optimism, Orpheus gives the workers a voice and sings *for* them rather than *with* them. Orpheus' voice therefore becomes a plural 'vocalic body' in the micro-voiceworld rather than an extension of any chorality from the macro-voiceworld.[133]

The particularities of this 'acoustic relationality' are heard sonically and semantically.[134] First, the workers' voices are slightly *sotto voce* to Orpheus overall, or otherwise delineated through digital phasing that places Orpheus in a different acoustic space using technologies reminiscent of the soundworld of *Phantom* and *Floyd Collins*.[135] Second, as Derrida heard in Echo's repetition of Narcissus, the expansion and plural vocality of Orpheus' words give voice to the workers' hope and anticipation for what might happen next.[136] 'Residual' and anticipatory, the 'acoustic relationality' of Orpheus' pluralized 'vocalic body' therefore gives voice to the utopian possibilities of change.

Hopes, nevertheless, are dashed. Orpheus fails in his mission, the industrialists win, and all seems dystopian for a moment. As the musical resets to begin again in the hope of a better outcome, Hermes begins the reprise of 'Road to Hell'. This time the tone and texture are different. While the lyrics are those heard at the beginning of the musical, Hermes sings the first half of the song almost entirely a cappella, except for a few notes on the piano at the beginning. The intensity and directness of solo voices have been well established to this point. Here, however, it becomes the sole aural focus without the additive of music or instrumentation.[137] As Hans-Thies Lehmann succinctly puts it: 'Looking at an individual speaker one experiences intensely that the sound belongs to the individual face'.[138] The power and directness of such focus can 'physically take hold of a listener', prompting an intense emotive response.[139]

This level of response to an a cappella voice may carry with it the weight of humanity itself. As noted in previous chapters, in recent years, anthropologists, biological scientists, and musical psychologists have speculated that melodic intonation could have even preceded the formal development of language as a means of human communication.[140] In other words, the directness and transparency of vocal melody go to the heart of human understanding and expression. Whatever the accuracy of this supposition, it nonetheless highlights the power of the solo voice to reach out and connect with an intensity and focus that is not accessible by any other means. The inherent vulnerability and emotional weight of an unaccompanied solo voice therefore offers a distillation of the power of solo vocality in the micro-voiceworld of a musical.

Reflecting on how the old song from long ago is sad and tragic, Hermes straightens himself up, pauses, and then makes a simple statement in speech rather than song: 'It's a sad song / but we sing it anyway'.[141] Having spent much of his narration freely exchanging melody for speech, or speak-singing, it is telling that the most important line in the whole musical—a declaration to continue and keep going—should be spoken. It is a small moment at the end of the musical, yet, as Sarah Whitfield has shown, this one act in the micro-voiceworld may be heard as a further utopian performative at the end of a tragedy. Citing Dolan, Whitfield suggests that 'small but profound moments' such as this one 'calls the attention of the audience in a way that lifts everyone slightly above the present'.[142] In particular, Whitfield responds in this way to the queer black actor André De Shields, who is now synonymous with the character of Hermes. As a small but profound moment, De Shields's use of speech offers a performance of black queer resistance to the hegemony of everything Hades—originated by an older white man—stands for in the world.[143]

Listening across this musical, perhaps the resistance goes even further, and might characterize the micro-voiceworld as a whole. The 'small moment' of one spoken line is clearly highlighted in De Shields's delivery of the song. In addition to a utopian performative related to identity, might the plural vocality of Orpheus—youthful, tender, powerful, and extraordinary—be heard as another form of subversive resistance? A decadent plurality in which an individual becomes an activist, and seeks to challenge the hegemony which leads to inequality, climate change, and labour exploitation? Heard in relation to the decline of utopian potential in the macro-voiceworld, as it slides from contingent chorality to the uncertainty and anxiety of liquid chorality to arrive at the oppressive hegemony of intentional chorality, could listening to the close-harmonies of the Fates reveal an urgency to consider the outcomes of social or political action and inaction? Does their neutrality in the micro-voiceworld offer listeners an exploration of the possible, beyond which a final moment of contingent chorality invites the audience to form a community which honours those who, like Orpheus, continue to fight for justice? Echoing José Esteban Muñoz, Whitfield notes: 'To consider the past events that have led to now and to tell their story "anyway" (to borrow from

Hermes) requires a resistant turn, a turn towards the future.'[144] Perhaps, one day, Orpheus might succeed after all.

'Why we tell the story': Choralities and Utopia

Returning to the assertion that the chorus is a 'manifestation of community',[145] listening across the changing relationships between choralities and individuals has revealed a fascinating—and surprising—characteristic of musical theatre. While the musical theatre chorus is commonly associated with a direct, transparent, idealized community; the macro-voiceworlds of chorus and ensemble—understood as intentional, contingent, or liquid choralities—may not be entirely utopian, after all. In particular, in a direct challenge to Dyer, Hughes, Taylor, and others, the paradoxical, exclusionary privileging heard in the intentional chorality of *The Arcadians* and *Oklahoma!* may offer a musical mirage of utopian possibility while the cultural meanings it encodes belie this claim; only 'We Raise Our Cups' at the end of *Hadestown* suggests there are exceptions that may yet prove this rule. Within the macro-voiceworld of musical theatre, only contingent chorality was heard to offer any momentary glimpse of collective utopianism, and this was only possible because of individual investment in its function. Perhaps, in this case, utopia is a world agreed by individuals rather than a collective—an assertion reinforced in the liquid choralities of *Company*.

This focus on the individual was prominent in the solo voices and smaller groupings of the micro-voiceworld in which empathy, melancholy, and the subversive resistance of a solo (yet plural) voice were heard to push ahead and offer the hope of 'something better'. In addition, a final act of spoken voice in *Hadestown* encoded the micro-voiceworld with a form of resistance that 'lifts everyone slightly above the present' and offers a glimpse of utopia through a moment which dispenses with the need for song.[146] Given all the reasons considered so far as to *why* musical theatre sings, and despite the poetic observations made by Whitfield, this moment nevertheless remains an outlier in the micro-voiceworld of *Hadestown*. If sung voice can be complex, paradoxical, and utopian, then in what ways might the spoken voice (albeit set in relief within a moment of unaccompanied song) be likewise encoded with utopian potential? Focussing on this as a specific aesthetic seam of musical theatre vocality, the next chapter will ask: what kind of voice is this?

4

Intermediate Vocalities

Between Speech and Song

'Don't think about singing [. . .] think about the words.'[1] Concerned that his singing voice was not strong enough, this advice did much to reassure classically trained English actor Rex Harrison that he would be able to succeed in playing the role of Professor Henry Higgins in Alan Jay Lerner's and Frederick Loewe's *My Fair Lady* (1956) (see Figure 4.1).[2] Harrison has since become synonymous with the irascible tutor of elocution who transforms Eliza Doolittle from a flower girl in the gutter to a well-mannered Duchess' at an Embassy ball. Originating the role on Broadway, in the West End, and in the 1964 Warner Brothers film adaptation, Harrison's performance as Higgins has become iconic as a protagonist who speaks more than sings in a musical.[3]

Seventeen years after Harrison gave voice to the professor, Stephen Sondheim would have a very long night indeed. Casting Glynis Johns as Desirée Armfeldt in *A Little Night Music* (1973), the writing of 'Send In the Clowns' in a hotel room after rehearsals during the first run-through in Boston has become Broadway lore. Written to be 'acted rather than sung', it was composed specifically to fit the limited contours of Johns's 'small, silvery voice', with short phrases and plentiful pauses for breath.[4] Reflecting on his compositional approach to this song, Sondheim later explained: 'You don't use open vowel sounds. You use little cut-off things so that the audience doesn't think it is the actress's fault.' Somewhat bluntly, he concluded that this approach 'makes the song specifically for someone who can't sing' (or, at least, may not have the vocal training of other performers).[5]

In previous chapters, we have listened to the possibilities and paradoxes of voices as utopian performatives, overcoming vulnerability through intensity and energy when characters burst into song. Yet, Harrison and Johns demonstrate that, at times, musical theatre protagonists or principal roles may be performed by actors who place more emphasis on the words than the singing. In doing so, they present a challenge to the relationship between

Singing Utopia. Ben Macpherson, Oxford University Press. © Oxford University Press 2024.
DOI: 10.1093/9780197557679.003.0005

Figure 4.1 Rex Harrison as Henry Higgins in *My Fair Lady,* 1956. Reproduced courtesy of Photofest.

singing and utopia in the musical, appearing to complicate or frustrate access to 'something better', resistant to the 'space of vulnerability' which comes with singing and avoiding the 'danger of failure' by circumventing the emotional expressivity of song.[6] This resistance may be felt at the 'level of sensibility' considered by Dyer, changing the affective properties of musical theatre vocality.[7] Yet, along with Rex Harrison's Henry Higgins and Glynis Johns's Desirée Armfeldt, we have listened to other examples which frustrate or alter the affective sensibility of the singing voice, including Sam Levene's Nathan Detroit, and the shift from speak-singing to the pure spoken word in the case of André De Shields's performance as Hermes in *Hadestown* (2019). As a recurring presence in the history of musical theatre performance, what kind of voice is this?

'Speech inflection' to 'intermediate voice': Travelling between Speech and Song

As considered in chapter 1, musical theatre has long been characterized by a particular emphasis on the clarity of words in performance. It has employed strategies of 'speech inflection' (or what Ana Flavia Zuim calls a 'speech-melody' approach to composition) in a way that distinguishes it from the overt privileging of vocal virtuosity in opera, even beyond the declamatory vocal setting of recitative.[8] In the early twentieth century, such 'speech inflection' was seen in the compositional approach of American composers including Irving Berlin, Jerome Kern, and George Gershwin, as they lowered tessiture, limited melodic ranges, shortened musical phrases, and played with metre, rhythm, and cadence to emphasize the words, somewhat as precursors of the kind of approach Sondheim would later take writing 'Send In the Clowns'.[9] In performance, actors such as Fred Astaire, Ivor Novello, or Jack Buchanan exuded a sense of laissez-faire sophistication or confidence through overt 'speech inflection' with minimal vibrato, clipped phrasing, and the presence of open cadences in delivery, even while their rounded vowels and select use of legato ensured they still adhered closely to the melody.[10]

This kind of 'speech-inflection' was not what Bill Low meant when advising Rex Harrison, or what Hal Prince and Stephen Sondheim had in mind when they cast Glynis Johns in *A Little Night Music*. The speak-singing aesthetic heard in these examples is indicative of something altogether different. Beginning in the 1930s, the introduction of microphone technologies and electronic amplification in playhouses facilitated a cultural shift which, at times, allowed for a change in emphasis to focus on an actor's dramatic—rather than vocal ability.[11] As a result, along with Harrison and Johns, Richard Burton lent his actorly voice to King Arthur in *Camelot* (1960), while a decade later Elaine Stritch—'a character actress of the highest calibre [whose] strength was never her mellifluous vocalizations'—embodied the disillusioned Joanne through a cynical drawl in *Company* (1970).[12] In each of these cases, the balance between melody and prosody becomes reoriented in favour of the latter. However, these are not voices which merely speak conversationally or casually; they are formal and deliberate, set in relief and organized by the tempi, rhythm, and metre of a musical accompaniment which serves to heighten the content of the performance and the drama of the moment.[13] At the same time, voices such as Harrison's, Johns's, or Levene's do not consistently bear the hallmarks of sung melody.[14] They do not exhibit an expansive scalar structure based on a musical key and do not always sustain stable pitch placement in relation to the melodic line—at times approximating, or even exceeding, the melody written in the score. This aesthetic is, therefore, marked by its difference from the 'speech inflection' which characterizes other kinds of musical theatre voice.

Borrowing from ethnographer George List, these voices might be understood as inhabiting an 'intermediate' space between speech and song, a space with its own pluralities and sonic differences.[15] After all, while Johns's voice was small, fragile, and careful, Harrison's 'heightened speech' showcased an impressive spoken vocal range which extended 'from falsetto to basso-profundo'.[16] As seen, however, neither voice speaks or sings entirely. How, then, might we listen across the 'intermediate voices' heard in musical theatre in a way that accounts for their variations while revealing something about their relationship to the notions of utopia commonly ascribed to the transparency, intensity, and energy of sung delivery? In his article 'The Boundaries of Speech and Song', List produced a chart on which a range of intermediate vocalities might be mapped (See Figure 4.2).[17]

Published over half a century ago, this chart nevertheless provides a useful way of examining voices which emphasize prosody over melody; in other words, those which might seem to 'think about the words' first.[18] Casual speech is placed at what List termed 'the north pole', while song is placed at the corresponding south. Travel between these two extremes is then mapped along contours of expansion and diminution of intonation, scalar structure, and pitch stability, while 'the use of lines of latitude and longitude permits the placement of forms at midpoints'.[19] In his article, List includes the midpoints of chant, monotone, and Sprechstimme, while mapping other examples which include the 'heightened speech' of 'dramatic presentations' and 'the delivery of sermons', the Maori Haka, the *spiel* of auctioneering, the ritual chants of Roman Catholic liturgy, the 'wangka' of the Nyangumata tribe of Western Australia, and the ritual lament of Tibetan lamas.[20]

Placing 'intermediate voices' from musical theatre along these lines may therefore include examples of Sprechstimme, chant, monotone, and liturgical or cantorial voice, but may also allow the possibility of including both older and more contemporary intermediate forms. For example, recalling Jacopo Peri's reflection on the word setting of *L'Euridice* in 1601, his consideration of a vocal delivery which 'took an intermediate form' in early opera suggests that recitative forms could be mapped using List's chart in any analysis of operatic vocalities.[21] Likewise, contemporary forms including rap as

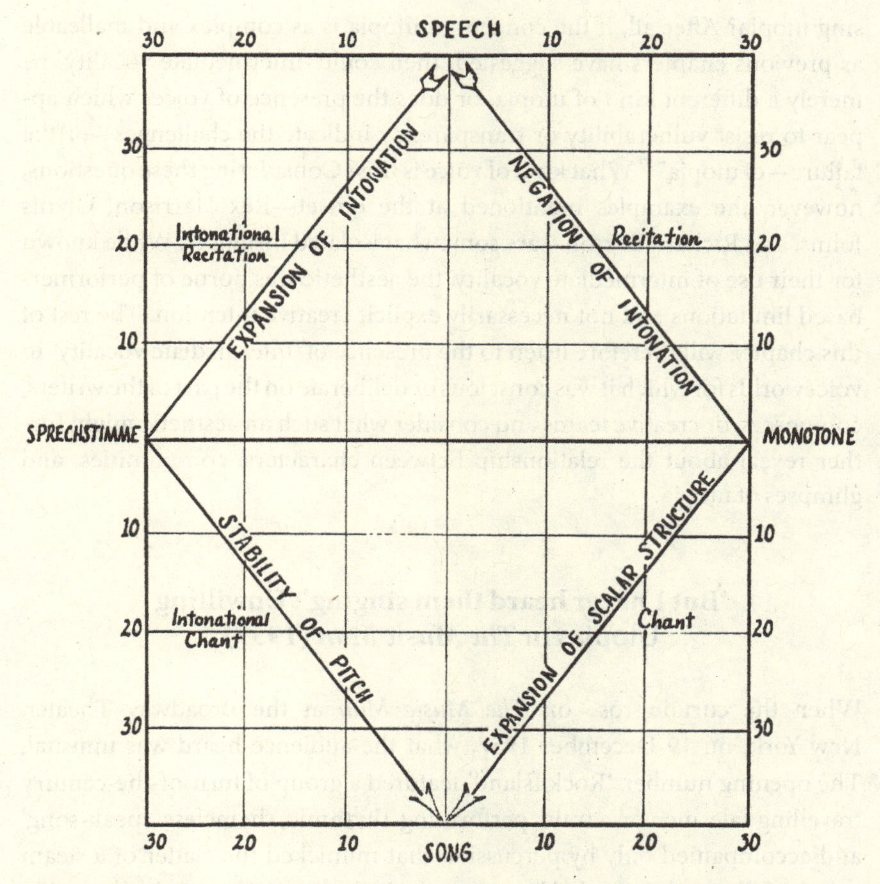

Figure 4.2 George List's 'Chart for Classifying Forms Intermediate to Speech and Song' (1963). Reproduced courtesy of the Society for Ethnomusicology.

heard in works such as *In the Heights* (2008), or the verbatim voiceworld of *London Road* (2011), may also be included. By listening to moments of intermediate voice in relation to speech, to each other, and to the utopian performative of song, some questions arise.

What does it mean for a character to be encoded with a predominantly intermediate vocality? What might the relative positions of these voices suggest about a given character's closeness to, or distance from, utopia? What happens when entire communities give voice in an intermediate space? In moments which see characters travel towards (or away from) either extreme of speech or song, what is revealed about musical theatre and its capacity to sing utopia? After all, if the concept of utopia is as complex and malleable as previous chapters have suggested, then could 'intermediate vocality' be merely a different kind of utopia, or does the presence of voices which appear to resist vulnerability or transparency indicate the challenges—or the failure—of utopia?[22] What kind of voice is this? Considering these questions, however, the examples mentioned at the outset—Rex Harrison, Glynis Johns, and Richard Burton—are somewhat isolated instances. While known for their use of intermediate vocality, the aesthetic was borne of performer-based limitations and not necessarily explicit creative intention. The rest of this chapter will therefore listen to the presence of 'intermediate vocality' in voiceworlds for which it was conscious or deliberate on the part of the writers, composers, or creative teams and consider what such an aesthetic might further reveal about the relationship between characters, communities, and glimpses of utopia.

'But I never heard them singing': Unwilling Utopias in *The Music Man* (1957)

When the curtain rose on *The Music Man* at the Broadway Theater, New York, on 19 December 1957, what the audience heard was unusual. The opening number, 'Rock Island', featured a group of turn-of-the-century travelling salesmen on a train, performing 'rhythmic, rhymeless, speak-song' and accompanied only by percussion that mimicked the clatter of a steam train at full speed. Intended by composer Meredith Willson to be 'pure *dialogue*, with *no melody* and *no rhyme*', *The Music Man* therefore begins with a contingent chorality and intermediate vocality.[23] Aping the patter and *spiel* of a travelling salesman, this aesthetic seems fitting, perhaps redolent of what List called the 'monotonic chant' of the auctioneer—with the need for speed to persuade potential consumers.[24] Yet, set in a quiet American city just before World War One, might the use of intermediate vocality in this musical serve a greater dramaturgical function than simply appropriating the vocal hallmarks of a particular profession?

Focussing on just one of the salesmen from the opening number, *The Music Man* tells the story of 'redeemable huckster' Professor Harold Hill, originally performed on Broadway by the actor Robert Preston, who was described by Willson as a 'high class hollerer'.[25] Alighting from the train in River City, Iowa, Hill poses as a travelling musician who sells the need for a marching band to the community, suggesting it will help keep the youth away from the rebellion, sin, and debauchery of the pool hall (and subsequent social vices). Convincing the townsfolk, Hill recruits the youth of River City to his marching band, with the promise of a civic parade in which they will play Beethoven's 'Minuet in G' on real instruments and in uniform. Hill, of course, cannot play a single note and has only the intention of conning the people out of money and moving to the next city before his scheme is discovered. Having to conceal his true thoughts, feelings, and fraudulent intent to cheat the townsfolk, the use of intermediate vocality by this character encodes Hill as duplicitous and dishonest in the voiceworld of this musical.

Early in act one, the song 'Ya Got Trouble' sees Hill work to persuade the community of the problem they need to address (the pool hall) so that, later, he can offer the solution (the marching band). Performed as a faux-revival meeting, complete with religious references in the lyrics, Hill assumes the role of a preacher to convince the townsfolk of the severity of potential youthful rebellion, changing from the 'monotonic chant' of a travelling salesman to the 'heightened speech' of a clergyman delivering a sermon, which may vary from 'speech' to a kind of 'intonational chant' on List's chart (See Figure 4.2). Delivering a song for which Willson had composed '*not a tune, [but] an accompaniment*', the number, therefore, builds to an almost-breathless 'evangelical fervor'.[26] Yet, despite the energy of his *spiel*, this fervour is constructed and Hill's intermediate vocality serves to position him at arm's length from the community in two specific ways.

First, the use of 'heightened speech' in this song affects the prominence of certain prosodic features in delivery. For example, the punchy and percussive highlighting of hard consonants not only serves as an authorial strategy for Willson but acts as a means by which the emphasis on voiceless plosives might produce a phonetic harshness through the change in airflow in performance:

HILL: YOU GOT TROUBLE, FOLKS, RIGHT HERE IN RIVER CITY, TROUBLE WITH A CAPITAL T/ AND THAT RHYMES WITH P/ AND THAT STANDS FOR POOL.[27]

As a result, Hill's vocal delivery configures his character as hard, perhaps even aggressive, as well as insincere and duplicitous. Second, the structure of the song charts a clear contrast between the macro-voiceworld of the Iowans and Hill's solo intermediate delivery. Using a call-and-response structure associated with evangelical sermons (and heard elsewhere in this book in relation to forms of African and African American folk song), Hill repeatedly sounds the call: 'Ya got trouble!' Whipped up into a frenzy, however, the townsfolk respond with a moment of contingent chorality rich in the same balance and blend that was heard when Oklahoma joined the Union, or when the race day attendees hedged their bets in *The Arcadians*. The community of River City, then, can sing utopia in a way that Hill's transient and fraudulent occupation does not allow. After all, he is an untrustworthy figure, an outsider who is never emotionally direct and is without scruples. When *The Music Man* first appeared—in the era of McCarthyism, American paranoia over global threats from communism, and suspicion of rock and roll rock and roll as a driver of youthful rebellion against the Christian conservatism of the American family—the intermediate vocality of Hill might even be heard as a sonic marker representing those who might infiltrate or challenge the cosy utopianism of the American Dream from the inside.[28]

Having convinced the townsfolk of the problem, Hill starts work on selling the idea of a boys' marching band in the song 'Seventy-Six Trombones'. Beginning with the same 'evangelical fervour' heard in 'Ya Got Trouble', Willson's lyrical setting emphasizes the voiced plosive 'B' in the repeated phrase '**B**oys' **B**and', while alternating between unvoiced and voiced plosives in the repetition of the word '**t**rom**b**one'. The phonation of these words has a forceful quality which keeps Hill at arm's length from the community when delivered in short, sharp phrases in the opening verse. Moving from the intermediate voice of a travelling salesman to a preacher of moral salvation, Hill's 'heightened speech' now positions him as bandleader or sergeant. The space between speech and song is, it seems, rich with possibilities for those who wish to avoid or frustrate the directness and vulnerability of song as a utopian performative. With the Iowans once again swept along by notions of American pride, embodied in the pomp and pageantry of a civic parade, they come together in another instance of contingent chorality to sing with the energy and intensity of the big parade.[29] However, as Hill leads the refrain, a change occurs. In his voice, we hear a stabilizing of pitch, expansion of scalar patterns, and emergent tonal centre. What has happened? Is this a moment of confected community on the part of Hill, designed to keep the townsfolk onside? Is Hill swept along by the deceptive delusions of his own sales pitch? Or is there more to this moment in the wider voiceworld of the musical?

While this momentary journey from intermediate vocality to song reveals that characters can travel from an intermediate space to ostensibly glimpse utopia, Hill cannot sustain it and quickly establishes a safe distance. He had flirted with Marian Paroo, the young unmarried librarian and River City's sole musician, early in the first act, and she once more rejects his advances as Hill reflects on the kind of girl he would like to marry. In the song 'The Sadder-but-Wiser Girl', he suggests that she must not be 'wide-eyed', 'wholesome', or someone who 'trades on purity'.[30] Yet, after joining the chorus momentarily to sing of seventy-six trombones, the casual intermediate vocality with which this song is performed sounds somehow different. Perhaps reminiscent of Rex Harrison's self-delusional musings as Henry Higgins in *My Fair Lady*, Hill's resistance to utopian vocality in this song is imbued with a sense of insecurity rather than insincerity. Intermediate vocality, then, may not only be for the conniving, contrary, or cynical; it may also be for the charming and clueless.

Hill is falling in love with Marian, yet it takes until the middle of the second act for Marian to admit she is also in love with Harold. Their duet, 'Till There Was You', finally renders Hill at the mercy of his heart rather than the hustle; a sensibility hinted at in 'Seventy-Six Trombones' but which takes until the end of the musical to be realizes fully. Following the lead of Marian (a role originated by Barbara Cook), Preston's huckster joins her in *singing* this penultimate ballad. Entering a utopian space of crooning baritone 'vulnerability', the hustler turns—presumably—into a husband, echoing Sky Masterson's journey in *Guys and Dolls* (1950). It becomes an apparent moment of willing intensity for a character whom Knapp suggests has changed from the morally bankrupt conman to someone reformed, redeemed, and domesticated.[31] In a poignant and devastating act of utopianism, the huckster whose artifice centred on saving the city's youth through the redemptive power of music is, himself, transformed by that very same power after falling in love with the city's only real musician.

Reflecting on this outcome as part of the broader narrative, Knapp suggests that 'music serves both as the literal and metaphoric basis of community-building'.[32] The community created is a sentimental and idealized vision of early-to-mid-twentieth-century America, heard in the John Philip Sousa–inspired marching tunes of the River City Boys' Band and the ageing schoolboard's parodic barbershop quartet—a group Hill formed early in act one, despite not singing himself.[33] If, as Knapp continues, 'redemption is always configured as acceptance by the larger group', then the finale of this show, in which the band performs in full marching colours and puts on a parade, reconfigures Hill from a threatening outsider to the living embodiment of the American Dream, a man who no longer needs intermediate vocality borne of insincerity or insecurity, but can enter the shared—*sung*—space of a utopian community. Put another way, the changes in Hill's voice may be encoded with a surrender to the American ideals he earlier sought to exploit.[34]

Yet, because voice can be a 'junction point of multiple encodings', and utopia itself is never a single ideal, then such a neat reading of the direction of travel from intermediate vocality to sung voice may be only one possibility.[35] What else might be revealed by listening again to the space between speech and song for Professor Harold Hill? In most readings of Willson's musical, the turn-of-the-century setting is considered to be nostalgic rather than utopian—performing a wistful remembrance of a simpler or more certain past. For example, Knapp suggests that *The Music Man* provides a 'nostalgic mythology of emerging community set in the past'.[36] What, though, is the relationship between nostalgia and idea(l)s of utopia? This question is developed in detail in the following chapter, but some aspects are worth considering here concerning other ways of listening to the intermediate voice of the redeemable huckster.

On a cultural continuum of the individual and collective popular imagination, utopia looks forward to imagine a better future, while nostalgia is wistful though not always innocent longing for the past.[37] While both nostalgia and utopia pull in opposing directions, these ideals also share several things in common. First, neither the imagined past nor the imagined future could ever actually exist; they are only ever wishes or ideals. Second, as Malcolm Chase and Christopher Shaw indicate, nostalgia arises out of a sense that the 'present is deficient', the same foundations upon which utopianism is built. Could it be, then, that the warm, safe feeling of nostalgia has a parallel in utopianism, as relative 'counterparts' of past and future?[38] Can a voice encode both at the same time or, at the very least, negotiate them somehow?

The 'nostalgic mythology' considered by Knapp is easy to understand. Set in 1912, but first performed in the 1950s, *The Music Man* portrays the redemption of an outsider and his eventual willingness to embrace traditional American values of community and domesticity as an idealized performance of utopia amid the anxieties of geopolitical threat and the emergence of youthful rebellion and rock 'n' roll in the immediate post-war and Cold War climate. Framed in the safe confines of an imagined, romanticized past where such conservative ideals of the American Dream were more fixed (nostalgia), it is tempting to suggest that Hill's gradual journey into a vocal utopia is a sonic 'counterpart' of nostalgia. However, while a utopian ideal is only an imagined possibility, any nostalgic construction of the past is also 'false' and 'prettified', with 'virtues exaggerated'.[39] In this case, what else might be going on here?

While it is true that Hill does succumb to Marian's charms in 'Till There Was You', and chooses to sing rather than speak, he never actually sings *to* her; he only sings *with* her. If utopia is experienced at the level of 'sensibility' or 'feelings', then Hill only offers an imitation of 'something better', mirroring Marian's feelings, rather than voicing any of his own. Hill no longer leads with his voice; he follows.[40] This complexity is summarized by Michael Schwartz, who sees the central love story in Willson's musical as a necessary anti-climax to a work which subverts narrative convention:

> For *The Music Man* to work as well as it possibly can, its perversion of musical comedy structure needs to remain in place—Hill is inevitably contained by the respectable domesticity of the love story [which] represents not the typical happy climax, but the somewhat deflating anticlimax.[41]

Surrendering to a vocal intensity that pushes towards utopian idealism—albeit in a mirror image of Marian—is Hill placing a limit on his dreams, settling for something else? While utopia trades on wish-fulfilment and an escape from reality, such wishes can never be fulfilled and reality is always present. In this case, Hill's redemption—settling and surrendering—may not be as utopian as it appears. At the same time, if he only succumbs and settles, then his apparent embrace of domesticity may be reluctant rather than genuine, undermining nostalgic idylls of romance and the contentment of community and family values in small-town turn-of-the-century America. In the post-war and Cold War era, the American Dream—encapsulated here by marching bands, parades, and the mythologies of domesticity and community—may not be all it seemed for those on the outside, or those on the inside either.

Hill's vocal trajectory, then, offers a multiplicity of potential encodings. It might be heard as utopian, offering a sense of redemption, conformity, and traditional American values. Yet it might also be heard as reluctant, unwilling, perhaps even still resistant, surrendering wish-fulfilment rather than achieving it. If this were the case, then Hill's journey from intermediate vocality to song reveals utopia to be a place of insincerity, reluctance, and disappointment. The presence of intermediate vocality in *The Music Man* therefore exposes the paradoxes, complexities, and ambiguities that characterize the relationship between utopia and nostalgia.

'Who will change the scene for me?': Resisting Utopia in *Oliver!* (1960)

Three years after *The Music Man* first played in New York, one of the most significant British works of the post-war period opened at the New Theatre, London, on 30 June 1960. Adapted from the novel *Oliver Twist* by Charles Dickens, Lionel Bart's musical *Oliver!* is set in the grimy underworld of London's Victorian East End. It tells the story of the eponymous orphan who gets thrown out of the workhouse after asking for more food. Fleeing the inhumane treatment of his foster family, Oliver escapes to the smog-ridden centre of the capital in search of a better life. Eventually, he is reunited with his respectable upper-middle-class extended family; in other words, he finds 'something better'.[42] Before that, he spends his time as the unwitting member of a street gang and is looked after by its ringleader and rogue Fagin, and Nancy—barmaid and mistress of violent criminal Bill Sykes.

Just as *The Music Man* borrowed a range of musical styles from Sousa-esque marching bands to barbershop quartets in its wistful evocation of turn-of-the-century America, *Oliver!* drew on traditions of English drinking songs, East End music hall culture, and folk music to conjure the world of Dickens's nineteenth-century melodrama. Since he was raised in a working-class East End neighbourhood, these were styles familiar to its composer. The market near where Bart grew up was rich with the sounds of 'barrel organs, one-man-bands, spoons and bones players, fiddlers and banjo-boys. The pubs had sing-songs [and] the Sally Army had tambourines'. His mother used to sing him 'lullabies and . . . street songs and kids nursery rhymes'.[43] These formative musical experiences imbued the macro-voiceworld of *Oliver!* with a '"shouty" [vocal] quality' which differed markedly from Willson's writing for *The Music Man* and the prim voices heard in previous British musical successes such as *The Boy Friend* (1953) or *Salad Days* (1954).

As a 'vernacular' aesthetic, it brought vividly to life both the taverns of Victorian London and more contemporary ideals of working-class Englishness which were celebrated in several notable 'Soho' musicals through the 1950s and 1960s. A 'shouty', 'vernacular' aesthetic of drinking songs and market traders therefore already locates *Oliver!* within an intermediate voiceworld somewhere between speech and song, with the chants of coster-mongers and the 'shouty' sounds of joyous pub sing-songs ringing in the air.[44] How entire communities inhabit and negotiate an intermediate macro-voiceworld is considered later in this chapter. Here, however, another influence on Bart's work offers a particular kind of intermediate vocality within the micro-voiceworld of *Oliver!* The son of a Jewish tailor, Bart remembers being taken to the Yiddish Theatre on Commercial Road in Stepney as a child. He would accompany his dad to the synagogue, recalling that: 'I loved the music. I loved the sound of that ram's horn on the Black Fast and Yom Kippur. It said something to me'.[45] While he was not a practising adherent of Judaism in later life, this cultural influence and Bart's clear love of Jewish art and music—both sacred and secular—found life in the character of Fagin.

In Dickens's novel, Fagin is irreligious. He eats sausages and rejects overt religious engagement even at the end of his life. Yet, he is described repeatedly as 'the Jew' or 'the villainous old Jew', as Dickens conflates his religious, ethnic, and social identity in a manifestation of the recurrent anti-Semitic stereotype of Jewish criminality in the nineteenth and early twentieth centuries.[46] While Bart's musical makes no explicit reference in the libretto or lyrics to Fagin's Jewishness, his music provides this identity, given voice in performance. Set at a time when a large portion of Jewish émigré entertainers worked in music halls, these influences make sense. Bart's writing therefore drew on East End working-class entertainment traditions, Yiddish folk song, and cantorial and liturgical music to re-imagine Fagin somewhere between a wizened music hall act and 'a Jewish mother-hen clucking away' as he took in orphans and urchins.[47] While he was originating the role, Jewish actor Ron Moody's experience in cabaret and comedy gave an added aged texture to the subsequent intermediate vocality of the character, sharing parallels with Harold Hill while also charting a very different trajectory between speech and song as a whole.[48]

While the entire macro-voiceworld of this musical can be characterized by a vernacular intermediacy that is not utopian (perhaps located broadly between 'intonational chant' and 'song' on List's chart, see Figure 4.2), Fagin's vocal character places him at a particular distance from any exploration of the possible through song. As a member of the criminal underworld, and a Jew in the East End, Fagin lives in the shadows and on the outskirts twice over. Like Harold Hill, he is therefore careful not to reveal his 'full self' to anyone—even his young employees.[49] While inducting Oliver into his gang in the humorous and playful 'You've Got to Pick a Pocket or Two', Fagin's delivery uses short, staccato statements which echo those of Hill's in 'Ya Got Trouble'. In a song set in a minor key typical of Jewish liturgical music, Fagin approximates the contours of the melody; his voice does not exhibit sustained pitch stability, positioning him near (or on) the coordinates of Sprechstimme on List's chart (see Figure 4.2). While Fagin lives in fear of arrest, reviling, and betrayal while acting *in loco parentis*, his intermediate vocality keeps him at a remove, even from his criminal companions, while the rhythm and tone of the music hint at the cultural identity of his character.[50] Concealing his exploitation and manipulation through the use of play and comedy, Fagin's repetition of the song title also sees him emphasize the same unvoiced plosives as Harold Hill when moralizing to the townsfolk of River City: 'With a capital **T** / and that rhymes with **P** / and that stands for **p**ool' becomes 'You've Got to **P**ick a **P**ocket or **T**wo'.[51] In combination with his intermediate delivery, Fagin keeps his distance, a suggestion further reinforced in the song 'Be Back Soon'.

As he employs inverse plosive alliteration in the titular refrain ('**S**eventy-**S**ix Trom**b**ones' and '**B**e **B**ack **S**oon'), it is Fagin's supposed paternal interest in the young ragamuffins that encourages them as they head off to pick pockets. Like Hill in 'Seventy-Six Trombones', Fagin is rhythmic in the delivery of short phrases in a military style. Yet, while the choral aesthetic of *Oliver!* is 'democratic . . . designed to represent the voices of the urban working-classes', the contingent chorality of the pickpockets only ever enters into a call-and-response with Fagin. At no time do they sing *together*.[52] As with the minor key of 'You've Got to Pick a Pocket or Two', this separation may even be a further example of Fagin's Jewishness as encoded in the music and vocal performance. As Jack Gottlieb noted, 'the music of the Jewish people has been pre-eminently single-line vocal melody for solo voice'; something which characterizes each of Fagin's songs.[53] The contrast between Fagin's solo voice and the contingent, unison chorality of the pickpockets in 'Be Back Soon' creates a tense sonic multiplicity, reinforcing Fagin's dislocation. Despite the children's adoration for their caregiver, he remains detached. Even when Fagin and his gang do briefly sing together, it is in a counterpoint comprised of unrefined, unbroken boys' voices and the constricted gruffness of Moody's closed vowel sound.

Yet, as Hill moved towards the utopian performative of song in *The Music Man*, Fagin also has a moment in which he fights with the temptation to reveal his 'full self'. In act two, Oliver is kidnapped by the villain Bill Sykes, and the ensuing panic prompts Fagin to consider his options by 'Reviewing the Situation' in a solo number that contains the most overt use of Jewish musical signifiers in Bart's work.[54] Once again in a minor key, the song combines free-tempo verses and a refrain that gathers and slows in momentum, as Fagin vacillates over whether or not to reform his ways. Gottlieb has observed that the verses of this song—in which Fagin asks rhetorical questions about life and death to process his fears of being caught by the police or Bill Sykes, of losing his treasures, or of Oliver coming to harm—derive from the Havdalah, the Hebrew chant sung to close the Sabbath. Meaning 'separation', this moment is bittersweet in its function as a liminal ritual between one end and another beginning. Fagin's musings are, similarly, bittersweet—a cocktail of emotions, anxieties, and unanswered questions—as his voice moves further towards speech than at any other moment in the show.[55]

Carried away on flights of fancy about marriage and responsibility, however, the refrain sections hear Fagin assume a more sustained melodic vocality, a kind of 'intonational chant' which travels towards song (See Figure 4.2). While still conversational, the structure of these sections has been compared with klezmer, an Eastern European dance of the Ashkenazy Jews, which gradually accelerates in tempo. As Fagin wonders what will happen when he reaches seventy years of age, however, everything seems to change. At this moment on the original cast recording (and, indeed, on several subsequent recordings), Moody's Fagin momentarily voices a 'vulnerability' through intimate, legato phrasing in a high register, as he speculates on a time when: 'You're old, and it's cold / And who cares if you live or you die?'[56] The phrase 'or you die' is voiced in a countertenor that creaks under its own lack of breath, coloured by a trace of anxious vocal fry, as if Moody might break into a sob at any moment. This sound is then echoed on the violin, evoking *drydlekh*—an ornamentation in klezmer music meaning 'tear in the voice'.[57] Quickly recanting and vowing to remain unreformed by a return to fast-paced patter and speak-singing, the realization of age, mortality, and the fright of being alone cause understandable vulnerability for Fagin, marked by shifts in his vocal aesthetic. At the level of the narrative, even the mere acknowledgement that he is vulnerable seems to imbue him with an intensity that is pitiable and a transparency that might hint at a longing for human connection. In other words, there seems to be a glimpse of utopia borne of the kind of melancholy heard in the previous chapter, an emotion of displacement as Fagin longs for an 'ideal' beyond the 'mundane world' he inhabits.[58] Yet, just as Hill's vocal trajectory into utopia seemed inevitable but may have been unwilling, Fagin's voice is likewise a 'junction point of multiple encodings' in which returning to the utopia of melancholy must be only one possibility.[59] What else might be revealed by listening again to the vocal dramaturgy of Fagin?

In 1960, *Oliver!* was a charming anachronism in a popular cultural climate that was moving on from variety shows to the thrill of the pop charts. While it had 'immediate appeal to a nostalgic audience who already knew the story', Robert Gordon suggests that in this context, *Oliver!* 'answered a need . . . to distance popular culture from the Victorian past by representing it as a mythic history'.[60] In other words, the operation of nostalgia served to reassure a nation ravaged by war and anxious to redefine its place in the world. Yet Fagin's configuration as a Yiddish music hall act—and Moody's vocal performance that gave life to him—suggests that things might be more complicated than this. When Nancy sings her torch song, 'As Long as He Needs Me', the musical style and vocal expressivity expand from her previous bar-room sing-along to a more conventional musical theatre ballad. Oliver's solo number ('Where Is Love?') is a lullaby-like love song with melisma in the vocal line, sung legato by an innocent treble voice. Bill Sykes's ode to his own reputation ('My Name') is a growling drawl of staccato exclamations. These characters each offer an intensity and directness in their vocal delivery, hovering around or reaching the utopian performative of song.

Fagin is different. As soon as he glimpses a vocal 'vulnerability' in his solo song, his retreat is almost immediate. Vowing to stay a villain, the character who places himself at a sonic distance—even from his closest companions—revels in his self-delusion and stubborn resistance to change. In other words, the East End music hall act—long held to symbolize an essence of English identity—cannot bear to take a bow. Perhaps it is truculence; perhaps it is insecurity. In either case, Marc Napolitano suggests that in this context, *Oliver!* functions less as a nostalgic marker for distance from the past than as an allegory for English post-war decline, a 'music-hall lament' in the vein of John Osborne's *The Entertainer* or *Look Back in Anger*.[61] In its resistance to change and quick return to the comfort of delusion, Fagin's vocal performance therefore may also represent a nation that, even now, struggles with its own sense of identity. This is a long way away from any exploration of the possible or the utopian performative of song.

Heard in this context, the closing reprise of 'Reviewing the Situation' at the end of the show—featuring only one verse, sung slowly and unconfidenty by Fagin—is almost unbearably poignant. Here, he becomes a lost music hall act with nothing to perform and a desperate desire for connection, much like English imperial identity in post-war Britain. Fagin's voice might sound vulnerable—encoded with a longing for the utopia of human connection in his old age—and yet, inherently, he resists. In this case, as with Hill, 'multiple encodings' of past and present, nostalgia and utopia, personal identity and national mythologies are heard in Fagin's intermediate vocality.[62] This is because voice never deals in 'pure, abstracted emotions [that are] expressed discretely'. The shifts to and from intermediate vocality to any glimpse of 'vocal utopia' evidence the plural complexities of voices as they contain 'a cocktail of several simultaneous feelings' shown through a complex range of transient physiological, acoustic, linguistic, and aural markers.[63]

The above examples have focused on two individuals in the micro-voiceworlds of the stories, both of whom are male. They have—unwittingly or momentarily—joined the macro-voiceworld of their given musical, as the form continues to glimpse utopia, yet their trajectory to achieve this seems characterized by a lack of willingness or even resistance. What happens, however, when these complexities characterize not simply individuals, but entire communities?

'Careful the things you say': Unfulfilled Utopia in *Into the Woods* (1987)

The change from a homogeneous or heterogeneous concept of society which may push towards utopia to a collective of individuals has already been heard in the liquid chorality of Sondheim's *Company*.[64] While this kind of chorality and its vocal grouping encoded the vocal dramaturgy of that work with a kind of dystopian utopia, what else might be heard by listening to the aesthetic of intermediate vocality in such 'fragmented' narratives, and the collectives of individual characters of which they are composed?

With music and lyrics by Stephen Sondheim and a book by James Lapine, *Into the Woods* opened at the Martin Beck Theater, New York, on 5 November 1987. The musical draws together well-known fairy tales into a larger, intertextual, 'quest' narrative.[65] Act one retells the familiar stories of Cinderella, Jack (complete with beanstalk), and Little Red Ridinghood, as they each venture into the woods to reach their 'happily ever after'. In a new fairy story developed by Lapine from the original opening to the Brothers

Grimm version of *Rapunzel*, these characters are joined by The Baker and his wife, who succeed in undoing their curse of infertility and act as the 'catalyst' for the interactions that take place between each of these well-known characters.[66] Act one, then, presents familiar 'images about the feasibility of utopian alternatives' to society and individual wish-fulfilment, as folklorist Jack Zipes has considered.[67] Act two, however, dramatizes the 'consequences' of wishing for a fairy-tale utopia, as the wife of the Giant murdered by Jack in act one visits the kingdom to avenge her husband's death. Heading into the woods once more, the townsfolk try to protect themselves and slay the Giant's wife, as the musical explores the moral and ethical complexities of murder, loss, retribution, deceit, grief, regret, infidelity, and what we each leave behind, considering 'action and the consequences of action' for individual characters and those around them.[68]

Bearing no initial familiarity with—or responsibility to—each other, characters exist as individuals (or a married couple) and encounter each other largely by chance, or in somewhat selfish pursuit of their desires. The exchanges and social interactions between them take place in a socially unstructured arena—the woods—where, as Cinderella's Prince remarks to The Baker's Wife, 'anything can happen'.[69] Ambiguous, and 'without a moral compass', feelings and experiences can never be discrete or complete among the trees. This is especially true in the first act, when each character has a deficit of something: their wishes are yet to be granted and few characters have the agency to reveal discrete or fully realized emotions in song, or otherwise. The moral and ethical dilemmas they face in the second act—for which there can be no defined solutions—also render them unable to voice 'pure, abstracted emotions . . . discretely'.[70]

If the woods are a liminal space between deficit, desire, and wish-fulfilment, it makes sense that the vocal dramaturgy of this musical may operate somewhere between speech and song. While *Into the Woods* is significantly closer to song than the voices of either Hill or Fagin, four specific aspects of its writing and performance configure the intermediacy of its voiceworlds. First, the majority of the story is told by a Narrator, framing the performance through the spoken word. Second, the musical score plays with the relationship between melodic line and musical accompaniment in a way that is 'mosaiclike', creating an 'odd disjuncture between melodic and harmonic structures'. As Raymond Knapp has considered, the relationship between the melodic lines and basslines is tonally functional while often accompanied by 'a complex of dissonant chordal structures'. The effect is such that in Sondheim's writing for this musical, the melodic lines are untethered from conventional tonal markers and often deny a sense of 'closure' in their resolutions or cadences.[71]

The third aspect of intermediate vocality relates to the word-setting of Sondheim's lyrics, as discussed elsewhere by Stephen Banfield. Pared down, utilizing monosyllabic 'list'-like constructions with a careful economy of language, the subsequent vocal delivery takes on a staccato quality, tilting towards the conversational, with only sparing use of multisyllabic word-setting across long-form melodic lines.[72] Fourth, echoing the casting priority of Hal Prince when developing *A Little Night Music*, Sondheim has also been quoted later in his career as saying: 'I don't really care how well the actors sing'.[73] While *Into the Woods* utilizes a range of vocal styles—including 'legit' voice for certain characters and moments—its regular use of intermediate vocality in various forms (heightened speech, chant, and Sprechstimme, see Figure 4.2) demands closer consideration for the ways in which the musicality of Sondheim's dramatic writing charts the complex and at times unresolved journeys of these characters into, and out of, the woods. Listening across moments of chorality in the macro- and micro-voiceworlds, how does intermediate vocality configure the social contract between the community and the individual in this musical? What might this reveal about the utopian performative of song in the process?

Framing the entire performance through the lens of oral storytelling, the musical begins with the Narrator speaking the traditional fairy-tale opening of 'Once upon a time . . .'. Introducing Cinderella, Jack, The Baker, and The Baker's wife, 'Prologue' sees each character expressing uncertainty or anxiety as they repeat, individually, the mantra: 'I wish . . .'. Delivered with either staccato or aspirate vocality, the monosyllabic sibilance of the phrase builds a spoken quality into the song, continued in the staccato rhythms and word-setting of the rest of the number. This kind of intermediate vocality, somewhere between 'Sprechstimme' and 'chant' on List's chart (see Figure 4.2)—perhaps at the halfway point in the lower hemisphere—gives voice to a sense of deficit or doubt. Cinderella wants to (but does not believe she will) go to the King's Festival. Jack (and his mother) need their pet cow to produce milk. The Baker and his wife long for a family. All of them desire 'utopian alternatives', as Zipes has considered. None is forthcoming and, in consequence, the stasis of their situations—a good distance from utopia—is encoded in the shared vocal aesthetic between speech and song.[74]

There is yet more to this opening number. During 'Prologue', the Witch visits The Baker and his wife and explains their childless existence. This moment of exposition from the Witch is designated in the musical score as the 'Witches' Rap' and is delivered using rhythmic, declamatory speech. Yet, while rap tends to embed a sense of 'flow' in its delivery (a technique considered in the final case study of this chapter), this passage remains 'remarkably static' in its metre and phrasing.[75] In this sense, it is more a 'chant' than a 'rap'. However, the fact that the reason for the plight of these characters is delivered using this kind of 'heightened speech' rather than the directness or emotional transparency of melody may be indicative of their hopelessness and, as it later transpires, that of the Witch as well. All is not lost for The Baker and his wife, however. To 'reverse the curse' of their barren marriage, they are told that they must find four ingredients to make a potion: a white cow, a red cape, a golden slipper, and a lock of yellow hair, and bring these to The Witch before midnight in three days. This becomes the motivation for their journey into the woods and, notably, the dramaturgical reason for the interactions between the couple and the rest of the characters—a conceit which 'explodes the insularity of each [fairy tale] and thereby confronts the infinite complexity of human interactions'.[76]

Despite the wider human appeal of their individual quests and the 'infinite complexity' of the overall narrative, however, 'Prologue' features no more than five voices singing at any given time, with a notable focus on The Baker, his wife, Cinderella, Jack, and his mother. As 'Prologue' segues into the title song, Little Red Ridinghood and Cinderella's family also add their voices to this opening number. Based on the delineations established in chapter 3, *Into the Woods* therefore begins with intermediate voices in liquid chorality as part of a micro-voiceworld. This, then, is a community that only comes together by happenstance; a collective of individuals whose sense of society exists beyond themselves, and to which they have no particular allegiance. In this musical, any understanding of 'community' is incidental to the pursuit of individual wish-fulfilment, a position reinforced at two central points in act one, as each character (or couple) takes stock of their quest.

In 'First Midnight' and 'Second Midnight', numerous characters express moral lessons or pearls of wisdom relating to their circumstances, in two of only four demonstrations of a macro-voiceworld in the musical. Building from solo utterances to a cacophony of voices, a liquid chorality once more sees a collective of individuals give voice to shared frustrations. Yet, while the micro-voiceworld of 'Prologue' and the title song might be mapped somewhere between 'Sprechstimme' and 'chant' on List's chart, 'First Midnight' and 'Second Midnight' are expressed through a 'heightened speech' which is nearer 'intonational recitation' (see Figure 4.2). It seems, then, that the cumulative effect of shared endeavour sees the collective placed even farther away from utopia than the individuals within it. Intermediate vocality therefore not only moves towards the utopian performative of song (as in the case of Harold Hill and, to an extent, Fagin) but also can move away as it charts the fragmentation or reorientation of the relationship between individuals and communities.

On either side of these moments, characters exhibit a range of intermediate vocalities along with the utopian performative of song, revealing further complexities about the relationship between speech, song, and vocal utopia. Cinderella's voice encodes her as 'ambivalent', a description echoed by Knapp's consideration of her actions.[77] Making the first distinction (of many) in the musical between 'good' and 'nice' in an exasperated outburst, Cinderella's voice mocks her parents with a sneering mimicry ('So be nice, Cinderella, / Good, Cinderella, / Nice good good nice—'), ending in a spoken repetition of 'Nice good nice kind good nice' with a descending cadence.[78] Standing, braiding her stepmother's hair in the 'Prologue', Cinderella does not know whether to be 'nice' or 'good', an ambivalence which is dramatized as she runs away from the 'very *nice* Prince' three times in the course of the musical.[79] Yet, when she visits her mother's grave, stating that she has been 'good' and 'kind' ('Cinderella at the Grave') or reflects on the peculiarity of leaving the prince a single slipper ('On the Steps of the Palace'), she enters a complex negotiation between intermediate voice and soprano sonority. As the first character to utter 'I wish', Cinderella perhaps betrays the least self-knowledge, with an aspirate ambivalence which characterizes her voice even when she sings. Knowing what she desires and knowing what she needs are different.[80] In contrast, when The Baker and his wife realize that 'It Takes Two' to complete their quest and get their wish, their duet moves gradually from a hesitant and aspirate intermediate vocality in the first verse to a directness and transparency in which their 'full selves' are given voice, ending the song in unison. Unlike Cinderella, the changes in their vocality, from aspirate to actualized, suggest self-awareness and personal growth are possible, even in the woods.

The moments in which the townsfolk *do* give voice through the intensity of song, therefore, become especially revealing for what they suggest about the individual human need for emotional connection and, more broadly, wish-fulfilment. Beyond the individual moments of song from Cinderella, Jack, or The Baker and his wife, one significant moment for the community comes at the end of act one. The curse has been lifted, The Baker's wife is pregnant, Jack and his mother have found riches beyond their dreams at the top of the beanstalk, and the Witch has lost her powers in exchange for beauty as a result of the spell being broken while also being instrumental in everyone else's happiness. All of them attend the wedding of Cinderella and Prince Charming.

Thanking the new Princess for the use of the slipper she left on the palace steps, The Baker and his wife sing, in harmony: 'I never thought I could be so happy'.[81] Having achieved Zipes's 'utopian alternative' to their childless existence, they can glimpse the 'something better' they had longed for.[82] This moment leads into the wedding song, 'Ever After'. Led for the first half by the Narrator, the song builds to the first moment of contingent chorality in the macro-voiceworld, complete with harmonies, 'legit' voices with synchronized breath, balance, blend, and uniform phonation, and all the intensity and energy of utopian vocality. Individually—and as a community—these characters have reached their respective happy endings. Yet, leading this song, the Narrator speak-sings with a staccato delivery in a clear vocal contrast to the wedding guests. While adhering to the broad melodic contours of the music, and with reasonable stability of pitch, the monosyllabic word-setting and narrow tessitura of the Narrator's lines serve to undercut the full-voiced intensity of the community from his external vantage point. A brief spoken interjection at the end of the song—'To be continued . . .'—seems to reinforce this sense of tension as act one ends.[83] In other words, the macro-voiceworld may be singing utopia, but the Narrator's vocal delivery suggests all is not as it appears.

In the second act, the realities of wishes fulfilled become apparent. The Narrator returns, and a new story begins: 'Once upon a time . . . later'.[84] Princess Cinderella, the rich young lad Jack, and The Baker and his wife—now new parents—each express dissatisfaction with their 'happy ever after' in some way. Once again sharing the opening motif, delivered with staccato or aspirate vocality and a monosyllabic sibilance which imbues their expressions with speech quality, Cinderella now wishes to host a Festival, Jack desires to return to the kingdom in the sky after the beanstalk was cut down in act one, and The Baker and his wife long for more room in their cottage. Having achieved their wishes, they find they are not entirely happy with their lot. The Narrator notes these 'minor inconveniences' as the characters commence singing the number 'So Happy'. The rise and fall of its legato lines, along with attendant balance, blend, synchronicity of breath, even phonation, and uniform dynamics in harmony momentarily evoke the utopian vocality heard earlier in 'Arcadians Are We' or even 'We Raise Our Cups'. From act one, then, there has been a definitive movement towards—and a glimpse of—utopia. The spoken word and intermediate vocality which frame this song, however, destabilize the sense of emotional transparency and directness. These characters may not be entirely revealing their full selves after all. In this case, the utopian performative of song might even begin to sound bitter-sweet; utopia may be somehow unfulfilling.

As rumours are confirmed of the Giant's wife visiting the kingdom to avenge her husband, any happiness experienced by the townsfolk begins to unravel completely. Utopia, it seems, cannot last. Together with the royal family, The Baker and his wife, Little Red Ridinghood, and Jack once more venture 'into the woods' to defend themselves and slay the Giant's wife. The first confrontation with her, however, changes everything. At a loss as to how to handle the threat, the community notice the Narrator for the first time. They bring him into the story, suspicious that he is always on the outside offering moral commentary. The Witch makes a hurried decision to throw him to the Giant to buy the community time. Suddenly the Narrator is gone; there is no one left to tell the story. How does this affect what is heard when listening across the voiceworlds of this musical, when the framing of the spoken word and the extra-diegetic narrator is removed?[85]

Three further fatalities occur after the death of the Narrator. Jack's mother is hit over the head by the Prince's Steward for defending her son from the giant, Rapunzel runs inadvertently towards the trouble and is crushed by the vengeful visitor to the kingdom, and The Baker's wife falls victim to an earthquake caused by the Giant's wife roaming the land in search of Jack. Riven with grief, confusion, and directionless without a narrator, Jack, Cinderella, Little Red Ridinghood, and The Baker turn on each other in search of someone to blame. The song 'Your Fault' is a rhythmically urgent four-part argument, delivered entirely in 'heightened speech'. Closest in aesthetic to the 'Witches' Rap' heard in the act one 'Prologue', it builds with expanded intonation and dynamic expressivity to the four characters shouting in unison at the Witch:

THE BAKER, CINDERELLA, JACK,
LITTLE RED RIDINGHOOD: YOU'RE RESPONSIBLE! [. . .]
IT'S YOUR FAULT![86]

Notwithstanding the formal rhythmic structure provided by the musical accompaniment, shouting exceeds the confines of musical utterance, and is no longer a form of intermediate vocality. Shouting has much in common with singing. It serves to expand the bodily presence of the shouter, 'inciting . . . collective experiences' and enabling individuals to move beyond 'the generative resonance [Adriana] Cavarero identifies at the core of being . . . to the raw tensions found in needing or commanding each other'.[87] In other words, shouting promotes community and a sense of relationships beyond oneself in the manner of song. As Brandon LaBelle observes, shouting can both empower the shouter through a call to action (in this case, that the Witch must take responsibility for the unravelling of things) and, at the same time, 'the shout is our suffering' under any kind of authoritarian regime, threat, or oppression (the Giant's wife seeking revenge).[88] Shouting is therefore encoded with a desire for 'something better' in a way which seems to parallel the same desires heard in song.[89] For characters who have only glimpsed utopia momentarily, and with an increasing lack of support or direction, this exclamation may be the only mode of expression left that is not intermediate. It does not even register on George List's chart. A shout may not necessarily be utopian, but as an extreme form of vocal expression, it nevertheless demands change. What changes, however, is the way these characters view themselves, each other, and the circumstances they face.

After the Witch leaves The Baker, Cinderella, Jack, and Little Red Ridinghood on their own ('Last Midnight'), they conspire between them to lure the Giant's wife to the steeple tower, hide in a tree, and fell her. While waiting, The Baker and Cinderella assume parental responsibility for Jack and Little Red Ridinghood. Singing 'No-one Is Alone', the four travel from the spoken argument and shouting match of 'Your Fault' to a tender melodic ballad. Bonded by a shared purpose, they each enter a 'space of vulnerability' to sing of 'something better'—the realization that no one needs to face life's hardships on their own.[90] With blend, balance, harmony, counterpoint, and legato vocal lines, the change in vocal aesthetic suggests that despite the bitterness, loss, regret, anger, and even moral ambiguities of life, it is human connection rather than individualism that offers the possibility for something better. In other words, the one moment of genuine vocal utopia in the musical presents a challenge to Lasch.

The sense of togetherness between the four townsfolk is what helps them to overcome their foe. Yet, with the wrongs avenged, having admitted his failures, and feeling that he is now 'alone', The Baker stands with Jack,

Cinderella, and Little Red Ridinghood, as the ghost of his wife urges him to take their young child in his arms and tell him the story of how all of this happened. Repeating the familiar fairy-tale opening in speech—'Once upon a time . . .'—the story is once more passed from father to son as the Witch sings the final song, 'Children Will Listen'.[91] An emotive ballad, with quiet legato phrasing, it builds from a solo verse to full contingent chorality in the macro-voiceworld, delivered with sincerity, directness, balance, blend, and harmony, urging parents to consider the spells they cast in life and the wishes they make for their children. As a lyrical caution about the dangers of narcissism and cultural fragmentation, the song offers a glimpse of utopia in its sonority. As with *The Music Man* and *Oliver!*, the musical stage succumbs to its utopian imperative for the closing number.

Of course, what utopia is for any of these characters at this point is largely undefined or open, but it points to the future and a caution of wishing too far. Sondheim, then, avoids any particular position, even if vocally, he allows the macro-voiceworld one moment of emotional directness and assuredness that was unattainable, undermined, or unsustainable previously, before shifting into reverse gear. 'Children Will Listen' segues into a final reprise of the title song, and while it is delivered in choral unison with some contrapuntal development, the audience is now very familiar with what happens when one ventures 'into the woods'. In a punchline that renders the entire performance once more intermediate and ambivalent, the very last line of *Into the Woods* comes from an aspirate, anxious, and uncertain Cinderella, as she once more exclaims: 'I wish!'[92] After all, if utopia is an ideal that can never be achieved, then there are always more wishes that remain just beyond reach. Beyond the desires of these simple townsfolk, however, some wishes come with much greater geo-political consequences.

'A beat without a melody': Political and Domestic Utopias in *Hamilton* (2015)

Based on a 2004 biographical study by Ron Chernow, *Hamilton* opened at the Richard Rodgers Theater, New York, on 6 August 2015, after a sell-out run Off-Broadway at the Public Theater (see Figure 4.3). With book, music, and lyrics by Lin-Manuel Miranda, the musical tells the story of the prodigious and precocious immigrant orphan Alexander Hamilton who would become one of the United States' founding fathers and first secretary of

Figure 4.3 Scene from *Hamilton* (Lin-Manuel Miranda, downstage centre). Photograph © Joan Marcus.

the US Treasury. Declaring he is 'young, scrappy, and hungry' for social change, Hamilton joins the fight against British colonialism, working with John Laurens, the Marquis de Lafayette, Hercules Mulligan, and George Washington to battle for independence.[93]

In telling the story of America's founding, *Hamilton* parallels the narrative structures of *Into the Woods.* Both musicals are 'quest' narratives which chart the fulfilment of wishes in act one, and explore their consequences and complexities in act two.[94] Act one of *Hamilton* stages key events in the American Revolution, including the Declaration of Independence, the battle of Yorktown, and victory against the British. In other words, it performs the utopian ideals of life, liberty, and the pursuit of happiness. It also depicts Hamilton's personal life including his marriage to Eliza(beth) Schuyler (daughter of a wealthy Dutch émigré) who falls pregnant, and his contentious relationship with Aaron Burr—portrayed as a misunderstood politician willing to trade his principles for political advancement. With the revolutionaries having achieved American independence from the British, *Hamilton*'s second act moves swiftly to the complex and contradictory machinations of political policy, portraying Hamilton's infidelity and his attempt to conceal this by fraud, acts of bribery in Congress, the death of Alexander and Eliza's son, and Hamilton's premature death at the hands of Aaron Burr in a duel. Like the townsfolk in the woods, the American revolutionaries also discover that wish-fulfilment comes with consequences.

First produced during the Obama presidency, *Hamilton* was described in interviews by its author as 'a story about America then told by America now'.[95] Reflecting the era of the first black President of the United States, its cast featured African American, Asian American, and Latinx performers in the roles of the (white) founding fathers and revolutionaries, trading on what Donatella Galella calls 'nationalist neoliberal multicultural inclusion'. *Hamilton* therefore presented an ostensible challenge to 'Broadway and America's whitewashing of American history'.[96]

This apparent challenge was heard in the score of *Hamilton*. Lauded for its contemporary and urban sound, its decadent appropriation of pop, rock, and musical theatre styles was underpinned by the energy of hip hop and rap, both of which are commonly associated with African American urban culture.[97] Often characterized by a 'tendency to eschew the precisely pitched vocals heard in most popular music', rap is a form of intermediate vocality which emphasizes rhythm over harmony, orality over melody, and operates by repetition and circularity in delivery.[98] As a genre, it also shares an 'improvisational aesthetic' with other African American forms including blues and jazz, a sensibility which 'manifests itself as freestyling' in rap, with an urgency or impetus in its rhyme scheme and pace, and an apparent spontaneity and flow in its delivery.[99] While the genre did not exist in its current form when George List explored the boundaries between speech and song, listening across its co-presence with other vocal forms in this musical reveals three further facets of intermediate vocality and its relationship with the utopian imperative of song. The first is dramaturgical.

Mapping rap on List's chart, the 'tendency to eschew' pitch does not mean the entire voiceworld of *Hamilton* can be placed on the same coordinates. While rap delivery places specific emphasis on rhythm, rhyme, orality, repetition, improvisational flow, and pace, pitch plays a central role. Adapting List's chart, music theorist Robert Komaniecki has identified five pitching techniques in rap, placing them on a similar continuum between speech and song. With the greatest instability of pitch (and therefore nearest to speech), 'rhyme strengthening' is a declamatory style which uses the same pitch on corresponding rhymed lyrics as a way of structuring vocal flow, perhaps equivalent to somewhere between 'speech' and 'intonational recitation' in Figure 4.2. This can be heard early in act one of *Hamilton*, as the revolutionaries plot their strategy and Hamilton introduces himself in the song 'My Shot'. With a driving rhythm and lyric characterized by titular repetition, the word 'shot'—complete with the same plosive ('T') which was heard' as an index of possible aggression in the voiceworlds of Hill and Fagin—is often placed on the same pitch, as if to evoke the dogged determination of a young man who is 'running out of time'.[100]

'Exaggerated declamation', Komaniecki's second pitch technique, is 'rather like the more familiar Sprechstimme in that both exaggerate typical speech patterns' (as seen on List's chart, see Figure 4.2).[101] Listening to 'Get Down Low' by American rap artist Snow Tha Product, Komaniecki notes that while 'rhyme strengthening' pitches rhyming words or syllables on the same note, 'exaggerated declamation' may raise or lower pitches depending on the lyrical content. The pitch changes need not be stepwise either way, and there need not be monotone delivery between the pitches. With the technique, however, the flow 'imbues the lyrics with a sense of urgency and building tension'.[102] Given its aesthetic imperatives, this kind of approach is heard throughout *Hamilton* to propel the drama. It is heard in the exchange between Hamilton and Burr when John Laurens meets to duel with Major General Charles Lee, leading to Hamilton's suspension from active duty ('Ten Duel Commandments'). It also characterizes the rap flow when George Washington realizes he needs Hamilton back in command ('Guns and Ships'), and adds tension and urgency to the intermediate vocality of Hamilton as he tries to reconcile his conscience over his affair with Maria Reynolds ('Say No to This').

Komaniecki's third pitch technique is 'pitch-based rhythmic layers', achieved by 'deliberately and markedly altering the pitch of one's voice at specific points in [the vocal] flow to create a separate [or secondary] rhythmic layer'.[103] The effect is that the rap flow creates two simultaneous rhythmic patterns and may not have a direct corollary on List's chart. As Paul Edwards notes, this kind of delivery is often used to 'create a structure for verses, in a similar way to how rhythm or rhyme is sometimes used'.[104] While it does not feature extensively in *Hamilton*, when Lafayette raps in 'Guns and Ships', the emphasis on selected downbeats throughout creates a sense of working against the grain of the song, creating a secondary rhythmic impetus. The effect is one of conflict and juxtaposition, musically encoding Lafayette's covert operations in his pitch flow.

The final two pitch techniques are 'sung interjections' and 'sung/chanted verses', both of which might be located between 'chant' and 'song' in Figure 4.2, and feature throughout *Hamilton* as it negotiates its complex and decadent blend of rap, hip hop, and other musical styles—an aesthetic characteristic to which we will return below. Listening across the foregoing examples, however, it is notable that while rap is a form of intermediate vocality, the variety of pitch techniques in rap flow allow moments in *Hamilton* to be located at different coordinates on List's chart. As heard in *Into the Woods*, then, intermediate vocality can itself be a plural space between speech and song—as characters, moments, or even entire communities negotiate their relative distances towards or away from the potential for song, and its utopian possibilities.

In the case of *Hamilton*, the above examples of intermediate vocality all take place in the public arenas of political discussion or military engagement, where ideals may be shared but one's emotions must be kept in check. Echoing the individual self-concern present in *Into the Woods*, the cutthroat world of competing political ideals and personal agendas forms a space in which these men dare not directly express their thoughts or feelings to those who may betray them. They cannot express their true selves in a public arena which is quite a way from utopia. This perhaps explains why Aaron Burr refuses to tell Hamilton what he stands for, revealing this—in song—only to the audience ('Wait for It'). These characters communicate with each other through spoken verbal competition, because in rap, 'the music . . . comes directly from the text itself'.[105] Revelling in wordplay, rhythm, flow, and rhyme, their expressive potential is guarded and detached in a manner that—on a larger scale—has echoes of the reasons Hill and Fagin could not express themselves fully in song. Intermediate vocality, then, makes dramaturgical sense as an aesthetic in this musical. Yet, two further aspects of this intermediate vocality are notable. Urban music scholars, including Nelson George and Imani Perry, have noted that rap (and hip hop more broadly) is connected inextricably with notions of African American masculinity in the popular consciousness.[106] What might a consideration of intermediate vocality and its relationship to both race and gender ideals further reveal about both the narrative of *Hamilton* and the cultural climate within which it was produced?

Performing 'blackness with roots in everyday urban struggles against marginalization', the determination, tension, and conflict heard in the above examples express 'the desire of young black people to reclaim their history' through voice. They challenge 'the powers of despair and economic depression that presently besiege the black community' in a sonic and embodied form of 'cultural resistance' (or 'subversive opposition', to return to Adam Alston's phrase from chapter 2).[107] In the case of *Hamilton*, two analogues can be identified. First, in the narrative of revolutionaries who contested the powers of despair and depression in the fight for independence against British hegemony. Second, as Tiffany Brooks has argued, the combination of contemporary urban music and diverse casting has the power to 'disrupt' cultural mythologies of white history in a further performance of resistance in the Obama era.[108]

Utilizing hip hop and rap in this way means that the use of voice in *Hamilton* is both politicized and political in a theatrical form associated with the white middle classes.[109] Reflecting on this aspect of *Hamilton's* cultural resistance, Leslie Odom Jr, who originated the role of Aaron Burr, suggests that: 'It is quite literally taking the history that someone has tried to exclude us from and reclaiming it. We are saying we have the right to tell it too', and to do so in the urban sounds of contemporary black resistance to white hegemony.[110] Echoing the title of Obama's second book—*The Audacity of Hope* (2006)—perhaps in this case, the presence of intermediate vocality on the musical stage may even seem to achieve its own kind of utopian exploration of the possible. 'But', as Nicole Hodges Persley asks, 'does it?'[111]

Beyond the initial plaudits for the apparent diversity of its casting and musical styles, Hodges Persley suggests that a musical 'about the pursuit of social and political freedom [in America], using actors of color who remain in a perpetual state of unfreedom as a result of system inequality and violence, is an ironic frame for *Hamilton*'.[112] Much has already been written about the difficulties in watching actors of colour 'playing' white founding fathers who, more troublingly, were slave owners.[113] In this case, the apparent revisionism remains understood through the lens of contemporary racial inequality. Heard through Morrison's 'Blacksound', this may even be viewed as a cynical ploy borne of the commodification and commercialization of black American musical styles within the white cultural frameworks of Broadway.[114] This kind of intermediate vocality, then, may appear quite a lot farther from utopia than its initial success suggested. How might this be confirmed or challenged when we consider the link between rap and masculinity?

Despite the image of *Hamilton* as a hip hop musical, the intermediate vocality of rap is used in approximately 60 per cent of the show, with the remaining songs more recognizable as contemporary musical theatre in their use of melody. As noted above, rap features most prominently in the public arena of politics and military action. This makes sense dramaturgically, but also genders the aesthetic: in the eighteenth century, the army and the government were masculine spaces. Could it be, then, that the intermediate vocality of *Hamilton* is not only paradoxical in its reification of a white mythology of founding fathers and its 'whitewashing' of difficult histories, but also perpetuates division between male-dominated spheres of public influence and the spaces to which women were allowed access? To borrow Stacy Wolf's words, does *Hamilton* have a 'woman problem', and how might this impact the way the voiceworld(s) of this musical may, or may not, chart a course to sing utopia?[115]

Early in act one, the three middle-class debutantes—Eliza(beth), Angelica, and Peggy Schuyler—are introduced in a song which mixes the final two pitch techniques from Komaniecki ('sung interjections' and 'sung/chanted verses') with moments of full song and rap ('The Schuyler Sisters'). The confident attitude of the three sisters, who move in and out of close three-part harmony, configure this trio as a pop group in the manner of Destiny's Child and other 'girl groups whose sound is familiar and empowering for feminist spectators'.[116] This initial introduction to the two principal female characters (and their sister Peggy) with insistent rhythmic phrasing and moments of belt may suggest that strong feminist ideals form a vital part of this musical's push towards utopia.

At one particular moment, Angelica shifts away from rhythmic and melodic delivery with her sisters and enters the masculine space. Employing 'rhyme strengthening', Angelica raps her feisty demands to 'include women in the sequel' to the Declaration of Independence (after all, it is not just men who were created equal). Echoing the cadences and phrasing of rappers and hip hop artists like Lauryn Hill or Nicki Minaj, Angelica appears to claim influence and independence.[117] The use of intermediate vocality once again seems apt, offering a sonic representation of the limitations placed upon women in such a patriarchal society. Further, when Angelica offers her version of Eliza's first encounter with Hamilton—'Satisfied'—she raps in a chant with sung interjections (see Figure 4.2), complex wordplay, and intricate rhythms. Intelligent and able to 'match wits' with men, Angelica nevertheless has limitations in her delivery. As she desires Alexander for herself, this song recounts her conspiring to match her sister with this rising star of American politics. Confident, defiant, and empowered though her vocal delivery may be—she is bound to employ it in the service of perpetuating politically beneficial marriage alliances, with all of the difficulties this will come to entail. Angelica, like Hamilton, will remain unsatisfied and has to conceal her feelings for Hamilton, encoded fittingly in the intermediate vocality of this number. The vocal character of Angelica, then, might suggest that while the narrative reflects the limits and inequalities of the pre-feminist struggle, there was a further 'independence' developing in society alongside the revolution.[118]

Angelica's transgression into the public sphere does not last. In act two, her only main song ('It's Quiet Uptown') is melodic, aspirate, and tender, as she turns narrator and sings of her sister forgiving Hamilton's infidelity as Eliza and Alexander adjust to life after the death of their son. In a moment of vocal 'vulnerability', Angelica is rendered as the meek facilitator of her sister's lack of agency in marriage, as Eliza forgives her husband in complete silence. Separate from the masculinized intermediate vocality of the public and political sphere, when the tender vulnerability of the 'full self' is heard, it codes utopian vocality as something private, familial, and domestic.

This appears to be reinforced in an earlier moment when Eliza tells Hamilton she is expecting a child and begs him to put his family first. With aspirate vocality, 'That Would Be Enough' may seem tender and intimate, but, it is notably one-sided. Eliza sings *to* Hamilton; as with Fagin and his gang, Bobby and April, and Harold Hill and Marian, they never share a vocal line or harmony at any moment of the performance. When they do sing together (heard briefly in 'Helpless' and later in act two), their vocal lines are contrapuntal, placing them in different emotional spaces. The individualized and ambitious world of Hamilton's career remains firmly separated, structurally, rhythmically, and vocally, from Eliza's utopian desire in the idealized, if not quite ideal, domestic sphere.

The separation between man and wife becomes even more acute when having won the war of independence, Burr and Hamilton share a duet about fatherhood ('Dear Theodosia') towards the end of act one, singing to their respective daughter and son with quiet optimism for the future. Like the townsfolk in the fairy tales, their wish for independence has been granted and, as Jeffery Severs puts it, 'rap [now] proves a largely inadequate language for the mature challenges Hamilton faces': parenthood, marriage, and work in the new national government.[119] Delivered in a light bari-tenor and often tilting into countertenor for both men, this gives voice to their dreams of a better life for their children and—unlike Eliza and Hamilton—includes a two-part harmony from the two rivals. Yet, even here, the vocal space is once more domestic; related to paternal aspirations and the way private lives may intersect with more public or societal developments, much in the same way that *Into the Woods* was preoccupied with children and the legacy parents leave behind.

At the end of act two, Burr and Hamilton have walked ten paces apart, pistols ready. As they turn, Hamilton delivers an extended monologue, presaging his own death. Accompanied and punctuated by sound, it is not, however, a song. Referring back to List's chart, it might be placed somewhere between speech and 'intonational recitation', more akin to the 'heightened speech' of a Shakespeare play (Figure 4.2). It is telling that in his moment of greatest anguish, Hamilton speaks. Perhaps utopia is not as achievable, after all. After Burr shoots Hamilton, the finale builds to Eliza leading the company in the concluding song, 'Who Lives, Who Dies, Who Tells Your Story'. Described as 'quiet and choir-like' by Stacy Wolf, it is delivered with balance, blend, and harmony in support of Eliza's lead vocal. This is a somewhat conventional Broadway finale 'at the end of a noisy, beat-driven, word-full, kinesthetically packed evening'. As such, it performs an apparent unity through a moment of intentional chorality. In other words, *Hamilton* appears to offer a glimpse of utopia, a 'hope that we are actually all working together to make a better America'. Yet, as Nicole Hodges Persley suggests, such a vision is 'fabricated' based on its performance of gender and race.[120]

First, it seems a 'profound' and empowered 'gesture of respect to Eliza' that she is the one who leads the closing number as Hamilton's widow, as an abolitionist, and founder of an orphanage.[121] Given her role in the final song, Wolf even suggests that Eliza may appear to be 'the entire reason that we have been here'.[122] Yet, despite appearances, she occupies 'a position with limited power'.[123] The story she tells is not hers. It celebrates her husband, the man who betrayed her and consistently denied her desire for closeness.

At the end of the song, looking out into the darkness of the auditorium, Eliza lets out an audible gasp as the lights fade. While hers is the last voice to be heard in the musical, a gasp is a sonic event which simultaneously 'evokes' while remaining ambivalent.[124] It is an expression which constructs a particular 'acoustic relationality',[125] 'fully aligned with certain external events or actions [as] an intensity of energy passes between the event and the body'. In other words, a person gasps when external events render them 'breathless, struck dumb'.[126] Just as Eliza's melodic 'space of vulnerability' in song is at the service of patriarchal history, this last gasp may further reinforce her lack of agency, as the 'helpless' yet supportive woman.[127] This is hardly a utopian vision of a better America.

Further, the voices of the company might be 'choir-like' with blend, synchronized breath, and unified dynamics as they repeat the title phrase and the word 'Time'. However, just like the exclusionary characteristics of intentional chorality in *The Arcadians, Oklahoma!*, or *Dear Evan Hansen*, Hodges Persley notes that any glimpse of unity or utopia here is only '"accessible" for predominantly White audiences' who attend the musical. She continues to assert that 'the culture of the Black and Brown people that made hip hop to speak truth to power [is] completely extracted' at the end of this musical, erased at the service of Broadway conventions dominated by whiteness.[128] Its chorality might 'fabricate' unity, while once more excluding or erasing those voices it purports to include. Perhaps, as the song ends with a repeat-to-fade of its titular question, the answer of who lives, who dies, and who tells your story, is implied in its own sonority: white men. Heard this way, utopia is not necessarily 'something better' after all.[129]

'The road you didn't take': Arriving at Utopia

What kind of voice is this? In both macro- and micro-voiceworlds, there are those who resist, deny, avoid, and frustrate. Through intermediate vocality—a plural and multifaceted space between speech and song—these characters are heard to travel towards and away from the utopian performative that characterizes the form. This voice gives a space to the dispossessed and those who do not know what to do for the best. This is the voice of the indirect, the outsider, the oppressed, the deceitful, and the lost. Yet, for Harold Hill, the townsfolk in their (not-so) fairy-tale kingdom, and for Eliza as she delivers a final homily to her husband, the journey to the utopian performative which characterizes musical theatre seems ineluctable. *Everyone* (except Fagin) sings utopia in the end. When they do, however, George List's ethnomusicological chart offers a means to map both the distance travelled and the route taken, each of which reveals further insights about what it means to (finally) sing in musical theatre.

It is true that Harold Hill falls in love with Marian and gets to lead the big parade. This may be the utopic American Dream in action, as an outsider—whether insincere or insecure—surrenders to the virtuous civic ideals he had sought to exploit.[130] Yet, the same vocal trajectory may be coloured by a sense of reluctant resignation; voice, after all, can contain a plural, complex and ambiguous 'cocktail of several simultaneous feelings'.[131] Hill may have entertained utopia, 'contained by the respectable domesticity of the love story', but given the fact he sings *to* Marian and never *with* her, following her lead and mirroring her vocal lines, Hill's voice remains detached, indirect. Perhaps the embrace of utopia is not always a willing one.[132] While possibly true for Hill, it is clearly the case for Fagin who resists and recants with a voice that longs for human connection and safety yet refuses, truculently, to reform. What of other characters who are seen as fraudulent, dishonest, or criminal such as Starbuck in *110 in the Shade* (1963) or the Thénardiers in *Les Misérables* (1985)?

Such complexities are not, however, limited to individual characters. In the latter half of the twentieth century, Sondheim and his collaborators created musical dramas of 'difference' that dealt with irony, anger, and uncertainty in 'complex' and 'multiple' ways.[133] Intermediate vocality gave voice to the townsfolk who ventured 'into the woods' to get their wishes only to find that—in the end—utopia can be unfulfilling and morally uncertain. Along the way, the complex emotions experienced even resulted in voices which travelled away from utopia, rather than towards it, mapping the changing relationships between individuals and communities. Even if—as with Harold Hill—this musical cannot resist a glimpse of utopia in the finale, it is shown to be unstable, a place which never really exists, as Cinderella ends the musical as it began: 'I wish.'[134] A similar performance of moral ambiguity, complicated emotions, and creeping sense of uncertainty might be heard in the intermediate vocality of the more recent musical *London Road* (2011), for which composer Adam Cork and creator Alecky Blythe crafted melodies out of verbatim interviews conducted with the residents of the eponymous street in Ipswich, England, after a number of prostitutes were murdered in their community.[135]

Elsewhere, the potential of intermediate vocality may even more closely reflect the complexity of lived experience, as audiences' lives became similarly fragmented and individualized and society, and what constitutes utopia, began to change. As a reflection of these changes, the presence of rap is revealing in *Hamilton*. While the genre was not recognized when George List mapped the boundaries between speech and song, the five pitch techniques to improve flow considered in this chapter located various moments of intermediate vocality within the vocal dramaturgy at different coordinates on List's chart. Journeying to utopia, then, is not the same for everyone. For Nicole Hodges Persley and others, the presence of rap in *Hamilton* was paradoxical in its celebration of African American music to perpetuate a white mythology of America's founding, far away from the utopian ideals the musical purported to represent. Can a similar paradox between representation, race, and reality be heard in the intermediate vocality of works with a similar vocal aesthetic such as *Bring in da Noise, Bring in da Funk* (1996), *In the Heights* (2008), or *Sylvia* (2018)?

Likewise, the configuration of vocal spaces in this musical suggests that while the complexities of community and history are determined by men in the public realm, utopian ideals are feminine, private, familial, and domestic. This implied gendering may be supported by the fact that when this aesthetic predominates, it is men like Hill, Fagin, and Hamilton who employ it. While women have moments of ambiguity or uncertainty (or, when they sing of sending in the clowns), they are often characterized as much more emotionally 'transparent'.[136] Whether or not this is a pejorative and patriarchal encoding is a matter of debate, but its persistent recurrence may reveal something about the way musical theatre configures and understands what it means for a character to be transparent and vulnerable.

As it developed beyond discrete emotional idealism and, from the mid-twentieth century onwards, offered audiences an emotionally multifaceted sound that gave voice to experiences and uncertainties very much like their own, intermediate vocality became a sonic space of resistance, denial, frustration, or challenge to the transparency and directness of wish-fulfilment through song. Yet, because utopian performatives are 'never finished gestures toward a potentially better future', might this not suggest that—even when unwilling, resistant, disappointed, gendered, or paradoxical—the very nature of intermediate vocality might, itself, be somehow utopian in its incompleteness?[137] After all, utopia is a place where wishes are imagined, but as it does not exist, can never be fulfilled. If this is the case, then the inevitably of vocal utopia at the conclusion of these works is not a reversal or sudden shift at all. Could it be that *this* voice—intermediate, at times ambiguous, and even ambivalent—is, in fact, the most utopian of them all?

5
Rediscovering Nostalgia
Whose Voice Is It, Anyway?

Singing utopia is complicated. For Nathan, Adelaide, Sky, and Sarah, the utopia of an American melting pot was only glimpsed through a 'tolerant accommodation of difference' as it was revealed to be plural and malleable rather than integrated or singular.[1] Likewise, Youth's search for 'The Real' in *Passing Strange* (2008) found the act of 'dreaming forward' to be 'unstable [and] in motion', characteristics which may also recall the dystopian utopia of liquid chorality in *Company*'s macro-voiceworld.[2] In the case of Harold Hill in *The Music Man* (1957), achieving utopia may even be heard as a failure. What happens, however, when utopia becomes more than just plural, complicated, or disappointing? Reflecting on the history of the twentieth century, Edward Rothstein observes that 'the worst horrors—including Nazi Germany, the Soviet regime, the Maoist Cultural Revolution—grew out of utopian visions'. Referencing the philosopher Isaiah Berlin, Rothstein more bluntly concludes that 'utopianism leads to . . . tyranny'.[3] Viewed this way, events ranging from the atrocities of World War One through to the terrorist attacks in New York City on 11 September 2001 might lead to one troubling conclusion: utopia is dangerous.[4]

Notwithstanding the characteristic imperatives of the musical to sing utopia through transparency, energy, and directness, how has the form also sought to navigate away from giving voice to an imagined future which may well become a nightmare? The answer may be found in the presence of nostalgia as a 'counterpart' to any threat of the utopian, a tendency through which the certainties of the past rather than the possibilities of the future allow an escape from a present somehow found wanting.[5] Beyond the nostalgic ambiguities heard in the micro-voiceworlds of *Oliver!* (1960) or *The Music Man*, however, nostalgia has become synonymous with a particular 'knockabout offshoot' of musical theatre: the 'jukebox musical'.[6] Ubiquitous in the latter half of the twentieth century, with a marked trend for these productions in the twenty-first century, jukebox musicals draw from an

Singing Utopia. Ben Macpherson, Oxford University Press. © Oxford University Press 2024.
DOI: 10.1093/9780197557679.003.0006

established catalogue of well-known popular songs, interpolating them into new (and often whimsical) narratives. Considering how musical theatre 'sings nostalgia' might therefore prove to be a fascinating and provocative coda to this story. In doing so, it is helpful to consider the cultural context and characteristics of the jukebox format and its association with tendencies towards nostalgia in more detail.

'I wasn't just made for these times': Jukebox Musicals, 'Retromania', and Singing Nostalgia

The practice of interpolating pre-existing popular songs into productions for which they were not written is not new. British musical comedy of the late nineteenth century saw star performers negotiate contracts to include their trademark song and dance routine, irrespective of whether the material bore anything but the scantest relationship to the storyline or narrative. North American vaudeville acts such as Florenz Ziegfeld's *Follies* (1907–1931) or the *George White Scandals* (1919–1927) likewise included popular songs in their programmes, many of which would form the basis for what became the Great American Songbook. Yet, where the Tin Pan Alley repertoire once achieved cultural reach via appropriated interpolation into contemporaneous revue and variety productions, the emergence of jukebox musicals in the second half of the twentieth century saw a reverse 'direction of travel' as music chart hits populated productions with little more than flimsy or fanciful storylines as a dramaturgical basis for their inclusion.[7]

In their recent 'interpretive history' of the jukebox musical, Kevin Byrne and Emily Fuchs identify three kinds of jukebox musical format. First, 'artist catalogue' jukebox musicals feature the work of a single performer or band, and include *Ain't Misbehavin'* (1978, featuring the music of Fats Waller), *Eubie!* (1978, featuring the music of Eubie Blake), *Mamma Mia!* (1999, featuring the music of ABBA), and *Jagged Little Pill* (2018, featuring the music of Alanis Morissette). Second, 'era-specific' jukebox productions draw from a style or genre connected with a particular zeitgeist or sound and include *Bubbling Brown Sugar* (1976, featuring music from the Harlem Renaissance), *Return to the Forbidden Planet* (1989, featuring various songs of the 1960s and 1970s), and *Motown: The Musical* (2013, featuring music from the Motown record label). Finally, 'biographical' jukebox musicals proffer a supposed 'biography' of an artist or group, with productions including *Elvis* (1977, featuring the music of Elvis Presley), *Buddy: The Buddy Holly Story* (1989, featuring the music of Buddy Holly), and *MJ: The Musical* (2021, featuring the music of Michael Jackson). The prevalence (if not always assured popularity) of these works—whether focussed on an artist, era, or biography—is characteristic of a turn towards the nostalgic.[8]

As popular culture becomes 'addicted' to the reassuring familiarity of borrowing from itself, the iconography of the jukebox—the large coin-operated playback machines symbolic of American popular music between the 1930s and 1960s—is fitting. Connected implicitly to the 'retromania' present in Western culture, the notion of the 'jukebox' evokes a world of optimistic youth, new musical trends, and the heyday of record companies that relied on jukeboxes as a significant source of exposure for new releases and subsequent income, as listeners were able to self-select their favourite song or artist to play at a diner, bar, arcade, or laundromat.[9] The nominal reference to a retro playback device from an earlier period, along with the celebration of music familiar to a broad audience demographic, therefore turns towards an (imagined) past, presented through the 'manufactured [retro] nostalgia' that jukebox musicals provide.[10] As such, Fred Davis has suggested that the jukebox musical format configures a wistful (mis)remembrance of a past in which even traumatic eras or events are imbued with, or filtered through, 'a kind of fuzzy, redeemingly benign aura'.[11] Throughout the twentieth and early twenty-first centuries, the world has experienced '[e]conomic transformations, technological innovations and sociocultural shifts', resulting in 'stark differences' between the world of a person's youth and that of their old age. Such an accelerated rate of change means that nostalgia for a more certain and bygone social order 'also intensified because the world [is] changing faster'.[12] By trading on nostalgia, jukebox musicals therefore appear to offer a return to a 'benign' or more certain past (irrespective of lived reality), challenging future-facing explorations of the possible.[13]

Yet, just as utopia has proven to be more complicated than a dream of 'something better', nostalgia is also far more complex than a wistful longing for the past.[14] While nostalgia has been applied in a broad sense in earlier chapters, cultural theorist Svetlana Boym suggests that it may be composed of two discrete but overlapping 'tendencies'. First, one may experience 'reflective nostalgia'—a tendency which 'lingers on ruins, the patina of time and history, in the dreams of another time and place'.[15] The reflective nostalgic experiences the past *through* the passage of time. It is a condition 'enamored of distance, not of the referent itself'.[16] Knowing the past is irrecoverable, this form of nostalgia 'cherishes shattered fragments of memory' as a means of reconciliation or meaning. It can therefore be 'ironic and humorous', but not sentimental.[17] Conversely, the second tendency of nostalgia is 'restorative'—best demonstrated in recent Western political narratives regarding the reclamation of national identities concerned with restoring 'greatness' or 'taking back control'. This harkening back to the past proposes to 'rebuild' or return, engaging in debates surrounding 'total reconstructions of [symbolic] monuments' in an effort to build a particular kind of present and future.[18] When 'nostalgia is an ache of distance and displacement', restorative nostalgia seeks to compensate for both by bringing condition of the past (distance) into the condition of the present (*re*-placement).[19] Considering these distinct but often interrelated tendencies, which kind of 'nostalgia' is manufactured in jukebox musicals, and how might this be given voice?

In 'artist catalogue' and 'era-specific' jukebox musicals, part of the audience appeal relates to the unabashed intertextuality that these works employ.[20] The joy for many audience members is found in the act of negotiating the evident mismatch of an actor, playing a fictional character, singing a well-known song that has a life beyond the world of the musical. For instance, interpolating songs from the band Queen into *We Will Rock You* (2002, book by Ben Elton) invites the audience to listen across two cultural inputs: the live experience of the musical in the present and the individual memory of a song and its singer from the past. While all performances 'embed traces of other performances', this particular kind of dualism is often explained with reference to Marvin Carlson's concept of 'ghosting', whereby the performance of an interpolated song is infused with the spectre of the original voice.[21] Freddie Mercury's distinct phrasing, tone, and style are therefore *always* present in any performance of *We Will Rock You*, affecting the way audiences listen to the performers on stage when they sing hits such as 'Radio Ga Ga' and 'Bohemian Rhapsody'. As Millie Taylor has argued, the intertextual excess and retro camp of such productions 'allow audiences the transcendental pleasure of attachment, intelligent interpretation and nostalgic recreation'.[22] This 'nostalgic recreation' may be experienced in moments of overlap between Boym's two tendencies, as an audience member negotiates a mismatch between the live performance and sonic spectre, 'enamored of distance', or 'ironic and humorous' (*reflective* nostalgia), while the playful intertextuality *restores* or 'replaces' the past in the here and now of the performance.[23]

For Boym, when such nostalgic recreations or negotiations occur, 'the past opens up a multitude of potentialities' in the constitution of present meaning and experience, facilitating the 'augmentation of self-continuity' between these two temporalities.[24] Is this a kind of exploration of the possible? If it is, the nostalgia(s) experienced in the moment of listening across present voices imbricated with past 'ghosts' is, to an extent, utopian. After all, if '[t]he counterpart to the imagined future is the imagined past', then the counterpart of nostalgia is utopia. Ricoeur elsewhere suggests that nostalgia is a 'pathology of utopia', its foundation or origin.[25] How might we explore this further? One way might be to consider the particular properties of Byrne and Fuchs's third kind of jukebox musical: the 'biographical' jukebox (or 'bio-musical' as it is more commonly known).

'So far away . . .': Bio-musicals and the Possibilities of Singing Nostalgia

Rather than placing artist-specific or era-specific songs at the service of flimsy and often irrelevant narratives, bio-musicals purport to validate the borrowings in context, offering a theatrical biography of a well-known band or artist by using their most popular songs as the basis for the score. In just the first two decades of the twenty-first century, this specific type of jukebox musical became increasingly prevalent in many theatre seasons on Broadway and the West End.[26] While 'artist catalogue' and 'era-specific' jukebox musicals elicit a sense of 'ghosting' through irony, playful fragmentation, and incongruity, bio-musical performances proffer a greater sense of fidelity to real life. Through costuming, design, and the theatricalizing of landmark concerts or television performances, bio-musicals construct a particular performance of 'retro' culture, including 'element[s] of exact recall' involving 'precision replication' of the look, physicality, and fashion of particular pop icons.[27] Such elements might include the distinctive red jackets of the Four Seasons, the trademark hairstyle and 'fierceness' of 1980s-era Tina Turner, or the changing fashions of Cher or Elvis. Yet, while tribute performances may be a primarily 'visual practice', the relationship between visual 'replication' and expectations of vocal 'replication' in the voiceworld(s) of a bio-musical performance is complicated.[28]

For example, reflecting on his development of the title role in *A Beautiful Noise: The Neil Diamond Musical* (2022, book by Anthony McCarten), actor Will Swenson stated in an interview that he was conscious to avoid impersonation: 'Neil has a gravely, gritty sound. If you go for absolute imitation, you run into trouble'. Instead, Swenson describes giving voice to Diamond on Broadway as a chance to 'honor his sound' rather than to try and produce an exact likeness, even while the costumes and hairstyles of the performance offered 'elements' of the look, physicality, and changing styles of Diamond through his career.[29] Nevertheless, writing in *Entertainment Weekly*, Dave Quinn boldly proclaimed that Swenson 'sounds nearly identical to Diamond in his raspy vocals', while on the website *Theatremania*, David Gordon claimed that Swenson 'doesn't look or sound like Diamond' yet acknowledged that the '60- and 70-year-olds exclaim at intermission' that '"He sounds *just* like him!"'.[30] Notwithstanding the problems of any conceit to vocal imitation (discussed in more detail below), it seems that even if audience members are well aware they are *not* watching or hearing the original pop star or even a professional tribute act who relies on crafting a form of vocal fidelity, their need to engage with the success (or apparent lack) of an actor's vocal likeness is a foundational concern in the operation and reception of the bio-musical.[31]

How, then, can we listen to these voices? What might the limitations and expectations of vocal similarity reveal about the ways in which such works construct a relationship between restorative nostalgia, reflective nostalgia, and the qualities and potential of utopian vocality?[32] What might listening across two discrete voiceworlds at once—as the voice of Tina Turner is channelled through Adrienne Warren, Carole King is channelled through Jessie Mueller, or Frankie Valli is channelled through John Lloyd Young—reveal about musical theatre vocality in an era where looking back seems to be all that is left? Such questions present knotty intangibilities in this final chapter. However, three approaches to vocal performance not yet considered in this book may prove useful in understanding a voiceworld which operates in the interstices between the stage, the studio, and the stadium on one level, and between fact and fiction on the other.

Conceiving these approaches as metaphorical audio filters, this chapter will first approach the voiceworld of bio-musicals through a focus on *lipsynching*, here termed 'vocal drag'. Self-conscious, knowingly referential, and operating through the 'mismatch' of what is seen and what is heard, this first approach will offer a way to consider what the camp artifice and reliance on collective and individual audience memory might suggest about such voices and their potential to be encoded with nostalgia or utopia. Second, it will listen through the filter of *ventriloquism*, asking what might be revealed about nostalgia or utopia when the spectral or uncanny voice of one being seems to 'speak' (or sing) through the body of another. Drawing findings from the previous two approaches together, the cultural politics of vocal *simulation* offers a third and final sonic 'junction point' through which the exploration of nostalgic cultural memory, utopian possibility, and the contemporary condition of pop culture might be heard.[33]

Audio Filter I: 'You watch the lips . . .'—Vocal Drag and the Illusion of Presence

Discussing the original Broadway production of *Beautiful: The Carole King Musical* (2014, book by Douglas McGrath), journalist Philip Fisher began his review for the *British Theatre Guide* by assessing Jessie Mueller's performance as the titular singer-songwriter:

> Jessie Mueller is a sensation. If viewers did not know that Carole King is now in her 70s, they would swear that she is participating in her own tribute on Broadway every night . . . you watch the lips like a hawk to see whether the actress is lip-synching.[34]

While employing hyperbole, Fisher's reference to lipsynching suggests that in performances such as this, there is a fundamental relationship between what is seen and what is heard.[35] As the reviews and experiences from *A Beautiful Noise* also attest, the debates surrounding vocal likeness remain a central component in the reception of bio-musical performances. What might a consideration of the hierarchy of visual and vocal fields reveal about the production of nostalgic tendencies in the bio-musical? The first metaphorical audio filter of lipsynching offers a possible answer to this question.

As a performance practice, lipsynching can be used to conceal or express the mechanisms of its production. When used to conceal, it enacts a primacy of the visual field, associated with synonyms including 'miming, dubbing, doubling, playback, ghosting [and] picturization'. Aside from the veneration of Mueller's performance by Fisher, this kind of lipsynching was seen during Hollywood's Golden Age, as 'ghost singers' lent their voices to the stars of many film musicals. These voices often went uncredited, 'concealed' so as not to distract from the film star *seen* on the screen. Singers including Marni Nixon and Bill Lee worked to align their vocal performance with the visual performance of the movie star onscreen (the movement of the lips, tongue, breath, swallowing, and even the shaping of unvoiced vowel formants).[36] When such mechanisms are concealed, film scholar Ruth Johnston suggests that the resulting 'loss of origin' renders ghost singing as 'a technologically produced form of drag', creating a false unity of what is heard and seen.[37] While there is no 'loss of origin' or material voice to 'conceal' in a musical where the performers sing live, a similar kind of 'false unity' of the visual and the vocal still occurs. Neuroscientific studies suggest that this is because when intersensory conflicts arise, they are resolved through the 'subjugation of the less reliable sense' and, in the spatial and embodied experience of live performance, auditory processing is the least dominant.[38]

Yet, as a metaphor, the concept of lipsynching has applications beyond the world of ghost singers and Hollywood films, offering a way in which we might listen across this false unity and critique its operation. This is because Johnston's use of drag might also invoke the second kind of lipsynching—one designed to express rather than conceal. Originating in New York in the 1960s, lipsynching to sound recordings became prevalent in drag acts when they were outlawed during the McCarthy era. Before their recent popularity in mainstream culture as a result of television shows such as *RuPaul's Drag Race* and *LipSync Battle*, changing audience tastes, a shrinking clientele, and the increased costs of professional musicians to accompany performances led to drag performers going underground and resorting to 'canned voices', miming silently to vinyl recordings of popular songs as a cynical, humorous, and economic alternative to live vocal performance. In this context, lipsynching became an expressive act of resistance for many, a decadent subversion against cultural and economic pressures to conform or fade.[39] In such performances, lipsynching is often acknowledged directly or implicitly, lending the dragged lipsynch (called 'vocal drag' from this point) a political knowingness as the performer self-consciously appropriates pop music from one cultural arena to another: this direction of travel 'enables the artist to translate recorded music into a theatrical performance'.[40]

From the cabaret clubs of New York to primetime television entertainment, part of the knowingness inherent in vocal drag is the self-conscious negotiation of the *mismatch* between the live and embodied visual and the 'canned' vocal from a recording—a negotiation that mirrors the kind Fisher engaged in when watching Jessie Mueller as Carole King. In addition, because of its cultural provenance, vocal drag is associated with the impersonation of gender as a critical or resistant practice. Sharing a 'historical alliance with [other forms of] subversion', the overt artifice of drag draws attention to the performance of gender—both of the drag artist and their alter ego. This means, as Judith Butler has argued, that the subversive nature of drag 'implicitly reveals the imitative structure of gender itself—as well as its contingency'.[41] In other words, drag subverts (or expresses) the concealing of personal identity through the self-conscious—and expressly visual—act of concealment itself.[42] When vocal drag forms part of this performance, the critical negotiation between the visual and vocal fields becomes ever more intense.

While vocal drag employs a pre-recorded voice in self-conscious artifice and bio-musical performers sing live, three aspects seem to suggest that vocal drag may be a suitable audio filter through which to listen to bio-musical vocality as it relates to what is seen onstage. First, the act of recrafting popular songs within a theatrical biography means that, in common with vocal drag, bio-musicals likewise 'translate recorded music into a theatrical performance'.[43] This results in the second aspect—the impersonation of pop culture icons with a theatrical knowingness. Both actor and audience know this is *not* the real performer and yet, as with drag performance, this knowledge functions in the visual field as an index of critique or contingency. Third, for most audience members, their direct association with an artist to whom an actor gives voice will be, predominantly, through the medium of recorded music. However, as with the historical practice of drag performance (and as Fisher's review of Mueller's performance attests), much of the fascination arises from the relationship between the 'precision replication' of visual elements onstage and the properties of the voice that is heard.[44] The 'amusement and charm' resulting from this combination suggests that vocal drag adheres to Reynolds's earlier definition of 'retro' cultural forms.[45] How might such an analogue be understood in relation to nostalgic (or utopian) vocality?

Just as drag expresses and subverts imitative gender structures knowingly, vocal drag expresses and subverts the relationship between the vocal and the visual performance. In further consideration of the 'technologically produced' vocal drag of playback and dubbing in cinema, Jennifer Fleeger borrows from film scholar Michel Chion to observe that '[w]hen we lip-synch, "it is the body that folds itself precisely to the voice" . . . fastening the body we see to the voice we hear' so that 'no matter how fictionalized it may appear, the [bodily] image is shouting at us to notice the [recorded] singer for herself'.[46] Expressing rather than concealing this mismatch between sight and sound, vocal drag therefore 'implicitly reveals' its own 'imitative structure'. As it does so, it challenges the dominance of the visual field, conferring great influence upon the recorded voice, and reducing the authority of the live bodily image which 'shouts at us' to direct our aural attention elsewhere.[47]

Forcing attention away from the present moment of live performance as an implicit condition *of* the live performance, vocal drag thus enacts a power struggle for audience members to listen simultaneously across extremes of two inputs—the visual understood as a spatial input, and the vocal, understood as a temporal input. 'Watching the lips' becomes a negotiation between the present and the past through what is seen and what is heard. This act of listening across is full of nostalgic potential because, as Boym further asserts, there is a direct relationship between the attempts of restorative nostalgia to 'spatialize time' through reconstructing the past and the fetishizing of exact details, and the parallel tendency of reflective nostalgia which 'temporalizes space' through an interplay of memory and distance (see Figure 5.1).[48] Vocal drag, then, maybe a useful way of understanding the manufacture of 'nostalgic vocality'.

In a similar manner to conventional vocal drag, bio-musical performances 'shout at us' to engage with spectral voices beyond the live moment heard

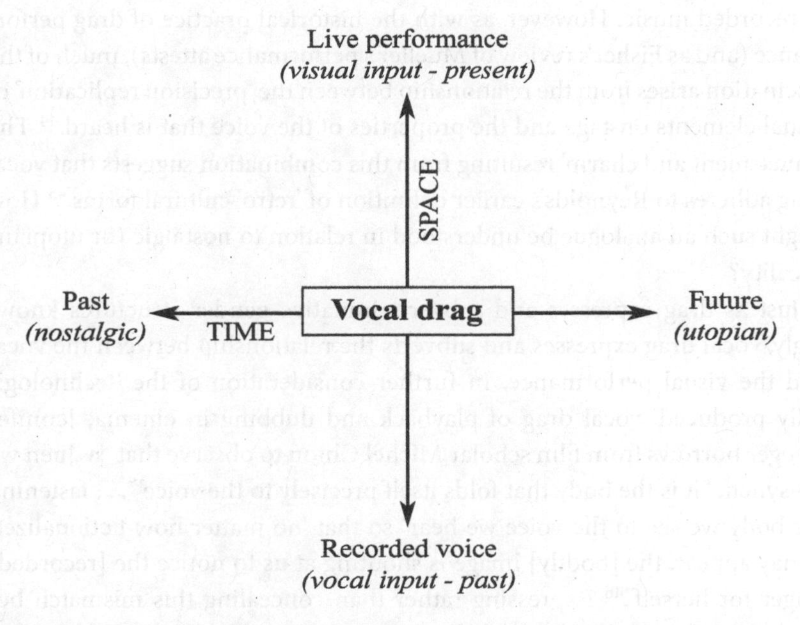

Figure 5.1 The characteristics of vocal drag. © Ben Macpherson.

through memories of a voice mediated on record. Often, this is achieved through the staged recreation of radio broadcasts or sessions in which titular characters are seen in the studio, immortalizing their voices in the act of recording. For example, in *Tina: The Tina Turner Musical* (2018, book by Katori Hall, Frank Ketelaar, and Kees Prins), the first act sees a young Turner being coached by producer Phil Spector during the recording of her breakout chart success, 'River Deep, Mountain High', in 1966. After time away from the top of the charts and feeling like an 'old black has-been',[49] act two sees Tina struggling to find the right version of a comeback single, as the audience witness several different short versions of her subsequent chart hit 'What's Love Got to Do with It?' before a performance of the final song.

In each case, as with other bio-musicals, the visual cue of a microphone in the present becomes metonymic of the *recorded* voice as a spectral presence from the past. Adrienne Warren metaphorically 'shouts at us' to notice—not her embodied presence—but a memory of the song as originally recorded. Drawing attention to its own historical reference points in this way, the vocal drag of the bio-musical invites spectres of past voices into a performance space full of visual replication, framing the real-life result of the recording sessions staged in these productions as an authority that both exceeds and sanctions the theatrical moment.[50] Recorded voices from the past therefore form the sonic foundation of the bio-musical. After all, while the immediacy of the live performance is thrilling, these productions are held to have such wide appeal because of their historic reference points, suggesting temporal rather than spatial experience might predominate.

Is vocal drag, then, a kind of nostalgic vocality asking audiences to listen across the recorded past and the live visual present? What tendency of nostalgia is present here? Due to the nature of recorded voices—long associated with auditory distress—the particularly localized attentiveness demanded by voices on record imbues them with a special kind of power, one which creates a new form of listening experience. '[M]oving uncontrollably through space as an invisible, immaterial body', the pre-recorded voice 'produces a direct, physical sensation on the listener'.[51] The overwhelming sense of the proximity to the past in this case creates a sense of temporal 'flux' between songs from another age and the immediacy of the live performance. Using the concept of queer futurity from José Esteban Muñoz, the affective potential inherent in this flux may also be understood as utopian. Muñoz argues that the concept of utopia 'rejects what already exists [and] always pursues the potential of not being *here*'.[52] The effective erasure of live and embodied singing in favour of a spectral voice on record in vocal drag might therefore enact a rejection of the present, perhaps to move *beyond* it rather than retreat to what went before. On this basis, vocal drag can be heard to offer a performance of 'potential', imbued with a sense of its own utopian futurity through an explicit disavowal of the now.[53] The 'availability of the desired object' (the past voice) is seemingly rebuilt in that moment, suggesting an equivalence between restorative nostalgia and the utopian impulse in listening to these voices as vocal drag.[54]

Yet, in any bio-musical, several characteristics are in evidence that might frustrate this position. First, while the recorded voice might have a vivid cultural agency in the 'horizon of expectation' attached to these productions, in the moment of hearing Warren-as-Turner or Mueller-as-King singing live, audience members are unlikely to be cognizant of any subversion of acousmatic pre-recorded dominance. Unlike Muñoz's 'rejection' of the 'now' inherent in its conventional iteration, vocal drag in the bio-musical seems to negotiate a tension between the present and the past precisely because of its liveness and immediacy.[55] Second, as a dramaturgical convention of the form, moments in recording studios are often incomplete glimpses that direct attention to the process and act of recording only in short or specific bursts, whether or not such songs are then heard in full. Such 'fragments of [vocal] memory' therefore perform a sense of deconstruction rather than restoration, de-stabilizing and challenging the dominance of the recorded voice and exposing what Rick Altman has called the 'illusion of presence' attributed to recordings through the embodied immediacy of the voice that is singing.[56] While 'drag implicitly reveals the imitative structure of gender' by exposing and subverting socially constructed norms or stereotypes, vocal drag forces the 'restored' memory of the recorded voice into its own erasure, diminished, de-constructed, and untethered from bittersweet memories of a lost past through the embodied immediacy of the live, fragmented moment.[57] In a reversal of the relationship between live performer and mediatized voice in conventional lipsynch performance, the metaphor of vocal drag in the bio-musical means that it is the voice on record which is now pursued for its potential of 'not being here'.[58]

This position is enhanced by a third characteristic related to the illusory nature of the recordings themselves. Even rudimentary engineering practices such as the ability to mix sound and use different microphones or spatial configurations in studios or booths mean that '[a]s soon as technology [is] used to record music, some aspects of artificiality [are] introduced', troubling any claim the 'original' recording may have to authenticity in its predominance. In other words, the voices that are emulated in bio-musicals are already known through an illusory and artificial medium.[59] Further, the vocal characteristics of certain performers are (or were) in themselves made up of their own imitative qualities and in-authenticities; among them are many whose lives have been theatricalized. For example, 'the cult that developed around the King [Elvis] was fully cognizant of Elvis's love for inauthenticity, for artifice' in his cultivated performance style and vocal affectations. As one of Presley's former girlfriends would remark: '"Elvis could imitate anybody. He could do Hank Snow, Dean Martin, Mario Lanza . . . anybody"', leading Hugo Barker and Yuval Taylor to ask: 'Would Elvis have spawned so many impersonators if he had sung just what came naturally to him?'[60] Elsewhere, the popularity of electronically produced disco music with its rhythmic aesthetic, increased use of synthesized instrumentation, and stylized production values was 'about an escape from everyday life'.[61] The vocal aesthetics of bio-musicals such as *Elvis: The Musical* (1977, book by Jack Good and Ray Cooney) or *Summer: The Donna Summer Musical* (2017, book by Dennis McAnuff and Robert Cary) therefore draw from sources already part of a popular recording culture which celebrates an escape or distortion of reality, even before being reframed theatrically.

The relationship between the spatial immediacy of live embodied performance and the disruption, de-construction, and subversion of the past recorded voice therefore creates a plural experience that manufactures a complex nostalgia rooted in the negotiation of a visual that offers a replica of the past but which, like the voices that are remembered, is merely an 'illusion of presence'.[62] How can anyone be nostalgic—either reflectively or restoratively—for a voice that was never actually there? While the audio filter of vocal drag has focussed on interactions between the visual and the vocal, a second approach might help reveal the particular qualities assigned to the aural 'illusions of presence' heard in the voices of Mueller, Warren, and others.

Audio Filter II: 'Where things lost become'—Aural Anachronisms and the Possibility of Nostalgia

Returning to Philip Fisher's review in which he praised Jessie Mueller's performance as Carole King, he mused further on the apparent vocal similarity beyond his mention of lipsynching, claiming that the 'vocal resemblance is uncanny'.[63] While listening to bio-musical voices as vocal drag suggests the complex relationship between the visual and the vocal in the configuration of nostalgia, the invocation of the uncanny—the strange or unsettlingly familiar—invites a greater focus on the properties of the voice apprehended beyond the 'precision replication' of costume, setting, or other material aspects of the production.

Popular as a lowbrow comedic form with a lineage from the eighteenth century via Victorian music halls to present-day comedy clubs, the practice of ventriloquism centres on the uncanny agency of a figure given a voice from elsewhere, as a performer skilfully animates an inanimate object via 'lip and tongue manipulation'. With barely perceptible movements of the mouth, the ventriloquist synchronizes their voice with 'the moving lips of a dummy [or another figure]', often appended to the ventriloquist as a kind of prosthetic.[64] The voice of the ventriloquist—'thrown' beyond the performer's body—activates the visual agency of the figure in a form of unsettling 'exchange'.[65] A ventriloquist's voice, 'having seemingly passed from one body through another, emerges' from the visual field of the animated object 'distorted, and yet still recognizable'.[66] In his pioneering study of ventriloquism, Steven Connor has considered the relationship between voicer and animate object as constructing a kind of twinning or '*alter ego*', an uncanny version of the self.[67] In bio-musical performances, the live performer imitating the celebrity may be conceived as a kind of prosthetic, activated by the voice of the 'original' which is channelled uncannily through them in the moment of performance. In this case, actors who seek to recreate well-known pop stars might become imbued with ventriloquial properties as defined by Connor, dependent on individual audience engagement. For example, for Fisher, Jessie Mueller sounded exactly like Carole King—and in this sense may register as an uncanny 'twin'.

As appealing as these equivalences might seem, extending this application of ventriloquism to the bio-musical also reveals the complexities of voices that are 'borrowed' or channelled from elsewhere. The popular understanding of the ventriloquial relationship between performer and figure implies what Connor has called a 'dialogue'; there is one who gives voice and one who receives it.[68] In the world of the bio-musical, the voice that is heard is never so direct or dualistic. Even while Tina Turner worked directly with Adrienne Warren to develop her vocal aesthetic, the 'likeness' that may (or may not) be heard in Warren's performance is a plural composite. It comprises the 'original' voice of Tina Turner, which 'ghosts' the live voice of

Warren. Both of these voices might be extended, conditioned, or disrupted by the sonic iconicity and memory of Turner's voice on various recordings or in moments of radio airplay on the part of the audience. They may be inflected with memories of Warren's voice from previous performances, or even that of Angela Bassett as Tina Turner in the 1993 biopic *What's Love Got to Do with It?* Notwithstanding the shared sense of indulgence and artifice, bio-musical vocality therefore exceeds the visual field, or a dualistic understanding of voices in 'dialogue', or 'twinned' in a two-way exchange. How, then, might we understand this excess? One possible approach is to consider historical manifestations and properties of ventriloquism beyond the dummies of popular entertainment.

As mentioned above, Carlson's concept of 'ghosting' has been used elsewhere to explore the means by which audience members might engage with the intertextuality of voices that are familiar to them in jukebox musicals, an experience even more vivid in the bio-musical. The term might even recall ideas more closely associated with voices of operatic metaphysicality discussed in chapter 1, as spectral vocality is related closely to ancient ritualistic practices that involved other forms of the ventriloquial. What might a brief return to ideas of metaphysical or mystical voices in this context reveal about these voices and their relationship to the past? If Adrienne Warren 'channels' the ghost of Tina Turner through her vocal performance, is the excess that accompanies it some kind of spectral ventriloquism? If it is (or is not), how might this relate to, or inform an understanding of, these voices in connection with utopia or its pathology?

Records from the ancient worlds of Greece, Babylon, Assyria, Egypt, Africa, India, Australia, and Iceland include numerous references to the religious ritual of fortune-telling, in which priests or diviners would give voice to prophecies from the gods in a trance-like state. In ancient Greece, this practice was known as gastromancy, from the word *engastrimythos* (literally 'stomach speaker'), as spirits were held to inhabit the deepest part of their human host. While gastromancy is a less familiar term, its Latin equivalent—ventriloquism—carries the same meaning, comprising a similar concatenation of 'venter' (stomach) and 'loqui' (speech). In his study of the origins of ventriloquism and religion, Walter Burkert suggests that as early as the second millennium BC, 'frenzied women from whose lips the God speaks' were recorded in Mari (now Syria), while the most influential example may be the Pythia—the priestess and mouthpiece of the oracle of Apollo at Delphi in Greece.[69]

With considerable reach in classical Greek culture, the Pythia (better known as the Delphic Oracle) was believed to utter otherworldly statements from Apollo, helping to shape both religious and civic life in Greece and abroad.[70] The concept of divine utterance in human form—as the human is 'ghosted' or inhabited by the spirit—therefore carried much power in the polytheistic world of antiquity and beyond. The exact origins of the Pythia and the oracle have been much debated by classical historians, and there are few direct mentions of the specific mechanisms of engastrimythic prophecy in ancient texts. However, in voicing a spirit that was held to inhabit the stomach, Connor has considered the resulting utterance in terms of both excretion and birth, highlighting the various values of this voice as execrable and earthly, violent and material, or maternal, vital, and life-giving.[71] This kind of ventriloquism is first a form of *bodily* excess, the kind that might be analogous with camp vocality in the musical.

However, another form of excess is found in further accounts of the Delphic Oracle. Connor points to a passage in Book Five of the poem *Pharsalia* by Roman writer Lucan, in which statesman Appius Claudius consults the Pythia and bears witness to her possession by Apollo. Recalling a similar account from Virgil's poem *Aeneid*, Appius experiences an oracular utterance comprising many 'voices, in the plural', even though they are achieved in this case by a struggle between the god and the Pythia, as Apollo seeks to 'block her throat'.[72] Ventriloquial excess, then, is not only bodily but polyphonic—rendering the voice that is heard as a plurality, a tension between the spirit and the one possessed, which becomes—in Connor's words—'a body in pieces'.[73] It may not be too tenuous to suggest that in application to the bio-musical, this polyphonic voice may include not only the 'original' voices of Turner and Warren but their multiple spectral traces, including Bassett and perhaps even other tribute acts. Is this, once more, a means of manufacturing reflective nostalgia, in which 'the past opens up a multitude of potentialities' through distance and interplay with the present moment?[74] Might it be that the manufacture of reflective nostalgia makes space for other imaginings—for the utopian?

In a literal demonstration of this kind of polyphonic vocality, *Summer: The Donna Summer Musical* features three 'versions' of disco star Donna Summer, as it charts her life and career. Duckling Donna (Storm Lever) represented Summer in her pre-teenage years, Disco Donna (originally played by Ariana DuBose, see Figure 5.2) represented her initial success, and Diva Donna (originally played by LaChanze) represented the singer in middle age, at

Figure 5.2 Ariana DuBose as Disco Donna. Photograph © Joan Marcus.

the peak of her fame. These three often featured in combination, singing in unison and harmony. For example, in the middle of act one, Disco Donna and Diva Donna share the song 'MacArthur Park', singing the second half in unison.

The song was Summer's first Billboard Hot 100 Number One in 1978, and therefore the performance by Disco Donna makes sense, perhaps even as a form of ventriloquial 'twinning'. However, after she died in 2012, a remixed version of the song was released by Ralphi Rosario and became Summer's first posthumous Number One on the Billboard Dance Club chart in December 2013. In this case, the inclusion of Diva Donna—played by an older actor with a different quality to Disco Donna—enacted a collapse of time: an aural anachronism. The younger and elder Summer, singing a song in unison that was twice a success for the original performer thirty-five years apart, invited numerous sonic 'spectres' into the performance, complicating, disrupting, and steering audience members' experiences at various points in the musical, in a performance of intense polyphony and anachronism.

The combination of excess and plurality in spectral ventriloquism therefore offers much to inform an understanding of the voice in bio-musical performance as manufacturing *reflective* nostalgia. A further area of comparison can be identified in terms of temporal anachronism. As seen in the example of *Summer*, the excess and plurality of spectral ventriloquism can change the relationship between the past, the present, and—by extension—the future, a relationship that was central to gastromantic utterances from the Oracle at Delphi and elsewhere.[75]

Other understandings of ventriloquism as a metaphysical act may yet offer a different sense of vocal plurality. Beyond the ancient world, these ventriloquial acts became understood as demonic possession, madness, or illusory hokum in the increasingly monotheistic world of the Judeo-Christian West, at least until the development of ventriloquism as a form of entertainment in the eighteenth century. In *The Discoverie of Witchcraft*, published in 1584 by Englishman Reginald Scot, 'ventriloquism' was defined as a historical process whereby actors would speak in a 'hollowe' voice to 'give oracles' or 'tell where things lost become'. Written from the position of a Christian sceptic, Scot's definition is notable for two reasons. First, in his book, the term 'ventriloqui'—a collective noun for those imbued with the superhuman ability to act as a channel for other voices—was interchangeable with the term 'Pythonists', in a direct critique of the perceived divinity of Pythia at Delphi, and in reference to the Devil's act of ventriloquism in the Garden of

Eden.[76] Second, the notion that prophetic oracles served to 'tell where things lost become' indicates a further function of such spectral ventriloquism. As Chase and Shaw suggest, '[w]hat we are nostalgic for is not the past as it was or even as we wish it was; but for the condition of *having been* . . . the past as reconstructed is always more coherent than when it happened'.[77] If ventriloquism 'tells where things lost become'—where what *has been* is reconstructed—then even with the anachronistic pluralities inherent in the bio-musical performances above, the celebration of *re*-locating voices from the past indicates a potential limit to reflective nostalgia and introduces the idea of reclamation or restoration, even if what is restored is only illusory.

Connor further suggests that at the intersection of paganism and the Christian world, the Delphic Oracle performed a 'mutilation of time' in which 'the future [was] revealed to the present in the mode of prophecy . . . from a past that has never been present except in the manner of its return'.[78] In other words, a reconstructed past (even one that is only imagined) offers a coherent sense of having been and as such has the potential to 'reveal the future'. If the voice of the Oracle functions as 'the passage through which . . . the past and the future can flood violently into the present', then this further changes the relationship between spatial experience (in which the visual predominates) and temporal experience (which confers greater authority on the aural). The spectral ventriloquism of the bio-musical may therefore act as a 'vocalic space' in which 'things lost' (the past) become the 'counterpart' (or pathology) of utopia. After all, '[n]ostalgia becomes possible at the same time as utopia'.[79] In this case, could it be that the bio-musical may not altogether eschew or reject the vocal utopia of earlier musical theatre but chart a different route (via temporal engagement) to the same place through the manufacture of restorative nostalgia? This would offer a fascinating boundary marker between utopia and its *past* rather than utopia and its possible failure, the voices of which were heard in the previous chapter. It would suggest that any discussion of the ways in which these musicals 'manufacture nostalgia' is imbued with a utopian tendency.

Such nostalgic vocality may therefore be reflective in one sense and restorative in another. In either tendency, utopia is implied if not entirely present, so further listening is required to better understand how bio-musicals might give voice to the rediscovery of a fondly remembered past, a live and immediate present, and a possible utopian future. Put another way, discussing the restorative or reflective nostalgia of vocal likeness in bio-musicals is to paradoxically talk about an experience of *rediscovery*, where not only 'lost

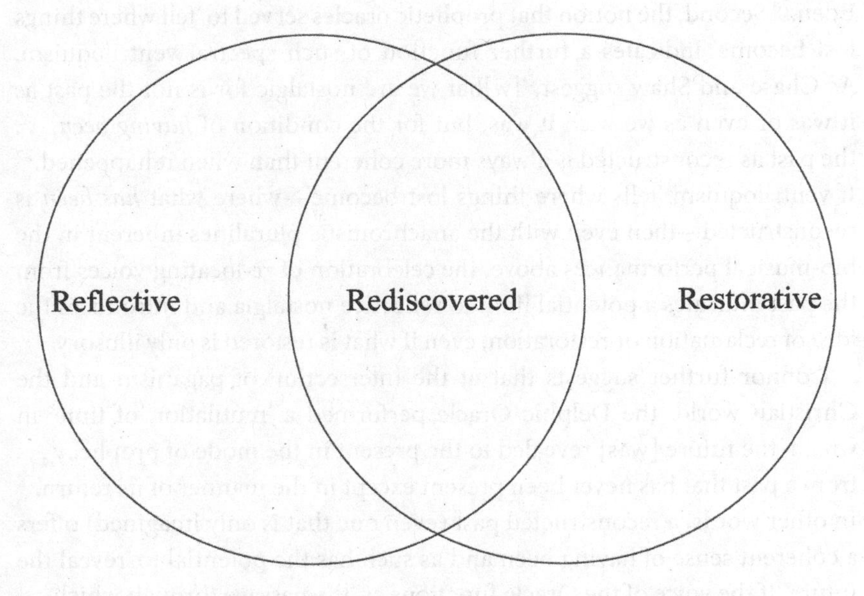

Figure 5.3 Venn diagram of nostalgic tendencies. © Ben Macpherson.

things become' but where other possibilities are unveiled. At the intersection of paradoxical tendencies to look forward while restoring the past through reflective critique, might *rediscovered nostalgia* constitute a third tendency which encapsulates the complexities of voices that are live on stage in the spatial field, but prompt memories of voices that were only ever 'illusions of presence' in the temporal field (see Figure 5.3)? How could we bring these concerns together, and consider rediscovered nostalgia as a holistic means to listen across the visual and the vocal, illusory and immediate, nostalgic and utopian? The third and final audio filter might offer a way to listen for the answer.

Audio Filter III: 'Remembering how we need to'—*Simuloquism* and the Possibility of Rediscovered Nostalgia

In his 1981 work *Simulacra and Simulation*, French philosopher Jean Baudrillard reflected on the pervasive proliferation of images and imagery across film, television, and advertising in postmodern culture. He argued that technological advances across various media (now including the internet and even augmented reality and AI) led to a blurring of the divisions between reality and illusion, authenticity and inauthenticity, originals and copies. The erosion of such distinctions has resulted in a culture Baudrillard called the 'hyperreal'—a world in which reality is distorted or perhaps replaced entirely by its representation or simulation. Demonstrating his point, Baudrillard reflected on the design and function of Disneyland: a place which is made to look entirely real but is only 'a play of illusions and phantasms' with no tangible origin. Disneyland is designed to make the mythology of America feel more of a reality than it is, to *mask* the absence of the American Dream and provide a 'social microcosm' of the possibility.[80]

This kind of hyperreality shares fundamental characteristics with many popular theatre forms, including musical theatre. By means of specific aesthetic, narrative, and participatory conventions such as realistic set design, vernacular dialogue, and conventions relating to modes of spectating, musical theatre often configures a 'portrayal of life with fidelity', creating a believable world which is, nonetheless, entirely separate from external realities.[81] Audiences willingly suspend disbelief, while at the same time they are always aware that any theatrical performance is only ever 'a play of illusions and phantasms'.[82] Musical theatre, like Disneyland, therefore offers a world that does not, and cannot, exist. In their direct reference to an external reality within the illusory world of theatrical performance, bio-musicals and their voiceworlds offer an intense form of hyperreality, aggregating 'the real' and its theatrical iteration. How, though, might the notion of hyperreality help draw together the properties of vocal performance heard in vocal drag and ventriloquism, or negotiate their limitations? Exploring this further, Baudrillard's notions of *simulation* and *simulacrum*—constituents of hyperreality—offer a fascinating way to listen.

In his consideration of hyperreality, simulation, and simulacrum, Baudrillard offers four 'successive phases' from reality to *simulacrum*:

1) The reflection of a profound reality, such as a painting;
2) Masking and denaturing of a profound reality, such as a painting that distorts the reality of its subject;
3) Masking the *absence* of a profound reality, such as the painting of a painting;
4) Pure simulacrum, with no relation to any reality whatsoever; an abstract painting with no immediate conceit to representation.[83]

While musical theatre might be a kind of hyperreality, bio-musicals offer a complex and intense negotiation of the first two of Baudrillard's phases. They reflect a sense of 'reality' in their subject matter while, at the same time, distorting the 'hyperreal' through a reflection, rather than a rejection, of the external world. This negotiation is manifest in three distinct ways. First, well-known songs are reframed or recrafted to fit the needs of a dramatic narrative. For example, Frankie and Mary Valli's marriage ended because of the strain of Frankie's touring and his persistent absenteeism as a father. Yet, while their divorce occurred in 1974, it is given dramatic heft in act two of *Jersey Boys* (2005, Rick Elice and Marshall Brickmann) when Frankie sings the 1975 US Billboard Number One 'My Eyes Adored You' to his former wife. Later, when the band seeks help from mobster Gyp DeCarlo to rescue bandmate Tommy DeVito from a $150,000 gambling debt, they perform 'Beggin''—a 1967 hit that lyrically had nothing to do with paying off loan sharks but which heightens the narrative intention of the scene. On this basis, the musical offers a reflection of 'profound reality' while the theatrical reframing of these moments 'denatures' reality. In scenes such as these, 'original' songs—stand-alone pop singles well known outside the world of the musical—are reframed dramatically, 'masked' within the theatrical hyperreal, even while their success still rests largely upon the recognition of these songs outside the world of the musical.[84]

Second, as heard through the audio filter of vocal drag, the staging of moments in recording studios offers a visual cue of a microphone that further distorts the reality presented, changing the relationship between the theatrical reality of live performance (held to represent an external reality) and memories of voices from popular recordings (external realities that are only ever illusory). Third, along with the theatricalizing of recording studios, another recurring trope of bio-musical productions is the recreation of landmark concerts or television appearances, such as the restaging of Carole King's famous 1971 Carnegie Hall concert, which bookends *Beautiful*. In many cases, these 'concerts' take place during or after the finale. Disarticulated from any conceit to narrative realism, such moments further denature or distort the very context within which the 'real' is referenced, facilitating a rediscovery through the uncanny ghosting of voices remembered—if not fully recreated. Bio-musicals therefore both reference *and* distort the supposed 'profound reality' of the singer-songwriters to whom they pay tribute. Yet, the denaturing or distortion of well-known voices goes further. As chapter 2 noted, the world of popular music upon which bio-musicals are based is also hyperreal, built on a complex practice of appropriation and recrafting.[85] In other words, the illusory voices of pop music icons that Warren, Swenson, DuBose and others are celebrated (or denigrated) for capturing in bio-musical performance are in themselves decadent hyperrealities—artificial in their sound and illusory in their presence.[86]

The vocal aesthetics of bio-musicals such as *Elvis: The Musical* or *Summer: The Donna Summer Musical* draw from sources that are already part of a hyperreal popular culture, one which celebrates a distortion of reality even before being reframed theatrically. The relationship between the external reality of a singer or band and their theatricalized biography onstage is therefore more complicated than a simple transposition from the presumed realm of 'the real' to the constructed hyperrealism of the stage. In resituating—borrowing, masking, and modifying—external sources from the realm of pop music within the conventions of the bio-musical, a theatrical hyperreality is required to both reference and distort *another* hyperreality that is nonetheless configured as external and 'original'. The voiceworld of bio-musicals is, therefore, the space of nostalgic rediscovery of 'real' voices which never actually existed, constituting the third phase of Baudrillard's 'precession of simulacra' as it masks the *absence* of a 'profound reality'. How does it do so, and what might this reveal about the possible experience of nostalgia for something that never was?

Reflecting on the cultural properties of vocal impersonation, Freya Jarman-Ivens offers a profound observation, suggesting that imitation 'relies on the absence of the real-original, and the persistence only of an *idea*-of-the-original'.[87] In the reception of bio-musical vocality, the 'original' voice on recording is illusory, absent. The 'original' properties of many popular voices are, like Elvis, artificial. Any memory of the 'original' will always be plural, fragmented, and informed by other vocal ghostings for each audience member. The perpetual absence of a real 'original' is, therefore, what facilitates the conceit that performers may 'sound like' their real-life counterparts. Such a position is pertinent because, while nostalgic ideas inherent in spectral ventriloquism or vocal drag presuppose a sense of fidelity in their restorative tendencies, a simple truism is inescapable: no matter how much a musical theatre performer seeks to sound like their 'twin' or 'alter ego', the results will always be limited.

From a Barthesian perspective, 'the materiality of the body speaking its mother tongue' renders the ineluctable, unquantifiable, but always-present 'grain' of the live voice more vital than the one they seek to emulate.[88] As the

Figure 5.4 'Portraying' Cher in *The Cher Show*. In common with *Summer: The Donna Summer Musical, The Cher Show* also featured a 'trio' of actors to depict various stages of Cher's career. Photograph © Joan Marcus.

director of *The Cher Show* (2018) acknowledged, 'we're portraying Cher but, ultimately, it's [actor] Stephanie J. Block that you are watching [and hearing]' (see Figure 5.4).[89]

Elsewhere, when playing the role of Al Jolson in *Jolson: The Musical* (1995, book by Francis Ellis and Rob Bettinson), British comedian and television personality Brian Conley elongated his vowels, assumed an appropriate accent, and imbued his vocal timbre with a rasp reminiscent of Jolson himself. Yet, even with these vectors of vocal similarity, Conley was still very much present, known for his own gravelly vocal texture. Such vocal limitations are supported by scientific research which demonstrates that the human capacity for phonetic mimicry has limited efficacy, with any attempt only including two or three key features or characteristics at one time.[90]

For example, a comparison of the first verse and refrain from Tina Turner's original recording of her 1966 breakout hit 'River Deep, Mountain High' with the *Tina* original cast recording vocal by Adrianne Warren offers moments of emulation along with stylistic and timbral differences. While the timing and phrasing of the opening line ('When I was a little girl') is phrased more or less identically by both Turner and Warren, a spectrographic visualization of the melodic range indicates that Warren's timbre is darker with a lower pitch range (see Figure 5.5.a). While Warren emulates the guttural texture of Turner's pop/rock sound (something Madison Moore has considered as a 'pleasant-sound straining' and 'raw sound' indexical of black female fierceness), she extends the ends of phrases in a more theatrical manner than Turner.[91] At the end of the lyric 'Only now my love has grown', Turner drops her cadence with a short final syllable. Conversely, Warren extends the note, shifting the sound forward with a brighter tone and employing a more controlled crescendo to move into the next phrase (see Figure 5.5.b). Aside from this, there is a similar use of vibrato between Turner and Warren on particular key notes in the melody ('say', 'my', 'why'). While Turner exhibits greater freedom with pitch bend and slide, Warren tends towards more precision and there are fewer instances of diphthongs in her vocal. In other words, Warren still exhibits elements of musical theatre style while evoking some indicative characteristics of the mediated voice of Turner (see Figure 5.5.c).[92]

Even when some similar aural or vocal features are present, the sonic markers they represent relate to voices that are in themselves absent, artificial, illusory, and hyperreal. In Baudrillardian terms, this means that such voices are *simulations* rather than imitations. Distinguishing these two categories, Baudrillard suggests that imitations such as mimicry (referred to as 'pretending') keep 'the principle of reality intact' and presume the presence of an 'original' against which a binary sense of likeness may be understood. Conversely, 'simulation threatens the difference between' the real and imaginary as they collapse into each other and the illusory replaces reality.[93] In the bio-musical, actors such as Warren, Young, Conley, Mueller, and others therefore employ vocal *simulacra*. Acknowledging the hyperreality of the theatrical context in which they are heard, they invoke sonic markers that may be identified with 'original' artists whose voices are already hyperreal. Here, it is the 'idea-of-the-original' that becomes the reference point, as it does if we listen to these voices as vocal drag. In this respect, perhaps it is no coincidence that when the 'original' in question is a sound recording that itself has already been exposed as another form of illusory hyperreality, the cultural currency of bio-musicals so readily involves discussions and anxieties about vocal likeness.

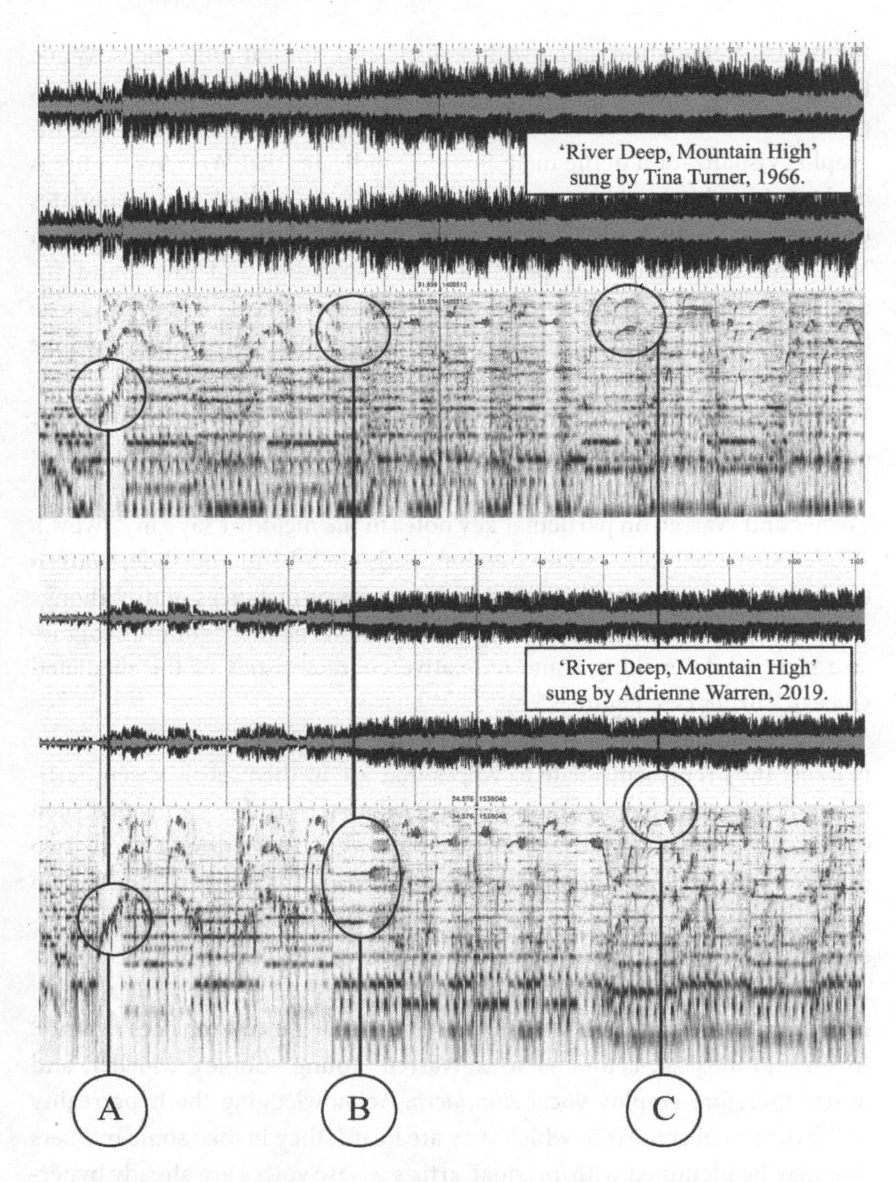

Figure 5.5 Comparative sonic visualization of Tina Turner and Adrienne Warren singing the first verse and refrain from 'River Deep, Mountain High'. © Ben Macpherson.

Echoing Baudrillardian concepts, sociologist Hillel Schwartz has reflected on the sense of instability or wavering uncertainty around the notion of 'originals' and 'copies' in postmodernity and beyond. With reality absent, the ensuing search for meaning beyond origin results in a culture where '[w]e use copies to certify originals [and] originals to certify copies'.[94] This negotiation further positions the fascination with voice in bio-musical performances at the heart of Western pop culture fetishism in the late twentieth and early twenty-first centuries. It also suggests that the capacity for meaning or experience in these performances depends on negotiating the interaction between the two forms of hyperreality considered above: the illusory 'original' voice as embodied by a theatricalized 'copy', and the 'copy' itself which offers a limited simulation of the (already hyperreal) 'original'. Schwartz notes that this negotiation—as audience members experience the simultaneous temporality of the present and the past, imbricated with the limitations of vocal simulation, results in a situation where listeners 'stand bewildered'.[95]

Often understood to mean confusion, bafflement, or quizzical dismay, the word 'bewildered' is poignant in Schwartz's description. Further, its etymology is particularly apt in this case. Derived from seventeenth-century English, the word is composed of 'be-', meaning 'thoroughly', and 'wilder-', meaning 'to go astray'. In other words, to be bewildered is to 'go thoroughly astray'—to be lost, without direction. Vocal simulation, with all its limitations and dual hyperreality, may therefore lead audience members thoroughly astray, bewildering ideas of what is original or simulated, challenging spatial and temporal experiences of memory, belonging, place, and cultural familiarity, such as those heard when listening through the audio filters of ventriloquism and vocal drag. Untethered from a clear sense of any 'profound reality', vocal simulation creates a fertile ground for the manufacture of rediscovered nostalgia through engagement with musical memory. After all, as Baudrillard states, it is only 'when the real is no longer what it was' that 'nostalgia assumes its full meaning'.[96]

During Tommy DeVito's direct address to the audience in the final moments of *Jersey Boys*, he draws together each of the quartet's differing versions of their story, which have formed and been retold throughout the course of the musical. With wistful and laconic resignation, he asks: 'Everyone remembers it how they need to, right?'[97] To what act of remembering was DeVito referring? At the level of narrative, he is referencing the divergent versions of a shared history as recounted by him and his bandmates in real-time during the performance. Yet, as a direct address, this question also points to individual or collective memories of the mediated voices, songs, and stories of the real Frankie Valli and the Four Seasons, in effect asking audience members: which version of this story, of these characters, songs, and voices, do *you* remember? It may be a throwaway remark, but it serves to draw attention to the ways in which bio-musicals play with, modify, or mask an audience's sense of time and cultural memory through a dual temporality of the past brought to life in the present by performers who engage in an act of simulated hyperreality. As with ventriloquism or vocal drag, vocal simulation therefore creates an experience of hyperreal 'shattered fragments' with which someone may either reflectively consider the 'ruins' of the past or seek to gather shards and threads together in an act of restoration.[98]

Sonic archaeologist José van Dijck notes that musical 'memories are constructed through stories *of* and *about*' favourite or familiar songs, memories which will depend on the intensity of an individual audience member's familiarity with the songs and voices in performance.[99] While one particular function of bio-musicals in popular culture may be to enable the promulgation of collective memory, this memory will always be a composite—a plurality that invites, includes, and negotiates the spectral traces of a multitude of other voices in a way that dilutes or obscures a tangible sense of objective reality. For some audience members, their desire to restore memories through the experience of vocal simulation will be vivid; for others, familiarity with musical material or voices will be more recent and less tethered to a particular kind of nostalgic tendency.

The experience of hearing a familiar or favourite song in the present moment—when playing an album, a playlist online, when it suddenly comes on the radio, or when attending a bio-musical—enacts a temporal flux in the manner of ventriloquism in which 'the past and present' become 'mixed in an apparently timeless suspension.'[100] This suspension, and its negotiation of dual hyperrealities (from the past recorded voice and the present live performance), is what allows both tendencies of nostalgia to co-exist, interact, and generate the possibility of rediscovery for all audience members. Perhaps this is the 'full meaning' of nostalgia intended by Baudrillard. This understanding of nostalgic vocality therefore extends beyond, but includes, the acknowledged limitations of the way performers simulate the voices of others, engaging in a fragmentary interplay of a hyperreal past and a hyperreal present, individual and collective memory, and competing but complementary nostalgic tendencies to restore, reflect, and rediscover. How might this complex plurality of performance and experience be articulated?

The answer might again be found at the level of linguistics, and the shared etymology of *simultaneity* (temporal flux or suspension) and *simulate* (vocal imitation). Both words contain the Latin adverb *simul*, meaning 'at the same time'. In other words, bio-musicals exist in a vocal in-between, a liminal space which fosters 'multiple encodings' at once.[101] Connor's notion of 'mutilated time' intimated a destructive element to the experience—removing any sense of here-and-now or there-and-then in favour of the present foretelling the future through reference to the past. Yet, even though 'mutilated time' implies a sense of finality in its aural anachronism, ventriloquism also offers the possibility of nostalgic rediscovery. Likewise, Muñoz's idea of 'temporal flux' in vocal drag indicated an active flow between the past and the present, the 'original' and its 'copy', or the recorded voice and its live counterpart, offering a way to listen to these voices across and in-between time and space, even while the recorded 'original' was found to be illusory and already in a sense of flux. The destruction of temporal and spatial boundaries and the free negotiation between them may therefore seem to occur simultaneously. Memories of a recorded voice might dominate at points only to enter their own deconstruction in the frustrated staging of studio sessions; the immediacy of a 'tribute concert' in an extra-diegetic encore may thrill some audience members while mutilating the hyperreality of the theatrical frame and intensifying the expectation of 'sounding like' the 'original'; a featured song may be more closely associated with another artist in popular culture, inviting sonic spectres from elsewhere into the process.

To negotiate these levels in the voice, and the fluid configurations of reception, culture, memory, and the manufacture of nostalgia which includes elements of material replication in the visual realm, it would seem a new term is needed. Here, as elsewhere, I use the term *simuloquism* to articulate the plural 'junction point' of nostalgic vocality in the bio-musical (see Figure 5.6).[102] As a neologism, this term comprises the Latin *simul* and *loqui*—the latter of which encompasses various facets, including the interaction of the text and language of culture, song lyrics, and dialogue across time and space. Just as Tommy DeVito's rhetorical question at the end of *Jersey Boys* resonates on the level of cultural narrative and vocal similarity, it also embodies the irreducible complexity that combines vocal simulation and temporal duality as the basis for the bio-musical phenomenon as a trend in pop culture. Simuloquism encapsulates all these facets as they operate

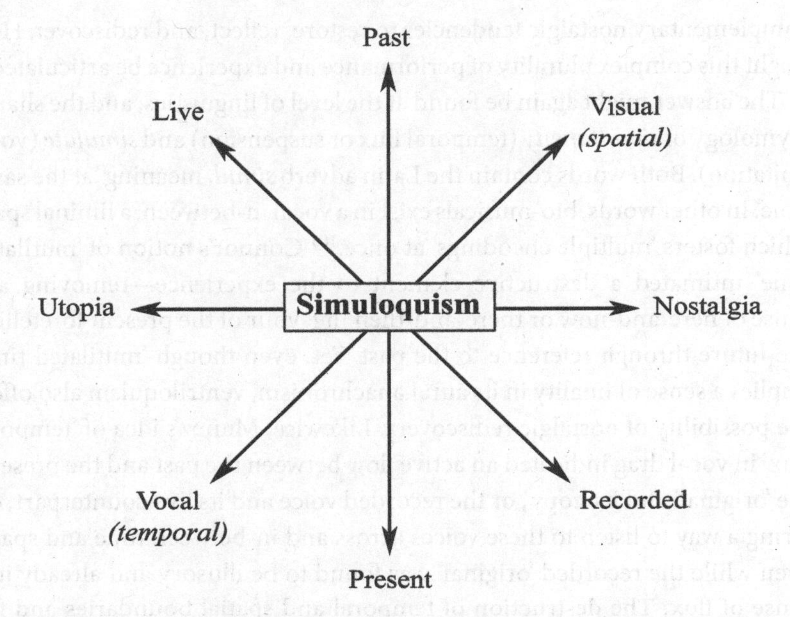

Figure 5.6 Conceptual and affective inputs which comprise 'simuloquism'. © Ben Macpherson.

metaphorically at the level of cultural memory and (con)text, and metonymically at the level of vocal similarity. It serves as a vocal index of cultural, nostalgic hyperreality, embracing bewilderment by negotiating and encoding an image of the 'original' through a shared knowledge that it is forever 'illusory', 'denatured', or absent.[103] Simuloquism is, therefore, a way to understand the 'full meaning' of nostalgic vocality as a means by which audience members might experience the past and the present, the 'original' and its simulation, as they are restored and reflected upon through a process of rediscovered nostalgia. Yet, simuloquism may also be a way to understand something else.

'If I could turn back time': *Simuloquism* and the Utopian Potential of Rediscovered Nostalgia

As noted above, Ricoeur defined nostalgia as the 'pathology' or origin of 'utopia'.[104] The tendency towards rediscovered nostalgia in the experience of bio-musicals must therefore suggest that simuloquism may even be the source, or origin, of utopian vocality. After all, as heard throughout this book, much like the absence of any original voice in bio-musical performances, utopia has not, does not, and can never, exist. It is only imagined, perhaps even remembered or (re)discovered in those moments that see characters burst into song.

Drawing on discussions of lipsynching and ventriloquism from voice studies, and developing these through notions of hyperreality and simulation, this chapter has considered bio-musical performances as they offer a space in which to negotiate notions of the past, the present, the future, the original, the simulation, and a dual experience of nostalgic rediscovery and utopic possibility. As the final neologism introduced in this book, simuloquism offers a way to listen across the multiple inputs at play in bio-musicals and helps to articulate the moment Boym's dual tendencies overlap, allowing for rediscovered nostalgia to point towards other possibilities through an engagement with the past. Because the 'retro' nature of many bio-musicals sees them theatricalizing voices that can be traced to a specific period of time, the concept of simuloquism may appear to have a limited application in analysing musical theatre voice at large. After all, when Jimmy told Frankie he loved her funny face (*Funny Face*, 1927), Tevye dreamt of being a rich man (*Fiddler on the Roof*, 1964), Chris asked God why (*Miss Saigon*, 1989), and Molina reflected on his skill as a window-dresser (*Kiss of the Spiderwoman*, 1992), none of the original performers—from Fred or Adele Astaire, Topol, Simon Bowman, or Brent Carver—was attempting to 'sound like' other people.

Yet, as part of the decadent appropriation by which we characterize musical theatre vocality, 'simuloquy' could be employed alongside other taxonomic categories such as the 'legit' voice, the Rock voice, or the Poperetta voice as a way of listening across voiceworlds which interact with, or acknowledge, a broader cultural familiarity beyond a particular musical.[105] While simuloquism has been developed through a focus on bio-musicals in this chapter, the term could be used as a way of re-evaluating the nostalgic and utopian potential of jukebox musicals more broadly. For example, what might be revealed through a close listening to the fictional input of a dramatic character that does not reference an external reality in the many 'artist catalogue' and 'era specific' productions that complement bio-musicals in this 'knockabout offshoot' of musical theatre?[106]

Extending beyond this sub-genre, simuloquism also offers a way to listen across the vocal indices of original productions and revivals as a means of evaluating their utopian potential through similarity and difference. For example, when Douglas Furber and Noel Gay's *Me and My Girl* was revised in London in 1985, much of its voiceworld was characterized by a clipped, affected delivery that 'aped' middle- and upper-class RP English accents heard on sound recordings from the 1930s—the time of its original production. In this and other instances, certain sounds, phrasing, and even the means of vocal production create a voiceworld that 'sounds like' another era in a way that extends beyond general stylistic traits. As such, the voiceworlds of many other musicals may be considered using the idea of simuloquy (or an application of its principles) to listen across vocal indices of pastiche and parody.

Likewise, the potential for simuloquism as an approach to listening across multiple iterations of the same song or character suggests that the tendency towards simulation inherent in the recreation of iconic vocality may also offer a glimpse of utopia. For example, in 2019, the Welsh tenor Michael Ball played Inspector Javert in a concert version of *Les Misérables* in London. Yet, the complexities inherent in this performance were multiple. The character of Javert had been played in earlier concert versions by Norm Lewis and Philip Quast. The role was originated in the West End by actor Roger Allam, alongside whom Ball had played the student Marius over three decades earlier. Given the multiple vocal inputs, whose voice was heard when Ball played Javert in 2019? Using Baudrillard's notion of simulacra, Susan Russell has elsewhere suggested that such voices become 'simulations of liveness' rather than live performances with an origin in the moment of embodied experience. Simuloquism, then, complements Russell's assertion while suggesting that even within the corporate, identikit, production practices of 'mass marketed and mass produced' musical theatre—first seen in the early twentieth century with producers such as George Edwardes, Charles Frohman, or Maurice Bandmann and epitomized in the late twentieth and early twenty-first centuries by Andrew Lloyd Webber, Cameron Mackintosh, and Disney—utopia may still be possible.[107]

Whether watching the lips like a hawk, hearing an uncanny resemblance, or experiencing the tensions between the spatial immediacy of a live performance and temporal flux as memories of other voices rush in, simuloquism offers a way of listening to the familiar in a range of circumstances or contexts. After all, rediscovering something already known to us may, in itself, be a moment in which we might remember 'how we need to'.

Conclusion
Keep Singing, Orpheus

The orchestra strikes up for the final moments as a scream rings out. Christine lay in Erik's arms, fatally wounded. The *dénouement* of *Love Never Dies* (2010) stands as a metonym for the utopian performative of voice in musical theatre—a gesture that remains fleeting and unfinished, but which nevertheless offers a glimpse of a 'potentially better future'.[1] After all, the Phantom *did* at least get to hear Christine sing once more before the dream was revealed as a phantasm in a manner analogous to the many illusions that became his stock-in-trade at the Opera Populaire and, latterly, Coney Island. As the best place never to have existed, musical theatre may sing utopia but, as heard through listening across voices and voiceworlds in this book, what this might mean is more complicated than the transparency, intensity, or escape suggested by Dyer.[2] While the idealism of Dyer's reasoning has provided a basis for consideration, the properties of utopian vocality are complex, complicated, and changeable. In Christine's death, it may also be possible to hear a confirmation that all utopian ideals end in disaster.

Yet, as Dolan has observed, utopia is only ever transient in performance, a mere 'index of the possible' rather than its realization.[3] Better, then, for the Phantom and the audience to have experienced a fleeting moment of 'impossible perfection' in an 'abstract utopia' than be left with only the disappointment of a material change that is never realized.[4] Perhaps, in the end, Christine and the Phantom were never really destined for anything other than this outcome. Beyond this bleak and seemingly nihilistic assertion, the erotic, dangerous, immediate, intimate, physical, familial, joyous, outsized, assertive, subversive, and politicized vocality of musical theatre nonetheless offers a richness and depth that is equally as compelling as the 'warbling voices' so prized in opera.[5] As such, it must be listened to on its own terms and not in relation to its older sibling. Borrowing from voice and sound studies, popular music studies, sociology, musicology, dramaturgy, the social sciences, narratology, linguistics, psychoanalysis, and ethnography, this book

Singing Utopia. Ben Macpherson, Oxford University Press. © Oxford University Press 2024.
DOI: 10.1093/9780197557679.003.0007

has attempted to develop a multidisciplinary approach to the study of voice in musical theatre, listening for the ways it may act as a utopian performative.

Introducing three neologisms, it proposed the following as a set of guiding principles for current and future analysis of voice in musical theatre—some of which, I hope, may also find application in other disciplinary areas such as dance, acting, dramaturgical analysis, and more.

1. Musical theatre vocality can be characterized by *decadent appropriation*.

In its musical parody, pastiche, and subsequent vocal inflections, *Love Never Dies* exhibits a rich plurality of vocal aesthetics, appropriated variously from operetta, vaudeville, early musical comedy, and even rock music. It builds on a tradition from the turn of the twentieth century, as musical comedy enacted a 'rupture' that allowed an exploration of the possible to be encoded in musical theatre vocality through the appropriation of styles from both high and low musical forms. As such, it has a richness and scope that extends beyond the ideological ossification of metaphysical aesthetics in opera.

This is more than a mere abundance of influences in a lush and romanticized 'poperetta' such as *Love Never Dies*. Drawing on tenets of stylistic plurality found in literary studies, popular music studies, and performance studies, the notion of 'decadent appropriation' proposed in chapter 2 enables us to listen across and understand the nature, function, and possibilities of the many vocal styles present across the whole history of musical theatre. In itself, such dynamic responsiveness may also be inherently utopian. This is because—just as musical styles have changed or shifted throughout the development of musical theatre—the nature of utopia is also apt to change. As Luke Martell observes, 'developments, intended or unforeseen, such as in technology or human nature' may alter the complexion of what is utopian.[6] Doing so, musical theatre encodes its voiceworlds with a complex, dynamic, and pluralistic blend of vernacular and highbrow styles, singing of ordinary people who, in moments of vulnerability, give voice to the pursuit of 'something better'.[7]

Since the 'rupture' enacted in early musical comedy, the popular musical stage has embraced stylistic developments which encompass opera, jazz, blues, gospel, pop, rock, punk, bluegrass, folk, country music, liturgical and cantorial song, hip hop, rap, and culturally specific vocal styles across the twentieth- and twenty-first centuries. In line with Martell's observation, not only is utopia a plural world 'to which alternatives are permitted', but the appropriation of so many styles is only possible through the embrace of sound technology.[8] Technology is therefore central to singing utopia and further offers a delineation with the aesthetic and performative properties of opera and operetta. It enabled the interrogation of race through Rock Voice in *Passing Strange*, 'recrafted' the metaphysicality of echo as a substance of material hope in *Floyd Collins*, and through visual representation allowed for an interrogation of the mismatch between the body that we see and the voice that hear in bio-musical performances. Amplification also facilitated the predominance of the Phantom's countertenor, influenced the aesthetic of crooning vulnerability in the case of Sky Masterson, and enabled Hamilton and his revolutionaries to be heard from the back row of the balcony as they rap their plans for American independence.

While utopian potential may be facilitated through such technology, the Phantom, Sky Masterson, and Hamilton in particular exhibit a further facet of decadence which may add to the sense of an exploration of the possible: resistance to the status quo through 'subversive opposition'. As part of the production of cultural meaning through musical theatre voices, this resistance exposes the dissimulation of established social structures through the uses of voice to critique the present in areas of 'taste, appearance, gender, sexuality, desire and behaviour', in a utopian act of exploring what might be possible.[9] This subversion was heard in the potential queering of the Phantom and the complex vocal character of Floyd Collins, through the overt presence of the countertenor voice for both, albeit appropriated from separate performance traditions (and in a manner that is heard differently to the pluralized 'vocalic body' of Orpheus' countertenor in *Hadestown*). Such challenges present an opportunity to further re-examine what the voices of other well-known musicals reveal about canonical characters, assumed identities, and, in doing so, what other explorations of the possible such an approach might yield.

In the case of Hamilton, Hill, Fagin, or the simple townsfolk who ventured into the woods, voices which exist somewhere between speech and song revealed that utopia—if reached—may be paradoxical, politicized, unwitting, unwilling, gendered, or even a disappointment. Yet, in the multifaceted intermediacy which gave voice to uncertainty, emotional fragility, deceit, insecurity, or a public persona which concealed the 'full self', this vocal aesthetic may also be characterized by its 'never finished [emotional] gestures': a 'utopian performative' which resists the very conventions of the form in which it functions.[10] Likewise, the 'vocally empty spaces' of Bobby and Marta were heard to be contradictory, giving voice to the dystopia of alienation and loneliness yet—like Hill and Hamilton—infused by possibilities beyond themselves.[11] In other words, while musical theatre voice might be heard as utopian in its desire to rupture and dream rather than reaffirm and dissimulate, such ruptures may also be imbricated with uncertainty, contradiction, or paradox. After all, utopia is never discrete or homogeneous.[12]

2. Musical theatre vocality can be understood as comprising two distinct 'in-between' spaces: the *macro*- and *micro-voiceworld*.

Chapter 2 also introduced the neologism 'voiceworld' as a way of describing the vocal properties and characteristics of specific musical productions.[13] While the term could be applied easily to a range of vocal or musical-theatrical practices, chapter 3 adapted it further to listen across various vocal groupings coherently. Understanding musical theatre to comprise two interrelated voiceworlds—a macro-voiceworld of choruses and ensemble, and a micro-voiceworld of small group and solo numbers, the chapter considered how these two worlds might be understood in relation to each other and ideals of utopian vocality.

Examining the macro-voiceworld of choruses and ensembles, Steven Connor's notion of 'choralities' offered a way of thinking more holistically about large group singing beyond the musicological definitions of a unified chorus or collaborative ensemble.[14] Drawing on various sociological theories of community, chapter 3 suggested that the macro-voiceworld of musical theatre is composed of three choralities: intentional, contingent, and liquid. Together, these might extend the ways in which the spectacle of multiple voices singing together is heard or understood in musical theatre. For example, while the spectacle of the chorus is paradigmatic of musical theatre in the popular imagination, and its utopian intensity, directness, energy, and emotional contagion have been considered at length, the concepts of 'intentional chorality' and 'liquid chorality' revealed a sense of the *dystopian* in *The Arcadians*, *Company*, and *Hadestown*.[15] Intentional chorality—in large chorus numbers—was heard as utopian in its aim while exclusionary in its manifestation, operating through the 'submergence of individual will' in pursuit of a monolithic ideal: hardly the hallmark of a utopia in which 'alternatives are permitted'.[16] This understanding may extend beyond the case studies here and offer a way of thinking about common readings of well-known musical choruses.

When the dancers sing 'One' in the finale of *A Chorus Line* (1975), the anonymity that results from their submerged uniformity and discipline undermines their personal success and the stories they tell through the show. In this sense, intentional chorality allows for a critical commentary about what it takes to achieve a dream, by consciously undermining its utopian characteristics. Likewise, liquid chorality gives voice to a macro-voiceworld that is fragmented, disillusioned, or ambivalent. It may not be as dystopian in its outlook as intentional chorality. Still, from Bobby's friends in *Company*, to 'Quintet' in *West Side Story* (1957), 'One Day More' in *Les Misérables* (1985), and 'Let's Have Lunch' in *Sunset Boulevard* (1993), it serves to frustrate through fragmentation, rather than submerge or exclude through discipline and expectation. Notwithstanding the revisionary potential of the foregoing choralities for how we listen to company numbers in other musicals, the presence of 'contingent chorality' offers a possibility of utopia through individual investment or acquiescence to the creation of a community. This can be heard at the races in *The Arcadians*, in the opening of *Hadestown*, and elsewhere: a plural space where 'alternatives are permitted'.[17]

Contingent chorality only functions because individuals facilitate its creation. Individual voices, then, are the primary means of singing utopia in musical theatre—not choruses or ensembles who perform a complex and often dystopian 'manifestation of community' in moments of apparent spectacle and intensity.[18] These individual voices are heard in the micro-voiceworld—from sextets to solo songs—encoding or negotiating everything from questions of gender, race, class, political views, and social standing, to affective qualities such as empathy and melancholy; emotions heard as utopian in *The Arcadians*, and which might likewise be identified in Tevye's 'If I Were a Rich Man' and 'Chaveleh (Little Bird)' (*Fiddler on the Roof*, 1964); Fosca's ballad 'Loving You' and Giorgio's response 'No One Has Ever Loved Me' (*Passion*, 1994); Mack's gentle rejection of Mabel, when he tells her 'I Won't Send Roses' (*Mack & Mabel*, 1974) or even 'Memory' (*Cats*, 1980). What, though, of musicals which only inhabit the micro-voiceworld as defined in this book? What might be revealed about individualism and utopian vocality in a close listening of *The Last Five Years* (2001), *Hedwig and the Angry Inch* (1998), or *Tell Me on a Sunday* (1982)? This is surely an area for future listening.

3. The concept of *simuloquism* offers a means of listening to nostalgic vocality, the counterpart of utopian vocality in musical theatre.

While intentional and liquid choralities, along with individual 'vocally empty spaces', may be shot through with dystopian ideals or disillusionment, and contingent choralities offer a glimpse of communal efforts towards something better, chapter 5 identified nostalgia as a 'counterpart' and pathology to utopia. Focussing on bio-musical performances, Svetlana Boym's tendencies of nostalgic vocality to restore or reflect the past were negotiated through the audio filters of vocal drag, ventriloquism, and Baudrillardian hyperreal simulation. As such, the concept of simuloquism was developed as a way to understand the nostalgic properties of voices that 'sound like' someone else.

Suggesting that the space or overlap between restorative nostalgia and reflective nostalgia offers the possibility of re-discovery, simuloquism offers a way to rediscover voices from the past in new ways. As such, simuloquy might be used alongside other vocal categories when discussing musical theatre voices in a way that complements those from the world of opera. For example, the simuloquial voice could form part of a lexicon that includes the 'legit' voice, the Rock Voice, or the belt voice, alongside others that have been coined or developed in recent discussions of musical theatre vocal taxonomies or categories.[19] In addition to the other approaches developed in this book, it also provides a means to articulate the complexities and contradictions that arise when listening to a familiar voice, even when we know it is *not* the voice we remember. This familiarity may be an external reference point (as Adrienne Warren looks like and 'sounds like' Tina Turner), or it may be due to the phonic palimpsests of one performer inhabiting a role familiar to audience members or who is in some way iconic. When, in 2018, Patti LuPone performed 'Ladies Who Lunch' in the *Company* revival at the Gielgud Theatre in London, to what extent did she open her mouth only to find that Elaine Stritch or Barbara Walsh could be heard?

In addition, while simuloquism was applied here to bio-musicals, how might it be applied to listen across the negotiations of utopia or nostalgia (or even dystopia) when real people are given fictional singing voices and original melodies? What nostalgic or utopian potential can be heard when Elaine Paige sang as Eva Perón in *Evita* (1978)? Is there an ethical dimension in such instances that forces a reconsideration of what world might be imagined, such as when Jeanna de Waal gave voice to Princess Diana in *Diana: The*

Musical (2019)? Beyond the scope of musical theatre, such questions suggest that simuloquism might also be applied in theatre, television, and film studies to consider the complex aesthetics or cultural reception of Michael Sheen's David Frost in the play *Frost/Nixon* (2006) or Meryl Streep's vocal embodiment of Margaret Thatcher in *The Iron Lady* (2011). To what extent do these voices negotiate facets of nostalgia and, therefore, to what extent might they even be considered as utopian?

From decadent appropriation, through the voiceworlds, choralities, and complexities of utopian, dystopian, and nostalgic vocalities, what kind of voice is *this*? Musical theatre may indeed sing utopia, but as has been revealed in listening across 130 years of musical theatre voice, it does so by negotiating the 'multiple encodings', paradoxes, contradictions, and possibilities given voice in moments of vulnerability, intensity, melancholy, empathy, or nostalgia.[20]

This book has offered several new approaches and neologisms, while nonetheless raising, or leaving open, many questions about voice in musical theatre and its utopian potential. For example, while suggesting that simuloquy might be a way to consider vocal ghosting in revivals or long-running productions, *Singing Utopia* has not explicitly considered the production of cultural meanings elicited through pastiche and parody as political performance practices, such as those which characterize the voiceworlds of *Little Mary Sunshine* (1959) and *Spamalot* (2004). Elsewhere, the use of 'Blacksound' has enabled a close listening to the influence of African and African American vocal styles in musical theatre, exposing some of the politicized and paradoxical discourses around race, appropriation, and utopia. In the case of Sam Levene's Nathan Detroit and Ron Moody's Fagin, Jewish vocal influences have also been heard, while indigenous vocalities were silenced in the voiceworlds of *Floyd Collins* and *Oklahoma!* What, though, of other cultures and vocal styles not covered in this book? For example, from *South Pacific* (1949), *The King and I* (1951), *Flower Drum Song* (1958), and *Miss Saigon* (1989) to *Pacific Overtures* (1976), *Allegiance* (2012), and *Soft Power* (2018), how might we listen to the political, cultural, and personal identities of Asian or Asian American characters through the voices that sing—or stereotype—them?[21] What utopias (or otherwise) might be heard? Listening across such works, 'Blacksound' would be an inexact methodology, so what other approaches could be taken?

Further, while moments of a cappella voice have been featured or mentioned in several case studies, what about characters who are featured but do not sing at all (Zach in *A Chorus Line*, or all adults in *Spring Awakening* [2008])? The relationship between real life and theatricalized representation was heard to be complex and compelling in the voices of bio-musicals, but where does that leave moments of verbatim vocality heard in *Oh What a Lovely War!* (1963) or *London Road* (2011)? Finally, how are we to understand the differences in utopian vocality between stage and screen performances? How might changes between overdubbing or ghost singing (Marni Nixon or Bill Lee) and live recordings (such as Eddie Redmayne in *Les Misérables* [2012]) affect what is encoded, what is heard, or what possibilities are explored? In any case, how are we to account for the 'blended vocals' of Elvis Presley and Austin Butler in Baz Luhrmann's *Elvis* (2022)?

Such questions demonstrate the breadth and possibility for further listening across stage, screen, and song, to hear what else might be revealed in the plural and provocative space of musical theatre voice. Yet, in *Singing Utopia*, I hope to have proposed a way to listen to the utopian performative of musical theatre voice. It is, after all, romantic, erotic, dangerous, immediate, intimate, physical, familial, joyous, outsized, assertive, subversive, politicized, vulnerable, energetic, empathetic, melancholy, intentional, contingent, liquid, resistant, nostalgic, utopian, and above all, absolutely thrilling. From spectacular choralities shot through with contradictions to soaring solo voices that push through to 'something better', musical theatre voiceworlds sing not-yet-finished glimpses that are full of contradictions and vulnerabilities, of the anxiety of being human, and what it means to raise our voices in the hope of what might be possible.[22] As Orpheus once said to Eurydice, the song is not yet finished, but when it is, the world will come back into tune.

Keep singing, Orpheus.

Author's Note

Under section 107 of the US Copyright Act 1976, allowance is made for 'fair use' for purposes such as criticism, comment, news reporting, teaching, scholarship, education, and research. Fair use is a use permitted by copyright statute that might otherwise be infringing. Every effort has therefore been made to keep citations or quotes from creative works to a minimum in order to fulfil the purposes of research and education. Full attribution has been given to each creative work used in recognition of their authorship.

Notes

Introduction

1. Throughout this book, where dates are cited in parenthesis, these refer to the date of the first production, in either London or New York.
2. For general reading of this sort, see examples including Joan Melton, ed., *Singing in Musical Theatre: The Training of Actors and Singers* (New York: Allworth Press, 2007); Paul Harvard, *Acting through Song: Techniques and Exercises for Musical Theatre Performers* (London: Nick Hern Books, 2013); Stephen Purdy, *Musical Theatre Song* (New York: Bloomsbury, 2016); Gillyanne Kayes, *Singing and the Actor* (London: Nick Hern Books, 2004).
3. Millie Taylor, ed., '"If I Sing": Voice and Excess', *Studies in Musical Theatre* 6, no. 1 (2012); Jake Johnson, *Mormons, Musical Theater, and Belonging in America* (Urbana: University of Illinois Press, 2019); Bruce Earnest, 'Male Belting: An Exploration of Technique and Style from 1967 to Current' (DMA diss., University of Southern Mississippi, 2018), https://aquila.usm.edu/cgi/viewcontent.cgi?article=2587&context=dissertations; Katrina Margaret Hunt, 'The Female Voice in American Musical Theater (1940–1955): Mary Martin and the Development of Integrated Vocal Style' (Doctoral thesis, Australian National University, 2016), https://openresearch-repository.anu.edu.au/handle/1885/101933; Colleen Ann Jennings, 'Belting Is Beautiful: Welcoming the Musical Theater Singer into the Classical Voice Studio' (DMA thesis, University of Iowa, 2014), https://ir.uiowa.edu/cgi/viewcontent.cgi?article=5379&context=etd.
4. Considering the character of Glinda in *Wicked*, Wolf understands the switching between soprano and mezzo vocal registers as an index of bisexuality in *Changed for Good: A Feminist History of the Broadway Musical* (New York: Oxford University Press, 2011). Morris and Knapp consider vocal style and register in terms of performance practice, in 'Singing', in *The Oxford Handbook of the American Musical*, ed. Raymond Knapp, Mitchell Morris, and Stacy Wolf (New York: Oxford University Press, 2011), 320–35.
5. For Taylor's chapter, 'Encoding the Voice', see *Musical Theatre, Realism and Entertainment*, Ashgate Interdisciplinary Studies in Opera (Farnham: Ashgate, 2012), 33–55. See also Jake Johnson, 'Building the Broadway Voice', in *The Oxford Handbook of Voice Studies*, ed. Nina Sue Eidsheim and Katherine Meizel (New York: Oxford University Press, 2019), 475–92; and Dominic Symonds, 'Capturing the "Sung" to Make It "Song"', in *Gestures of Music Theater: The Performativity of Song and Dance*, ed. Dominic Symonds and Millie Taylor (New York: Oxford University Press, 2014), 9–21.
6. Stacy Wolf, 'Introduction', in *The Oxford Handbook to the American Musical*, ed. Raymond Knapp, Mitchell Morris, and Stacy Wolf (New York: Oxford University Press, 2011), 3.
7. See Oliver Double, 'Introduction: What Is Popular Performance?', in *Popular Performance*, ed. Adam Ainsworth, Oliver Double, and Louise Peacock (London: Bloomsbury Methuen, 2017), 1–29.
8. David Savran, 'Toward a Historiography of the Popular', *Theatre Survey* 45, no. 2 (2004): 213–15.
9. Virginia Woolf, 'Middlebrow', in *The Death of the Moth, and Other Essays* (London: Hogarth Press Ltd, 1942), 176–87.
10. For one particularly complex example of genre indeterminacy in this regard, see David Horn, 'Who Loves You Porgy? The Debates Surrounding Gershwin's Musical', in *Approaches to the American Musical*, ed. Robert Lawson-Peebles (Exeter: University of Exeter Press, 1996), 109–26.
11. Wolf, 'Introduction', 3; *The Empty Space*, Modern Classics (London: Penguin, 2008), 76–77. For a further discussion of Brook's 'Rough Theatre' and contemporary discussions of popular performance, see Double et al., 'Introduction: What Is Popular Performance?'.
12. Konstantinos Thomaidis, *Theatre and Voice* (Basingstoke: Palgrave, 2017), 11.
13. Key theoretical tenets from this body of work are then transposed into the realm of theatre, music, and performance studies. Such transposition is not unusual or new, giving evidence of

the interdisciplinary nature of the theatrical arts, but it is nonetheless worthy of note when so much theatrical endeavour depends upon the use of voice as a medium or apparatus.

14. Adriana Cavarero, *For More than One Voice: A Philosophy of Vocal Expression* (Stanford, CA: University of Stanford Press, 2005); Jacques Derrida, *Of Grammatology*, trans. Gayatri Chakravorty Spivak (Baltimore: Johns Hopkins University Press, 1997); Jacques Derrida, *Voice and Phenomenon: Introduction to the Problem of the Sign in Husserl's Phenomenology*, trans. Leonard Lawlor (Evanston, IL: Northwestern University Press, 2010).
15. Roland Barthes, 'The Grain of the Voice', in *Image, Music, Text*, trans. Stephen Heath (London: Fontana, 1977), 179–89; Roland Barthes, 'The Death of the Author', in *Image, Music, Text*, trans. Stephen Heath (London: Fontana, 1977), 142–48; Mladen Dolar, *A Voice and Nothing More*, Short Circuits (Cambridge, MA: MIT Press, 2006); Steven Connor, 'Voice, Ventriloquism and the Vocalic Body', in *Psychoanalysis and Performance*, ed. Patrick Campbell and Adrian Kear (London: Routledge, 2000), 75–93; Steven Connor, *Dumbstruck: A Cultural History of Ventriloquism* (London: Oxford University Press, 2001); Michel Chion, *The Voice in Cinema*, trans. Claudia Gorbman (New York: Columbia University Press, 1999); Jennifer Fleeger, *Mismatched Women: The Siren's Song through the Machine* (New York: Oxford University Press, 2014); Brian Kane, *Sound Unseen: Acousmatic Sound in Theory and Practice* (New York: Oxford University Press, 2014).
16. Konstantinos Thomaidis and Ben Macpherson, 'Introduction: Voice(s) as a Method and an In-between', in *Voice Studies: Critical Approaches to Process, Performance and Experience*, ed. Konstantinos Thomaidis and Ben Macpherson (Oxford: Routledge, 2015), 4. In fact, we might locate a consolidated 'vocal turn' in scholarship to the year 2015; a few months after *Voice Studies* was published, Duke University Press also published Nina Sun Eidsheim's *Sensing Sound: Singing and Listening as Vibrational Practice* (Durham, NC: Duke University Press, 2015).
17. Simon Frith, 'The Voice as a Musical Instrument', in *Music, Words and Voice: A Reader*, ed. Martin Clayton (Manchester: Manchester University Press, 2008), 68. For a similar sense of vocal layers, see Edward Cone, 'Song and Performance', in *Music, Words and Voice: A Reader*, ed. Martin Clayton (Manchester: Manchester University Press, 2008), 230–41.
18. Mary Ann Smart, ed., *Siren Songs: Representations of Gender and Sexuality in Opera* (Princeton, NJ: Princeton University Press, 2000); Catherine Clément, *Opera, or the Undoing of Women* (London: Virago, 1989); Carolyn Abbate, *In Search of Opera* (Princeton, NJ: Princeton University Press, 2001); Carolyn Abbate, *Unsung Opera: Opera and Musical Narrative in the Nineteenth Century* (Princeton, NJ: Princeton University Press, 1991); Wayne Koestenbaum, *Queen's Throat: Opera, Homosexuality and the Mystery of Desire* (New York: Da Capo, 2001); Michel Poizat, *The Angel's Cry: Beyond the Pleasure Principle in Opera*, trans. Arthur Denner (Ithaca, NY: Cornell University Press, 1992); Gary Tomlinson, *Metaphysical Song: An Essay in Opera* (Princeton, NJ: Princeton University Press, 1999).
19. Thomaidis and Macpherson, 'Introduction: Voice(s) as a Method and an In-between', 4.
20. Scott McMillin, *The Musical as Drama* (Ithaca, NY: Cornell University Press, 2006); Carey Wall, 'There's No Business Like Show Business: A Speculative Reading of the Broadway Musical', in *Approaches to the American Musical*, ed. Robert Lawson-Peebles (Exeter: University of Exeter Press, 1996), 30–31. For a critique of McMillin's binary reading of the way 'book time' and 'lyric time' operate in performance, see Matthew Lockitt, '"Love, Let Me Sing You": The Liminality of Song and Dance in LaChiusa's "Bernarda Alba" (2006)', in *Gestures of Music Theater: The Performativity of Song and Dance*, ed. Dominic Symonds and Millie Taylor (New York: Oxford University Press, 2014), 91–108.
21. Jake Johnson et al., 'Divided by a Common Language: Musical Theater and Popular Music Studies', *Journal of Popular Music Studies* 31, no. 4 (2019): 36, https://doi.org/10.1525/jpms.2019.31.4.32.
22. Richard Dyer, 'Entertainment and Utopia', in *The Cultural Studies Reader*, ed. Simon During (London: Routledge, 1993), 273. Dyer's use of the terms 'intensity', 'energy', and 'directness' are foundational to this discussion, and I use them within the lexicon of this book without direct attribution each time from this point. This is for the clarity of reading and matters of length. In each case, however, their application relates directly to Dyer's discussion in his essay.
23. The energy and directness of song and dance in musical theatre is, of course, not the sum total of utopia in theatrical performance. For example, Siân Adiseshiah's book *Utopian Drama: In Search of a Genre* (London: Bloomsbury, 2022) offers a rigorous consideration of utopianism in Western drama from antiquity to the present day.

24. Dyer, 'Entertainment and Utopia', 271–83.
25. McMillin, *The Musical as Drama*, 141, 149.
26. Dyer, 'Entertainment and Utopia', 273. The complex relationship between text, structure, affect, and the production of utopia in musical film is also explored in Katy Jayasuriya in 'Femininity and Utopia in MGM's Adaptation of Sally Benson's "Meet Me in St. Louis"', *Studies in Musical Theatre* 18, no. 1 (2024): 21–35, https://doi.org/10.1386/smt_00147_1.
27. Jill Dolan, *Utopia in Performance: Finding Hope at the Theater* (Ann Arbor: University of Michigan Press, 2005), 13–14, 8; Dyer, 'Entertainment and Utopia', 273.
28. Ernst Bloch, *The Principle of Hope* (Oxford: Basil Blackwell, 1986). In his seminal utopian work, Bloch contrasts *abstract* utopias with *concrete* utopias—ones which thrive of a tangible hope of future change. For a development of this contrast and a consideration of this from the perspective of Marxist social ideals, see Ruth Levitas, *The Concept of Utopia* (Hertfordshire: Philip Allan, 1990).
29. Dolan, *Utopia in Performance*, 13–14, 8; Dyer, 'Entertainment and Utopia', 273.
30. Salomé Voegelin, *Sonic Possible Worlds: Hearing the Continuum of Sound* (London: Bloomsbury, 2014).
31. Thomaidis and Macpherson, 'Voice(s) as a Method and an in-Between', 4.
32. Plato, *Republic*, trans. John Llewelyn Davies and David James Vaughan (Hertfordshire: Wordsworth Editions, 1997); Thomas More, 'Utopia', in *Three Early Modern Utopias*, ed. Susan Bruce (New York: Oxford University Press, 1999), 1–148.
33. Edward Rothstein, 'Utopia and Its Discontents', in *Visions of Utopia*, ed. Furaha D. Norton (New York: Oxford University Press, 2003), 3.
34. Dolan, *Utopia in Performance*, 2.
35. Krishan Kumar, *Utopianism* (Milton Keynes: Open University Press, 1991), 77; Lyman Tower Sargent, *Utopianism: A Very Short Introduction* (New York: Oxford University Press, 2010), 21. As demonstrated by the geo-political purview of this book, along with being inherently human, utopian thought is also a tradition of writing and discourse peculiar to the Western world in its prevalence, traditions, and ideas. See Kumar, *Utopianism*, 33.
36. Rothstein, 'Utopia and Its Discontents', 16.
37. Kumar, *Utopianism*, 84.
38. Rothstein, 'Utopia and Its Discontents', 16.
39. Dyer, 'Entertainment and Utopia', 273.
40. Sargent, *Utopianism*, 21.
41. Luke Martell, 'Utopianism and Social Change: Materialism, Conflict and Pluralism', *Capital and Class* 42, no. 3 (2018): 446, https://doi.org/10.1177/0309816818759230.
42. Martell, 'Utopianism and Social Change', 448, 447.
43. Dyer, 'Entertainment and Utopia', 271–83.
44. Martell, 'Utopianism and Social Change', 447.
45. Dyer, 'Entertainment and Utopia', 273.
46. Dyer, 'Entertainment and Utopia', 273.
47. Konstantinos Thomaidis, 'Editorial: Listening Across', *Journal of Interdisciplinary Voice Studies* 4, no. 1 (2019): 3–6. From this point, I will proceed to use the term 'listening across' within the lexicon of this book without direct attribution each time, for the purposes of clarity and length. Nonetheless, I hope this is a sufficient attribution of its source.
48. Thomaidis, *Theatre and Voice*, 72–73. For a parallel (if somewhat more broadly articulated) consideration of a similar position, see Nina Sun Eidsheim, *The Race of Sound: Listening, Timbre, and Vocality in African American Music* (Durham, NC: Duke University Press, 2019).
49. Salome Voegelin, *The Political Possibility of Sound: Fragments of Listening* (New York: Bloomsbury, 2018), 155–56.
50. For Steven Mithen, the notion that melodic sound was a pre-historic means of communication that preceded the development of language among humans has anthropological significance, echoing philosophical themes developed in the philosophy of Maurice Merleau-Ponty. Irrespective of its accuracy, this idea nonetheless demonstrates the universal human imperative to communicate through sound and tone. See *The Singing Neanderthals: The Origins of Music, Language, Mind and Body* (Cambridge, MA: Harvard University Press, 2005).
51. Eidsheim, *The Race of Sound*, 1, 11.
52. Jennifer Lynn Stoever, *The Sonic Color Line: Race and the Cultural Politics of Listening* (New York: New York University Press, 2016), 11.

53. Matthew D. Morrison, 'Race, Blacksound, and the (Re)Making of Musicological Discourse', *Journal of the American Musicological Society* 72, no. 3 (2019): 783, https://doi.org/10.1525/jams.2019.72.3.781.
54. Stoever, *The Sonic Color Line*, 15.
55. Morrison, 'Race, Blacksound, and the (Re)Making of Musicological Discourse', 783.
56. Paul Ricoeur, 'The Creativity of Language', in *Dialogues with Contemporary Continental Thinkers: The Phenomenological Heritage*, ed. Richard Kearney (Manchester: Manchester University Press, 1984), 29; Martell, 'Utopianism and Social Change', 448, 447. As with Thomaidis's term 'listening across', Ricoeur's concept of utopianism as an 'exploration of the possible' will be employed throughout this discussion without constant reattribution.
57. Bethany Hughes, 'Singing the Community: The Musical Theater Chorus as Character', in *Gestures of Music Theater: The Performativity of Song and Dance*, ed. Dominic Symonds and Millie Taylor (New York: Oxford University Press, 2014), 263.
58. Dyer, 'Entertainment and Utopia', 273.
59. Malcolm Chase and Christopher Shaw, *The Imagined Past: History and Nostalgia* (Manchester: Manchester University Press, 1989), 3, 9.

Chapter 1

1. Pietro Bardi, 'Pietro Bardi on the Birth of Opera', in *Opera: A History in Documents*, ed. Piero Weiss (New York: Oxford University Press, 2002), 8–10.
2. It has to be acknowledged that while such differences persist, access and affordability are changing inversely in recent years. Broadway and West End ticket prices have increased markedly in the last two decades, while the advent of live-streaming to cinemas, such as 'The Metropolitan Opera: Live in HD' series (which began in 2006), has allowed opera to reach new audiences at affordable prices.
3. In common with several opera scholars, I use the term 'operatic voice' here as a point of reference, while acknowledging the limitations of its use. Aside from closing down four centuries of practice to one singular idea, Michal Grover-Friedlander notes that developments in other musical-dramatic forms, along with artistic changes relating to 'other signifying systems (text, scenery, etc.)', demonstrate the insufficiency of the term as a synecdoche of opera more broadly (Michal Grover-Friedlander, 'Voice', in *The Oxford Handbook of Opera*, ed. Helen M. Greenwald [New York: Oxford University Press, 2014], 318–19). For a complementary discussion, see Lawrence Kramer, 'The Voice of/in Opera', in *On Voice*, (Leiden: Brill, 2014), 43–55. While using 'operatic voice' to establish the terms of reference on which the rest of this discussion operates, the phrase is limited in its application through the rest of this book. Where it does appear, it is through direct citation or in a way that acknowledges its insufficiency.
4. Carolyn Abbate and Roger Parker, *A History of Opera: The Last Four Hundred Years* (London: Penguin Books, 2012), 25; Scott McMillin, *The Musical as Drama* (Ithaca, NY: Cornell University Press, 2006). A similar consideration of aesthetic and generic similarity and difference could also be considered with regard to divergent understandings of opera, musical theatre, and 'music theatre' (sometimes called 'composed theatre' or 'new music theatre'). As a genre, music theatre often approaches text, score, movement, language, duration, and audience engagement in ways which challenge the conventions of traditional performance modes. Rooted in the historical avant-garde, works ranging from Arnold Schoenberg's *Pierrot Lunaire* (1912) to Robert Wilson's and Philip Glass's *Einstein on the Beach* (1976) and Michael Thalheimer's *Die Wildente* (2008) may all be considered works of 'music theatre'. Such work, however, often includes varieties of text, music, and movement in musical and theatrical performance. While exceeding the scope of this book, it is nonetheless worth noting the complexities in segregating genres in this way.
5. Grover-Friedlander, 'Voice', 318–19. It is perhaps telling that in considering the way character is written in opera, Carolyn Abbate and Roger Parker also distinguish between *plot-character* and *voice-character* (rather than 'musical' or 'melodic character') in their analysis (Abbate and Parker, *A History of Opera*, 15.)
6. For a scientific exploration of the differences in vocal demand between opera and musical theatre singing, see Eva Björkner, 'Why So Different?—Aspects of Voice Characteristics in Operatic and Musical Theatre Singing' (Stockholm, Sweden, KTH School of Computer Science and Communication, 2006), http://www.diva-portal.org/smash/get/diva2:11182/FULLTEXT01.pdf; Kramer, 'The Voice of/in Opera', 43.
7. Ana Flavia Zuim, 'Speech Inflection in American Musical Theatre Compositions' (PhD diss., Florida Atlantic University, 2012); Tracy Bourne, Maeve Garnier, and Diana Kenny,

'Music Theater Voice: Production, Physiology and Pedagogy', *Journal of Singing* 67, no. 4 (2011): 437–44.

8. Tom Vallance, 'Celeste Holm: Oscar-Winning Actress Best Known for "All About Eve" and "High Society"', *The Independent* online, 16 July 2012, https://www.independent.co.uk/news/obituaries/celeste-holm-oscarwinning-actress-best-known-for-all-about-eve-and-high-society-7946744.html.
9. John Potter and Neil Sorrell, *A History of Singing* (Cambridge: Cambridge University Press, 2014), 245.
10. Potter and Sorrell, *A History of Singing*, 242. This was the case until the age of electronic amplification on Broadway, which some sources suggest became nascent in live performance in 1937 with *The Wookie* (see Harold C. Schonberg, 'Stage View: The Surrender of Broadway to Amplified Sound', *New York Times*, 15 March 1981).
11. Bourne, Garnier, and Kenny, 'Music Theater Voice', 438.
12. In an interview with Elliot Norton on the 'Elliot Norton Reviews', Merman recalled Gershwin's words to her in paraphrase. 'Elliot Norton Interview with Ethel Merman', *Elliot Norton Reviews* (Boston: WGBH, 1976), Alexander Street Collection, Sound and Moving Image Collection.
13. Colleen Ann Jennings, 'Belting Is Beautiful: Welcoming the Musical Theater Singer into the Classical Voice Studio' (DMA thesis, University of Iowa, 2014), https://ir.uiowa.edu/cgi/viewcontent.cgi?article=5379&context=etd, 4.
14. LoVetri in Melton, *Singing in Musical Theatre: The Training of Actors and Singers* (New York: Allworth Press, 2007), 48.
15. Ricoeur, 'The Creativity of Language', 29.
16. Ricoeur, 'The Creativity of Language', 29.
17. Paul Ricoeur, *Lectures on Ideology and Utopia*, ed. George H. Taylor (New York: Columbia University Press, 1986), 17. Given that musical theatre began to develop in the 1890s, the operatic practices considered in this book are therefore centred on the nineteenth century and informed by historical discussion from the preceding three centuries. Because of this, the work of more modern composers such as Alban Berg or Karl Stockhausen fall outside the bounds of this study.
18. Claude V. Palisca, *The Florentine Camerata: Documentary Studies and Translations* (New Haven, CT: Yale University Press, 1989), 3, 5.
19. B. Zelechow, 'The Opera: The Meeting of Popular and Elite Culture in the Nineteenth Century', *History of European Ideas* 16 (1993): 101.
20. Ricoeur, 'The Creativity of Language', 29.
21. Abbate and Parker, *A History of Opera*, 44.
22. Zelechow, 'The Opera', 261; H. Raynor, *A Social History of Music: From the Middle Ages to Beethoven* (London: Barrie and Jenkins, 1972), 171.
23. Abbate and Parker, *A History of Opera*, 39; Tim Carter, 'What Is Opera?', in *The Oxford Handbook of Opera*, ed. Helen M. Greenwald (New York: Oxford University Press, 2015), 17.
24. Abbate and Parker, *A History of Opera*, 40.
25. Chris Balme, 'The Bandmann Circuit: Theatrical Networks in the First Age of Globalization', *Theatre Research International* 40, no. 1 (2015): 19–36.
26. Daniel Snowman, *The Gilded Stage: A Social History of Opera* (London: Atlantic Books, 2009), 203–5.
27. For a more detailed discussion of this history, see Ben Macpherson, *Cultural Identity in British Musical Theatre 1890–1939: Knowing One's Place* (Basingstoke: Palgrave, 2018).
28. While not exact in their correspondence, these terms echoed ideas from English essayist Matthew Arnold's 1869 work *Culture and Anarchy*, in which he distinguished between the 'Barbarians' (elite), 'Philistines' (broad middle-class), and 'Populace' (mass lower class) in terms of cultural strata. See Matthew Arnold, *Culture and Anarchy* (Oxford: Oxford University Press, 2009). For an exhaustive and incisive discussion of this cultural stratification on opera, see Lawrence W. Levine, *Highbrow-Lowbrow: The Emergence of Cultural Hierarchy in America* (Cambridge, MA: Harvard University Press, 1990).
29. Eric Hobsbawn and Terence Ranger, eds., *The Invention of Tradition* (Cambridge: Cambridge University Press, 2012).
30. John Sullivan Dwight (1870) cited in Levine, *Highbrow-Lowbrow*, 200.
31. Bruce A. McConachie, 'New York Operagoing, 1825–50: Creating an Elite Social Ritual', *American Music* 6 (1988): 182.
32. Zelechow, 'The Opera', 262; Levine, *Highbrow-Lowbrow*, 98, 101.

33. John Storey, '"Expecting Rain": Opera as Popular Culture?', in *High-Pop: Making Culture into Popular Entertainment*, ed. J. Collins (Malden, MA: Blackwell, 2002), 33–34. The new opera houses became 'monuments to the institution of opera', designed to reinforce its peculiar status in culture (Dominic Symonds and Pamela Karantonis, 'Introduction: Empty Houses, Booming Voices', in *The Legacy of Opera: Reading Music Theatre as Experience and Performance*, ed. Dominic Symonds and Pamela Karantonis [Amsterdam: Rodopi, 2011], 11).
34. Slavoj Žižek and Mladen Dolar, *Opera's Second Death* (New York: Routledge, 2001), 3; Symonds and Karantonis, 'Introduction: Empty Houses, Booming Voices', 13; see also Abbate and Parker, *A History of Opera*, 44.
35. Ricoeur, *Lectures on Ideology and Utopia*, 23–26; Storey, '"Expecting Rain"', 37; Symonds and Karantonis, 'Introduction', 12.
36. David Cannadine, *Ornamentalism: How the British Saw Their Empire* (London: Penguin, 2001), 122.
37. Jennifer Hall-Witt, *Fashionable Acts: Opera and Elite Culture in London, 1780–1880* (Lebanon, NH: University of New Hampshire Press, 2007), 3.
38. The very name—Royal *Italian* Opera—reflected Victoria's keen interest but also highlighted an ongoing tension in broader nineteenth-century British culture between the dominance of continental repertoire from Italy, Germany, and France and the native form of English lyric opera that Paul Rodmell suggests struggled to gain traction at Covent Garden or in the West End while nevertheless playing a significant role in the regions (*Opera in the British Isles, 1875–1918* [Farnham: Ashgate, 2013]).
39. Hermann Klein, *The Golden Age of Opera* (London: G. Routledge and Sons, 1933), xiii.
40. See the introduction and chapter 1 in Macpherson, *Cultural Identity in British Musical Theatre*.
41. Hall-Witt, *Fashionable Acts*.
42. Rodmell, *Opera in the British Isles, 1875–1918*, 5.
43. Paul Ricoeur, 'Ideology and Utopia as Cultural Imagination', *Philosophic Exchange* 7, no. 1 (1976): 23–26; Ricoeur, 'The Creativity of Language', 17.
44. Jacopo Peri, 'Peri's Dedication of the Score and Letter to the Reader', in *Opera: A History in Documents*, ed. Piero Weiss (New York: Oxford University Press, 2002), 15.
45. The term *stile rappresentativo* was used by Peri, while other variations relating to vocal utterance heightened from ordinary speech included *recitar cantando*, *stile monodico*, *stile detto narrativo*, *stile detto expressivo*, and later, *secco recitativo* (or 'simple recitative') which was melodically rudimentary, with a fixed time signature but great freedom of expression to enable conversations between characters. While the complexities of recitative have already been much discussed elsewhere, the nature of 'intermediate' vocality in musical theatre is considered in depth in chapter 4. For a brief overview of recitative, see F. W. Sternfeld, 'A Note on "Stile Recitativo"', *Proceedings of the Royal Musical Association* 110 (1983): 41–44.
46. By 1783, Peri's 'opinion of many' on this subject had even become received wisdom, with Thomas Iriarte's history of music authoritatively stating that opera was invented in ancient Greece and revived in Italy in 1600.
47. Tomlinson, *Metaphysical Song*, 28, 10.
48. Ficino in Tomlinson, *Metaphysical Song*, 11–12.
49. Abbate and Parker, *A History of Opera*, 46; Tomlinson, *Metaphysical Song*, ix.
50. Tomlinson, *Metaphysical Song*, 4.
51. Abbate and Parker, *A History of Opera*, 8.
52. René Descartes, 'Meditations on First Philosophy', in *Descartes: Key Philosophical Writings*, ed. Enrique Chavez-Arvizo (London: Wordsworth Editions, 1997), 143.
53. René Descartes et al., 'The Passions of the Soul', in *Descartes: Key Philosophical Writings* (London: Wordsworth Editions, 1997), 362.
54. In Tomlinson, *Metaphysical Song*, 34.
55. Charles de Saint-Évremond, 'Saint-Évremond's Views on Opera', in *Opera: A History in Documents*, ed. Piero Weiss (New York: Oxford University Press, 2002), 53.
56. Tomlinson, *Metaphysical Song*, 41.
57. Jairo Moreno, *Musical Representations, Subjects, and Objects: The Construction of Musical Thought in Zarlino, Descartes, Rameau, and Weber* (Bloomington: Indiana University Press, 2004), 57.
58. Abbate, *Unsung Opera*, 6.
59. Abbate and Parker, *A History of Opera*, 58; Tomlinson, *Metaphysical Song*, 41.
60. Carter, 'What Is Opera?', 17.

61. Michal Grover-Friedlander, 'Voice', in *The Oxford Handbook of Opera*, ed. Helen M. Greenwald (New York: Oxford University Press, 2014), 318-19.
62. Saint-Évremond, 'Saint-Évremond's Views on Opera'.
63. Geoffrey Burgess, 'Revisiting Atys', *Early Music* 34 (2006): 465–78.
64. For further discussion see Philip Gossett, 'Writing the History of Opera', in *The Oxford Handbook of Opera* (New York: Oxford University Press, 2015), 1032–48.
65. Tomlinson, *Metaphysical Song*, 43.
66. Carter, 'What Is Opera?', 24. This perspective is prevalent in much operatic scholarship. For example, Edward T. Cone, *The Composer's Voice* (Oakland: University of California Press, 1988) suggests that characters are, in effect, the composer of their own musical expression, which gives voice to their internal emotional states through song.
67. In Edward A. Lippman, *The Philosophy and Aesthetics of Music* (Lincoln: University of Nebraska Press, 1999), 111.
68. Tomlinson, *Metaphysical Song*, 65.
69. K. Mitchells, "Operatic Characters and Voice Type," *Proceedings of the Royal Musical Association* 97 (1970): 49.
70. Catherine Clément, 'Through Voices, History', in *Siren Songs: Representations of Gender and Sexuality in Opera*, ed. Mary Ann Smart (Princeton, NJ: Princeton University Press, 2000), 23.
71. Abbate and Parker, *A History of Opera*, 153, 218–21. For a more detailed consideration of the *castrati*, see Patrick Barbier, *The World of the Castrati: The History of an Extraordinary Operatic Phenomenon* (London: Souvenir Press, 1998). Naomi Andre also offers a fascination consideration of early nineteenth-century *castrati* and *travesti* in *Voicing Gender: Castrati, Travesti, and the Second Woman in Early-Nineteenth-Century Italian Opera* (Bloomington: Indiana University Press, 2006).
72. Clément, 'Through Voices, History'.
73. Clément, 24.
74. Tomlinson, *Metaphysical Song*, 65.
75. Of course, Mozart also played with types. In his 1782 work *Die Entführung aus dem Serail* (*The Abduction from the Seraglio*), the character Osmin is a bass-baritone but also a comic buffoon.
76. Abbate and Parker, *A History of Opera*, 155.
77. Jason R. D'Aoust, 'Posthumanist Voices in Literature and Opera', in *The Oxford Handbook of Sound and Imagination*, Vol. 2, ed. Mark Grimshaw-Agaard, Mads Walther-Hansen, and Martin Knakkergaard (New York: Oxford University Press, 2019), 637.
78. Dolar, *A Voice and Nothing More*, 43.
79. Abbate, *In Search of Opera*, 70. For an alternative reading, see Abbate's later discussion on pp. 90–94. It is worth noting that even in this case, the Queen of the Night's arias were, at this time, already a form of parody—written as Baroque *opera seria*.
80. Poizat, *The Angel's Cry*, 65.
81. Abbate, *Unsung Opera*, 4. We might also think of moments from Brünnhilde in Wagner's *Die Valküre* (1867) and *Götterdämmerung* (1876).
82. Tomlinson, *Metaphysical Song*, 85–86.
83. Dolar, *A Voice and Nothing More*.
84. Carlo Zuccarini, 'The (Un)Pleasure of Song: On the Enjoyment of Listening in Opera', in *Gestures of Music Theater: The Performativity of Song and Dance*, ed. Dominic Symonds and Millie Taylor (New York: Oxford University Press, 2014), 26; Steven Mithen, *The Singing Neanderthals: The Origins of Music, Language, Mind and Body* (Cambridge, MA: Harvard University Press, 2005).
85. Žižek and Dolar, *Opera's Second Death*, 3.
86. Carter, 'What Is Opera?', 23; Abbate, *In Search of Opera*, 1.
87. Hall-Witt, *Fashionable Acts*, 3; Katherine K. Preston, 'American Musical Theatre before the Twentieth Century', in *The Cambridge Companion to the Musical*, ed. William A. Everett and Paul R. Laird, 2nd ed. (Cambridge: Cambridge University Press, 2002), 3.
88. Abbate and Parker, *A History of Opera*, 40; Preston, 'American Musical Theatre before the Twentieth Century', 3.
89. Cited in Preston, 'American Musical Theatre before the Twentieth Century', 3.
90. Ann Dhu Shapiro, 'Music in American Pantomime and Melodrama, 1730–1913', *American Music* 2, no. 4 (1984): 50.

91. These 'vocal stars' tended to tour on the theatrical circuit with their straight-theatre counterparts, such as British actors Edmund Kean and Charles Kemble, or otherwise formed vocal troupes, such as that of Jane Shirreff, John Wilson and Anne and Edward Seguin, who arrived in New York in 1838.
92. Raymond Knapp, *The American Musical and the Formation of National Identity* (Princeton, NJ: Princeton University Press, 2005), 59.
93. Knapp, *The American Musical and the Formation of National Identity*, 62. For a further history of blackface and minstrel performance, see W. T. Lhamon Jr., *Raising Cain: Black Performance from Jim Crow to Hip Hop* (Cambridge, MA: Harvard University Press, 1998).
94. Matthew D. Morrison, 'The Sound(s) of Subjection: Constructing American Popular Music and Racial Identity through Blacksound', *Women & Performance: A Journal of Feminist Theory* 27, no. 1 (2017): 14, https://doi.org/10.1080/0740770X.2017.1282120.
95. Morrison, 'The Sound(s) of Subjection', 14; Allan Woll, *Black Musical Theatre from 'Coontown' to 'Dreamgirls'* (New York: Da Capo, 1991), 1; William J. Mahar, *Behind the Burnt Cork Mask: Early Blackface Minstrelsy and Antebellum American Popular Culture* (Urbana: University of Illinois Press, 1998), 9. As Morrison elsewhere notes, 'Blackface was the first popular entertainment export from the United States to travel internationally' ('Race, Blacksound, and the (Re)Making of Musicological Discourse', 783).
96. Woll, *Black Musical Theatre from 'Coontown' to 'Dreamgirls'*, 1; Preston, 'American Musical Theatre before the Twentieth Century', 18; Mahar, *Behind the Burnt Cork Mask*, 9.
97. Woll, *Black Musical Theatre from 'Coontown' to 'Dreamgirls'*, 2.
98. Richard Crawford, *America's Musical Life: A History* (New York: W. W. Norton, 2001), 208; Morrison, 'The Sound(s) of Subjection', 14.
99. See Macpherson, *Cultural Identity in British Musical Theatre.*
100. John Culme and Matthew Lloyd, '"An Opinion of Musical Halls" from "The Tomahawk" (14 September 1867)', 14 September 1867, http://www.arthurlloyd.co.uk/AboutMusicHall.htm.
101. Stefanie Leigh Batiste, *Darkening Mirrors: Imperial Representation in Depression-Era African American Performance* (Durham, NC: Duke University Press, 2011), 4; for a broader discussion of mechanisms and resistance and radical empowerment, see Fred Moten, *In the Break: The Aesthetics of the Black Radical Tradition* (Minneapolis: University of Minnesota Press, 2003).
102. Eileen Southern, *The Music of Black Americans*, 2nd ed. (New York: W. W. Norton, 1983), 107–10.
103. Woll, *Black Musical Theatre from 'Coontown' to 'Dreamgirls'*, 5.
104. Thomas L. Riis, 'The Experience and Impact of Black Entertainers in England, 1895–1920', *American Music* 4, no. 1 (1986): 53.
105. Sarah Whitfield and Sean Mayes have tried to redress the perception that 'Black-British musical theatre' is either a marginal designation or somehow only came to maturity as a result of immigration following World War Two. In particular, their work examines both familiar productions, performers, and writers such as Will Marion Cook, Belle Davis, and William Garland, while also uncovering and revealing the network of black theatrical and musical practice in Britain beyond the West End in the first half of the twentieth century. See *An Inconvenient Black History of British Musical Theatre 1900–1950* (London: Methuen, 2021).
106. Richard Traubner, *Operetta: A Theatrical History* (London: Victor Gollancz Ltd, 1984), xi.
107. Morris and Knapp, 'Singing', 320, 326; Taylor, *Musical Theatre, Realism and Entertainment*, 38–39. As such, operetta routinely referenced both operatic and popular styles in a practice that anticipated the development of musical comedy. The genetic resemblance of the two forms in the first twenty-years of musical comedy, for example, saw a plethora of interchangeable descriptions (see Traubner, *Operetta: A Theatrical History*, x–xvi; Preston, 'American Musical Theatre before the Twentieth Century', 3–28).
108. Michael Goron, *Gilbert and Sullivan's 'Respectable Capers': Class, Respectability and the Savoy Operas, 1877–1909* (Basingstoke: Palgrave, 2016), 25. Crucially, it would be a Gilbert and Sullivan comic opera—*HMS Pinafore*—that would also exert a profound influence on the American musical theatre, following its 1878 premiere in Boston. Knapp suggests that its wry critique of British naval abuses would have resonated with American audiences, a little after the Centenary of independence from the British Empire.
109. Ricoeur, 'Ideology and Utopia as Cultural Imagination', 25, italics mine.

110. Ricoeur, *Lectures on Ideology and Utopia*, 310; Ricoeur, 'Ideology and Utopia as Cultural Imagination', 25; Jill Dolan, *Utopia in Performance: Finding Hope at the Theater* (Ann Arbor: University of Michigan Press, 2005), 2.
111. Preston, 'American Musical Theatre before the Twentieth Century', 3.
112. Cecil Smith, *Musical Comedy in America* (New York: Theatre Arts Books, 1950), 20.
113. Knapp, *The American Musical and the Formation of National Identity*, 23, 27.
114. In his recent survey of British musical theatre on Broadway, Thomas Hischak casts doubt on *In Town* as the first musical comedy. However, his assertion relies on defining success in New York as a benchmark for British musical comedy and its subsequent development and influence. Considering the impact of *In Town* as a landmark of modern, consumer-driven, urbane popular musical theatre, it seems to offer as good a point as can be achieved that might be suitably deemed the beginning of the popular musical. See Thomas S. Hischak, *The Mikado to Matilda: British Musicals on the New York Stage* (Lanham, MD: Rowman & Littlefield, 2020), 125–27.
115. It was the first work by Edwardes to feature explicit product placement, with costumes being provided by local department stores, designed to appeal to the newly leisured middle-class audiences who may spend time in London watching new theatrical fare and then buying the fashions they saw on stage. See Len Platt, *Musical Comedy on the West End Stage, 1890–1939* (Basingstoke: Palgrave, 2004), 49.
116. Ricoeur, 'Ideology and Utopia as Cultural Imagination', 25.
117. As a term, 'the middlebrow' was not in common use until the interwar period, coined in the 1920s as a 'dirty word' in the manner described by Virginia Woolf in the introduction. However, for the purposes of locating a particular cultural sphere within which the musical has long resided, I am using it here with respect to a broader period of time. For a further discussion and definition, see Nicola Humble, *The Feminine Middlebrow Novel 1920s to 1950s: Class, Domesticity, and Bohemianism* (Oxford: Oxford University Press, 2001), 1.
118. Pierre Bourdieu, *Distinction: A Social Critique of the Judgement of Taste*, trans. Richard Nice (Cambridge: Cambridge University Press, 1984), 323; Humble, *The Feminine Middlebrow Novel 1920s to 1950s*, 11, 12.
119. Humble, *The Feminine Middlebrow Novel 1920s to 1950s*, 11, 12.
120. Morrison, 'Race, Blacksound, and the (Re)Making of Musicological Discourse'; Morrison, 'The Sound(s) of Subjection'.
121. As Abbate and Parker observe in *A History of Opera*, 153–56, 215–21, by the time of Mozart, the operatic designation of voice type to character was codified, with the heroic Italian tenor coming to dominate the early nineteenth century even as the *castrati*, for example, had fallen out of fashion. Since this time—like the repertoire these voices give life to—voice character and type in opera has also been, to borrow from Dolar and Žižek, 'historically closed'. By contrast, contemporary musical theatre voice is more malleable and pluralized. In a 2014 article that explored trends in musical theatre audition requirements, it was found that between October 2012 and April 2013, only 5 percent of job postings on the *Backstage* website in the United States specified 'legit' (meaning a 'legitimate' vocal set-up that leads to a voice quality close to opera) as a requirement. Of the remaining 95 percent, over half of the vocal styles needed were listed as contemporary/pop/rock, while the rest were listed as 'traditional', a term which refers to the speech-inflected sound that perhaps most distinguishes musical theatre from opera). Therefore, new ways of thinking about voice are needed; ones that acknowledge—but move beyond—the parameters drawn from analysis of a 400-year-old form. See Kathryn Green et al., 'Trends in Musical Theatre Voice: An Analysis of Audition Requirements for Singers', *Journal of Voice* 28, no. 3 (2014): 324–27.
122. Green et al., 'Trends in Musical Theatre Voice', 324.
123. Wolf, *Changed for Good: A Feminist History of the Broadway Musical* (New York: Oxford University Press, 2011), 7.
124. Wolf, *Changed for Good*, 46.
125. Wolf, *Changed for Good*, 212–13.
126. Tomlinson, *Metaphysical Song*, 65.
127. Wolf's discussion is later referenced in Michelle Boyd's article 'Alto on a Broomstick' (2010), in which she examines the way G(a)linda's vocal character both conforms to, and subverts, traditional gendered configurations—singing with a feminine soprano as the 'good' witch of Oz, and yet joining her fellow witch as an alto in their shared and private moments of friendship. In other words, the analysis of voice type—drawn from opera—allows for a musical

hermeneutic of this character that suggests a fluidity in the definition of 'good', 'wicked', and—in this instance—of gender and sexuality as well. Beyond Wolf's analysis, Boyd's consideration expressly draws on Clément's chapter mentioned above, which uses the very same definitions of voice types as seen in Wolf.

128. Abbate cited in Wolf, *Changed for Good*, 7.
129. For examples, see Taylor, *Musical Theatre, Realism and Entertainment*, 52; Symonds, 'Capturing the "Sung" to Make It "Song"', 12–13; Alison L. McKee, '"Think of Me Fondly": Voice, Body, Affect and Performance in Prince/Lloyd Webber's *The Phantom of the Opera*', *Studies in Musical Theatre* 7, no. 3 (2013): 309–25; Ben Macpherson, 'A Voice and So Much More (or When Bodies Say Things That Words Cannot)', *Studies in Musical Theatre* 6, no. 1 (2012): 43–57.
130. See Dolar, *A Voice and Nothing More*; Macpherson, 'A Voice and so Much More (or When Bodies Say Things That Words Cannot)'.
131. Cavarero, *For More than One Voice: A Philosophy of Vocal Expression* (Stanford, CA: University of Stanford Press, 2005), 37.
132. McKee, '"Think of Me Fondly"'.
133. See Ben Macpherson, 'Sing: Musical Theater Voices from *Superstar* to *Hamilton*', in *The Routledge Companion to the Contemporary Musical*, ed. Jessica Sternfeld and Elizabeth L. Wollman (New York: Routledge, 2020), 70.
134. Taylor, *Musical Theatre, Realism and Entertainment*, 53.
135. Bourne, Garnier, and Kenny, 'Music Theater Voice', 437.
136. Masi Asare, 'Vocal Colour in Blue: Early Twentieth-Century Black Women Singers as Broadway's Voice Teachers', *Performance Matters* 6, no. 2 (2020): 52.
137. Richard Schechner, *Between Theater and Anthropology* (Philadelphia: Pennsylvania University Press, 1985), 35; Asare, 'Vocal Colour in Blue', 52, 63.
138. In this case, by Stephen De Rosa, of a song from William Finn's *Falsettos*. Derek Miller, 'Polyvocally Perverse; or, the Disintegrating Pleasures of Singing Along', *Studies in Musical Theatre* 6, no. 1 (2012): 89–98; Wayne Koestenbaum, *Queen's Throat: Opera, Homosexuality and the Mystery of Desire* (New York: Da Capo, 2001).
139. Dominic Symonds, 'The Corporeality of Musical Expression: The Grain of the Voice and the Actor-Musician', *Studies in Musical Theatre* 1, no. 2 (2007): 167–81.
140. Lockitt, '"Love, Let Me Sing You": The Liminality of Song and Dance in LaChiusa's "Bernarda Alba" (2006)', in *Gestures of Music Theater: The Performativity of Song and Dance*, ed. Dominic Symonds and Millie Taylor (New York: Oxford University Press, 2014), 102–4. Elsewhere, Lockitt also employs Wagnerian and Nietzschean ideas regarding voice and opera to examining the non-singing actor in musical theatre. This is an aesthetic trope to which we return in chapter 6. See Matthew Lockitt, '"Proposition": To Reconsider the Non-Singing Character and the Songless Moment', *Studies in Musical Theatre* 6, no. 2 (2012): 187–98.

Chapter 2

1. Billy Rowe, 'Difference between "Hot" and "Swing" Mikados—Billy Rowe Gives Courier Readers the Real Low Down', *Pittsburgh Courier*, 20 May 1939, 20; Brooks Atkinson, 'Chicago Unit of the Federal Theatre Comes In Swinging the Gilbert and Sullivan Mikado', *New York Times*, 2 March 1939, 18.
2. Roy Shuker, *Popular Music—The Key Concepts*, 4th ed. (Oxford: Routledge, 2017), 19–20.
3. Julie Sanders, *Adaptation and Appropriation*, 2nd ed. (Oxford: Routledge, 2016), 36, 38. Appropriation is therefore a process related to a range of other practices—adaptation, translation, transposition, homage, emulation, travesty, burlesque, echo, *bricolage*, pastiche, pasticcio, parody, and even plagiarism—all of which are at times identifiable traits of the musical theatre voice.
4. John Potter, *Vocal Authority: On Singing Style and Ideology* (Cambridge: Cambridge University Press, 1998), 190, 194; Antonio Gramsci, *Selections from Prison Notebooks*, trans. Quentin Hoare and Geoffrey Nowell Smith (London: Lawrence & Wishart, 1986), 107.
5. Potter, *Vocal Authority*, 194.
6. Potter, 194.
7. Potter, 194.
8. Potter, 194.
9. Adam Alston, '"Burn the Witch": Decadence and the Occult in Contemporary Feminist Performance', *Theatre Research International* 46, no. 3 (2021): 286; Adam Alston, 'Carnal

Acts: Decadence in Theatre, Performance and Live Art', *Volupte: Interdisciplinary Journal of Decadence Studies* 4, no. 2 (2021): iv, https://doi.org/10.25602/GOLD.v.v4i2.1598.g1712.

10. Weir cited in Alston, 'Carnal Acts', ii.
11. Nicola Humble, *The Feminine Middlebrow Novel 1920s to 1950s: Class, Domesticity, and Bohemianism* (New York: Oxford University Press, 2001), 11, 12.
12. The neologism 'voiceworld' is the second new term in this chapter, and will be used throughout the rest of this book, offering a more specific rendering of the term 'soundworld', often used to describe or locate the musical or sonic properties of a range of musical-theatrical productions or sensory experiences. See, e.g., 'Vernacular Soundworlds, Narratives and Stardom', Part 3 in *The Routledge Research Companion to Popular Music and Gender*, ed. Stan Hawkins (Abingdon: Routledge, 2017), 133–210; Susan J. Smith, 'Performing the (Sound)World', *Environment and Planning: Society and Space* 18, no. 5 (2000): 615–37; Millie Taylor, *Theatre Music and Sound at the RSC* (Basingstoke: Palgrave, 2018), 1–10.
13. In the United States, the production spawned such things as a film (*The Florodora Girl*, 1930), an eponymous cocktail, and the iconographic 'Florodora Girl', who quickly became a reference point in popular culture. See Ben Macpherson, 'The Sweet Smell of Success: "Florodora" as Victorian Megamusical', in *Blockbusters of Victorian Theater, 1850–1910: Critical Essays*, ed. Paul Fryer (Jefferson, NC: McFarland, 2023), 88–98.
14. Such was its success that recording historian Tim Brooks notes that by the summer of 1901, there were 'at least twenty *Florodora* recordings available on cylinder and disc' including a Columbia recording of highlights from the show, released on a series of 78rpm gramophone records and even featuring a full libretto of the production. See Tim Brooks, 'Early Recordings of Songs from Florodora: Tell Me, Pretty Maiden . . . Who Are You?—A Discographical Mystery', *Association for Recorded Sound Collections Journal* 31 (2000): 55.
15. Evie Greene, *Queen of the Philippine Islands*, Shellac disc (London: Opal, 1910), D1 S2 BD4, British Library. In fact, beyond the practical and circumstantial presence of vocal aesthetics, the very subject of Greene's performance may have also situated *Florodora* in the realms of operetta, as it sought to evoke a 'distant time and place' (the Philippines) in common with the exoticism of other operettas at the time. See Mitchell Morris and Raymond Knapp, 'Singing', in *The Oxford Handbook of the American Musical*, ed. Raymond Knapp, Mitchell Morris, and Stacy Wolf (New York: Oxford University Press, 2011), 326.
16. W. Louis Bradfield, *Phrenology*, Wax cylinder (London: Berliner, 1900), 28 4522, British Library. In fact, W. Louis Bradfield was the first performer to record any song from *Florodora*. On 27 September 1900, he and composer Leslie Stuart recorded 'I Want to Be a Military Man' at Maiden Lane Studios in London. Even here, his limited vocal range and unrefined style can be heard. The fact that Bradfield originated the role of Lord Coddington in George Edwardes's 1890 production *In Town* also indicates the more speech-inflected aesthetics of earlier musical farce and musical comedy.
17. Luke Martell, 'Utopianism and Social Change: Materialism, Conflict and Pluralism', *Capital and Class* 42, no. 3 (2018): 447.
18. Alston, '"Burn the Witch"', 286.
19. *Tell Me Pretty Maiden (Are There Any More at Home like You?)*, Shellac disc (London: Columbia, 1902), British Library Shelfmark 1LP0002808, British Library.
20. Andrew Lamb, *Leslie Stuart—Composer of Florodora* (Oxford: Routledge, 2002), 91.
21. Lamb, *Leslie Stuart*, 91.
22. In a further performance of these complexities, the parody song 'Tell Me, Dusky Maiden' featured in the African American musical comedy *The Sleeping Beauty and the Beast* (1901) by Bob Cole and J. Rosamond Johnson just one year after *Florodora* opened on Broadway. With uneven phrase lengths echoing those in Stuart's original composition, and a refrain which shares a broad melodic similarity to the number in *Florodora*, this song was popularized by African American artists Pete Hampton and Laura Bowman, and recorded in London in September 1906. Employing speech-quality throughout, showcasing Hampton's conversational phrasing and Bowman's light lyric soprano, this parody serves as an example of subversive appropriation from a production imported from England into the ecosystem of American entertainment—and, in particular, one way in which black musical comedy productions and voices borrowed back to critique social structures, as is also heard later in examples from *Passing Strange*. See Pete Hampton and Laura Bowman, *Tell Me, Dusky Maiden (1906)*, CD, vol. 1, *Black Europe—The Sounds and Images of Black People in Europe Pre-1927* (London: Bear Family Records BCD 16095, 2013), 1SS0009976 D3 BD20, British Library.

23. David Chandler quotes Jerrold Hogle in the first description, while he inverts Cathleen Myers in the second quote. See '"What Do We Mean by Opera, Anyway?": Lloyd Webber's Phantom of the Opera and "High-Pop" Theatre', *Journal of Popular Music Studies* 21, no. 2 (2009): 154, 155, https://doi.org/10.1111/j.1533-1598.2009.01186.x.
24. Jim Collins, 'High-Pop: An Introduction', in *High-Pop: Making Culture into Popular Entertainment*, ed. Jim Collins (Malden, MA: Blackwell, 2002), 1–31.
25. The cultural juxtaposition inherent in this term not only encapsulates the synthesis of tradition (nineteenth century opera and operetta) and contemporary commercial appeal (popular music) that became the hallmark of the *Phantom* and other works such as *Les Misérables* (1985), *Miss Saigon* (1989), *Sunset Boulevard* (1993) and more recently *Wicked* (2003), but also aligns with the socio-political era of its production. For a discussion of the moral and economic implications of the work's traditionalism, sense of the past, and the clearly commercial imperatives of the production, see Amanda Eubanks Winkler, 'Politics and the Reception of Andrew Lloyd Webber's *The Phantom of the Opera*', *Cambridge Opera Journal* 26, no. 3 (2014): 271–87.
26. With respect to this moment, Dominic Symonds's analysis of amplification and sound design as acoustic dramaturgy in *Phantom* and *Starlight Express* (1984) opens as follows: 'It's a striking acoustic opening. . . . From silence, the crack of a gavel hitting its block, and the assertive announcement of an auctioneer: "Sold!", the voice cries into the void'. Symonds develops his discussion of acoustic dramaturgy by noting that much of this affect is via technology: 'reverb and amplification—far too much for the scenario (the empty stage of an opera house), and certainty for the period setting (1911)'. In many ways, Symonds's consideration relates more specifically to concerns in the following chapter, but is relevant when read in conjunction with this case study. See 'Starlight Expression and Phantom Operatics: Technology, Performance, and the Megamusical's Aesthetic of the Voice', in *The Routledge Companion to the Contemporary Musical*, ed. Jessica Sternfeld and Elizabeth L. Wollman (Oxford: Routledge, 2020), 87.
27. Jessica Sternfeld, *The Megamusical* (Bloomington: Indiana University Press, n.d.), 236.
28. John Snelson, *Andrew Lloyd Webber* (New Haven, CT: Yale University Press, 2004), 106–8.
29. Chandler, '"What Do We Mean by Opera, Anyway?", 158.
30. Chandler, 106. In this sense, there are parallels between *Phantom* and Cole Porter's pastiche of operetta in *Kiss Me, Kate* (see Morris and Knapp, 'Singing').
31. As Richard Dyer has elsewhere noted: 'Pastiche is always an imitation of an imitation'. *Pastiche* (Oxford: Routledge, 2007), 2.
32. For a cultural consideration of the megamusical and, in particular, *Phantom*, see Sternfeld, *The Megamusical*, 1–7, 225–72.
33. Brandon LaBelle, *Lexicon of the Mouth: Poetics and Politics of Voice and the Oral Imaginary* (London: Bloomsbury, 2014), 58–59, 60. For more on the *object voice* in opera, see Carolyn Abbate, *Unsung Opera: Opera and Musical Narrative in the Nineteenth Century* (Princeton, NJ: Princeton University Press, 1991); Abbate, *In Search of Opera* (Princeton, NJ: Princeton University Press, 2001); Mladen Dolar, *A Voice and Nothing More* (Cambridge, MA: MIT Press, 2006).
34. Snelson, *Andrew Lloyd Webber*, 109; Symonds, 'Starlight Expression and Phantom Operatics', 93. This aesthetic can certainly be heard on the Original London Cast Recording, in Sarah Brightman's performance as Christine; see Michael Crawford, Sarah Brightman, and Steve Barton, *The Phantom of the Opera (Original Cast Recording)*, Vinyl (London: EMI, 1986).
35. Lloyd Webber in George Perry, *The Complete Phantom of the Opera* (London: Pavilion Books, 1987), 72.
36. I have considered the properties of this voice elsewhere, referring to it as the 'Poperetta Voice' of the megamusical in Ben Macpherson, 'Sing: Musical Theater Voices from *Superstar* to *Hamilton*' in *The Routledge Companion to the Contemporary Musical*, ed. Jessica Sternfeld and Elizabeth L. Wollman (New York: Routledge, 2000), 69–77.
37. Sternfeld, *The Megamusical*, 240–41.
38. Symonds, 'Starlight Expression and Phantom Operatics', 94; Freya Jarman-Ivens, *Queer Voices: Technologies, Vocalities, and the Musical Flaw*, (Basingstoke: Palgrave, 2011), 44. For a brief discussion of the Phantom's falsetto, see Sternfeld, *The Megamusical*, 238–41. For discussion of attitudes to falsetto, see Victoria Malawey, *A Blaze of Light in Every Word: Analyzing the Popular Singing Voice* (New York: Oxford University Press, 2021), 49.
39. Alston, 'Carnal Acts', iv.
40. Chandler, '"What Do We Mean by Opera, Anyway?"'.

41. Deborah J. Thompson, 'Searching for Silenced Voices in Appalachian Music', *GeoJournal* 65 (2006): 67; George Revill and John R. Gold, '"Far Back in American Time": Culture, Region, Nation, Appalachia, and the Geography of Voice', *Annals of the American Association of Geographers* 108, no. 5 (2018): 1409, https://doi.org/10.1080/24694452.2018.1431104.
42. Thompson, 'Searching for Silenced Voices in Appalachian Music', 67. The musical begins with 'The Ballad of Floyd Collins', introducing the audience to the story and protagonist. Ostensibly, such balladeering may derive from the European traditions of travelling troubadours and may easily elicit connections with practices such as the Epic Theatre of Brecht. However, telling stories through balladry is also found in the *griot* tradition of West Africa, with its simple accompaniment of a guitar or banjo (see Thompson, 71; see also G. Milnes, *Play of a Fiddle: Traditional Music, Dance, and Folklore in West Virginia* [Lexington: University Press of Kentucky, 1999]). Around 90 per cent of Appalachia's earliest European settlers were from areas in England like the Cumberland, Northumberland, and Yorkshire, with others from the Scottish counties of Ayrshire, Berwickshire, and elsewhere in the British Isles. There was also a strong Germanic presence with some influence from the Finns and Swedish cultures in the development of logging as important to the mountainous regions, along with communities from Africa since the eighteenth century and Native tribes including the Cherokee, Melungeon, Powhatan, and Shawnee peoples; see Jean Haskell, ed., *Encyclopedia of Appalachia* (Knoxville: University of Tennessee Press, 2006).
43. Revill and Gold, '"Far Back in American Time"', 1409; Alston, 'Carnal Acts', ii. It is not the subject of this book to examine the politics and legacies of oppression and displacement in the history, for example, of indigenous tribal peoples in American history. However, it is only right to acknowledge this difficult and contested history in the context of this discussion.
44. David Spencer, 'Floyd Collins: Review', *Aisle Say—New York* (blog), 1994, http://www.aislesay.com/NY-FLOYD-COLLINS.html.
45. Catherine Clément, 'Through Voices, History', , in *Siren Songs: Representations of Gender and Sexuality in Opera*, ed. Mary Ann Smart (Princeton, NJ: Princeton University Press, 2000), 23.
46. Tina Landau, Adam Guettel, and Wiley Hausam, 'Floyd Collins', in *The New American Musical: An Anthology from the End of the Century* (New York: Theatre Communications Group, 2003), 62. Elsewhere, Floyd's brother Homer—a supporting character in the musical—is the tenor male voice, traditionally associated with '[y]oung, courageous, imprudent, heroes of a rebellion against the social order, fighting for love' (Clement, 'Through Voices, History', 23).
47. See Adam Guettel and Tina Landau, *Floyd Collins: Vocal Score* (New York: Williamson Music, 2001), 77–78, bb. 101–104 and 113–114. The rest of this case study will also be based on the Off-Broadway cast album *Floyd Collins (Original Cast Recording)*, Compact Disc (New York: Nonesuch, 1996).
48. See Guettel and Landau, *Floyd Collins*, 174–175, bb. 8–19, delivered with the performance instruction: 'Plaintive legato'.
49. I have considered the presence of vocalise in Guettel's *The Light in the Piazza* (2005) in Macpherson, 'A Voice and So Much More (or When Bodies Say Things That Words Cannot)', *Studies in Musical Theatre* 6, no. 1 (2012): 43–57.
50. Tim Wise, 'Yodel Species: A Typology of Falsetto Effects in Popular Music Vocal Styles', *Radical Musicology* 2 (2007), http://www.radical-musicology.org.uk/2007/Wise.htm. Wise has elsewhere considered the presence of the yodel in both classical and folk music from Beethoven's Sixth Symphony and Rossini's *Guillaume Tell* to 'traditional' song, while acknowledging its tendency to be pastiche in classical form in 'How the Yodel Became a Joke: The Vicissitudes of a Musical Sign', *Popular Music* 31, no. 3 (2012): 464.
51. Wise, 'How the Yodel Became a Joke', 464.
52. Bart Plantenga, *Yodel-Ay-Ee-Oooo* (London: Routledge, 2004), 13.
53. Plantenga, 157. It is notable that unlike Deborah J. Thompson, Plantenga and elsewhere Charlotte J. Frisbie identify the influence of Native American musical practice on Appalachian vocal performance. See Charlotte J. Frisbie, 'Vocables in Navajo Ceremonial Music', *Ethnomusicology* 24, no. 3 (1980): 347–92.
54. Julian F. Henriques and Hillegonda Rietveld, 'Echo', in *The Routledge Companion to Sound Studies*, ed. Michael Bull (London: Routledge, 2018), 275–82. See also Jean-François Augoyard and Henri Torgue, eds., *Sonic Experience: A Guide to Everyday Sounds* (Montreal: McGill-Queen's University Press, 2005), 111.

55. Alan Locket cited in Henriques and Rietveld, 'Echo'. While not directly considered here, echo has also long been gendered and understood in the light of patriarchal anxiety about unruly female voices, with emphasis on the regularity of echo patterns as measurable and containable.
56. Abbate, *In Search of Opera*, 27.
57. See Leendert van der Miesen, 'Studying the Echo in the Early Modern Period: Between the Academy and the Natural World', *Sound Studies: An Interdisciplinary Journal (Special Issue: Sonic Things—Knowledge Formation in Flux)* 6, no. 2 (2020): 201.
58. Steven Connor, *Dumbstruck: A Cultural History of Ventriloquism* (Oxford: Oxford University Press, 2001), 35–43.
59. The notion of the 'fleshness' of the voice in sonic exchange is used by Salome Voegelin, *Listening to Noise and Silence: Toward a Philosophy of Sound Art* (London: Bloomsbury, 2010), 73. Elsewhere, I have explored the somatic properties of voice and listening in Ben Macpherson, 'The Somaesthetic In-between: Six Statements on Vocality, Listening and Embodiment', in *Somatic Voices in Performance Research and Beyond*, ed. Christina Kapachoda (London: Routledge, 2021), 212–26.
60. Lynne Kendrick, *Theatre Aurality* (Basingstoke: Palgrave, 2017), 63; Barry Blesser and Linda-Ruth Salter, *Spaces Speak, Are You Listening?: Experiencing Aural Architecture* (Cambridge, MA: MIT Press, 2006), 49. For a development of these ideas in contemporary architectural acoustics, see Joseph Clarke, *Echo's Chambers: Architecture and the Idea of Acoustic Space* (Pittsburgh: University of Pittsburgh Press, 2021).
61. Kendrick, *Theatre Aurality*, 63.
62. Guettel and Landau, *Floyd Collins*, 216–18 (bb. 89–99).
63. On the musical stage, the 1918 musical play *The Beauty Spot* also had a mock-yodelling duet.
64. Wise, 'How the Yodel Became a Joke: The Vicissitudes of a Musical Sign', 467.
65. Guettel and Landau, *Floyd Collins*, 227 (b. 132).
66. Cavarero, *For More Than One Voice: A Philosophy of Vocal Expression* (Stanford, CA: University of Stanford Press, 2005), 166–67. For a consideration of the gendered origin of echo, see van der Miesen, 'Studying the Echo in the Early Modern Period'.
67. Cavarero, 167, 170, emphasis mine.
68. This physicality is also heard in the closing moments with respect to the cave. As Blesser and Salter further observe, '[t]he vastness of an enclosed space is revealed by decaying reverberation', an effect heard in the final vocal canon of 'How Glory Goes'; see *Spaces Speak, Are You Listening?*, 56.
69. Jacques Derrida, *Rogues: Two Essays on Reason*, ed. Pascale-Anne Brault and Michael Naas (Stanford, CA: Stanford University Press, 2005), xi–xii.
70. I note here the closeness of this Derridean reading of Echo to that offered by Pleshette DeArmitt, 'Resonances of Echo: A Derridean Allegory', *Mosaic: An Interdisciplinary Critical Journal (Special Issue: Sound, Part II)* 42, no. 2 (2009): 89–100.
71. Alston, 'Carnal Acts', ii; Revill and Gold, '"Far Back in American Time"', 1409.
72. The sixteen genre categories they identified were rendered manageable through macro-grouping into three genre complexes and categorized as Niche, Rock/Pop, and Hip Hop, in Daniel Silver, Monica Lee, and C. Clayton Childress, 'Genre Complexes in Popular Music', *PloSOne* 11, no. 5 (2016), https://doi.org/10.1371/journal.pone.0155471.
73. Slavoj Žižek and Mladen Dolar, *Opera's Second Death* (New York: Routledge, 2001), 2–3.
74. See Robert Alda et al., *Guys and Dolls: A Musical Fable of Broadway (A Decca Original Cast Album)*, Compact Disc, Broadway Gold (California: MCA Classics, 1991).
75. Frank Loesser in Susan Loesser, *A Most Remarkable Fella: Frank Loesser and the Guys and Dolls in His Life* (New York: Hal Leonard, 1993), 118.
76. Millie Taylor, *Musical Theatre, Realism and Entertainment* (Farnham: Ashgate, 2012), 48.
77. Raymond Knapp, *The American Musical and the Formation of National Identity* (Princeton, NJ: Princeton University Press, 2005), 139.
78. As Knapp has observed, in comparison with the bitter ironies and twists in Runyon's original *Guys and Dolls* stories, this ending is sentimentalized for the musical stage.
79. As noted in the introduction, while not every case study will focus individual or specific performances of a song or character, the creative process of *Guys and Dolls* is noteworthy for the crafting of certain roles for well-known performers as discussed. While Sky was not crafted specifically for Alda in the same way that Detroit was for Levene or Adelaide was for Blaine, the voices of the original cast have become a template for all other incarnations, perhaps because of the way in which the creation of key characters was so closely bound with the actors themselves.

80. Malawey, *A Blaze of Light in Every Word*, 35–36.
81. Matthew D. Morrison, 'Race, Blacksound, and the (Re)Making of Musicological Discourse', *Journal of the American Musicological Society* 72, no. 3 (2019): 789.
82. See Zuim, 'Speech Inflection in American Musical Theatre Compositions' (Florida Atlantic University, 2012), 125. For a further consideration of flexibility in rhythm and delivery, see Samuel Floyd, cited in Matthew D. Morrison, 'The Sound(s) of Subjection: Constructing American Popular Music and Racial Identity through Blacksound', *Women & Performance: A Journal of Feminist Theory* 27, no. 1 (2017): 15.
83. Ron Byrnside, '"Guys and Dolls": A Musical Fable of Broadway', *Journal of American Culture* 19, no. 2 (1996): 28. See also Malawey, *A Blaze of Light in Every Word*, 71–79.
84. Richard Middleton, 'Rock Singing', in *The Cambridge Companion to Singing*, ed. John Potter (Cambridge: Cambridge University Press, 2000), 55.
85. Morrison, 'Race, Blacksound, and the (Re)Making of Musicological Discourse', 791.
86. Allison McCracken, *Real Men Don't Sing: Crooning in American Culture* (Durham, NC: Duke University Press, 2015), 11; John Potter and Neil Sorrell, *A History of Singing* (Cambridge: Cambridge University Press, 2014), 244.
87. McCracken, *Real Men Don't Sing*, 210. Despite prejudices in this regard, crooning was still a popular style of singing. In fact, as McCracken notes, 'The romantic crooner persona was so popular in 1929–30 that Hollywood even promoted some homegrown singers with crooning qualities' (215).
88. McCracken, 16, 210. In this sense, crooning is heard as an 'in-between' vocal marker—simultaneously primal and visceral, and somewhat redolent of the magical and metaphysical.
89. Excerpt of 'My Time of Day' from Alda et al., *Guys and Dolls: A Musical Fable of Broadway (A Decca Original Cast Album)*, with Robert Alda's speech-inflection and croon in bold and italicized.
90. McCracken, *Real Men Don't Sing*, 8. On this point, Malawey notes that crooning offers a direct contrast with opera because it 'emerged in the 1920s with the popularization of phonograph records and radio broadcasts'; *A Blaze of Light in Every Word*, 138.)
91. Martell, 'Utopianism and Social Change', 447.
92. Taylor, *Musical Theatre, Realism and Entertainment*, 49; Frank Loesser in Loesser, *A Most Remarkable Fella*, 118.
93. Josh Kun, *Audiotopia: Music, Race, and America* (Berkeley: University of California Press, 2005), 50.
94. Brandon LaBelle, *Acoustic Territories: Sound Culture and Everyday Life* (New York: Continuum, 2010), 136.
95. Knapp, *The American Musical and the Formation of National Identity*, 137–38.
96. Alston, 'Carnal Acts', iv.
97. Masi Asare, 'Vocal Colour in Blue: Early Twentieth-Century Black Women Singers as Broadway's Voice Teachers', *Performance Matters* 6, no. 2 (2020): 52. As Taylor notes, the nasal one-octave range of Adelaide's melodic lines was also apt to convey her status as an older showgirl (*Musical Theatre, Realism and Entertainment*, 48).
98. Alexandra Apolloni, 'The Lollipop Girl's Voice: Respectability, Migration, and Millie Small's "My Boy Lollipop"', *Journal of Popular Music Studies* 28, no. 4 (2016): 466.
99. Stacy Wolf, *Changed for Good: A Feminist History of the Broadway Musical* (New York: Oxford University Press, 2011), 36. Sarah's 'legit' vocal set-up is related to the plain and simple vocal aesthetic of the hymn 'Follow the Fold', while subverted or 'reworked' in the original production by the fact that Brother Arvide Abernathy (a paternal figure to Sarah) was performed by Pat Rooney Jr., an established vaudevillian with a limited vocal range.
100. Wolf, 36–41.
101. Wolf, 40.
102. Wolf, 40–41.
103. LaBelle, *Lexicon of the Mouth* (London: Bloomsbury, 2014), 124.
104. Wolf, *Changed for Good*, 25–53.
105. Knapp, *The American Musical and the Formation of National Identity*, 144; Martell, 'Utopianism and Social Change', 447.
106. Kun, *Audiotopia*, 50.
107. Developed at the Sundance Institute Theatre Laboratory in 2004, the musical played in California and Off-Broadway prior to its Broadway engagement, where it would run for 165 performances.

108. Stew, Heidi Rodewald, and Annie Dorsen, *Passing Strange (Script)* (New York: Dramatists Play Service Inc., 2008), 21. Reflecting on this notion, Saidiya Hartman writes that it 'inadequately contends with the history of racial subjection and enslavement, since the texture of freedom is laden with the vestiges of slavery, and abstract equality is utterly enmeshed in the narrative of black subjection, given that slavery undergirded the rhetoric of the republic and equality defined so as to sanction subordination and segregation' (*Scenes of Subjection: Terror, Slavery and Self-Making in Nineteenth-Century America* [New York: Oxford University Press, 1997], 116).
109. Gayle Wald, 'Passing Strange and Post–Civil Rights Blackness', *Humanities Research* 16, no. 1 (2010): 13.
110. Tommie Shelby and Paul Gilroy, 'Cosmopolitanism, Blackness, and Utopia', *Transition* 98 (2008): 133.
111. Stew, Rodewald, and Dorsen, *Passing Strange (Script)*, 10.
112. A small but instructive study was published in the *Journal of Voice* in 2016 that found a higher subglottal pressure but lower sound level and much shorter tone length in soul singing than in traditional musical theatre vocal production. The authors concluded that: 'This can be interpreted as a support for the assumption that soul as compared with musical theatre was sung in a somewhat heavier register and with greater vocal resistance. This suggests that soul was produce with firmer glottal adduction, and hence would be vocally more demanding than musical theatre' (Hanna Hallqvist, Filipa M.B. Lã, Johan Sundberg, 'Soul and Musical Theater: A Comparison of Two Vocal Styles', *Journal of Voice* 31, no. 2 (2016): 235). Victoria Malawey considers the nature of 'genre-specific prosodic markers' in popular music in *A Blaze of Light in Every Word*, 90.
113. See Kim Chandler, 'Teaching Popular Music Styles', in *Teaching Singing in the 21st Century*, ed. Scott D. Harrison and Jessica O'Bryan (New York: Springer, 2014), 49.
114. Stew, Rodewald, and Dorsen, *Passing Strange (Script)*, 15.
115. Stew, Rodewald, and Dorsen, 15.
116. See Morrison, 'The Sound(s) of Subjection', 15.
117. Nina Sun Eidsheim, *The Race of Sound: Listening, Timbre and Vocality in African American Music* (Durham, NC: Duke University Press, 2019), 27; Brandon Woolf, 'Negotiating the "Negro Problem": Stew's Passing (Made) Strange', *Theatre Journal* 62, no. 2 (May 2010): 198.
118. Woolf, 'Negotiating the "Negro Problem"', 198.
119. Woolf, 198.
120. Stew, Rodewald, and Dorsen, *Passing Strange (Script)*, 15.
121. Morrison, 'The Sound(s) of Subjection', 15. Further to this, Jennifer Lynn Stoever argues that the commodification allowed for the 'control' of 'cross-racial aural traffic' to the extent that gospel song—even in 'composite' forms inclusive of European structures—is still Othered by race. See *The Sonic Color Line: Race and the Cultural Politics of Listening* (New York: New York University Press, 2016), 27.
122. Woolf, 'Negotiating the "Negro Problem"', 198.
123. As Edward Rothstein has simply stated: 'one man's utopia is another man's dystopia' ('Utopia and Its Discontents', in *Visions of Utopia*, ed. Furaha D. Norton [New York: Oxford University Press, 2003], 4.)
124. Woolf, 'Negotiating the "Negro Problem"', 203.
125. W. T. Lhamon Jr., *Raising Cain: Black Performance from Jim Crow to Hip Hop* (Cambridge, MA: Harvard University Press, 1998), 142–43.
126. Stoever, *The Sonic Color Line*, 279.
127. Lee B. Brown, 'Can American Popular Vocal Music Escape the Legacy of Blackface Minstrelsy?', *Journal of Aesthetics and Art Criticism* 71, no. 1 (2013): 96–97, https://doi.org/10.1111/j.1540-6245.2012.01545.x.
128. Stew, Rodewald, and Dorsen, *Passing Strange (Script)*, 56–57.
129. Stew, Rodewald, and Dorsen, 80–81.
130. Alston, 'Carnal Acts', iv. The notion of the 'listening ear' comes from Stoever, *The Sonic Color Line*, 8.
131. Morrison, 'The Sound(s) of Subjection', 22. In a similar vein, as discussed in chapter 4, a broader discussion of the politics of such performance is developed by Nicole Hodges Persley in her monograph *Sampling and Remixing Blackness in Hip-Hop Theater and Performance* (Ann Arbor: University of Michigan Press, 2021).
132. Woolf, 'Negotiating the "Negro Problem"', 106.

133. Woolf, 106.
134. Louis Chude-Sokei, *The Last "Darky": Bert Williams, Black-on-Black Minstrelsy, and the African Diaspora* (Durham, NC: Duke University Press, 2006), 44.; Morrison, 'Race, Blacksound, and the (Re)Making of Musicological Discourse', 783.
135. 'Nobody' was written by Williams (music) and Alex Rogers (lyrics) in 1905. Disc 1, Track 6, *Really the Blues?—A Blues History 1893–1959*, CD, vol. 1, 4 vols. (Toronto: West Hill Radio Archives, 2010), 1SS0010415 D1 BD6 WHRA, British Library.
136. Fred Moten, *In the Break: The Aesthetics of the Black Radical Tradition* (Minneapolis: University of Minnesota Press, 2003), 1. In a further act of vocal subversion and resistance, Youth's white German friends are all played by actors of colour who assume the vocal affectations of a Central European accent. Perhaps in these moments, re-evaluation becomes a renegotiation of cultural and racial agency, a position examined further in chapter 4.
137. Morrison, 'Race, Blacksound, and the (Re)Making of Musicological Discourse', 783.
138. Stew, Rodewald, and Dorsen, *Passing Strange (Script)*, 10.
139. Considering the loudness of *Passing Strange*, Brian D. Valencia writes that 'There is, no doubt, great excitement to be had in what is very large, very loud. The intensity, affect and meaning of what is very loud grows, however, not in demonstrating that it can be louder still, but in hearing what it is louder than. Outsized rock musician Stew comes to recognize this acutely in the published preface to his 2006/2008 theatre-rumbling concert-play *Passing Strange*, when he acknowledges the essential, countervailing contributions of his collaborator Heidi Rodewald. There he writes, "[L]ike any good musician, Heidi always tried to get us to remember how beautiful the silences were"'. Brian D. Valencia, 'What a Crescendo—Not to Be Missed: Loudness on the Musical Stage', *Studies in Musical Theatre* 10, no. 1 (2016): 14, https://doi.org/10.1386/smt.10.1.7_1. In Sing: Musical Theater Voices from *Superstar* to *Hamilton*. I consider other aspects of 'The Rock Voice' in musical theatre.
140. Taylor, *Musical Theatre, Realism and Entertainment*, 51, 50. Frictive vocalizing is contrasted with the discipline of European classical singing by Theo van Leeuwen, *Speech, Music, Sound* (Basingstoke: Macmillan, 1999), 132.
141. Peter Kivy, *Authenticities: Philosophical Reflections on Musical Performance* (Ithaca, NY: Cornell University Press, 2012), 3. As Richard Middleton puts it: '"real experience", expressed with "sincerity", is regarded as the indispensable basis of good (that is, "honest") [rock] singing' (Middleton, 'Rock Singing', 38).
142. Theo van Leeuwen suggests that 'roughness' is associated with assertiveness in popular music (*Speech, Music, Sound*, 132).
143. Jacob Smith, *Vocal Tracks: Performance and Sound Media* (Berkeley: University of California Press, 2008), 9.
144. Kivy, *Authenticities*, 3.
145. As Elizabeth L. Wollman says in her review of *Passing Strange*, 'black musicals weren't marketed as rock musicals or rock operas because "rock" was for white people. *Jesus Christ Superstar* was a "rock opera"; *The Wiz* was a "soul musical"'; 'Passing Strange (Review)', *Theatre Journal* 60, no. 4 (2008): 635. This is borne out in Wollman's book *The Theater Will Rock* (2009) in which she considers rock and roll and rock musicals from *Bye Bye Birdie* (1960) and *Hair* (1968) to *Rent* (1996) and *The Full Monty* (2000)—all of which were written by white people—see *The Theater Will Rock: A History of the Rock Musical, from Hair to Hedwig* (Ann Arbor: University of Michigan Press, 2009).
146. See Jack Hamilton, *Just around Midnight: Rock and Roll and the Racial Imagination* (Cambridge, MA: Harvard University Press, 2016); Matthew Bannister, *White Boys, White Noise: Masculinities and 1980s Indie Guitar Rock* (Farnham: Ashgate, 2006); Maureen Mahon, *Right to Rock: The Black Rock Coalition and the Cultural Politics of Race* (Durham, NC: Duke University Press, 2004); Simon Frith, *Performing Rites: Evaluating Popular Music* (Oxford: Oxford University Press, 1996).
147. Taylor, *Musical Theatre, Realism and Entertainment*, 51, 50; Frith, *Performing Rites*, 130.
148. Woolf, 'Negotiating the "Negro Problem": Stew's Passing (Made) Strange', 193
149. Woolf, 198.
150. Martell, 'Utopianism and Social Change', 447.
151. Martell, 448, 447.
152. Martell, 447.
153. Alston, '"Burn the Witch"', 286; Morrison, 'Race, Blacksound, and the (Re)Making of Musicological Discourse', 783.

154. Woolf, 'Negotiating the "Negro Problem"', 193.

Chapter 3

1. The term 'vocal dramaturgy' here is adapted from 'acoustic dramaturgy' used in Dominic Symonds, 'Starlight Expression and Phantom Operatics: Technology, Performance, and the Megamusical's Aesthetic of the Voice', in *The Routledge Companion to the Contemporary Musical*, ed. Jessica Sternfeld and Elizabeth L. Wollman (Oxford: Routledge, 2020), 94.
2. Bethany Hughes, 'Singing the Community: The Musical Theater Chorus as Character', in *Gestures of Music Theater: The Performativity of Song and Dance*, ed. Dominic Symonds and Millie Taylor (New York: Oxford University Press, 2014), 263. In opera studies, Catherine Clément uses a parallel term when she refers to a 'society of voices', in 'Through Voices, History', in *Siren Songs: Representations of Gender and Sexuality in Opera*, ed. Mary Ann Smart (Princeton, NJ: Princeton University Press, 2000), 19.
3. Scott McMillin, *The Musical as Drama* (Ithaca, NY: Cornell University Press, 2006), 68.
4. Erika Fischer-Lichte, *The Transformative Power of Performance: A New Aesthetics*, trans. Saskya Iris Jain (Oxford: Routledge, 2008), 127.
5. See Lynne Kendrick, *Theatre Aurality* (Basingstoke: Palgrave, 2017); Ben Macpherson, 'A Voice and So Much More (or When Bodies Say Things That Words Cannot)', *Studies in Musical Theatre* 6, no. 1 (2012): 43–57. Previously, I have explored the notion of 'corporeal vocality' in a challenge to the often-paradoxical Lacanian perspectives of Mladen Dolar in *A Voice and Nothing More* (2006), extending this to consider 'somaesthetic vocality', a term which is related to, and underpins this analysis (see Macpherson, 'The Somaesthetic In-between: Six Statements on Vocality, Listening and Embodiment', in *Somatic Voices in Performance Research and Beyond*, ed. Christina Kapachoda [London: Routledge, 2021], 212–26.) Elsewhere, I have suggested that even in the notation of vocal music there in an implied or implicit sense of corporeality (see Ben Macpherson, '"Body Musicality": The Visual, Virtual, Visceral Voice', in *Voice Studies: Critical Approaches to Process, Performance and Experience*, ed. Konstantinos Thomaidis and Ben Macpherson [Oxford: Routledge, 2015], 149–61). As Anne Tarvainen further observes: 'the artist's body is strongly present' in vocal performance, often becoming the 'object of experience' for audience or listeners ('Singing, Listening, Proprioceiving: Some Reflections on Vocal Somaesthetics', in *Aesthetic Experience and Somaesthetics*, ed. Richard Shusterman [Leiden: Brill, 2018], 120).
6. For an alternative reading, see Jonathan Burston, 'Theatre Space as Virtual Place: Audio Technology, the Reconfigured Singing Body, and the Megamusical', *Popular Music* 17, no. 2 (1999): 205–18.
7. For a discussion of these terms and their application, see John Martin, 'Characteristics of the Modern Dance', in *The Twentieth-Century Performance Reader*, ed. M. Huxley and N. Witts, 2nd ed. (London: Routledge, 2002), 295–302; Christian Keysers and Vincent Gazzola, 'Social Neuroscience: Mirror Neurons Recorded in Humans', *Current Biology* 20, no. 8 (2010): 353–54. For an application of these ideas to musical theatre performance, see Ben Macpherson, 'Dynamic Shape: The Dramaturgy of Song and Dance in Lloyd Webber's *Cats*', in *Gestures of Music Theater—The Performativity of Song and Dance*, ed. Dominic Symonds and Millie Taylor (New York: Oxford University Press, 2014), 54–70.
8. Antonio Damasio, *Self Comes to Mind: Constructing the Conscious Brain* (London: Vintage, 2010), 104.
9. McMillin, *The Musical as Drama*, 79.
10. Millie Taylor, Singing and Dancing Ourselves: The Politics of the Ensemble in *A Chorus Line*', in *Gestures of Music Theater: The Performativity of Song and Dance*, ed. Dominic Symonds and Millie Taylor (New York: Oxford University Press, 2014), 277.
11. McMillin, *The Musical as Drama*, 141, 149.
12. For the purposes of this discussion, micro-voiceworlds are composed of any song from a solo to a sextet. This is an arbitrary designation; a septet or octet may just as easily be a smaller grouping dependent on cast size and scale. This is then a simple measure of efficacy in this discussion rather than adhering to a specific definition drawn from accepted musicological or performative conventions.
13. Hughes, 'Singing the Community', 271.
14. See Ben Macpherson, *Cultural Identity in British Musical Theatre 1890–1939: Knowing One's Place* (Basingstoke: Palgrave, 2018), 35.

15. Edison Light Opera Company, *Favorite Airs from The Arcadians*, Wax cylinder (New York City: Edison [Amberol], 1913), 1CYL0002091 BD1 Black Amberol, British Library, http://www.library.ucsb.edu/OBJID/Cylinder0401. This recording (issue number Edison Blue Amberol: 2051) was a reissue of Edison 4-minute Amberol 476 (1913) and includes excerpts from 'Arcadians Are We', 'The Girl with a Brogue', 'Arcady Is Ever Young', 'Charming Weather', 'Bring Me a Rose', and 'Truth Is So Beautiful'; June Bronhill, Ann Howard, and Andy Cole, *The Arcadians*, Vinyl, Studio 2 Stereo (London: Columbia, 1968).
16. Lionel Monckton, Howard Talbot, and Arthur Wimperis, *The Arcadians (Vocal Score)* (London: Chappell & Co., 1909), 4–5.
17. Opening Chorus—Arcadians Are We' (London: Blue Amberol 2051, Unknown), C1816/D1 BD Paleophonics, British Library.
18. Hughes, 'Singing the Community', 263.
19. McMillin, *The Musical as Drama*, 68.
20. In their discussions of community, e.g., both Gerhard Delanty (2003) and Tony Blackshaw (2013) suggest it can be understood as a shared place or place, personal identity, or political ideology. See Gerhard Delanty, *Community* (Oxford: Routledge, 2003); Tony Blackshaw, *Key Concepts in Community Studies* (London: SAGE, 2013).
21. Robert Nisbet, *The Sociological Tradition* (London: Heinemann, 1967), 47–48.
22. Hughes, 'Singing the Community', 263.
23. Lyman Tower Sargent, 'The Three Faces of Utopianism Revisited', *Utopian Studies* 5, no. 1 (1994): 15. Given its peculiarly political ideal in contrast with the metropolitan corruption of London, we might also apply Benedict Anderson's notion of the 'imagined community' to Arcadia, defined as a national sensibility rather than a personal or tangible grouping of individuals. See Benedict Anderson, *Imagined Communities* (London: Verso, 1983).
24. McMillin, *The Musical as Drama*, 71.
25. Krishan Kumar, *Utopianism* (Oxford: Open University Press, 1991), 27.
26. Kumar, 24.
27. In another mid-twentieth-century article by George A. Hillery, 'community' was found to have ninety-four separate meanings. Consequently, Hillery advocated abandoning it in common discourse and social thought, in 'Definitions of Community: Areas of Agreement', *Rural Sociology* 20 (1955): 111–23.
28. Nisbet, *The Sociological Tradition*, 47.
29. Andrea Most, '"We Know We Belong to the Land": The Theatricality of Assimilation in Rodgers and Hammerstein's *Oklahoma!*', *PMLA Journal* 113, no. 1 (1998): 82.
30. Most, 82.
31. In an alternative reading, Jud is also indexical of Jewishness. For Derek Miller, 'Rodgers and Hammerstein present two versions of the Jew: the foreign, assimilable Ali Hakim and the assimilated, but essentially other, Jud', in 'Underneath the Ground: Jud and the Community in *Oklahoma!*', *Studies in Musical Theatre* 2, no. 2 (2008): 172.
32. Martell, 'Utopianism and Social Change: Materialism, Conflict and Pluralism', *Capital and Class* 42, no. 3 (2018): 447. See also Sargent, 'The Three Faces of Utopianism Revisited'.
33. Lyman Tower Sargent, *Utopianism: A Very Short Introduction* (Oxford: Oxford University Press, 1994), 21.
34. Jill Dolan, *Utopia in Performance: Finding Hope at the Theater* (Ann Arbor: University of Michigan Press, 2005), 2.
35. See Victor Turner, *Dramas, Fields, and Metaphors: Symbolic Action in Human Society* (Ithaca, NY: Cornell University Press, 1974), 273–74.
36. This is the same community heard configured in the song 'Plant Your Posies' at the top at act three, set in the now-famous Arcadian Restaurant, established by James 'Simplicitas' Smith.
37. Steven Connor, 'Choralities', *Twentieth-Century Music* 13, no. 1 (2016): 3.
38. Connor, 3.
39. Connor, 6.
40. McMillin, *The Musical as Drama*, 68, 71.
41. Adriana Cavarero, *For More than One Voice: A Philosophy of Vocal Expression* (Stanford, CA: Stanford University Press, 2005), 37; 'Death of Miss Florence Smithson', *The Times*, 13 February 1936, 10. For a recording of this song, see Florence Smithson, *The Pipes of Pan* (London: Columbia 542 6467, 1915), C1816/4 DL BD4 Paleophonics, British Library. This version demonstrates Smithson's occasional alveolar trills and awkward passaggio, while including a cadenza in her higher soprano range. Discussions of this decoration in later works

of musical theatre can be found in Taylor, *Musical Theatre, Realism and Entertainment*, 52; Symonds, 'Capturing the "Sung" to Make It "Song"', 12–13; Alison L. McKee, '"Think of Me Fondly": Voice, Body, Affect and Performance in Prince/Lloyd Webber's The Phantom of the Opera', *Studies in Musical Theatre* 7, no. 3 (2013): 309–25; Macpherson, 'A Voice and So Much More'; Cavarero, *For More Than One Voice*, 37.

42. There may even be a faint parallel to the presence of cry and echo in *Floyd Collins*, as heard in chapter 2.
43. As a point of comparison, Jeremy Rifkin suggests that empathy is not compatible with utopia. Jeremy Rifkin, *The Empathetic Civilization: The Race to Global Consciousness in a World in Crisis* (New York: Penguin, 2009).
44. Nancy L. Nester, 'The Empathetic Turn: The Relationship of Empathy to the Utopian Impulse', in *The Individual and Utopia: A Multidisciplinary Study of Humanity and Perfection*, ed. Clint Jones and Cameron Ellis (Oxford: Ashgate, 2015), 122, 127.
45. Numerous musical and scientific studies have explored the contentious notion of emotional response in listeners, both from a programmatic and an absolutist standpoint. For example, the work of Deniz Peters ('Musical Empathy, Emotional Co-Constitution, and the "Musical Other"', *Empirical Musicology Review* 10, no. 1 [2015]: 2–15) has explored how listening to music can allow listeners to experience emotions that are not their own to experience a form of vicarious empathy. Elsewhere, mirroring responses, affective empathy, and contagion in relation to musical response have been considered in Stephen Davies, 'Infection Music: Music-Listener Emotional Contagion', in *Empathy: Philosophical and Psychological Perspectives*, ed. A. Coplan and P. Goldie (New York: Oxford University Press, 2011), 134–48; Clemens Wollner, 'Audience Responses in the Light of Perception-Action Theories of Empathy', in *Music and Empathy*, ed. Elaine King and Caroline Waddington (London: Routledge, 2017), 139–56.
46. Alfred Lester, 'My Motter'. (London: Columbia 544 6474, 1915), C1816/4 D1 BD10 Paleophonics, British Library. Lester's delivery is clearly affected music hall speak-singing. At one moment, he stops the orchestra to direct them to be more 'lively' and 'merry' in the dance section, laconically requesting that they '[b]ring out that twiddly bit, that's a fine bit that is . . .'
47. 'Shaftesbury Theatre', *The Times*, 29 April 1909, 10.
48. 'Mr Alfred Lester—From Melodrama to Revue', *Manchester Guardian*, 7 May 1925, 10.
49. Onur Acaroglu, *Rethinking Marxist Approaches to Transition: Theory of Temporal Dislocation* (Leiden: Brill, 2021), 103.
50. McMillin, *The Musical as Drama*, 141, 149.
51. Nester, 'The Empathetic Turn', 122, 127.
52. In a recording of 'I'm a Jonah Man' from 1904, African American actor Pete Hampton clearly employed vocal cry and sob qualities in his overtly melodramatic delivery. British Library Sound and Image Archives, Shelfmark 1SS0009976 *'I'm A Jonah Man' (14 Jan 1904, recorded London), Orig. issue no: G&T GC 32041*. Accessed 20 July 2022.
53. Jermaine Singleton, *Cultural Melancholy: Readings of Race, Impossible Mourning and African American Ritual* (Champaign: University of Illinois Press, 2015), 2–3; see also Anne Anlin Cheng, *The Melancholy of Race: Psychoanalysis, Assimilation, and Hidden Grief* (New York: Oxford University Press, 2020).
54. Singleton, *Cultural Melancholy*, 10.
55. Martell, 'Utopianism and Social Change', 447.
56. Christopher Lasch, *The Culture of Narcissism: American Life in an Age of Diminishing Expectations* (New York: W. W. Norton, 1991).
57. John Bush Jones, *Our Musicals, Ourselves: A Social History of American Musical Theater* (Hanover, NH: University Press of New England, 2003), 269–70. More conventionally, these works are termed 'concept musicals'. However, Bush Jones's term is useful here, as it demonstrates the shift in structural priorities and frameworks that this chapter considers.
58. Sondheim cited in Meryle Secrest, *Stephen Sondheim: A Life* (London: Bloomsbury, 1998), 192.
59. Cited in Secrest, 199. The 2018 revisal, which changed Bobby's gender, may offer a different cultural reading of the character, but this falls beyond the scope of this discussion.
60. Bush Jones, *Our Musicals, Ourselves*, 276–77.
61. Hughes, 'Singing the Community', 263.
62. Sondheim cited in Secrest, *Stephen Sondheim*, 192.
63. George Furth and Stephen Sondheim, 'Company (Playscript)', in *Ten Great Musicals of the American Theatre*, ed. Stanley Richards (Ontario: Chilton Book Company, 1973), 649.

64. Steve Swayne, *How Sondheim Found His Sound* (Ann Arbor: University of Michigan Press, 2005), 30–31.
65. Hughes, 'Singing the Community', 263; Taylor, 'Singing and Dancing Ourselves', 277.
66. Sondheim cited in Secrest, *Stephen Sondheim*, 192.
67. Bush Jones, *Our Musicals, Ourselves*, 270. Groups numbers such as 'Company', 'Side by Side', and 'What Would We Do without You?' portray dysfunctional individuals riddled with contradictions and paradoxes.
68. Dolan, *Utopia in Performance*, 74.
69. In this way, it challenges any notion of even *imagined* communities of the kind Benedict Anderson has explored.
70. Zygmunt Bauman, *Liquid Modernity* (Malden, MA: Polity, 2012), viii.
71. Zygmunt Bauman, *Liquid Life* (Malden, MA: Polity, 2005).
72. Blackshaw, *Key Concepts in Community Studies*.
73. Most prominent in the restless, transitory, and fragmentary work of Stephen Sondheim ('The Day Off' and 'Putting It Together' in *Sunday in the Park with George* [1984]; 'Everybody's Got the Right' and 'Another National Anthem' in *Assassins* [1991]; and 'A Weekend in the Country' in *A Little Night Music* [1973]), it is also the chorality which gives voice to teenagers gossiping ('The Telephone Hour', *Bye Bye Birdie*, 1960), the anxieties of the inhabitants of 'Skid Row' (*Little Shop of Horrors*, 1982) and *London Road* (2011), and the nervous musings of hopeful hoofers ('I Hope I Get It', *A Chorus Line*, 1975).
74. Scholars and journalists alike have noted the contemporaneity of *Company* when it was first produced in 1970. It was a 'show about contemporary upper-middle-class New Yorkers, presented to contemporary upper-middle-class New Yorkers' (E. Bristow and K. Butler cited in Jeffrey Rubel, "You Never Need an Analyst with Bobby Around": The Mid-20th Century Human Sciences in Sondheim and Furth's Musical *Company*', *History of the Human Sciences* 35 [2021]: 2.) For others, '*Company* is one of the few Broadway [shows] to reflect the environment and lives of its original audiences' (John Olson, '*Company*—25 Years Later', in *Stephen Sondheim: A Casebook*, ed. Joanne Gordon [New York: Garland, 2000], 47.)
75. Salomé Voegelin, *Sonic Possible Worlds: Hearing the Continuum of Sound* (London: Bloomsbury, 2014).
76. The micro-voiceworld of *Company* includes moments of parody and specific aesthetic appropriation, with patter songs, hymnals, and a parody of the vocal trio the Andrews Sisters. However, given the discussion of stylistic appropriation and their decadent function in singing utopia, they will not be considered in full here.
77. Blackshaw, *Key Concepts in Community Studies*.
78. Furth and Sondheim, 'Company (Playscript)', 676, 703.
79. Blackshaw, *Key Concepts in Community Studies*.
80. Stacy Ellen Wolf, 'Keeping Company with Sondheim's Women', in *The Oxford Handbook of Sondheim Studies*, ed. Robert Gordon (New York: Oxford University Press, 2014), 372.
81. Matthew Beaumont, 'Socially Empty Space and Dystopian Utopianism in the Late Nineteenth Century', in *Utopian Spaces of Modernism: British Literature and Culture 1885–1945*, ed. Rosalyn Gregory and Benjamin Kohlmann (Basingstoke: Palgrave, 2012), 19–34.
82. Beaumont, 19.
83. Wolf, 'Keeping Company with Sondheim's Women', 372.
84. McMillin, *The Musical as Drama*, 141, 149; Beaumont, 'Socially Empty Space and Dystopian Utopianism in the Late Nineteenth Century', 21.
85. Perhaps it is utopian by dint of the fact that a solo character enters the 'space of vulnerability' in the moment of performance (a fact reinforced by the complex vocal demands in Sondheim's writing); McMillin, *The Musical as Drama*, 141, 149. Perhaps it is utopian through its lyrical focus on the opportunities of the big city. While both readings have merit, this is also not a voice which arises from a moment of emotional transparency or intensity. It is not a voice which sings about anyone or anything. It does not enact a sonic 'exploration of the possible', instead giving voice to a condition in the here and now.
86. Barbara Means Fraser, 'Revisiting Greece: The Sondheim Chorus', in *Stephen Sondheim: A Casebook*, ed. Joanne Gordon (New York: Garland, 2000), 223–50; McMillin, *The Musical as Drama*, 96–98; Bruce Kirle, *Unfinished Showbusiness: Broadway Musicals as Works-in-Process* (Carbondale: Southern Illinois University Press, n.d.), 121–22.
87. As McMillin continues to note, 'The ensemble has a grip in *Company* . . . not so much in the book or the lyrics, but in the performance of the numbers', in *The Musical as Drama*, 97.

88. Bauman, *Liquid Modernity*, 169.
89. Mark Jendrysik, 'Fundamental Oppositions: Utopia and the Individual', in *The Individual and Utopia: A Multidisciplinary Study of Humanity and Perfection*, ed. Clint Jones and Cameron Ellis (Abingdon: Ashgate, 2015), 28.
90. Furth and Sondheim, 'Company (Playscript)', 719.
91. McMillin, *The Musical as Drama*, 80.
92. Morrison, 'Race, Blacksound, and the (Re)Making of Musicological Discourse', 783.
93. Nia Wilson, '*Hadestown*: Nontraditional Casting, Race, and Capitalism', *TDR: The Drama Review* 65, no. 1 (2021): 188–92.
94. Due to the complex development of the work, this case study will consider the cast first seen on Broadway in 2019.
95. Richard Schechner, 'The Director's Process: An Interview with Rachel Chavkin', *TDR: The Drama Review* 65, no. 1 (2021): 79–94.
96. Morrison, 'Race, Blacksound, and the (Re)Making of Musicological Discourse', 789.
97. This is based on the premise that of the forty songs on the Original Broadway Cast Recording, twenty of them include more than eight vocalists; *Hadestown (Original Broadway Cast Recording)*, Compact Disc (Sing It Again Records, 2019). This recording formed the primary basis for the analysis of the musical.
98. Samuel Floyd in Matthew D. Morrison, 'The Sound(s) of Subjection: Constructing American Popular Music and Racial Identity through Blacksound', *Women & Performance: A Journal of Feminist Theory* 27, no. 1 (2017): 15, https://doi.org/10.1080/0740770X.2017.1282120.
99. See Malawey, *A Blaze of Light in Every Word*, 123.
100. Steven Connor, *Beyond Words: Sobs, Hums, Stutters and Other Vocalizations* (London: Reaktion Books, 2014), 91–95.
101. Connor, 91–95.
102. Anais Mitchell, *Working on a Song: The Lyrics of Hadestown* (New York: Plume, 2020), 100.
103. Jarman-Ivens, *Queer Voices: Technologies, Vocalities, and the Musical Flaw* (Basingstoke: Palgrave, 2011), 44.
104. Clément, 'Through Voices, History', 24.
105. Valerie Lynn Schrader, '"Why We Build the Wall": Hegemony, Memory and Current Events in *Hadestown*', *Studies in Musical Theatre* 16, no. 2 (2022): 125, https://doi.org/10.1386/smt_00093_1.
106. Mitchell, *Working on a Song*, 134.
107. Nisbet, *The Sociological Tradition*, 47–48.
108. In line with Blackshaw, it is therefore the *function* of the community to enact the exclusion through the building of a wall—something which had profound social resonance in America at the time of *Hadestown*'s first production during the 2016-2020 presidential administration of Donald Trump.
109. Mitchell, *Working on a Song*, 250.
110. Wilson, 'Hadestown', 191–92.
111. Mitchell, *Working on a Song*, 253.
112. Notwithstanding the fact that 'the musical pretends that the racial difference can be overcome in the spirit of exuberant singing', small glimpses of a progressive contingent chorality can also be found in early works such as *Show Boat* (1928) (McMillin, *The Musical as Drama*, 71). In a 1946 performance of 'Can't Help Lovin' Dat Man', for example, the mixed-race trio of Carol Bruce, Helen Dowdy, and Kenneth Spencer are joined by a mixed chorus (Carol Bruce, Helen Dowdy, and Kenneth Spencer, Can't Help Lovin' Dat Man, Compact Disc [New York City: Columbia, 1946], 1CD0187652 D2 BD10 Pearl, British Library). Given the intention, if not entire success, of *Show Boat* in challenging segregation on the musical stage, there is nonetheless a sense of 'honoring' the intention in a way that, decades later, might find a parallel in 'We Raise Our Cups'.
113. Mitchell, *Working on a Song*, 11.
114. Mitchell, 117.
115. Mitchell, 171.
116. It should be noted that not all Fates in all casts are African American, even while the vocal tropes in the musical draw on this influence. For example, the original Broadway cast featured African American performer Jewelle Blackman, Filipino-American Kay Trinidad, and Cuban-American Yvette Gonzalez-Nacer.

117. Goosman, *Group Harmony*, 3. As Goosman has explored elsewhere, there is a direct link between the roots of African American culture and popularity of vocal trios, in 'The Black Authentic: Structure, Style and Values in Group Harmony', *Black Music Research Journal* 17, no. 1 (1997): 81–99.
118. African American female vocal harmony groups were not always relegated to backing or support for white artists. Popular examples from the 1960s include the Crystals and the Ronettes, leading to the prominence of so-called girl groups of the 1990s and early 2000s (such as Destiny's Child and TLC)—an aesthetic and trope which returns in the following chapter.
119. Maureen Mahon, *Black Diamond Queens: African American Women and Rock and Roll* (Durham, NC: Duke University Press, 2020), 108.
120. Mahon, 106; Mitchell, *Working on a Song*, 11.
121. Stoever, *The Sonic Color Line*, 2016, 11.
122. Morrison, 'Race, Blacksound, and the (Re)Making of Musicological Discourse', 783.
123. Asare, 'Vocal Colour in Blue', 52, 63.
124. Mahon, *Black Diamond Queens*, 106; Susan Fast, 'Genre, Subjectivity and Back-Up Singing in Rock Music', in *The Ashgate Research Companion to Popular Musicology*, ed. Derek B. Scott (Surrey: Ashgate, 2009), 178.
125. Mahon, *Black Diamond Queens*, 109.
126. Mahon, 111.
127. Mahon, 111.
128. Asare, 'Vocal Colour in Blue', 61.
129. Means Fraser, 'Revisiting Greece', 223. The American musical stage has often had a complicated relationship with the notion of a Greek chorus, evident in the criticism levelled at Rodgers and Hammerstein's *Allegro* (1947), for example. This is because '[t]he Greek conception of character is the opposite of American sensibilities', celebrating individualism as part of the community, rather than *apart* from the community. For further discussion on this subject, see Zachary Dunbar, '"How Do You Solve a Problem like the Chorus?": Hammerstein's *Allegro* and the Reception of the Greek Chorus on Broadway', in *Choruses, Ancient and Modern*, ed. Joshua Billings, Felix Budelmann, and Fiona Macintosh (Oxford: Oxford University Press, 2013), 243–58; Hughes, 'Singing the Community'.
130. Mitchell, *Working on a Song*, 33.
131. Kendrick, *Theatre Aurality*, 63; Barry Blesser and Linda-Ruth Salter, *Spaces Speak, Are You Listening?: Experiencing Aural Architecture* (Cambridge, MA: MIT Press, 2006), 49.
132. Cavarero, *For More than One Voice*, 170.
133. Steven Connor, *Dumbstruck: A Cultural History of Ventriloquism* (Oxford: Oxford University Press, 2001), 35–43.
134. Cavarero, *For More Than One Voice*, 167, 170, emphasis mine.
135. This 'acoustic relationality' is particularly evidence in moments of falsetto, as Orpheus' voice soars above the workers' echoes.
136. Jacques Derrida, *Rogues: Two Essays on Reason* (Stanford, CA: Stanford University Press, 2005), xi–xii.
137. Notably, several musical theatre works have been performed entirely using a cappella voices. These include *Avenue X*, which written by John Jiler and Ray Leslee was seen Off-Broadway in 1994, drawing on the a cappella aesthetic in a story about Doo-Wop singers. In December 2016, *In Transit* became the first entirely a cappella musical on Broadway, having premiered Off-Broadway in 2010. In both cases, multiple voices provided textures and rhythms along with melodic performances.
138. Hans-Thies Lehmann, *Postdramatic Theatre* (Abingdon: Routledge, 2006), 130.
139. Fischer-Lichte, *The Transformative Power of Performance*, 127.
140. See, e.g., Daniel J. Levitin, *This Is Your Brain on Music: The Science of a Human Obsession* (London: Atlantic Books, 2008); chapters 4 and 5 of Isabelle Peretz and Robert Zatorre, eds., *The Cognitive Neuroscience of Music* (Oxford: Oxford University Press, 2003); Michael H. Thaut, *Rhythm, Music, and the Brain: Scientific Foundations and Clinical Applications* (Oxford: Routledge, 2007); Mithen, *The Singing Neanderthals: The Origins of Music, Language, Mind and Body* (Cambridge, MA: Harvard University Press, 2005).
141. Mitchell, *Working on a Song*, 246.
142. Dolan, *Utopia in Performance*, 6.
143. Sarah K. Whitfield, 'Disrupting Heteronormative Temporality through Queer Dramaturgies: *Fun Home, Hadestown and A Strange Loop*', *Arts (MDPI)* 9, no. 2 (2020): 69,

https://doi.org/10.3390/arts9020069. This reading, of course, changes when we listen across new cast members of the Broadway production; in August 2022 it was announced that Lilias White—an African American female—would take over as Hermes, while in late 2023, the black actor Phillip Boykin would take on the role of Hades and white, openly queer performer Betty Who would play Persephone. These changes in the personal identities of the performers may alter radically the way in which their micro-voiceworlds may be heard.

144. Whitfield, 70.
145. Hughes, 'Singing the Community', 263.
146. Richard Dyer, 'Entertainment and Utopia', in *The Cultural Studies Reader*, ed. Simon During (London: Routledge, 1993), 273; Dolan, *Utopia in Performance*, 6.

Chapter 4

1. Stephen Citron, *The Wordsmiths* (London: Vintage, 1996), 262.
2. In one review of the Original Broadway Cast Recording, Harrison's singing was described as something of a 'sideline' ('"Fair Lady" Album Off to Hot Start', *Billboard*, 7 April 1956, 22).
3. For further discussion, see Dominic McHugh, *Loverly: The Life and Times of 'My Fair Lady'* (New York: Oxford University Press, 2012); Ben Macpherson, '"Eliza, Where the Devil Are My Songs?": Negotiating Voice, Text and Performance Analysis in Rex Harrison's Henry Higgins', *Studies in Musical Theatre* 2, no. 1 (2008): 235–44; 'Part II: Production, Reproduction, and the case of My Fair Lady', in Tim Anderson, *Making Easy Listening: Material Culture and Postwar American Recording* (Minneapolis: University of Minnesota Press, 2006), 49–102.
4. Susan Loesser, *A Most Remarkable Fella: Frank Loesser and the Guys and Dolls in His Life* (New York: Hal Leonard, 1993), 18; Meryle Secrest, *Stephen Sondheim: A Life* (London: Bloomsbury, 1998), 251; Stephen Sondheim et al., *Four by Sondheim, Wheeler, Lapine, Shevelove and Gelbart* (New York: Hal Leonard, 2000), 170.
5. Secrest, *Stephen Sondheim*, 253.
6. Scott McMillin, *The Musical as Drama* (Ithaca, NY: Cornell University Press, 2006), 141, 149.
7. Dyer, 'Entertainment and Utopia', in *The Cultural Studies Reader*, ed. Simon During (London: Routledge, 1993), 273.
8. Ana Flavia Zuim, 'Speech Inflection in American Musical Theatre Compositions' (Florida Atlantic University, 2012); Tracy Bourne, Maeve Garnier, and Diana Kenny, 'Music Theater Voice: Production, Physiology and Pedagogy', *Journal of Singing* 67, no. 4 (2011): 437–44.
9. See Zuim, 'Speech Inflection in American Musical Theatre Compositions'. This sort of shift also happened in the mid-nineteenth century, when the verismo aesthetic became vogueish. In this case, it led to what Andreas Giger termed a rejection of the emotional 'monumentality' (or 'transparency') of Romantic opera in favour of something altogether more ambiguous. See Andreas Giger, 'Verismo: Origin, Corruption, and Redemption of an Operatic Term', *Journal of the American Musicological Society* 60, no. 2 (2007): 297.
10. See Fred Astaire and George Gershwin, 'The Half-of-It Dearie Blues' (London: Columbia, 1926), 1CS0025324 2 Columbia, British Library; Jack Buchanan and Ray Noble, 'Jack Buchanan Medley #1: Sunny / Goodnight Vienna / Stand Up and Sing' (London: HMV, 1933), 1CD0048488 D1 S1 BD16 Living Era, British Library; Ivor Novello and Dorothy Dickson, 'Used to You' from *Crest of a Wave* (London: Rococo S2 BD6, Unknown), 1LP0118740, British Library. In tandem with African American influences as described by Matthew D. Morrison and others, moments of speak-singing have therefore formed a recurrent presence throughout much of the twentieth and twenty-first centuries in both musical theatre and popular music at large.
11. As noted in the introduction, this may have been first introduced on Broadway in *The Wookie* (1937); Harold C. Schonberg, 'Stage View: The Surrender of Broadway to Amplified Sound', *New York Times*, 15 March 1981. See also Arreanna Rostosky, 'Amplifying Broadway after the Golden Age', in *The Routledge Companion to the Contemporary Musical*, ed. Jessica Sternfeld and Elizabeth L. Wollman (New York: Routledge, n.d.), 78. Later, composer John Kander reflected: 'My memory is that when I did the dance music for 'Gypsy' on the road, one day Jule Styne turned on the foot mikes without telling Ethel Merman. I say it's been downhill all the way from that moment' (cited in Ben Macpherson, 'Sing: Musical Theater Voices from *Superstar* to *Hamilton*', in *The Routledge Companion to the Contemporary Musical*, ed. Jessica Sternfeld and Elizabeth L. Wollman [New York: Routledge, 2020], 69).
12. Jude Dry, 'DA Pennebaker's "Original Cast Album: Company" Is the Best Musical Theater Documentary Ever', *IndieWire*, 5 August 2019, https://www.indiewire.com/features/general/da-pennebaker-original-cast-album-company-sondheim-elaine-stritch-1202163427/.

13. George List, 'The Boundaries of Speech and Song', *Ethnomusicology* 7, no. 1 (1963): 3; Raymond Knapp, *The American Musical and the Formation of National Identity* (Princeton, NJ: Princeton University Press, 2005), 12.
14. George List identifies three common characteristics of speech and song: they are both vocally produced, [often] linguistically meaningful, and both are melodic. In common with List's approach, the points of similarity and divergence with respect to melody is the most provocative focus in this chapter. List, 'The Boundaries of Speech and Song', 1.
15. List, 9. See also Konstantinos Thomaidis and Ben Macpherson, 'Voice(s) as a Method and an In-Between', in *Voice Studies: Critical Approaches to Process, Performance and Experience*, ed. Thomaidis and Macpherson (Oxford: Routledge, 2015), 3–0.
16. Citron, *The Wordsmiths*, 262.
17. The production of List's chart is credited to Sheridan Schroeter.
18. Citron, *The Wordsmiths*, 262.
19. List, 'The Boundaries of Speech and Song', 7–9.
20. List, 2–5.
21. Jacopo Peri, 'Peri's Dedication of the Score and Letter to the Reader', in *Opera: A History in Documents*, ed. Piero Weiss (New York: Oxford University Press, 2002), 15. As Abbate and Parker outline, *secco recitativo* in particular is a style in which 'the pitches tend to follow the intonations of speech' (*A History of Opera: The Last Four Hundred Years* [London: Penguin, 2012], 26). Notwithstanding the ideological imperatives in opera, this kind of analysis might present fascinating opportunities for revisiting the kind of declamatory vocal writing in operas, beyond arias, duets, or other discrete musical numbers.
22. Edward Rothstein, 'Utopia and Its Discontents', in *Visions of Utopia*, ed. Furaha D. Norton (New York: Oxford University Press, 2003), 1–28; Krishan Kumar, *Utopianism* (Oxford: Open University Press, 1991).
23. Meredith Willson, *'But He Doesn't Know the Territory'—The Making of Meredith Willson's 'The Music Man'* (Minneapolis: University of Minnesota Press, 2009), 48, italics mine. Yet, the style was a creative decision by composer and lyricist Willson, who had 'an abiding conviction... that in a musical comedy the musical numbers ought to grow out of the dialogue'. (Willson, 43.)
24. List, 'The Boundaries of Speech and Song', 6.
25. Willson, *'But He Doesn't Know the Territory'*, 176; Michael Schwartz, 'The Music Man Cometh: The Tuneful Pipe Dreams of Professor Harold Hill', in *Text and Presentation*, ed. Stratos E. Constantinidis (Jefferson, NC: McFarland, 2008), 174. In this analysis, I refer primarily to the 1992 re-issue of the Original Broadway Cast Recording (Robert Preston and Barbara Cook, *The Music Man [Original Broadway Cast]*, Compact Disc, Vol. 3, Broadway Classics [Hayes, Middlesex: Angel Records, 1992]).
26. Willson, *'But He Doesn't Know the Territory'*, 61 original emphasis; Schwartz, 'The Music Man Cometh', 173.
27. Track 3: 'Ya Got Trouble', *The Music Man (Original Broadway Cast)*.
28. Such characters are part of a tradition of the conman or greedy hustler on the musical stage including Anthony Tweedlepunch in *Florodora* (1899), Ali Hakim in *Oklahoma!* (1943), General Bullmoose in *Li'l Abner* (1956), or Starbuck in *110 in the Shade* (1963).
29. For an extensive consideration of the ways in which civic parades—with marching bands—helped forge various American social identities in the nineteenth century and beyond, see Mary Ryan, 'The American Parade: Representations of the Nineteenth-Century Social Order', in *The New Cultural History*, ed. Lynn Hunt (Berkeley: University of California Press, 1989), 131–53; Kenneth Moss, 'St. Patrick's Day Celebrations and the Formation of Irish-American Identity, 1845–1875', *Journal of Social History* 29, no. 1 (1995): 125–48; Patrick Warfield, 'The March as Musical Drama and the Spectacle of John Philip Sousa,' *Journal of the American Musicological Society* 64, no. 2 (2011): 289–318; Jürgen Heideking, Genevieve Fabre, and Kai Dreisbach, *Celebrating Ethnicity and Nation: American Festive Culture from the Revolution to Early 20th Century* (Oxford: Berghahn Books, 2001), specifically chapter 2.
30. Track 8, *The Music Man (Original Broadway Cast)*.
31. Knapp, *The American Musical and the Formation of National Identity*, 144–51. Along with 'The Sadder-but-Wiser Girl', Hill also performs the song 'Marian the Librarian'. Taken together, these form a vocal transition from conman to reformed huckster, as Meredith gives the character increasingly elongated vowel sounds on the words 'Marian' and 'Librarian', allowing Preston to sonically perform a vocal litmus test of her willingness to let him be vulnerable and finally surrender in song.

32. Knapp, 146.
33. For a social history of barbershop quartets, including their link to African American song forms, see Vic Hobson, *Louis Armstrong and Barbershop Harmony* (Jackson: University of Mississippi Press, 2018); Richard Mook, 'White Masculinity in Barbershop Quartet Singing', *Journal of the Society for American Music* 1, no. 4 (2007): 453–83; Gage Averill, *Four Parts, No Waiting: A Social History of American Barbershop Harmony* (New York: Oxford University Press, 2003).
34. Knapp, *The American Musical and the Formation of National Identity*, 146.
35. Thomaidis and Macpherson, 'Voice(s) as a Method and an In-Between', 4.
36. Knapp, *The American Musical and the Formation of National Identity*, 145; Robert Gordon, Olaf Jubin, and Millie Taylor, *British Musical Theatre since 1950* (London: Bloomsbury Methuen, 2016), 127.
37. It would appear that such a feeling is culturally determined, and therefore might apply more intensely to American musicals in America and British musicals in Britain.
38. Malcolm Chase and Christopher Shaw, *The Imagined Past: History and Nostalgia* (Manchester; Manchester University Press, 1989), 3, 9.
39. David Lowenthal, 'Nostalgia Tells It like It Wasn't', in *The Imagined Past: History and Nostalgia*, ed. Malcolm Chase and Christopher Shaw (Manchester: Manchester University Press, 1989), 29.
40. Dyer, 'Entertainment and Utopia', 273. Specifically, Hill follows the lead of Marian, a girl-next-door American ideal, but nevertheless, a woman, and a *real* musician, in a performance of shifting gender ideals as part of the post-war American Dream.
41. Schwartz, 'The Music Man Cometh', 165.
42. Dyer, 'Entertainment and Utopia', 273.
43. David Stafford and Caroline Stafford, *Fings Ain't Wot They Used T'Be: The Lionel Bart Story* (London: Omnibus Press, 2011), 17–18.
44. I borrow the term 'vernacular' here from Millie Taylor, as a way of describing the quality of the intermediate vocality in these East End British musicals. While Harold Hill uses heightened speech, his transitions from travelling salesman to revival-meeting preacher and bandleader do not exhibit the same 'vernacular' properties; Millie Taylor, 'Lionel Bart: British Vernacular Musical Theatre', in *The Oxford Handbook of the British Musical*, ed. Robert Gordon and Olaf Jubin (New York: Oxford University Press, 2016), 500. This unrefined vocality typified Bart's musical but is also heard in works such as *Make Me an Offer* (1959) and *Fings Ain't Wot They Used T'Be* (1960). Elizabeth Wells suggests that the casual and unrefined style that characterized the communities in these 'Soho musicals'—including their vocal aesthetics—was in part a defence of English working-class identities against a newly dominant American popular culture. In other words, while speak-singing characterized individuals as they resisted conformity on Broadway and the West End, it might also come to characterize entire communities, as discussed later in this chapter. See Wells, 'After Anger: The British Musical of the Late-1950s', in *The Oxford Handbook of the British Musical*, ed. Robert Gordon and Olaf Jubin (New York: Oxford University Press, 2016), 273–90.
45. Cited in Stafford and Stafford, *Fings Ain't Wot They Used T'Be*, 18.
46. Charles Dickens, *Oliver Twist* (Barcelona: Fabbri Publishing, 1990).
47. As one essay remarked in a theatrical magazine from 1880, 'Jews are so exceedingly fond of dramatical and musical entertainments . . . they furnish so many aspirants for music-hall honours', in Marc Napolitano, *Oliver! A Dickensian Musical* (New York: Oxford University Press, 2014), 116.
48. This analysis primarily refers to the following: *Oliver! (Original London Production)*, LP vinyl (London: Decca (SKL4105), 1960). Like Preston's Hill and Moody's Fagin, Danny Sewell's original performance as Bill Sykes was also quasi-prosodic in his song 'My Name'—both in its sonority and its aesthetic. However, given Fagin's centrality to the broader narrative, Moody's performance yields more insights.
49. Carey Wall, 'There's No Business like Show Business: A Speculative Reading of the Broadway Musical', in *Approaches to the American Musical*, ed. Robert Lawson-Peebles (Exeter: University of Exeter Press, 1996), 30–31. In fact, Oliver's unbroken juvenile voice (particularly in the song 'Where Is Love?') may be the only 'full self' on display in the voiceworld of the entire musical.
50. Fagin's Jewish identity is also heard in the seemingly improvised cadenza on the word 'boys' at the end, typical of Jewish cantorial music. At times, this cadenza is heard at the end of 'Reviewing the Situation' rather than 'You've Got to Pick a Pocket or Two'.
51. Track 3: 'Ya Got Trouble', Preston and Cook, *The Music Man (Original Broadway Cast)*.

52. Taylor, 'Lionel Bart', 500.
53. Jack Gottlieb, *Funny, It Doesn't Sound Jewish: How Yiddish Songs and Synagogue Melodies Influenced Tin Pan Alley, Broadway, and Hollywood* (Albany: State University of New York Press, 2004), 12.
54. This song is also 'purely a creation for Bart's Fagin; Dicken's "merry old gentleman" would never consider leaving the criminal underworld'; see Napolitano, *Oliver!*, 155.
55. Gottlieb, *Funny, It Doesn't Sound Jewish*, 149.
56. Lionel Bart, *Oliver! (Full Conductor's Score)* (New York: TRO Hollis Music Ltd, 1963), 118; Track 18: 'Reviewing the Situation', *Oliver! (Original London Production)*.
57. Mark Slobin, *Fiddler on the Move: Exploring the Klezmer World* (Oxford: Oxford University Press, 2000), 98–122.
58. Rothstein, 'Utopia and Its Discontents', 3.
59. Thomaidis and Macpherson, 'Voice(s) as a Method and an In-Between', 4.
60. Gordon, Jubin, and Taylor, *British Musical Theatre since 1950*, 127, 45.
61. Napolitano, *Oliver!*, 119.
62. Thomaidis and Macpherson, 'Voice(s) as a Method and an In-Between', 4.
63. Anne Karpf, *The Human Voice: How This Extraordinary Instrument Reveals Essential Clues about Who We Are* (New York: Bloomsbury, 2006), 139. Karpf further observes that while 'emotions produce changes in muscle tension, breathing patterns, . . . psychomotor activity [and alter] our laryngeal muscles' and the limbic area responsible for our feelings and emotions, any suggestion that the binary equivalence between certain voice patterns and clear emotions is inherently flawed (Karpf, 134–35). See also Swati Johar, 'Psychology of Voice', in *Emotion, Affect and Personality in Speech: The Bias of Language of Paralanguage* (Cham, Switzerland: Springer International, 2016), 11.
64. Chistopher Lasch, *The Culture of Narcissism: American Life in an Age of Diminishing Expectations* (New York: W. W. Norton, 1991).
65. Craig Zadan, *Sondheim & Co.*, 2nd ed. (London: Nick Hern Books, 1990), 337.
66. Knapp, *The American Musical and the Performance of Personal Identity*, 151.
67. Jack Zipes, *Breaking the Magic Spell: Radical Theories of Folk and Fairy Tales*, 2nd ed. (Lexington: University Press of Kentucky, 2002), 3.
68. Mari Cronin, 'Sondheim: The Idealist', in *Stephen Sondheim: A Casebook*, ed. Joanne Gordon (Oxford: Garland, 2000), 144–45.
69. Track 15: 'Any Moment/Moments in the Woods', *Into the Woods (Original Broadway Cast Recording)*, Compact Disc, Masterworks Broadway (Sony BMG, 1990). The following analysis is based primarily on the Original Broadway Cast Recording and the filmed DVD release of the original production (*Into the Woods*, DVD [New York: Image Entertainment, 1997]). As with other analyses, references to individual audio tracks will only be made where lyrics have been cited from a recording rather than libretto.
70. Karpf, *The Human Voice*, 139.
71. Knapp, *The American Musical and the Performance of Personal Identity*, 159–60. For a brief consideration of Sondheim's 'modular' approach to composition in *Into the Woods*, see Steve Swayne, *How Sondheim Found His Sound* (Ann Arbor: University of Michigan Press, 2005), 230–32.
72. Stephen Banfield, *Sondheim's Broadway Musicals* (Ann Arbor: University of Michigan Press, 1995), 393.
73. Sondheim cited in Tavi Gevinson, 'The Special Panic of Singing Sondheim', *New Yorker*, 23 December 2021, https://www.newyorker.com/culture/culture-desk/the-special-panic-of-singing-sondheim. Elsewhere in this article, Gevinson recalls working on an Off-Broadway production of Sondheim's 1991 musical *Assassins*. Reflecting on the 'special panic' of singing Sondheim's words and music, she notes that he wrote songs 'allowing characters' desires to come with caveats and second-guessing. His curlicued melodies are those thoughts' sonic equivalents.
74. Zipes, *Breaking the Magic Spell*, 3.
75. Swayne, *How Sondheim Found His Sound*, 94; see also Robert Komaniecki, 'Vocal Pitch in Rap Flow', *Integral* 34 (2020): 25–45.
76. Knapp, *The American Musical and the Performance of Personal Identity*, 156.
77. Knapp, 152.
78. Track 1: 'Prologue: Into the Woods', *Into the Woods (Original Broadway Cast Recording)*. As Knapp has suggested, there is a direct parallel in Cinderella's ambivalence with the Witch, who later tells the Baker, Jack, Cinderella, and Little Red Ridinghood that they are 'not good . . .just nice' (Knapp, *The American Musical and the Performance of Personal Identity*, 152; Track 16, *Into the Woods [Original Broadway Cast Recording]*).

79. Track 1: 'Prologue: Into the Woods'; Track 6: 'A Very Nice Prince/First Midnight/Giants in the Sky', *Into the Woods (Original Broadway Cast Recording).*
80. Ben Francis offers a slightly different reading, suggesting that Cinderella's desire to live 'in-between' is not ambivalence, but a desire to escape two forms of repression—'the slavery of her past and the fantasy of the Prince's palace'—and live a life she chooses and desires. Read this way, Kim Crosby's aspirate aesthetic in the original production might offer a way of listening to Cinderella's changeable vocality in relation to her circumstances. See Ben Francis, Ben Francis, '"Careful the Spell You Cast": *Into the Woods* and the Uses of Disenchantment', in *The Oxford Handbook of Sondheim Studies*, ed. Robert Gordon (New York: Oxford University Press, 2014), 358.
81. Track 12: 'Act II Prologue: So Happy', *Into the Woods (Original Broadway Cast Recording).*
82. Dyer, 'Entertainment and Utopia', 273.
83. Track 11: 'Ever After', *Into the Woods (Original Broadway Cast Recording).*
84. Track 12: 'Act II Prologue: So Happy', *Into the Woods (Original Broadway Cast Recording).*
85. While tangential to this discussion, the death of the narrator invites clear parallels with Barthes' concept of the death of the author and birth of the reader. In the case of *Into the Woods*, when the narrator is removed, both characters and audience members are given agency in how the story develops. As Barthes says, without the narrator/author figure, a text is revealed to be 'made up of multiple writings'. As if to reinforce the centrality of the listener in how we might understand musical theatre voiceworlds, Barthes continues to assert that 'the reader [or, audience member] is the space on which all the quotations that make up a writing are inscribed without any of them being lost; a text's unity lies not in its origin but in its destination' (see 'The Death of the Author', in *Image, Music Text*, trans. Stephen Heath [London: Fontana, 1977], 148).
86. Track 16: 'Your Fault/Last Midnight', *Into the Woods (Original Broadway Cast Recording).*
87. Brandon LaBelle, *Lexicon of the Mouth: Poetics and Politics of Voice and the Oral Imaginary* (London: Bloomsbury, 2014), 45, 56.
88. LaBelle, 58.
89. Dyer, 'Entertainment and Utopia', 273.
90. McMillin, *The Musical as Drama*, 141, 149; Dyer, 'Entertainment and Utopia', 273.
91. Central to the entire musical is the triangulation of storytelling, fathers, and sons. The Narrator is often cast as The Mysterious Man in the woods, who turns out to be The Baker's father. The Baker, then, tells his son the story, passing on the moral lessons from his own father.
92. Track 19: 'Finale: Children Will Listen', *Into the Woods (Original Broadway Cast Recording).*
93. This analysis will refer to *Hamilton* (New York: Disney+, 2020) and *Hamilton (Original Broadway Cast Recording)*, Compact Disc (Atlantic Records, 2016).
94. Zadan, *Sondheim & Co.*, 337.
95. Edward Delman, 'How Lin-Manuel Miranda Shapes History', *The Atlantic*, 29 September 2015, https://www.theatlantic.com/entertainment/archive/2015/09/lin-manuel-miranda-hamilton/408019/. The development of *Hamilton* was interconnected to Obama's presidency. Lin-Manuel Miranda first presented the title song in an evening of poetry and music, hosted by President Obama and the First Lady, at the White House on 12 May 2009. Seven years later—as a 'firm favourite' of the Obama family—the White House hosted a concert performance of *Hamilton* (with the Broadway cast) on 14 March 2016. On the same day, First Lady Michelle Obama had also joined cast members in workshops with high school students, based on the musical. See The Obama White House, '"President Obama Welcomes the Broadway Cast of 'Hamilton'"', YouTube, 14 March 2016, https://www.youtube.com/watch?v=V3bNmhbvU2o.
96. Donatella Galella, 'Being in "The Room Where It Happens": *Hamilton*, Obama, and Nationalist Neoliberal Multicultural Inclusion', *Theatre Survey* 59, no. 3 (2018): 363–85; Hodges Persley, *Sampling and Remixing Blackness in Hip-Hop Theater and Performance* (Ann Arbor: University of Michigan Press), 201.
97. See Imani Perry, *Prophets of the Hood: Politics and Poetics in Hip Hop* (Durham, NC: Duke University Press, 2004); Tricia Rose, *Black Noise: Rap Music and Black Culture in Contemporary America* (Middletown, CT: Wesleyan University Press, 1994).

98. Because of these properties, some analyses draw a direct connection between rap delivery and the aesthetics of recitative; see Nataliia Kravchencko, Olena Zhykharieva, and Yuliia Konenets, 'Rap Artists' Identity in Archetypal Roles of Hero and Seeker: A Linguistic Perspective', *Journal of Language and Linguistic Studies* 17, no. 1 (2021): 646–61; Rob Weiner-Kendt, 'From Rags to Revolutionary: "Hamilton" Tells a True American Story'. *America Magazine* (2015), https://www.americamagazine.org/rags-revolutionary#:~:text=Born%20out%20of%20wedlock%20in,for%20the%20budding%20American%20Revolution. However, the emphasis on rhyme through repetition in rap, and its strict metre to support flow in delivery differs from much recitative—particularly *secco recitativo* (simple recitative). While often delivered with rapidity, it did not always exhibit repetition or rhyme, and often had 'no sense of a regular beat'; see Carolyn Abbate and Roger Parker, *A History of Opera: The Last Four Hundred Years* (London: Penguin, 2012), 26.
99. Komaniecki, 'Vocal Pitch in Rap Flow', 25; see also Rose, *Black Noise*; Perry, *Prophets of the Hood*.
100. Lin-Manuel Miranda, *Hamilton: The Revolution—Being the Complete Libretto of the Broadway Musical, with a True Account of Its Creation, and Concise Remarks on Hip-Hop, the Power of Stories, and the New America* (New York: Grand Central, 2016), 137.
101. Komaniecki, 'Vocal Pitch in Rap Flow', 33.
102. Komaniecki, 36.
103. Komaniecki, 36.
104. Paul Edwards, *How to Rap 2: Advanced Flow and Delivery Techniques* (Chicago: Chicago Review Press, 2013), 106.
105. John Potter, *Vocal Authority: On Singing Style and Ideology* (Cambridge: Cambridge University Press, 1998), 155.
106. Nelson George, *Hip Hop America* (New York: Penguin, 2005), see chapter 5 in particular); Perry, *Prophets of the Hood*, see Chapter 5 in particular.
107. John L. Jackson in Regina Bradley, 'Contextualising Hip Hop Sonic Cool Pose in Late Twentieth- and Twenty-First-Century Rap Music', *Current Musicology* 93 (2012): 57; Michael Dyson, *The Michael Eric Dyson Reader* (New York: Basic Civitas Books, 2004), 410; Adam Alston, '"Burn the Witch": Decadence and the Occult in Contemporary Feminist Performance', *Theatre Research International* 46, no. 3 (2021): 286.
108. Tiffany Brooks, 'Staging a Revolution: The Cultural Tipping Points of John Gay and Lin-Manuel Miranda', *Studies in Musical Theatre* 12, no. 2 (2018): 205. It should be noted that this view is not universal. Many scholars have also expressed concern about the politics of black performers playing white characters, instead of playing the slaves that were held by these white men, as discussed below.
109. For the specific cultural heritage often attributed to Broadway, see Stuart J. Hecht, *Transposing Broadway: Jews, Assimilation and the American Musical* (Basingstoke: Palgrave, 2011). For an additional study of the associated with the Latter-day Saints, see Jake Johnson, *Mormons, Musical Theater, and Belonging in America* (Urbana: University of Illinois Press, 2019).
110. Odom cited in Mark Binelli, '"Hamilton" Creator Lin-Manuel Miranda: The Rolling Stone Interview', *Rolling Stone*, 1 June 2016, 10, http://www.rollingstone.com/music/features/hamilton-creator-lin-manuel-miranda-the-rolling-stone-interview-20160601.
111. Barack Obama, *The Audacity of Hope: Thoughts on Reclaiming the American Dream* (New York: Crown, 2006); Persley, *Sampling and Remixing Blackness in Hip-Hop Theater and Performance*, 201.
112. Persley, *Sampling and Remixing Blackness in Hip-Hop Theater and Performance*, 213.
113. See, among others, Galella, 'Being in "The Room Where It Happens"'; Elissa Harbert, 'Embodying History: Casting and Cultural Memory in *1776* and *Hamilton*', *Studies in Musical Theatre* 13, no. 3 (2019): 251–67; Persley, *Sampling and Remixing Blackness in Hip-Hop Theater and Performance*.
114. Matthew D. Morrison, 'Race, Blacksound, and the (Re)Making of Musicological Discourse', *Journal of the American Musical Society* 72, no. 3 (2019): 781–823. As Hodges Persley poignantly concludes, 'Hip-hop is voided of its political power in *Hamilton* because the musical is not intended for audiences comprised of people of color' (*Sampling and Remixing Blackness in Hip-Hop Theater and Performance*, 247).
115. Stacy Wolf, 'Hamilton's Women', *Studies in Musical Theatre* 12, no. 2 (2018): 169.
116. Wolf, 170.

117. Lin-Manuel Miranda, *Hamilton: The Revolution—Being the Complete Libretto of the Broadway Musical, with a True Account of Its Creation, and Concise Remarks on Hip-Hop, the Power of Stories, and the New America* (New York: Grand Central Publishing, 2016), 44; Persley, *Sampling and Remixing Blackness in Hip-Hop Theater and Performance*, 220.
118. Hodges Persley argues that Angelica's vocal character may serve to oversimplify the 'pre-feminist narrative' of black women: 'having women of color sing these lyrics absolutely invokes the ghosts of history's past, as Black women such as Harriet Tubman, Sojourner Truth, Ida B. Wells, and many other fought and died for Black women to be legible as women in emerging feminist narratives. As Black female slaves took care of the homes, children, and sexual desires of slave owners, the pre-feminist narrative of Black women was swallowed by trauma' (*Sampling and Remixing Blackness in Hip-Hop Theater and Performance*, 220).
119. Jeffrey Severs, 'Is It like a Beat without a Melody?: Rap and Revolution in *Hamilton*', *Studies in Musical Theatre* 12, no. 2 (2018): 146.
120. Wolf, 'Hamilton's Women', 177; Persley, *Sampling and Remixing Blackness in Hip-Hop Theater and Performance*, 251.
121. Wolf, 'Hamilton's Women', 177.
122. Wolf, 167–68.
123. Catherine Allgor, '"Remember . . . I'm Your Man": Masculinity, Marriage and Gender in *Hamilton*', in *Historians on Hamilton: How a Blockbuster Musical Is Restaging America's Past*, ed. Renee C. Romano and Claire Bond Potter (New Brunswick, NJ: Rutgers University Press, 2018), 101.
124. LaBelle, *Lexicon of the Mouth*, 175. For Wolf, Eliza may be gasping as she sees an apparition of her husband, an premonition of her own death, or some other kind of future vision (see 'Hamilton's Women', 167).
125. Adriana Cavarero, *For More Than One Voice: A Philosophy of Vocal Expression* (Stanford, CA: Stanford University Press, 2005), 170.
126. LaBelle, *Lexicon of the Mouth*, 75, 77.
127. McMillin, *The Musical as Drama*, 141, 149; Wolf, 'Hamilton's Women', 177, 169.
128. Persley, *Sampling and Remixing Blackness in Hip-Hop Theater and Performance*, 251.
129. Dyer, 'Entertainment and Utopia', 273.
130. Knapp, *The American Musical and the Formation of National Identity*, 146.
131. Karpf, *The Human Voice*, 139.
132. Schwartz, 'The Music Man Cometh', 165.
133. McMillin, *The Musical as Drama*, 210
134. Track 15: 'Finale: Children Will Listen', *Into the Woods (Original Broadway Cast Recording)*.
135. For consideration of the vocal aesthetic used in this work, and the subsequent film adaptation, see Lib Taylor, 'Voice, Body and the Transmission of the Real in Documentary Theatre', *Contemporary Theatre Review* 23, no. 3 (2013): 368–79; Konstantinos Thomaidis, *Theatre and Voice* (Basingstoke: Palgrave, 2017), 49.
136. Such moments might also include Joanne's 'Ladies Who Lunch' in *Company* (1970) or Kathy's tirade at Jamie in 'See, I'm Smiling' (*The Last Five Years*, 2001).
137. Jill Dolan, *Utopia in Performance: Finding Hope at the Theater* (Ann Arbor: University of Michigan Press, 2005), 13–14, 8.

Chapter 5

1. Raymond Knapp, *The American Musical and the Formation of National Identity* (Princeton, NJ: Princeton University Press, 2005), 144; Martell, 'Utopianism and Social Change: Materialism, Conflict and Pluralism', *Capital and Class* 42, no. 3 (2018): 447.
2. Brandon Woolf, 'Negotiating the "Negro Problem": Stew's Passing (Made) Strange', *Theatre Journal* 62, no. 2 (May 2010): 193.
3. Edward Rothstein, 'Utopia and Its Discontents', in *Visions of Utopia*, ed. Furaha D. Norton (New York: Oxford University Press, 2003), 5.
4. As heard in previous chapters, the cases of *Floyd Collins* and *Oklahoma!* demonstrate that this danger may also be manifest in the absenting of Native American voices, or in the cultural appropriation of Jewish and African American vocal styles across multiple voiceworlds.
5. Malcolm Chase and Christopher Shaw, *The Imagined Past: History and Nostalgia* (Manchester: Manchester University Press, 1989), 3, 9.
6. Kevin Byrne and Emily Fuchs, *The Jukebox Musical: An Interpretive History* (London: Routledge, 2022), 4.

7. Millie Taylor, *Musical Theatre, Realism and Entertainment* (Farnham: Ashgate, 2012), 150.
8. Byrne and Fuchs, *The Jukebox Musical*, 5.
9. Simon Reynolds, *Retromania: Pop Culture's Addiction to Its Own Past* (London: Faber & Faber, 2012). Reynolds explicitly notes that part of the condition for work to be considered 'retro' is that it deliberately draws upon pop culture icons, objects, and images, not admitting high cultural reference points in its content or aesthetic (xxx). The casual self-selection and lack of long-form listening in the era of jukeboxes was also, perhaps, prophetic of the shift to 'playlists' in an era of online streaming. For a detailed history of jukeboxes in popular culture, see Kerry Segrave, *Jukeboxes: An American Social History* (Jefferson, NC: McFarland, 2002).
10. John Bush Jones, *Our Musicals, Ourselves: A Social History of American Musical Theater* (Hanover, NH: University Press of New England, 2003), 312. Scholars who have dismissed them include Bush Jones, 312–14; and Barbara Ellen, 'I Want to Break Free . . . Now', *The Observer*, 16 April 2006, http://www.the-guardian.com/stage/2006/apr/16/theatre.musicals. For more nuanced explorations of the cultural agency and nostalgic appeal of this format, see George Rodosthenous, '*Mamma Mia!* And the Aesthetics of the Twenty-First-Century Jukebox Musical', in *The Oxford Handbook of the British Musical*, ed. Robert Gordon and Olaf Jubin (New York: Oxford University Press, 2017), 613–31; Kelly Kessler, *Destabilizing the Hollywood Musical: Music, Masculinity and Mayhem* (Basingstoke: Palgrave Macmillan, 2010); Naomi Graber, 'Memories That Remain: *Mamma Mia!* and the Disruptive Potential of Nostalgia', *Studies in Musical Theatre* 9, no. 2 (2015): 187–98.
11. Fred Davis, *Yearning for Yesterday: A Sociology of Nostalgia* (New York: Free Press, 1979), 14; Ricoeur, 'Ideology and Utopia as Cultural Imagination', *Philosophic Exchange* 7, no. 1 (1976): 26.
12. Reynolds, *Retromania*, 11.
13. Davis, *Yearning for Yesterday*, 14; Ricoeur, 'Ideology and Utopia as Cultural Imagination', 26.
14. Richard Dyer, 'Entertainment and Utopia', in *The Cultural Studies Reader*, ed. Simon During (London: Routledge, 1993), 273.
15. Svetlana Boym, *The Future of Nostalgia* (New York: Basic Books, 2001), 41.
16. Susan Stewart, *On Longing* (Baltimore: Johns Hopkins University Press, 1985), 145.
17. Boym, *The Future of Nostalgia*, 49.
18. Boym, 41.
19. Boym, 44.
20. Adam Rush, 'Recycled Culture: The Significance of Intertextuality in Twenty-First Century Musical Theatre' (Unpublished thesis, Lincolnshire, University of Lincoln, 2017), http://eprints.lincoln.ac.uk/27701/1/27701%20RUSH%20ADAM%20-%20PERFORMING%20ARTS%20-%20JUNE%202017.pdf; Taylor, *Musical Theatre, Realism and Entertainment*.
21. Elin Diamond, *Writing Performances* (London: Routledge, 1995), 2; Marvin Carlson, *The Haunted Stage: The Theatre as Memory Machine* (Ann Arbor: University of Michigan Press, 2003).
22. Taylor, *Musical Theatre, Realism and Entertainment*, 165.
23. Boym, *The Future of Nostalgia*, 49, 44.
24. Boym, 50; Constantine Sedikides and Tim Wildschut, 'Finding Meaning in Nostalgia', *Review of General Psychology* 22, no. 1 (2018): 48.
25. Ricoeur, 'Ideology and Utopia as Cultural Imagination', 26.
26. Douglas Mayo, 'Are Bio-Musicals Taking Over Broadway and the West End?', British Theatre, 18 April 2018, https://britishtheatre.com/are-bio-musicals-taking-over-broadway-west-end/. The list of bio-musicals seen in the United States and the UK since 2000 includes *Lennon* (2005); *Jersey Boys: The Story of Frankie Valli and the Four Seasons* (2005); *Beautiful: The Carole King Musical* (2014); *Sunny Afternoon* (2014, based on the story of the Kinks); *On Your Feet! The Story of Emilio and Gloria Estefan* (2015); *Summer: The Donna Summer Musical* (2017); *Cilla The Musical* (2017); *Tina: The Tina Turner Musical* (2018); *The Cher Show* (2018), *Dusty—the Dusty Springfield Musical* (2018); and *Ain't Too Proud: The Life and Times of the Temptations* (2019).
27. Reynolds, *Retromania*, 12.
28. Reynolds, 12; Madison Moore, 'Tina Theory: Notes on Fierceness', *Journal of Popular Music Studies* 24, no. 1 (2012): 71–86; Tracy McMullen, *Haunthenticity: Musical Replay and the Fear of the Real* (Middletown, CT: Wesleyan University Press, 2019), 6.
29. P. Scott Reedy, 'Meet Will Swenson. He's Playing Neil Diamond in the Jukebox Musical "A Beautiful Noise"', *Patriot Ledger*, 16 June 2022, https://eu.patriotledger.com/story/entertainm

ent/2022/06/16/broadway-bound-neil-diamond-musical-ready-boston-world-premiere-beautiful-noise/7621678001/; Reynolds, *Retromania*, 12.

30. Dave Quinn, 'A Beautiful Noise Review: Neil Diamond Pulls Back the Curtain on His Catalog of Hits for New Broadway Musical', *Entertainment Weekly*, 6 December 2022, https://ew.com/theater/theater-reviews/a-beautiful-noise-review-neil-diamond/; David Gordon, 'Review: Neil Diamond Musical A Beautiful Noise Is So Meh, So Meh, So Meh', *Theatremania*, 4 December 2022, https://www.theatermania.com/broadway/reviews/review-neil-diamond-musical-a-beautiful-noise_94623.html. Elsewhere, in *Variety*, A. D. Amorosi heard in Swenson a 'Diamond-inspired' vocal performance ('"A Beautiful Noise" Review: Neil Diamond Musical Unpacks Hitmaker's Life in Therapy and Song', *Variety*, 5 December 2022, https://variety.com/2022/legit/reviews/a-beautiful-noise-review-neil-diamond-musical-broadway-1235449537/), a sensibility that echoes an interview with actor Stephanie J. Block who played one of the Chers in *The Cher Show.* Reflecting on the development of the character, she noted how the director Jason Moore told her that she should focus on being a storyteller rather than seeking to be a direct impersonator (Casey Mink, 'Why Broadway's "The Cher Show" Cast 3 Different Actors to Play the Iconic Diva', *Backstage.com*, 2 December 2018, https://www.backstage.com/magazine/article/cher-show-broadway-director-jason-moore-interview-66145/).
31. This expectation of vocal similarity differs from works of musical theatre that tell the story of real people using original scores and songs, such as *Evita* (1978) or *London Road* (2011). I have written on this subject elsewhere; see Macpherson '(Re)Authoring the 27 Club: Bewildered Voices, Acousmatic Audiophilia, and the Dangers of Listening-In', *Journal of Interdisciplinary Voice Studies* 1, no. 2 (2016): 131–42.
32. Reflecting on the definition of tribute bands, Gregory notes that the term 'tribute' has more positive connotations than 'impersonation', suggesting admiration rather than inauthentic mimicry (*Send in the Clones: A Cultural Study of the Tribute Band* [Sheffield: Equinox, 2012], 23).
33. Konstantinos Thomaidis and Ben Macpherson, 'Voice(s) as a Method and an In-Between', in *Voice Studies: Critical Approaches to Process, Performance and Experience*, ed. Thomaidis and Macpherson (Oxford: Routledge, 2015), 4. These ways of listening to vocal impersonation—lipsynching (vocal drag), ventriloquism, and simulation—have been mentioned or partially explored by a number of excellent scholars including Jennifer Fleeger, *Mismatched Women: The Siren's Song through the Machine* (New York: Oxford University Press, 2014); Katherine Meizel, *Multivocality* (New York: Oxford University Press, 2020), 71–89; Freya Jarman-Ivens, *Queer Voices: Technologies, Vocalities, and the Musical Flaw* (Basingstoke: Palgrave, 2011), 44–57. However, drawing them together in a consideration of the cultural politics of these voices in musical theatre, this chapter extends beyond the ideas in these texts. With respect to the relationship between bio-musical, the aesthetics of 'camp', and the construction of nostalgia, see the brief commentary by Taylor, *Musical Theatre, Realism and Entertainment*, 151–52.
34. Philip Fisher, 'Beautiful—The Carole King Musical (Review)', British Theatre Guide, accessed 21 December 2019, https://www.britishtheatreguide.info/reviews/beautifulthe-stephen-sondhei-11086.
35. There are many variations of the spelling of this term. For consistency, I employ the spelling as used by Merrie Snell in her recent study of this art form.
36. Merrie Snell, *Lipsynching* (London: Bloomsbury, 2020), 4, 7. In fact, psychological and scientific studies suggest that when this happens in a situation with a predominantly visual frame (a theatre auditorium, e.g.), visual cues tend to dominate aural ones in the way an audience processes the information; see Collins Opoku-Baah et al., 'Visual Influences on Auditory Behavioral, Neural, and Perceptual Processes: A Review', *Journal of the Association for Research in Otolaryngology* 22 (2021): 265–86, https://doi.org/10.1007/s10162-021-00789-0; Kingson Man et al., 'Seeing Objects Improves Our Hearing of the Sounds They Make', *Neuroscience of Consciousness* 6, no. 1 (2020): 1–8, https://doi.org/10.1093/nc/niaa014; Sharon E. Guttman, Lee A. Gilroy, and R. Blake, 'Hearing What the Eyes See: Auditory Encoding of Visual Temporal Sequences', *Psychological Science* 16, no. 3 (2005): 228–35, https://doi.org/10.1111/j.0956-7976.2005.00808.x). Elsewhere, the same sense of concealment was an open secret or actively acknowledged, with the clear mismatch between sung voice and stars on screen in mid-twentieth-century Hindi cinema forming part of the audio-visual pleasure of 'Bollywood' movies, even while it led to a complicated status for 'ghost' and playback singers. For an in-depth study of this practice, see Kiranmayi Indraganti, *Her Majestic Voice: South Indian Female Playback Singers and Stardom, 1945–1955* (New York: Oxford University Press, 2016); Amanda Weidman, *Brought to Life by the Voice: Playback Singing and Cultural Politics in South India*

(Oakland: University of California Press, 2021). The practice of ghosting might be heard in the mismatched voice and body designed to elicit comedic effect, such as in advertising. In what Snell calls its most amateur and 'vernacular' form, this form of vicarious vocality is seen in lipsynched covers on YouTube and other online video hosting platforms.

37. Ruth Johnston, 'Technologically Produced Forms of Drag in "Singin' in the Rain" and "Radio Days"', *Quarterly Review of Film and Video 21*, no. 2 (2004): 121.
38. This argument is developed through a review of studies in Guttman, Gilroy, and Blake, 'Hearing What the Eyes See', 2.
39. Jacob Mallinson Bird, 'Haptic Aurality: On Touching the Voice in Drag Lip-Sync Performance', *Sound Studies: An Interdisciplinary Journal* 6, no. 1 (2020): 46. In his history of theatrical drag, Laurence Senelick even notes that lipsynching 'became the rage' because it was so cheap it 'obviated both professional musicians and drag artistes'; *The Changing Room: Sex, Drag and Theatre* (London: Routledge, 2000), 384.
40. Carol Langley, 'Borrowed Voice: The Art of Lip-Synching in Sydney Drag', *Australasian Drama Studies* 48 (2006): 8; see also Snell, *Lipsynching*. The term 'vocal drag' in this context is not the same as 'sonic drag', the term used in Wayne Koestenbaum's discussion of operatic voices on record (*Queen's Throat: Opera, Homosexuality and the Mystery of Desire* [New York: Da Capo, 2001], 49.)
41. Jarman-Ivens, *Queer Voices*, 56; Judith Butler, *Gender Trouble* (London: Routledge, 1990), 137.
42. For Johnston, this application in 'technological form' is typified in the closing scene of *Singin' in the Rain* during which the character Cosmo, played by Donald O'Connor, replaces love-interest Cathy Selden (Debbie Reynolds) at a microphone in order to draw attention to the fact that the 'unwitting' film star Lina Lamont (Jean Hagen) is lipsynching. Johnston suggests that in this case, 'one form of drag [Cosmo and Lina] displaces another [Cathy and Lina]' and expresses the gender and class politics that underpin the narrative of the film; 'Technologically Produced Forms of Drag in "Singin' in the Rain" and "Radio Days"', 121.
43. Langley, 'Borrowed Voice', 8; see also Snell, *Lipsynching*.
44. Reynolds, *Retromania*, 12.
45. Reynolds, xxxi, xxx.
46. Fleeger, *Mismatched Women*, 90–91.
47. Butler, *Gender Trouble*, 137; Fleeger, *Mismatched Women*, 91.
48. Boym, *The Future of Nostalgia*, 49.
49. This line is quoted from notes taken during a performance of *Tina* that I attended on 19 June 2019, at the Aldwych Theatre, London.
50. For a related discussion of this subject, see Jessica E. Teague's analysis of the staging of recording studio practice in August Wilson's play *Ma Rainey's Black Bottom*. See 'The Recording Studio on Stage: Liveness in "Ma Rainey's Black Bottom"', *American Quarterly* 63, no. 3 (2011): 555–71.
51. Pieter Verstraete, 'The Frequency of Imagination: Auditory Distress and Aurality in Contemporary Music Theatre' (Doctoral thesis, University of Amsterdam, 2009), 228.
52. José Esteban Muñoz, *Cruising Utopia: The Then and There of Queer Futurity* (New York: New York University Press, 2009), 97.
53. Muñoz, 97.
54. Boym, *The Future of Nostalgia*, 44.
55. Muñoz, *Cruising Utopia*, 97.
56. Reynolds, *Retromania*, xxxi; Boym, *The Future of Nostalgia*, 49; As Altman further notes, recorded voice is only ever a 'representation' of the original performance, and never a 'reproduction'; 'The Material Heterogeneity of Recorded Sound', in *Sound Theory, Sound Practice*, ed. Rick Altman (New York: Routledge, 1992), 29.
57. Butler, *Gender Trouble*, 137.
58. Muñoz, *Cruising Utopia*, 97.
59. Hugo Barker and Yuval Taylor, *Faking It: The Quest for Authenticity in Popular Music* (London: Faber, 2007), 247.
60. Barker and Taylor, 141, 149.
61. Barker and Taylor, 237.
62. Boym, *The Future of Nostalgia*, 50; Sedikides and Wildschut, 'Finding Meaning in Nostalgia', 48.
63. Fisher, 'Beautiful—The Carole King Musical (Review)'.
64. Sarah Kessler, 'Anachronism Effects: Ventriloquism and Popular Media' (Doctoral thesis, California, University of California, Irvine, 2016), 4, https://escholarship.org/uc/item/6x08k529; Steven Connor, *Dumbstruck: A Cultural History of Ventriloquism* (Oxford: Oxford University Press, 2001), 407.

65. David Goldblatt, 'Ventriloquism: Ecstatic Exchange and the History of Artwork', *Journal of Aesthetics and Art Criticism* 51, no. 3 (1993): 299, https://doi.org/10.2307/431511.
66. Kessler, 'Anachronism Effects', 4.
67. Connor, *Dumbstruck*, 398.
68. Connor, 398.
69. Walter Burkert, *Greek Religion* (Cambridge, MA: Harvard University Press, 1985), 116–18.
70. William J. Broad, *The Oracle: Ancient Delphi and the Science behind Its Lost Secrets* (London: Penguin, 2007), 43.
71. Connor, *Dumbstruck*, 51.
72. Connor, 64.
73. Connor, 74.
74. Boym, *The Future of Nostalgia*, 50.
75. Boym, 50.
76. Reginald Scot, *The Discoverie of Witchcraft* (London: Rowman & Littlefield, 1973), 101. The early modern vocabulary for soothsaying and divination was very rich; other terms used for one given to prophetic, demonic, or ventriloquial speech included *ob*, *python* or *pythonist*, *engastrimyth*, and *gastriloquist*.
77. Chase and Shaw, *The Imagined Past*, 29–30.
78. Connor, *Dumbstruck*, 74.
79. Connor, 74; Chase and Shaw, *The Imagined Past*, 9.
80. Jean Baudrillard, *Simulacra and Simulation*, trans. Sheila Faria Glaser (Ann Arbor: University of Michigan Press, 1994), 12–13.
81. Taylor, *Musical Theatre, Realism and Entertainment*, 112, 115.
82. Baudrillard, *Simulacra and Simulation*, 12.
83. Baudrillard, 6.
84. Baudrillard, 6. For other examples of Baudrillardian principles with respect to impersonation and vocal likeness, see Jarman-Ivens, *Queer Voices*; Macpherson, '(Re)Authoring the 27 Club'; Ben Macpherson, 'Baudrillard on Broadway: Bio-Musicals, the Hyperreal and the Cultural Politics of "Simuloquism"', *Journal of Interdisciplinary Voice Studies* 5, no. 1 (2020): 43–57; Meizel, *Multivocality*; Gregory, *Send In the Clones*.
85. Roy Shuker, *Popular Music: The Key Concepts*, 4th ed. (Oxford: Routledge, 2017).
86. Barker and Taylor continue to note that the vocal artifice of popular singers was exacerbated by the nature of recording: '[a]s soon as technology was used to record music, some aspects of artificiality were introduced' (*Faking It*, 247). Well-known recordings of Elvis, the Four Seasons, Tina Turner, and others are therefore all technologically mediated, 'denaturing' original performances in the recording studio or elsewhere.
87. Jarman-Ivens, *Queer Voices*, 49, emphasis mine.
88. Roland Barthes, 'The Grain of the Voice', in *Image, Music, Text*, ed. Stephen Heath (London: Fontana, 1977), 182.
89. Mink, 'Why Broadway's "The Cher Show" Cast 3 Different Actors to Play the Iconic Diva'.
90. Nolan in Jody Kreiman and Diana Sidtis, *Foundations of Voice Studies: An Interdisciplinary Approach to Voice Production and Perception* (Hoboken, NJ: Wiley Blackwell, 2011), 247.
91. Moore, 'Tina Theory', 79.
92. This method of sonic visualization was produced using Sonic Visualiser 4.3 (www.sonicvisualiser.org) and employs a method outlined by musicologist Nicholas Cook in 'Methods for Analysing Recordings', in *The Cambridge Companion to Recorded Music*, ed. Nicholas Cook et al. (Cambridge: Cambridge University Press, 2009), 221–45.
93. Baudrillard, *Simulacra and Simulation*, 3.
94. Hillel Schwartz, *The Culture of the Copy: Striking Likenesses, Unreasonable Fascimiles* (New York: Zone Books, 2014), 176.
95. Schwartz, 176.
96. Baudrillard, *Simulacra and Simulation*, 6.
97. This line is quoted from notes taken during a performance of *Jersey Boys* that I attended on 5 May 2019 at the Mayflower Theatre Southampton, England.
98. Boym, *The Future of Nostalgia*, 49, 44.
99. José van Dijck, 'Remembering Songs through Telling Stories: Pop Music as a Resource for Memory', in *Sound Souvenirs: Audio Technologies, Memories and Cultural Practices*, ed. Karin

Bijsterveld and José van Dijck (Amsterdam: Amsterdam University Press, 2009), 107, original emphasis.

100. William Howland Kenney, *Recorded Music in American Life: The Phonograph and Popular Memory, 1890–1945* (New York: Oxford University Press, 1999), xix.
101. Thomaidis and Macpherson, 'Voice(s) as a Method and an In-Between', 4.
102. Thomaidis and Macpherson, 4.
103. Baudrillard, *Simulacra and Simulation*, 6.
104. Ricoeur, 'Ideology and Utopia as Cultural Imagination', 26.
105. See Ben Macpherson, 'Sing: Musical Theater Voices from *Superstar* to *Hamilton*', in *The Routledge Companion to the Contemporary Musical*, ed. Jessica Sternfeld and Elizabeth L. Wollman (New York: Routledge, 2000), 69–77.
106. Byrne and Fuchs, *The Jukebox Musical*, 4.
107. Susan Russell, 'The Performance of Discipline on Broadway', *Studies in Musical Theatre* 1, no. 1 (2006): 97, https://doi.org/10.1386/smt.1.1.97_1.

Chapter 6

1. Dolan, *Utopia in Performance: Finding Hope at the Theater* (Ann Arbor; University of Michigan Press, 2005), 74.
2. Dyer, 'Entertainment and Utopia', in *The Cultural Studies Reader*, ed. Simon During (London: Routledge, 1993), 271–83.
3. Dolan, *Utopia in Performance*, 13–14.
4. Krishan Kumar, *Utopianism* (Oxford: Open University Press, 1991), 77; Ernst Bloch, *The Principle of Hope* (Oxford: Basil Blackwell, 1986).
5. Tim Carter, 'What Is Opera?', in *The Oxford Handbook of Opera*, ed. Helen M. Greenwald (New York: Oxford University Press, 2015), 17.
6. Luke Martell, 'Utopianism and Social Change: Materialism, Conflict and Pluralism', *Capital and Class* 42, no. 3 (2018): 447.
7. Dyer, 'Entertainment and Utopia', 273.
8. Martell, 'Utopianism and Social Change', 448, 447.
9. Alston, '"Burn the Witch": Decadence and the Occult in Contemporary Feminist Performance', *Theatre Research International* 46, no. 3 (2021): 286.
10. Dolan, *Utopia in Performance*, 13–14, 8.
11. Stacy Wolf, 'Keeping Company with Sondheim's Women', in *The Oxford Companion of Sondheim Studies*, ed. Robert Gordon (New York: Oxford University Press, 2014), 372.
12. Martell, 'Utopianism and Social Change', 448, 447.
13. Throughout this book, the idea of the 'voiceworld' has also been used as a broader term of reference for the qualities of musical theatre vocality as distinct from other genres.
14. Steven Connor, 'Choralities', *Twentieth-Century Music* 131, no. 1 (2016): 3–23, https://doi.org/10.1017/S1478572215000158.
15. Dyer, 'Entertainment and Utopia'.
16. Martell, 'Utopianism and Social Change', 448, 447.
17. Martell, 447.
18. Bethany Hughes, 'Singing the Community: The Musical Theater Chorus as Character', in *Gestures of Music Theatre: The Performativity of Song and Dance*, ed. Dominic Symonds and Millie Taylor (New York: Oxford University Press, 2014), 263.
19. For a discussion of such categories beyond the concepts and approaches discussed here, see Masi Asare, 'The Singing Voice', in *The Routledge Companion to Musical Theatre*, ed. Laura MacDonald, Ryan Donovan, and William A. Everett (New York: Routledge, 2022), 54–67; Ben Macpherson, 'Sing: Musical Theater Voices from *Superstar* to *Hamilton*', in *The Routledge Companion to the Contemporary Musical*, ed. Jessica Sternfeld and Elizabeth L. Wollman (New York: Routledge, 2020), 69–77; Jake Johnson, 'Building the Broadway Voice', in *The Oxford Handbook of Voice Studies*, ed. Nina Sue Eidsheim and Katherine Meizel (New York: Oxford University Press, 2019), 475–92.
20. Konstantinos Thomaidis and Ben Macpherson, 'Voice(s) as a Method and an In-Between', in *Voice Studies: Critical Approaches to Process, Performance and Experience*, ed. Thomaidis and Macpherson (Oxford: Routledge, 2015), 4.

21. With respect to the representations of Asian and Asian American characters in musical theatre see, among others, Hye Won Kim, 'Performing Asian/American Women: Labor, Resistance, and (De)Compression in *The King and I* and *KPOP*', *TDR: The Drama Review* 67, no. 3 (2023): 151–72, https://doi.org/10.1017/S1054204323000308; Broderick D. V. Chow, 'Seeing as a Filipino: *Here Lies Love* (2014) at the National Theatre', in *Reframing the Musical: Race, Culture and Identity*, ed. Sarah K. Whitfield (London: Methuen, 2021), 17–34; Donatella Galella, 'Feeling Yellow: Responding to Contemporary Yellowface in Musical Performance', *Journal of Dramatic Theory and Criticism* 32, no. 2 (2018): 67–77.
22. Dyer, 'Entertainment and Utopia', 273.

Bibliography

Abbate, Carolyn. *In Search of Opera*. Princeton, NJ: Princeton University Press, 2001.

Abbate, Carolyn. *Unsung Opera: Opera and Musical Narrative in the Nineteenth Century*. Princeton, NJ: Princeton University Press, 1991.

Abbate, Carolyn, and Roger Parker. *A History of Opera: The Last Four Hundred Years*. London: Penguin, 2012.

Acaroglu, Onur. *Rethinking Marxist Approaches to Transition: Theory of Temporal Dislocation*. Leiden: Brill, 2021.

Adiseshiah, Siân. *Utopian Drama: In Search of a Genre*. London: Bloomsbury, 2022.

Alda, Robert, Vivian Blaine, Sam Levene, and Isabel Bigley. *Guys and Dolls: A Musical Fable of Broadway (A Decca Original Cast Album)*. Compact Disc. Broadway Gold. California: MCA Classics, 1991.

Allgor, Catherine. '"Remember . . . I'm Your Man": Masculinity, Marriage and Gender in *Hamilton*'. In *Historians on Hamilton: How a Blockbuster Musical Is Restaging America's Past*, edited by Renee C. Romano and Claire Bond Potter, 94–118. New Brunswick, NJ: Rutgers University Press, 2018.

Alston, Adam. '"Burn the Witch": Decadence and the Occult in Contemporary Feminist Performance'. *Theatre Research International* 46, no. 3 (2021): 285–302.

Alston, Adam. 'Carnal Acts: Decadence in Theatre, Performance and Live Art'. *Volupte: Interdisciplinary Journal of Decadence Studies* 4, no. 2 (2021): ii–xxiii. https://doi.org/:10.25602/GOLD.v.v4i2.1598.g1712.

Altman, Rick. 'The Material Heterogeneity of Recorded Sound'. In *Sound Theory, Sound Practice*, edited by Rick Altman, 15–31. New York: Routledge, 1992.

Amorosi, A. D. '"A Beautiful Noise" Review: Neil Diamond Musical Unpacks Hitmaker's Life in Therapy and Song'. *Variety*, 5 December 2022. https://variety.com/2022/legit/reviews/a-beautiful-noise-review-neil-diamond-musical-broadway-1235449537/.

Anderson, Benedict. *Imagined Communities*. London: Verso, 1983.

Anderson, Tim. *Making Easy Listening: Material Culture and Postwar American Recording*. Minneapolis: University of Minnesota Press, 2006.

Andre, Naomi. *Voicing Gender: Castrati, Travesti, and the Second Woman in Early-Nineteenth-Century Italian Opera*. Bloomington: Indiana University Press, 2006.

Apolloni, Alexandra. 'The Lollipop Girl's Voice: Respectability, Migration, and Millie Small's "My Boy Lollipop"'. *Journal of Popular Music Studies* 28, no. 4 (2016): 460–73.

Arnold, Matthew. *Culture and Anarchy*. Oxford World's Classics. Oxford: Oxford University Press, 2009.Asare, Masi. 'The Singing Voice'. In *The Routledge Companion to Musical Theatre*, ed. Laura MacDonald, Ryan Donovan, and William A. Everett, 54–67. New York: Routledge, 2022.

Asare, Masi. 'Vocal Colour in Blue: Early Twentieth-Century Black Women Singers as Broadway's Voice Teachers'. *Performance Matters* 6, no. 2 (2020): 52–66.

Astaire, Fred, and George Gershwin. 'The Half-of-It Dearie Blues'. London: Columbia, 1926. 1CS0025324 2 Columbia. British Library.

Atkinson, Brooks. 'Chicago Unit of the Federal Theatre Comes In Swinging the Gilbert and Sullivan Mikado'. *New York Times*, 2 March 1939.

Augoyard, Jean-François, and Henri Torgue, eds. *Sonic Experience: A Guide to Everyday Sounds*. Montreal: McGill-Queen's University Press, 2005.

Averill, Gage. *Four Parts, No Waiting: A Social History of American Barbershop Harmony*. American Musicspheres. New York: Oxford University Press, 2003.

Balme, Chris. 'The Bandmann Circuit: Theatrical Networks in the First Age of Globalization'. *Theatre Research International* 40, no. 1 (2015): 19–36.

Banfield, Stephen. *Sondheim's Broadway Musicals*. Michigan American Music. Ann Arbor: University of Michigan Press, 1995.

Bannister, Matthew. *White Boys, White Noise: Masculinities and 1980s Indie Guitar Rock*. Ashgate Popular and Folk Music Series. Farnham: Ashgate, 2006.

Barbier, Patrick. *The World of the Castrati: The History of an Extraordinary Operatic Phenomenon*. London: Souvenir Press, 1998.

Bardi, Pietro. 'Pietro Bardi on the Birth of Opera'. In *Opera: A History in Documents*, edited by Piero Weiss, 8–10. New York: Oxford University Press, 2002.

Barker, Hugo, and Yuval Taylor. *Faking It: The Quest for Authenticity in Popular Music*. London: Faber, 2007.

Bart, Lionel. *Oliver! (Full Conductor's Score)*. New York: TRO Hollis Music Ltd, 1963.

Barthes, Roland. 'The Death of the Author'. In *Image, Music, Text*, translated by Stephen Heath, 142–48. London: Fontana, 1977.

Barthes, Roland. 'The Grain of the Voice'. In *Image, Music, Text*, translated by Stephen Heath, 179–89. London: Fontana, 1977.

Batiste, Stefanie Leigh. *Darkening Mirrors: Imperial Representation in Depression-Era African American Performance*. Durham, NC: Duke University Press, 2011.

Baudrillard, Jean. *Simulacra and Simulation*. Translated by Sheila Faria Glaser. Ann Arbor: University of Michigan Press, 1994.

Bauman, Zygmunt. *Liquid Life*. Malden, MA: Polity, 2005.

Bauman, Zygmunt. *Liquid Modernity*. Malden, MA: Polity, 2012.

Beaumont, Matthew. 'Socially Empty Space and Dystopian Utopianism in the Late Nineteenth Century'. In *Utopian Spaces of Modernism: British Literature and Culture 1885–1945*, edited by Rosalyn Gregory and Benjamin Kohlmann, 19–34. Basingstoke: Palgrave, 2012.

Billboard. '"Fair Lady" Album Off to Hot Start'. 7 April 1956.

Binelli, Mark. '"Hamilton" Creator Lin-Manuel Miranda: The Rolling Stone Interview'. *Rolling Stone*, 1 June 2016. http://www.rollingstone.com/music/features/hamilton-creator-lin-manuel-miranda-the-rolling-stone-interview-20160601.

Bird, Jacob Mallinson. 'Haptic Aurality: On Touching the Voice in Drag Lip-Sync Performance'. *Sound Studies: An Interdisciplinary Journal* 6, no. 1 (2020): 45–64.

Bjorkner, Eva. 'Why So Different?—Aspects of Voice Characteristics in Operatic and Musical Theatre Singing'. KTH School of Computer Science and Communication, 2006. http://www.diva-portal.org/smash/get/diva2:11182/FULLTEXT01.pdf.

Blackshaw, Tony. *Key Concepts in Community Studies*. London: SAGE, 2013.

Blesser, Barry, and Linda-Ruth Salter. *Spaces Speak, Are You Listening?: Experiencing Aural Architecture*. Cambridge, MA: MIT Press, 2006.

Bloch, Ernst. *The Principle of Hope*. Oxford: Basil Blackwell, 1986.

Bourdieu, Pierre. *Distinction: A Social Critique of the Judgement of Taste*. Translated by Richard Nice. Cambridge, MA: Cambridge University Press, 1984.

Bourne, Tracy, Maeve Garnier, and Diana Kenny. 'Music Theater Voice: Production, Physiology and Pedagogy'. *Journal of Singing* 67, no. 4 (2011): 437–44.

Boym, Svetlana. *The Future of Nostalgia*. New York: Basic Books, 2001.

Bradfield, W. Louis. 'Phrenology', Wax cylinder. London: Berliner, 1900. 28 4522. British Library.

Bradley, Regina. 'Contextualising Hip Hop Sonic Cool Pose in Late Twentieth- and Twenty-First-Century Rap Music'. *Current Musicology* 93 (2012): 55–70.

Broad, William J. *The Oracle: Ancient Delphi and the Science Behind Its Lost Secrets*. London: Penguin, 2007.

Bronhill, June, Ann Howard, and Andy Cole. *The Arcadians.* Vinyl. Studio 2 Stereo. London: Columbia, 1968.

Brook, Peter. *The Empty Space.* Modern Classics. London: Penguin, 2008.

Brooks, Tiffany. 'Staging a Revolution: The Cultural Tipping Points of John Gay and Lin-Manuel Miranda'. *Studies in Musical Theatre* 12, no. 2 (2018): 199–212.

Brooks, Tim. '"Early Recordings of Songs from *Florodora*: Tell Me, Pretty Maiden . . . Who Are You?—A Discographical Mystery"'. *Association for Recorded Sound Collections Journal* 31 (2000): 51–64.

Brown, Lee B. 'Can American Popular Vocal Music Escape the Legacy of Blackface Minstrelsy?' *Journal of Aesthetics and Art Criticism* 71, no. 1 (2013): 91–100. https://doi.org/10.1111/j.1540-6245.2012.01545.x.

Bruce, Carol, Helen Dowdy, and Kenneth Spencer. 'Can't Help Lovin' Dat Man'. Compact Disc. New York City: Columbia, 1946. 1CD0187652 D2 BD10 Pearl. British Library.

Buchanan, Jack, and Ray Noble. 'Jack Buchanan Medley #1: Sunny / Goodnight Vienna / Stand Up and Sing'. London: HMV, 1933. 1CD0048488 D1 S1 BD16 Living Era. British Library.

Burgess, Geoffrey. 'Revisiting Atys'. *Early Music* 34 (2006): 465–78.

Burkert, Walter. *Greek Religion.* Cambridge, MA: Harvard University Press, 1985.

Burston, Jonathan. 'Theatre Space as Virtual Place: Audio Technology, the Reconfigured Singing Body, and the Megamusical'. *Popular Music* 17, no. 2 (1999): 205–18.

Bush Jones, John. *Our Musicals, Ourselves: A Social History of American Musical Theater.* Hanover, NH: University Press of New England, 2003.

Butler, Judith. *Gender Trouble.* London: Routledge, 1990.

Byrne, Kevin, and Emily Fuchs. *The Jukebox Musical: An Interpretive History.* London: Routledge, 2022.

Byrnside, Ron. '"Guys and Dolls": A Musical Fable of Broadway'. *Journal of American Culture* 19, no. 2 (1996): 25–33.

Cannadine, David. *Ornamentalism: How the British Saw Their Empire.* London: Penguin, 2001.

Carlson, Marvin. *The Haunted Stage: The Theatre as Memory Machine.* Ann Arbor: University of Michigan Press, 2003.

Carter, Tim. 'What Is Opera?' In *The Oxford Handbook of Opera*, edited by Helen M. Greenwald, 15–32. New York: Oxford University Press, 2015.

Cavarero, Adriana. *For More than One Voice: A Philosophy of Vocal Expression.* Stanford, CA: University of Stanford Press, 2005.

Chandler, David. '"What Do We Mean by Opera, Anyway?": Lloyd Webber's *Phantom of the Opera* and "High-Pop" Theatre'. *Journal of Popular Music Studies* 21, no. 2 (2009): 152–69. https://doi.org/10.1111/j.1533-1598.2009.01186.x.

Chandler, Kim. 'Teaching Popular Music Styles'. In *Teaching Singing in the 21st Century*, edited by Scott D. Harrison and Jessica O'Bryan, 35–51. New York: Springer, 2014.

Chase, Malcolm, and Christopher Shaw. *The Imagined Past: History and Nostalgia.* Manchester: Manchester University Press, 1989.

Cheng, Anne Anlin. *The Melancholy of Race: Psychoanalysis, Assimilation, and Hidden Grief.* New York: Oxford University Press, 2020.

Chion, Michel. *The Voice in Cinema.* Translated by Claudia Gorbman. New York: Columbia University Press, 1999.

Chow, Broderick D. V. 'Seeing as a Filipino: *Here Lies Love* (2014) at the National Theatre'. In *Reframing the Musical: Race, Culture and Identity*, edited by Sarah K. Whitfield, 17–34. London: Methuen, 2021.

Chude-Sokei, Louis. *The Last "Darky": Bert Williams, Black-on-Black Minstrelsy, and the African Diaspora.* Durham, NC: Duke University Press, 2006.

Citron, Stephen. *The Wordsmiths.* London: Vintage, 1996.

Clarke, Joseph. *Echo's Chambers: Architecture and the Idea of Acoustic Space.* Pittsburgh: University of Pittsburgh Press, 2021.

Clément, Catherine. *Opera, or the Undoing of Women*. London: Virago, 1989.
Clément, Catherine. 'Through Voices, History'. In *Siren Songs: Representations of Gender and Sexuality in Opera*, edited by Mary Ann Smart, 17–28. Princeton, NJ: Princeton University Press, 2000.
Collins, Jim. 'High-Pop: An Introduction'. In *High-Pop: Making Culture into Popular Entertainment*, edited by Jim Collins, 1–31. Malden, MA: Blackwell, 2002.
Cone, Edward T. *The Composer's Voice*. Oakland: University of California Press, 1988.
Cone, Edward. 'Song and Performance'. In *Music, Words and Voice: A Reader*, edited by Martin Clayton, 230–41. Manchester: Manchester University Press, 2008.
Connor, Steven. *Beyond Words: Sobs, Hums, Stutters and Other Vocalizations*. London: Reaktion Books, 2014.
Connor, Steven. 'Choralities'. *Twentieth-Century Music* 131, no. 1 (2016): 3–23. https://doi.org/10.1017/S1478572215000158.
Connor, Steven. *Dumbstruck: A Cultural History of Ventriloquism*. Oxford: Oxford University Press, 2001.
Connor, Steven. 'Voice, Ventriloquism and the Vocalic Body'. In *Psychoanalysis and Performance*, edited by Patrick Campbell and Adrian Kear, 75–93. London: Routledge, 2000.Cook, Nicholas. 'Methods for Analysing Recordings'. In *The Cambridge Companion to Recorded Music*, edited by Nicholas Cook, Eric Clark, Daniel Leech-Wilkinson, and John Rink, 221–45. Cambridge Companions. Cambridge: Cambridge University Press, 2009.
Cook, Nicholas, and Nicola Dibben. 'Musicological Approaches to Emotion'. In *Music and Emotion: Theory and Research*, 45–70. New York: Oxford University Press, 2001.
Crawford, Michael, Sarah Brightman, and Steve Barton. *The Phantom of the Opera (Original Cast Recording)*. Vinyl. London: EMI, 1986.
Crawford, Richard. *America's Musical Life: A History*. New York: W. W. Norton, 2001.
Cronin, Mari. 'Sondheim: The Idealist'. In *Stephen Sondheim: A Casebook*, edited by Joanne Gordon, 143–52. Oxford: Garland, 2000.
Culme, John, and Matthew Lloyd. '"An Opinion of Musical Halls" from "The Tomahawk" (14 September 1867)', 14 September 1867. http://www.arthurlloyd.co.uk/AboutMusicHall.htm.
Damasio, Antonio. *Self Comes to Mind: Constructing the Conscious Brain*. London: Vintage, 2010.
D'Aoust, Jason R. 'Posthumanist Voices in Literature and Opera'. In *The Oxford Handbook of Sound and Imagination*, Vol. 2, edited by Mark Grimshaw-Agaard, Mads Walther-Hansen, and Martin Knakkergaard, 629–51. New York: Oxford University Press, 2019.
Davies, Stephen. 'Infection Music: Music-Listener Emotional Contagion'. In *Empathy: Philosophical and Psychological Perspectives*, edited by A. Coplan and P. Goldie, 134–48. New York: Oxford University Press, 2011.
Davis, Fred. *Yearning for Yesterday: A Sociology of Nostalgia*. New York: Free Press, 1979.
DeArmitt, Pleshette. 'Resonances of Echo: A Derridean Allegory'. *Mosaic: An Interdisciplinary Critical Journal (Special Issue: Sound, Part II)* 42, no. 2 (2009): 89–100.
Delanty, Gerhard. *Community*. Oxford: Routledge, 2003.
Delman, Edward. 'How Lin-Manuel Miranda Shapes History'. *The Atlantic*, 29 September 2015. https://www.theatlantic.com/entertainment/archive/2015/09/lin-manuel-miranda-hamilton/408019/.
Derrida, Jacques. *Of Grammatology*. Translated by Gayatri Chakravorty Spivak. Baltimore: Johns Hopkins University Press, 1997.
Derrida, Jacques. *Rogues: Two Essays on Reason*. Edited by Pascale-Anne Brault and Michael Naas. Stanford, CA: Stanford University Press, 2005.
Derrida, Jacques. *Voice and Phenomenon: Introduction to the Problem of the Sign in Husserl's Phenomenology*. Translated by Leonard Lawlor. Evanston, IL: Northwestern University Press, 2010.

Descartes, René. 'Meditations on First Philosophy'. In *Descartes: Key Philosophical Writings*, edited by Enrique Chavez-Arvizo, 134–90. Wordsworth Classics of World Literature. London: Wordsworth Editions, 1997.

Descartes, René, Enrique Chavez-Arvizo, Elizabeth S. Haldane, and G. R. T. Ross. 'The Passions of the Soul'. In *Descartes: Key Philosophical Writings*, 358–83. Wordsworth Classics of World Literature. London: Wordsworth Editions, 1997.

Diamond, Elin. *Writing Performances*. London: Routledge, 1995.

Dickens, Charles. *Oliver Twist*. Classic Adventures. Barcelona: Fabbri Publishing, 1990.

Dijck, José van. 'Remembering Songs through Telling Stories: Pop Music as a Resource for Memory'. In *Sound Souvenirs: Audio Technologies, Memories and Cultural Practices*, edited by Karin Bijsterveld and José van Dijck, 107–22. Amsterdam: Amsterdam University Press, 2009.

Dolan, Jill. *Utopia in Performance: Finding Hope at the Theater*. Ann Arbor: University of Michigan Press, 2005.

Dolar, Mladen. *A Voice and Nothing More*. Short Circuits. Cambridge, MA: MIT Press, 2006.

Double, Oliver. 'Introduction: What Is Popular Performance?' In *Popular Performance*, edited by Adam Ainsworth, Oliver Double, and Louise Peacock, 1–29. London: Bloomsbury Methuen, 2017.

Dry, Jude. 'DA Pennebaker's "Original Cast Album: Company" Is the Best Musical Theater Documentary Ever'. *IndieWire*, 5 August 2019. https://www.indiewire.com/features/general/da-pennebaker-original-cast-album-company-sondheim-elaine-stritch-1202163427/.

Dunbar, Zachary. '"How Do You Solve a Problem like the Chorus?": Hammerstein's *Allegro* and the Reception of the Greek Chorus on Broadway'. In *Choruses, Ancient and Modern*, edited by Joshua Billings, Felix Budelmann, and Fiona Macintosh, 243–58. Oxford: Oxford University Press, 2013.

Dyer, Richard. 'Entertainment and Utopia'. In *The Cultural Studies Reader*, edited by Simon During, 271–83. London: Routledge, 1993.

Dyer, Richard. *Pastiche*. Oxford: Routledge, 2007.

Dyson, Michael. *The Michael Eric Dyson Reader*. New York: Basic Civitas Books, 2004.

Earnest, Bruce. 'Male Belting: An Exploration of Technique and Style from 1967 to Current'. DMA diss., University of Southern Mississippi, 2018. https://aquila.usm.edu/cgi/viewcontent.cgi?article=2587&context=dissertations.

Edwards, Paul. *How to Rap 2: Advanced Flow and Delivery Techniques*. Chicago: Chicago Review Press, 2013.

Eidsheim, Nina Sun. *The Race of Sound: Listening, Timbre, and Vocality in African American Music*. Durham, NC: Duke University Press, 2019.

Eidsheim, Nina Sun. *Sensing Sound: Singing and Listening as Vibrational Practice*. Durham, NC: Duke University Press, 2015.

Ellen, Barbara. 'I Want to Break Free . . . Now'. *The Observer*, 16 April 2006. http://www.theguardian.com/stage/2006/apr/16/theatre.musicals.

'Elliot Norton Interview with Ethel Merman'. *Elliot Norton Reviews*. Boston: WGBH, 1976. Alexander Street Collection. Sound and Moving Image Collection.

Fast, Susan. 'Genre, Subjectivity and Back-Up Singing in Rock Music'. In *The Ashgate Research Companion to Popular Musicology*, edited by Derek B. Scott, 171–89. Surrey: Ashgate, 2009.

Fischer-Lichte, Erika. *The Transformative Power of Performance: A New Aesthetics*. Translated by Saskya Iris Jain. Oxford: Routledge, 2008.

Fisher, Philip. 'Beautiful—The Carole King Musical (Review)'. British Theatre Guide. Accessed 21 December 2019. https://www.britishtheatreguide.info/reviews/beautifulthe-stephen-sondhei-11086.

Fleeger, Jennifer. *Mismatched Women: The Siren's Song through the Machine*. New York: Oxford University Press, 2014.

Floyd Collins (Original Cast Recording). Compact Disc. New York: Nonesuch, 1996.

Francis, Ben. '"Careful the Spell You Cast": *Into the Woods* and the Uses of Disenchantment'. In *The Oxford Handbook of Sondheim Studies*, edited by Robert Gordon, 350–61. New York: Oxford University Press, 2014.

Frisbie, Charlotte J. 'Vocables in Navajo Ceremonial Music'. *Ethnomusicology* 24, no. 3 (1980): 347–92.

Frith, Simon. *Performing Rites: Evaluating Popular Music*. Oxford: Oxford University Press, 1996.

Frith, Simon. 'The Voice as a Musical Instrument'. In *Music, Words and Voice: A Reader*, edited by Martin Clayton, 65–71. Manchester: Manchester University Press, 2008.

Furth, George, and Stephen Sondheim. 'Company (Playscript)'. In *Ten Great Musicals of the American Theatre*, edited by Stanley Richards, 643–720. Ontario: Chilton Book Company, 1973.

Galella, Donatella. 'Being in "The Room Where It Happens": *Hamilton*, Obama, and Nationalist Neoliberal Multicultural Inclusion'. *Theatre Survey* 59, no. 3 (2018): 363–85.

Galella, Donatella. 'Feeling Yellow: Responding to Contemporary Yellowface in Musical Performance'. *Journal of Dramatic Theory and Criticism* 32, no. 2 (2018): 67–77.

George, Nelson. *Hip Hop America*. New York: Penguin, 2005.

Gevinson, Tavi. 'The Special Panic of Singing Sondheim'. *The New Yorker*, 23 December 2021. https://www.newyorker.com/culture/culture-desk/the-special-panic-of-singing-sondheim.

Giger, Andreas. 'Verismo: Origin, Corruption, and Redemption of an Operatic Term'. *Journal of the American Musicological Society* 60, no. 2 (2007): 271–315.

Goldblatt, David. 'Ventriloquism: Ecstatic Exchange and the History of Artwork'. *Journal of Aesthetics and Art Criticism* 51, no. 3 (1993): 389–98. https://doi.org/10.2307/431511.

Goosman, Stuart L. *Group Harmony: The Black Urban Roots of Rhythms & Blues*. Philadelphia: University of Pennsylvania Press, 2010.

Goosman, Stuart L. 'The Black Authentic: Structure, Style and Values in Group Harmony'. *Black Music Research Journal* 17, no. 1 (1997): 81–99.

Gordon, David. 'Review: Neil Diamond Musical A Beautiful Noise Is So Meh, So Meh, So Meh'. *Theatremania*, 4 December 2022. https://www.theatermania.com/broadway/reviews/review-neil-diamond-musical-a-beautiful-noise_94623.html.

Gordon, Robert, Olaf Jubin, and Millie Taylor. *British Musical Theatre since 1950*. Methuen Critical Companions. London: Bloomsbury Methuen, 2016.

Goron, Michael. *Gilbert and Sullivan's 'Respectable Capers': Class, Respectability and the Savoy Operas, 1877–1909*. Palgrave Studies in British Musical Theatre. Basingstoke: Palgrave, 2016.

Gossett, Philip. 'Writing the History of Opera'. In *The Oxford Handbook of Opera*, 1032–48. New York: Oxford University Press, 2015.

Gottlieb, Jack. *Funny, It Doesn't Sound Jewish: How Yiddish Songs and Synagogue Melodies Influenced Tin Pan Alley, Broadway, and Hollywood*. Albany: State University of New York Press, 2004.

Graber, Naomi. 'Memories That Remain: *Mamma Mia!* and the Disruptive Potential of Nostalgia'. *Studies in Musical Theatre* 9, no. 2 (2015): 187–98.

Gramsci, Antonio. *Selections from Prison Notebooks*. Translated by Quentin Hoare and Geoffrey Nowell Smith. London: Lawrence & Wishart, 1986.

Green, Kathryn, Warren Freeman, Matthew Edwards, and David Meyer. 'Trends in Musical Theatre Voice: An Analysis of Audition Requirements for Singers'. *Journal of Voice* 28, no. 3 (2014): 324–27.

Greene, Evie. *Queen of the Philippine Islands*. Shellac disc. London: Opal, 1910. D1 S2 BD4. British Library.

Gregory, Georgina. *Send In the Clones: A Cultural Study of the Tribute Band*. Sheffield: Equinox, 2012.

Grover-Friedlander, Michal. 'Voice'. In *The Oxford Handbook of Opera*, edited by Helen M. Greenwald, 318–34. New York: Oxford University Press, 2014.

Guettel, Adam, and Tina Landau. *Floyd Collins: Vocal Score.* New York: Williamson Music, 2001.

Guttman, Sharon E., Lee A. Gilroy, and R. Blake. 'Hearing What the Eyes See: Auditory Encoding of Visual Temporal Sequences'. *Psychological Science* 16, no. 3 (2005): 228–35. https://doi.org/10.1111/j.0956-7976.2005.00808.x.

Hadestown (Original Broadway Cast Recording). Compact Disc. Sing It Again Records, 2019.

Hall-Witt, Jennifer. *Fashionable Acts: Opera and Elite Culture in London, 1780–1880.* Becoming Modern: New Nineteenth-Century Studies. Lebanon, NH: University of New Hampshire Press, 2007.

Hallqvist, Hanna, Filipa M.B. Lã, and Johan Sundberg, 'Soul and Musical Theater: A Comparison of Two Vocal Styles'. *Journal of Voice* 31, no. 2 (2016): 229–235.

Hamilton. New York: Disney+, 2020. *Hamilton (Original Broadway Cast Recording).* Compact Disc. Atlantic Records, 2016.

Hamilton, Jack. *Just around Midnight: Rock and Roll and the Racial Imagination.* Cambridge, MA: Harvard University Press, 2016.

Hampton, Pete, and Laura Bowman. 'Tell Me, Dusky Maiden' (1906). CD. Vol. 1. *Black Europe—The Sounds and Images of Black People in Europe Pre-1927.* London: Bear Family Records BCD 16095, 2013. 1SS0009976 D3 BD20. British Library.

Harbert, Elissa. 'Embodying History: Casting and Cultural Memory in *1776* and *Hamilton*'. *Studies in Musical Theatre* 13, no. 3 (2019): 251–67.

Hartman, Saidiya. *Scenes of Subjection: Terror, Slavery and Self-Making in Nineteenth-Century America.* New York: Oxford University Press, 1997.

Harvard, Paul. *Acting through Song: Techniques and Exercises for Musical Theatre Performers.* London: Nick Hern Books, 2013.

Haskell, Jean, ed. *Encyclopedia of Appalachia.* Knoxville: University of Tennessee Press, 2006.

Hawkins, Stan, ed. *The Routledge Research Companion to Popular Music and Gender.* Abingdon: Routledge, 2017.

Hecht, Stuart J. *Transposing Broadway: Jews, Assimilation and the American Musical.* Basingstoke: Palgrave, 2011.

Heideking, Jurgen, Genevieve Fabre, and Kai Dreisbach. *Celebrating Ethnicity and Nation: American Festive Culture from the Revolution to Early 20th Century.* European Studies in American History. Oxford: Berghahn Books, 2001.

Henriques, Julian F., and Hillegonda Rietveld. 'Echo'. In *The Routledge Companion to Sound Studies,* edited by Michael Bull, 275–82. London: Routledge, 2018.

Hillery, George A. 'Definitions of Community: Areas of Agreement'. *Rural Sociology* 20 (1955): 111–23.

Hischak, Thomas S. *The Mikado to Matilda: British Musicals on the New York Stage.* Lanham, MD: Rowman & Littlefield, 2020.

Hobsbawn, Eric, and Terence Ranger, eds. *The Invention of Tradition.* Cambridge: Cambridge University Press, 2012.

Hobson, Vic. *Louis Armstrong and Barbershop Harmony.* Jackson: University of Mississippi Press, 2018.

Hodges Persley, Nicole. *Sampling and Remixing Blackness in Hip-Hop Theater and Performance.* Ann Arbor: University of Michigan Press, 2021.

Horn, David. 'Who Loves You Porgy? The Debates Surrounding Gershwin's Musical'. In *Approaches to the American Musical,* edited by Robert Lawson-Peebles, 109–26. Exeter: University of Exeter Press, 1996.

Hughes, Bethany. 'Singing the Community: The Musical Theater Chorus as Character'. In *Gestures of Music Theater: The Performativity of Song and Dance,* edited by Dominic Symonds and Millie Taylor, 263–75. New York: Oxford University Press, 2014.

Humble, Nicola. *The Feminine Middlebrow Novel 1920s to 1950s: Class, Domesticity, and Bohemianism.* New York: Oxford University Press, 2001.

Hunt, Katrina Margaret. 'The Female Voice in American Musical Theatre (1940–1955): Mary Martin and the Development of Integrated Vocal Style'. Doctoral thesis, Australian National University, 2016. https://openresearch-repository.anu.edu.au/handle/1885/101933.

Indraganti, Kiranmayi. *Her Majestic Voice: South Indian Female Playback Singers and Stardom, 1945–1955*. New York: Oxford University Press, 2016.

Into the Woods. DVD. New York: Image Entertainment, 1997.

Into the Woods (Original Broadway Cast Recording). Compact Disc. Masterworks Broadway. Sony BMG, 1990.

Jarman-Ivens, Freya. *Queer Voices: Technologies, Vocalities, and the Musical Flaw*. Critical Studies in Gender, Sexuality, and Culture. Basingstoke: Palgrave, 2011.

Jayasuriya, Katy. 'Femininity and Utopia in MGM's Adaptation of Sally Benson's Meet Me in St. Louis', *Studies in Musical Theatre*, 18, no. 1 (2024): 21–35. https://doi.org/10.1386/smt_00147_1.

Jendrysik, Mark. 'Fundamental Oppositions: Utopia and the Individual'. In The Individual and Utopia: A Multidisciplinary Study of Humanity and Perfection, edited by Clint Jones and Cameron Ellis, 27–43. Abingdon: Ashgate, 2015.

Jennings, Colleen Ann. 'Belting Is Beautiful : Welcoming the Musical Theater Singer into the Classical Voice Studio'. Doctoral thesis, University of Iowa, 2014. https://ir.uiowa.edu/cgi/viewcontent.cgi?article=5379&context=etd.

Johar, Swati. 'Psychology of Voice'. In *Emotion, Affect and Personality in Speech: The Bias of Language of Paralanguage*, 9–15. Cham, Switzerland: Springer International, 2016.

Johnson, Jake. 'Building the Broadway Voice'. In *The Oxford Handbook of Voice Studies*, edited by Nina Sue Eidsheim and Katherine Meizel, 475–92. New York: Oxford University Press, 2019.

Johnson, Jake. *Mormons, Musical Theater, and Belonging in America*. Urbana: University of Illinois Press, 2019.

Johnson, Jake, Masi Asare, Amy Coddington, Daniel Goldmark, Raymond Knapp, Oliver Wang, and Elizabeth Wollman. 'Divided by a Common Language: Musical Theater and Popular Music Studies'. *Journal of Popular Music Studies* 31, no. 4 (2019): 32–50. https://doi.org/10.1525/jpms.2019.31.4.32.

Johnston, Ruth. 'Technologically Produced Forms of Drag in "Singin' in the Rain" and "Radio Days"'. *Quarterly Review of Film and* Video 21, no. 2 (2004): 119–29.

Kane, Brian. *Sound Unseen: Acousmatic Sound in Theory and Practice*. New York: Oxford University Press, 2014.

Karpf, Anne. *The Human Voice: How This Extraordinary Instrument Reveals Essential Clues About Who We Are*. New York: Bloomsbury, 2006.

Kayes, Gillyanne. *Singing and the Actor*. London: Nick Hern Books, 2004.

Kendrick, Lynne. *Theatre Aurality*. Basingstoke: Palgrave, 2017.

Kenney, William Howland. *Recorded Music in American Life: The Phonograph and Popular Memory, 1890–1945*. New York: Oxford University Press, 1999.

Kessler, Kelly. *Destabilizing the Hollywood Musical: Music, Masculinity and Mayhem*. Basingstoke: Palgrave Macmillan, 2010.

Kessler, Sarah. 'Anachronism Effects: Ventriloquism and Popular Media'. Doctoral thesis, University of California, Irvine, 2016. https://escholarship.org/uc/item/6x08k529.

Keysers, Christian, and Vincent Gazzola. 'Social Neuroscience: Mirror Neurons Recorded in Humans'. *Current Biology* 20, no. 8 (2010): 353–54.

Kim, Hye Won. 'Performing Asian/American Women: Labor, Resistance, and (De) Compression in *The King and I and KPOP*'. *TDR: The Drama Review* 67, no. 3 (2023): 151–72. https://doi.org/10.1017/S1054204323000308.

Kirle, Bruce. *Unfinished Showbusiness: Broadway Musicals as Works-in-Process*. Carbondale: Southern Illinois University Press, n.d.

Kivy, Peter. *Authenticities: Philosophical Reflections on Musical Performance*. Ithaca, NY: Cornell University Press, 2012.

Klein, Hermann. *The Golden Age of Opera*. London: G. Routledge & Sons, 1933.
Knapp, Raymond. *The American Musical and the Formation of National Identity*. Princeton, NJ: Princeton University Press, 2005.
Knapp, Raymond. *The American Musical and the Performance of Personal Identity*. Princeton, NJ: Princeton University Press, 2006.
Koestenbaum, Wayne. *Queen's Throat: Opera, Homosexuality and the Mystery of Desire*. New York: Da Capo, 2001.
Komaniecki, Robert. 'Vocal Pitch in Rap Flow'. *Integral* 34 (2020): 25–45.
Kramer, Lawrence. 'The Voice of/in Opera'. In *On Voice*, 43–55.. Word and Music Studies. Leiden: Brill, 2014.
Kravchencko, Nataliia, Olena Zhykharieva, and Yuliia Konenets. 'Rap Artists' Identity in Archetypal Roles of Hero and Seeker: A Linguistic Perspective'. *Journal of Language and Linguistic Studies* 17, no. 1 (2021): 646–61.
Kreiman, Jody, and Diana Sidtis. *Foundations of Voice Studies: An Interdisciplinary Approach to Voice Production and Perception*. Hoboken, NJ: Wiley Blackwell, 2011.
Kumar, Krishan. *Utopianism*. Oxford: Open University Press, 1991.
Kun, Josh. *Audiotopia: Music, Race, and America*. Berkeley: University of California Press, 2005.
LaBelle, Brandon. *Acoustic Territories: Sound Culture and Everyday Life*. New York: Continuum, 2010.
LaBelle, Brandon. *Lexicon of the Mouth: Poetics and Politics of the Oral Imaginary*. London: Bloomsbury, 2014.
Lamb, Andrew. *Leslie Stuart—Composer of Florodora*. Forgotten Stars of the Musical Theatre. Oxford: Routledge, 2002.
Landau, Tina, Adam Guettel, and Wiley Hausam. 'Floyd Collins'. In *The New American Musical: An Anthology from the End of the Century*, 1–98. New York: Theatre Communications Group, 2003.
Langley, Carol. 'Borrowed Voice: The Art of Lip-Synching in Sydney Drag'. *Australasian Drama Studies* 48 (2006): 5–17.
Lasch, Christopher. *The Culture of Narcissism: American Life in an Age of Diminishing Expectations*. New York: W. W. Norton, 1991.
Leeuwen, Theo van. *Speech, Music, Sound*. Basingstoke: Macmillan, 1999.
Lehmann, Hans-Thies. *Postdramatic Theatre*. Abingdon: Routledge, 2006.
Lester, Alfred. 'My Motter'. London: Columbia 544 6474, 1915. C1816/4 D1 BD10 Paleophonics. British Library.
Levine, Lawrence W. *Highbrow-Lowbrow: The Emergence of Cultural Hierarchy in America*. Cambridge, MA: Harvard University Press, 1990.
Levitas, Ruth. *The Concept of Utopia*. Hertfordshire: Philip Allan, 1990.
Levitin, Daniel J. *This Is Your Brain on Music: The Science of a Human Obsession*. London: Atlantic Books, 2008.
Lhamon, W. T., Jr. *Raising Cain: Black Performance from Jim Crow to Hip Hop*. Cambridge, MA: Harvard University Press, 1998.
Lippman, Edward A. *The Philosophy and Aesthetics of Music*. Lincoln: University of Nebraska Press, 1999.
List, George. 'The Boundaries of Speech and Song'. *Ethnomusicology* 7, no. 1 (1963): 1–16.
Lockitt, Matthew. '"Love, Let Me Sing You": The Liminality of Song and Dance in LaChuisa's "Bernarda Alba" (2006)'. In *Gestures of Music Theater: The Performativity of Song and Dance*, edited by Dominic Symonds and Millie Taylor, 91–108. New York: Oxford University Press, 2014.
Lockitt, Matthew. '"Proposition": To Reconsider the Non-Singing Character and the Songless Moment'. *Studies in Musical Theatre* 6, no. 2 (2012): 187–98.
Loesser, Susan. *A Most Remarkable Fella: Frank Loesser and the Guys and Dolls in His Life*. New York: Hal Leonard, 1993.

Lowenthal, David. 'Nostalgia Tells It like It Wasn't'. In *The Imagined Past: History and Nostalgia*, edited by Malcolm Chase and Christopher Shaw, 18–32. Manchester: Manchester University Press, 1989.

Macpherson, Ben. 'Baudrillard on Broadway: Bio-Musicals, the Hyperreal and the Cultural Politics of "Simuloquism"'. *Journal of Interdisciplinary Voice Studies* 5, no. 1 (2020): 43–57.

Macpherson, Ben. '"Body Musicality": The Visual, Virtual, Visceral Voice'. In *Voice Studies: Critical Approaches to Process, Performance and Experience*, edited by Konstantinos Thomaidis and Ben Macpherson, 149–61. Oxford: Routledge, 2015.

Macpherson, Ben. *Cultural Identity in British Musical Theatre 1890–1939: Knowing One's Place*. Basingstoke: Palgrave, 2018.

Macpherson, Ben. 'Dynamic Shape: The Dramaturgy of Song and Dance in Lloyd Webber's "*Cats*"'. In *Gestures of Music Theater—The Performativity of Song and Dance*, edited by Dominic Symonds and Millie Taylor, 54–70. New York: Oxford University Press, 2014.

Macpherson, Ben. '"Eliza, Where the Devil Are My Songs?": Negotiating Voice, Text and Performance Analysis in Rex Harrison's Henry Higgins'. *Studies in Musical Theatre* 2, no. 1 (2008): 235–44.

Macpherson, Ben. '(Re)Authoring the 27 Club: Bewildered Voices, Acousmatic Audiophilia, and the Dangers of Listening-In'. *Journal of Interdisciplinary Voice Studies* 1, no. 2 (2016): 131–42.

Macpherson, Ben. 'Sing: Musical Theater Voices from *Superstar to Hamilton*'. In *The Routledge Companion to the Contemporary Musical*, edited by Jessica Sternfeld and Elizabeth L. Wollman, 69–77. New York: Routledge, 2020.

Macpherson, Ben. 'The Somaesthetic In-Between: Six Statements on Vocality, Listening and Embodiment'. In *Somatic Voices in Performance Research and Beyond*, edited by Christina Kapachoda, 212–26. Routledge Voice Studies. London: Routledge, 2021.

Macpherson, Ben. 'The Sweet Smell of Success: "*Florodora*" as Victorian Megamusical'. In *Blockbusters of Victorian Theater, 1850–1910: Critical Essays*, edited by Paul Fryer, 88–98. Jefferson, NC: McFarland, 2023.

Macpherson, Ben. 'A Voice and So Much More (or When Bodies Say Things That Words Cannot)'. *Studies in Musical Theatre* 6, no. 1 (2012): 43–57.

Mahar, William J. *Behind the Burnt Cork Mask: Early Blackface Minstrelsy and Antebellum American Popular Culture*. Urbana: University of Illinois Press, 1998.

Mahon, Maureen. *Black Diamond Queens: African American Women and Rock and Roll*. Refiguring American Music. Durham, NC: Duke University Press, 2020.

Mahon, Maureen. *Right to Rock: The Black Rock Coalition and the Cultural Politics of Race*. Durham, NC: Duke University Press, 2004.

Malawey, Victoria. *A Blaze of Light in Every Word: Analyzing the Popular Singing Voice*. Oxford Studies in Music Theory. New York: Oxford University Press, 2021.

Man, Kingson, Gabriela Melo, Antonio Damasio, and Jonas Kaplan. 'Seeing Objects Improves Our Hearing of the Sounds They Make'. *Neuroscience of Consciousness* 6, no. 1 (2020): 1–8. https://doi.org/10.1093/nc/niaa014.

The Manchester Guardian. 'Mr Alfred Lester—From Melodrama to Revue'. 7 May 1925.

Martell, Luke. 'Utopianism and Social Change: Materialism, Conflict and Pluralism'. *Capital and Class* 42, no. 3 (2018): 435–52. https://doi.org/10.1177/0309816818759230.

Martin, John. 'Characteristics of the Modern Dance'. In *The Twentieth-Century Performance Reader*, edited by M. Huxley and N. Witts, 295–302. 2nd ed. London: Routledge, 2002.

Mayo, Douglas. 'Are Bio-Musicals Taking Over Broadway and the West End?' *British Theatre*, 18 April 2018. https://britishtheatre.com/are-bio-musicals-taking-over-broadway-west-end/.

McConachie, Bruce A. 'New York Operagoing, 1825–50: Creating an Elite Social Ritual'. *American Music* 6 (1988): 181–92.

McCracken, Allison. *Real Men Don't Sing: Crooning in American Culture*. Durham, NC: Duke University Press, 2015.

McHugh, Dominic. *Loverly: The Life and Times of 'My Fair Lady'*. Broadway Legacies. New York: Oxford University Press, 2012.
McKee, Alison L. '"Think of Me Fondly": Voice, Body, Affect and Performance in Prince/Lloyd Webber's *The Phantom of the Opera*'. *Studies in Musical Theatre* 7, no. 3 (2013): 309–25.
McMillin, Scott. *The Musical as Drama*. Ithaca, NY: Cornell University Press, 2006.
McMullen, Tracy. *Haunthenticity: Musical Replay and the Fear of the Real*. Middletown, CT: Wesleyan University Press, 2019.
Means Fraser, Barbara. 'Revisiting Greece: The Sondheim Chorus'. In *Stephen Sondheim: A Casebook*, edited by Joanne Gordon, 223–50. New York: Garland, 2000.
Meizel, Katherine. *Multivocality*. New York: Oxford University Press, 2020.
Melton, Joan, ed. *Singing in Musical Theatre: The Training of Actors and Singers*. New York: Allworth, 2007.
Middleton, Richard. 'Rock Singing'. In *The Cambridge Companion to Singing*, edited by John Potter, 28–42. Cambridge: Cambridge University Press, 2000.
Miesen, Leendert van der. 'Studying the Echo in the Early Modern Period: Between the Academy and the Natural World'. *Sound Studies: An Interdisciplinary Journal (Special Issue: Sonic Things—Knowledge Formation in Flux)* 6, no. 2 (2020): 196–214.
Miller, Derek. 'Polyvocally Perverse; or, the Disintegrating Pleasures of Singing Along'. *Studies in Musical Theatre* 6, no. 1 (2012): 89–98.
Miller, Duncan. 'Underneath the Ground: Jud and the Community in *Oklahoma!*' *Studies in Musical Theatre* 2, no. 2 (2008): 163–74.
Milnes, G. *Play of a Fiddle: Traditional Music, Dance, and Folklore in West Virginia*. Lexington: University Press of Kentucky, 1999.
Mink, Casey. 'Why Broadway's "The Cher Show" Cast 3 Different Actors to Play the Iconic Diva'. *Backstage.com*, 2 December 2018. https://www.backstage.com/magazine/article/cher-show-broadway-director-jason-moore-interview-66145/.
Miranda, Lin-Manuel. *Hamilton: The Revolution—Being the Complete Libretto of the Broadway Musical, with a True Account of Its Creation, and Concise Remarks on Hip-Hop, the Power of Stories, and the New America*. New York: Grand Central Publishing, 2016.
Mitchell, Anais. *Working on a Song: The Lyrics of Hadestown*. New York: Plume, 2020.
Mitchells, K. 'Operatic Characters and Voice Type'. *Proceedings of the Royal Musical Association* 97 (1970): 47–58.
Mithen, Steven. *The Singing Neanderthals: The Origins of Music, Language, Mind and Body*. Cambridge, MA: Harvard University Press, 2005.
Monckton, Lionel, Howard Talbot, and Arthur Wimperis. *The Arcadians (Vocal Score)*. London: Chappell & Co., 1909.
Mook, Richard. 'White Masculinity in Barbershop Quartet Singing'. *Journal of the Society for American Music* 1, no. 4 (2007): 453–83.
Moore, Madison. 'Tina Theory: Notes on Fierceness'. *Journal of Popular Music Studies* 24, no. 1 (2012): 71–86.
More, Thomas. 'Utopia'. In *Three Early Modern Utopias*, edited by Susan Bruce, 1–148. Oxford World's Classics. New York: Oxford University Press, 1999.
Moreno, Jairo. *Musical Representations, Subjects, and Objects: The Construction of Musical Thought in Zarlino, Descartes, Rameau, and Weber*. Bloomington: Indiana University Press, 2004.
Morris, Mitchell, and Raymond Knapp. 'Singing'. In *The Oxford Handbook of the American Musical*, edited by Raymond Knapp, Mitchell Morris, and Stacy Wolf, 320–35. New York: Oxford University Press, 2011.
Morrison, Matthew D. 'Race, Blacksound, and the (Re)Making of Musicological Discourse'. *Journal of the American Musicological Society* 72, no. 3 (2019): 781–823. https://doi.org/10.1525/jams.2019.72.3.781.

Morrison, Matthew D. 'The Sound(s) of Subjection: Constructing American Popular Music and Racial Identity through Blacksound'. *Women & Performance: A Journal of Feminist Theory* 27, no. 1 (2017): 13–24. https://doi.org/10.1080/0740770X.2017.1282120.

Moss, Kenneth. 'St. Patrick's Day Celebrations and the Formation of Irish-American Identity, 1845–1875'. *Journal of Social History* 29, no. 1 (1995): 125–48.

Most, Andrea. '"We Know We Belong to the Land": The Theatricality of Assimilation in Rodgers and Hammerstein's *Oklahoma!*'. *PMLA Journal* 113, no. 1 (1998): 77–89.

Moten, Fred. *In the Break: The Aesthetics of the Black Radical Tradition*. Minneapolis: University of Minnesota Press, 2003.

Muñoz, José Esteban. *Cruising Utopia: The Then and There of Queer Futurity*. New York: New York University Press, 2009.

Napolitano, Marc. *Oliver! A Dickensian Musical*. New York: Oxford University Press, 2014.

Nester, Nancy L. 'The Empathetic Turn: The Relationship of Empathy to the Utopian Impulse'. In *The Individual and Utopia: A Multidisciplinary Study of Humanity and Perfection*, edited by Clint Jones and Cameron Ellis, 117–32. Oxford: Ashgate, 2015.

Nisbet, Robert. *The Sociological Tradition*. London: Heinemann, 1967.

Novello, Ivor, and Dorothy Dickson. *Used to You from 'Crest of a Wave'*. London: Rococo S2 BD6, Unknown. 1LP0118740. British Library.

Obama, Barack. *The Audacity of Hope: Thoughts on Reclaiming the American Dream*. New York: Crown, 2006.

The Obama White House. '"President Obama Welcomes the Broadway Cast of 'Hamilton'"'. YouTube, 14 March 2016. https://www.youtube.com/watch?v=V3bNmhbvU2o.

Oliver! (Original London Production). LP vinyl. London: Decca (SKL4105), 1960.

Olson, John. '*Company*—25 Years Later'. In *Stephen Sondheim: A Casebook*, edited by Joanne Gordon, 47–68. New York: Garland, 2000.

'Opening Chorus—Arcadians Are We'. London: Blue Amberol 2051, Unknown. C1816/D1 BD Paleophonics. British Library.

Opera Company, Edison Light. *Favorite Airs from The Arcadians*. Wax cylinder. New York: Edison (Amberol), 1913. 1CYL0002091 BD1 Black Amberol. British Library. http://www.library.ucsb.edu/OBJID/Cylinder0401.

Opoku-Baah, Collins, Adriana M. Schoenhaut, Sarah G. Vassall, David A. Tovar, Ramnarayan Ramachandran, and Mark T. Wallace. 'Visual Influences on Auditory Behavioral, Neural, and Perceptual Processes: A Review'. *Journal of the Association for Research in Otolaryngology* 22 (2021): 265–86. https://doi.org/10.1007/s10162-021-00789-0.

Palisca, Claude V. *The Florentine Camerata: Documentary Studies and Translations*. New Haven, CT: Yale University Press, 1989.

Peretz, Isabelle, and Robert Zatorre, eds. *The Cognitive Neuroscience of Music*. Oxford: Oxford University Press, 2003.

Peri, Jacopo. 'Peri's Dedication of the Score and Letter to the Reader'. In *Opera: A History in Documents*, edited by Piero Weiss, 14–17. New York: Oxford University Press, 2002.

Perry, George. *The Complete Phantom of the Opera*. London: Pavilion Books, 1987.

Perry, Imani. *Prophets of the Hood: Politics and Poetics in Hip Hop*. Durham, NC: Duke University Press, 2004.

Peters, Deniz. 'Musical Empathy, Emotional Co-Constitution, and the "Musical Other"'. *Empirical Musicology Review* 10, no. 1 (2015): 2–15.

Plantenga, Bart. *Yodel-Ay-Ee-Oooo*. London: Routledge, 2004.

Plato. *Republic*. Translated by John Llewelyn Davies and David James Vaughan. Wordsworth Classics of World Literature. Hertfordshire: Wordsworth Editions, 1997.

Platt, Len. *Musical Comedy on the West End Stage, 1890–1939*. Basingstoke: Palgrave, 2004.

Poizat, Michel. *The Angel's Cry: Beyond the Pleasure Principle in Opera*. Translated by Arthur Denner. Ithaca, NY: Cornell University Press, 1992.

Potter, John. *Vocal Authority: On Singing Style and Ideology*. Cambridge: Cambridge University Press, 1998.

Potter, John, and Neil Sorrell. *A History of Singing*. Cambridge: Cambridge University Press, 2014.

Preston, Katherine K. 'American Musical Theatre before the Twentieth Century'. In *The Cambridge Companion to the Musical*, edited by William A. Everett and Paul R. Laird, 3–28. 2nd ed. Cambridge: Cambridge University Press, 2002.

Preston, Robert, and Barbara Cook. *The Music Man (Original Broadway Cast)*. Compact Disc. Vol. 3. Broadway Classics. Hayes, Middlesex: Angel Records, 1992.

Purdy, Stephen. *Musical Theatre Song*. New York: Bloomsbury, 2016.

Quinn, Dave. '*A Beautiful Noise* Review: Neil Diamond Pulls Back the Curtain on His Catalog of Hits for New Broadway Musical'. *Entertainment Weekly*, 6 December 2022. https://ew.com/theater/theater-reviews/a-beautiful-noise-review-neil-diamond/.

Raynor, H. *A Social History of Music: From the Middle Ages to Beethoven*. London: Barrie & Jenkins, 1972.

Reedy, P. Scott. 'Meet Will Swenson. He's Playing Neil Diamond in the Jukebox Musical "A Beautiful Noise"'. *Patriot Ledger*, 16 June 2022. https://eu.patriotledger.com/story/entertainment/2022/06/16/broadway-bound-neil-diamond-musical-ready-boston-world-premiere-beautiful-noise/7621678001/.

Revill, George, and John R. Gold. '"Far Back in American Time": Culture, Region, Nation, Appalachia, and the Geography of Voice'. *Annals of the American Association of Geographers* 108, no. 5 (2018): 1406–21. https://doi.org/10.1080/24694452.2018.1431104.

Reynolds, Simon. *Retromania: Pop Culture's Addiction to Its Own Past*. London: Faber & Faber, 2012.

Ricoeur, Paul. 'The Creativity of Language'. In *Dialogues with Contemporary Continental Thinkers: The Phenomenological Heritage*, 15–35. edited by Richard Kearney. Manchester: Manchester University Press, 1984.

Ricoeur, Paul. 'Ideology and Utopia as Cultural Imagination'. *Philosophic Exchange* 7, no. 1 (1976): 17–28.

Ricoeur, Paul. *Lectures on Ideology and Utopia*. Edited by George H. Taylor. New York: Columbia University Press, 1986.

Rifkin, Jeremy. *The Empathetic Civilization: The Race to Global Consciousness in a World in Crisis*. New York: Penguin, 2009.

Riis, Thomas L. 'The Experience and Impact of Black Entertainers in England, 1895–1920'. *American Music* 4, no. 1 (1986): 50–58.

Rodmell, Paul. *Opera in the British Isles, 1875–1918*. Music in Nineteenth-Century Britain. Farnham: Ashgate, 2013.

Rodosthenous, George. '*Mamma Mia!* and the Aesthetics of the Twenty-First-Century Jukebox Musical'. In *The Oxford Handbook of the British Musical*, edited by Robert Gordon and Olaf Jubin, 613–31. New York: Oxford University Press, 2017.

Rose, Tricia. *Black Noise: Rap Music and Black Culture in Contemporary America*. Middletown, CT: Wesleyan University Press, 1994.

Rostosky, Arreanna. 'Amplifying Broadway after the Golden Age'. In *The Routledge Companion to the Contemporary Musical*, edited by Jessica Sternfeld and Elizabeth L. Wollman, 78–86. New York: Routledge, n.d.

Rothstein, Edward. 'Utopia and Its Discontents'. In *Visions of Utopia*, edited by Furaha D. Norton, 1–28. New York: Oxford University Press, 2003.

Rowe, Billy. 'Difference between "Hot" and "Swing" Mikados—Billy Rowe Gives Courier Readers the Real Low Down'. *Pittsburgh Courier*, 20 May 1939.

Rubel, Jeffrey. '"You Never Need an Analyst with Bobby Around": The Mid-20th Century Human Sciences in Sondheim and Furth's Musical *Company*'. *History of the Human Sciences* 35 (2021): 1–25.

Rush, Adam. 'Recycled Culture: The Significance of Intertextuality in Twenty-First Century Musical Theatre'. Unpublished thesis, University of Lincoln, 2017. https://repository.lincoln.ac.uk/articles/thesis/Recycled_culture_the_significance_of_intertextuality_in_twenty-first_century_musical_theatre/24325726?file=42747697.

Russell, Susan. 'The Performance of Discipline on Broadway'. *Studies in Musical Theatre* 1, no. 1 (2006): 97–108. https://doi.org/10.1386/smt.1.1.97_1.

Ryan, Mary. 'The American Parade: Representations of the Nineteenth-Century Social Order'. In *The New Cultural History*, edited by Lynn Hunt, 131–53. Studies on the History of Society and Culture. Berkeley: University of California Press, 1989.

Saint-Évremond, Charles de. 'Saint-Évremond's Views on Opera'. In *Opera: A History in Documents*, edited by Piero Weiss, 51–59. New York: Oxford University Press, 2002.

Sanders, Julie. *Adaptation and Appropriation*, 2nd ed. Oxford: Routledge, 2016.

Sargent, Lyman Tower. 'The Three Faces of Utopianism Revisited'. *Utopian Studies* 5, no. 1 (1994): 1–37.

Sargent, Lyman Tower. *Utopianism: A Very Short Introduction*. Very Short Introductions. New York: Oxford University Press, 2010.

Savran, David. 'Toward a Historiography of the Popular'. *Theatre Survey* 45, no. 2 (2004): 211–17.

Schechner, Richard. *Between Theater and Anthropology*. Philadelphia: Pennsylvania University Press, 1985.

Schechner, Richard. 'The Director's Process: An Interview with Rachel Chavkin'. *TDR: The Drama Review* 65, no. 1 (2021): 79–94.

Schonberg, Harold C. 'Stage View: The Surrender of Broadway to Amplified Sound'. *New York Times*, 15 March 1981.

Schrader, Valerie Lynn. '"Why We Build the Wall": Hegemony, Memory and Current Events in *Hadestown*'. *Studies in Musical Theatre* 16, no. 2 (2022): 117–31. https://doi.org/10.1386/smt_00093_1.

Schwartz, Hillel. *The Culture of the Copy: Striking Likenesses, Unreasonable Fascimiles*. New York: Zone Books, 2014.

Schwartz, Michael. 'The Music Man Cometh: The Tuneful Pipe Dreams of Professor Harold Hill'. In *Text and Presentation*, edited by Stratos E. Constantinidis, 169–78. Jefferson, NC: McFarland, 2008.

Scot, Reginald. *The Discoverie of Witchcraft*. London: Rowman & Littlefield, 1973.

Secrest, Meryle. *Stephen Sondheim: A Life*. London: Bloomsbury, 1998.

Sedikides, Constantine, and Tim Wildschut. 'Finding Meaning in Nostalgia'. *Review of General Psychology* 22, no. 1 (2018): 48–61.

Segrave, Kerry. *Jukeboxes: An American Social History*. Jefferson, NC: McFarland, 2002.

Senelick, Laurence. *The Changing Room: Sex, Drag and Theatre*. London: Routledge, 2000.

Severs, Jeffrey. '"Is It like a Beat without a Melody?: Rap and Revolution in *Hamilton*'. *Studies in Musical Theatre* 12, no. 2 (2018): 141–52.

Shapiro, Ann Dhu. 'Music in American Pantomime and Melodrama, 1730–1913'. *American Music* 2, no. 4 (1984): 49–72.

Shelby, Tommie, and Paul Gilroy. 'Cosmopolitanism, Blackness, and Utopia'. *Transition* 98 (2008): 116–35.

Shuker, Roy. *Popular Music: The Key Concepts*. 4th ed. Oxford: Routledge, 2017.

Silver, Daniel, Monica Lee, and C. Clayton Childress. 'Genre Complexes in Popular Music'. *PloSOne* 11, no. 5 (2016): 1–23. https://doi.org/10.1371/journal.pone.0155471.

Singleton, Jermaine. *Cultural Melancholy: Readings of Race, Impossible Mourning and African American Ritual*. Champaign: University of Illinois Press, 2015.

Slobin, Mark. *Fiddler on the Move: Exploring the Klezmer World.* Oxford: Oxford University Press, 2000.

Smart, Mary Ann, ed. *Siren Songs: Representations of Gender and Sexuality in Opera.* Princeton, NJ: Princeton University Press, 2000.

Smith, Cecil. *Musical Comedy in America.* New York: Theatre Arts Books, 1950.

Smith, Jacob. *Vocal Tracks: Performance and Sound Media.* Berkeley: University of California Press, 2008.

Smith, Susan J. 'Performing the (Sound)World'. *Environment and Planning: Society and Space* 18, no. 5 (2000): 615–37.

Smithson, Florence. *The Pipes of Pan.* London: Columbia 542 6467, 1915. C1816/4 DL BD4 Paleophonics. British Library.

Snell, Merrie. *Lipsynching.* Bloomsbury Studies in Sound. London: Bloomsbury, 2020.

Snelson, John. *Andrew Lloyd Webber.* Yale Broadway Masters. New Haven, CT: Yale University Press, 2004.

Snowman, Daniel. *The Gilded Stage: A Social History of Opera.* London: Atlantic Books, 2009.

Sondheim, Stephen, Bert Shevelove, Larry Gelbart, and James Lapine. *Four by Sondheim, Wheeler, Lapine, Shevelove and Gelbart.* New York: Hal Leonard, 2000.

Southern, Eileen. *The Music of Black Americans.* 2nd ed. New York: W. W. Norton, 1983.

Spencer, David. 'Floyd Collins: Review'. *Aisle Say—New York* (blog), 1994. http://www.aislesay.com/NY-FLOYD-COLLINS.html.

Stafford, David, and Caroline Stafford. *Fings Ain't Wot They Used T'Be: The Lionel Bart Story.* London: Omnibus, 2011.

Sternfeld, F. W. 'A Note on "Stile Recitativo"'. *Proceedings of the Royal Musical Association* 110 (1983): 41–44.

Sternfeld, Jessica. *The Megamusical.* Bloomington: Indiana University Press, n.d.

Stew, Heidi Rodewald, and Annie Dorsen. *Passing Strange (Script).* New York: Dramatists Play Service, 2008.

Stewart, Susan. *On Longing.* Baltimore: Johns Hopkins University Press, 1985.

Stoever, Jennifer Lynn. *The Sonic Color Line: Race and the Cultural Politics of Listening.* New York: New York University Press, 2016.

Storey, John. '"Expecting Rain": Opera as Popular Culture?' In *High-Pop: Making Culture into Popular Entertainment*, edited by J. Collins, 32–55. Malden, MA: Blackwell, 2002.

Stuart, Leslie, E. Boyd-Jones, Paul Rubens, and Owen Hall. *Florodora: A Musical Comedy (Vocal Score).* London: Francis, Day & Hunter, 1899.

Swayne, Steve. *How Sondheim Found His Sound.* Ann Arbor: University of Michigan Press, 2005.

Symonds, Dominic. 'Capturing the "Sung" to Make It "Song"'. In *Gestures of Music Theater: The Performativity of Song and Dance*, edited by Dominic Symonds and Millie Taylor, 9–21. New York: Oxford University Press, 2014.

Symonds, Dominic. 'The Corporeality of Musical Expression: The Grain of the Voice and the Actor-Musician'. *Studies in Musical Theatre* 1, no. 2 (2007): 167–81.

Symonds, Dominic. 'Starlight Expression and Phantom Operatics: Technology, Performance, and the Megamusical's Aesthetic of the Voice'. In *The Routledge Companion to the Contemporary Musical*, edited by Jessica Sternfeld and Elizabeth L. Wollman, 87–97. Oxford: Routledge, 2020.

Symonds, Dominic, and Pamela Karantonis. 'Introduction: Empty Houses, Booming Voices'. In *The Legacy of Opera: Reading Music Theatre as Experience and Performance*, edited by Dominic Symonds and Pamela Karantonis, 11–24. Amsterdam: Rodopi, 2011.

Tarvainen, Anne. 'Singing, Listening, Proprioceiving: Some Reflections on Vocal Somaesthetics'. In *Aesthetic Experience and Somaesthetics*, edited by Richard Shusterman, 1:120–44. Studies in Somaesthetics. Leiden: Brill, 2018.

Taylor, Lib. 'Voice, Body and the Transmission of the Real in Documentary Theatre'. *Contemporary Theatre Review* 23, no. 3 (2013): 368–79.

Taylor, Millie, ed. *Studies in Musical Theatre* 6, no. 1, Special Themed Issue: "If I Sing": Voice and Excess'. (2012).

Taylor, Millie. 'Lionel Bart: British Vernacular Musical Theatre'. In *The Oxford Handbook of the British Musical*, edited by Robert Gordon and Olaf Jubin, 483–506. New York: Oxford University Press, 2016.

Taylor, Millie. *Musical Theatre, Realism and Entertainment*. Ashgate Interdisciplinary Studies in Opera. Farnham: Ashgate, 2012.

Taylor, Millie. 'Singing and Dancing Ourselves: The Politics of the Ensemble in "*A Chorus Line*"'. In *Gestures of Music Theater: The Performativity of Song and Dance*, edited by Dominic Symonds and Millie Taylor, 276–92. New York: Oxford University Press, 2014.

Taylor, Millie. *Theatre Music and Sound at the RSC*. Palgrave Studies in British Musical Theatre. Basingstoke: Palgrave, 2018.

Teague, Jessica E. 'The Recording Studio on Stage: Liveness in "Ma Rainey's Black Bottom"'. *American Quarterly* 63, no. 3 (2011): 555–71.

'Tell Me Pretty Maiden (Are There Any More at Home like You?)', Shellac disc. London: Columbia, 1902. British Library Shelfmark 1LP0002808. British Library.

Thaut, Michael H. *Rhythm, Music, and the Brain: Scientific Foundations and Clinical Applications*. Oxford: Routledge, 2007.

Thomaidis, Konstantinos. 'Editorial: Listening Across'. *Journal of Interdisciplinary Voice Studies* 4, no. 1 (2019): 3–6.

Thomaidis, Konstantinos. *Theatre and Voice*. Basingstoke: Palgrave, 2017.

Thomaidis, Konstantinos, and Ben Macpherson. 'Introduction: Voice(s) as a Method and an In-Between'. In *Voice Studies: Critical Approaches to Process, Performance and Experience*, edited by Konstantinos Thomaidis and Ben Macpherson, 3–9. Oxford: Routledge, 2015.

Thompson, Deborah J. 'Searching for Silenced Voices in Appalachian Music'. *GeoJournal*, 65 (2006): 67–78.

The Times. 'Death of Miss Florence Smithson'. 13 February 1936.

The Times. 'Shaftesbury Theatre'. 29 April 1909.

Tomlinson, Gary. *Metaphysical Song: An Essay in Opera*. Princeton, NJ: Princeton University Press, 1999.

Traubner, Richard. *Operetta: A Theatrical History*. London: Victor Gollancz, 1984.

Turner, Victor. *Dramas, Fields, and Metaphors: Symbolic Action in Human Society*. Ithaca, NY: Cornell University Press, 1974.

Valencia, Brian D. 'What a Crescendo—Not to Be Missed: Loudness on the Musical Stage'. *Studies in Musical Theatre* 10, no. 1 (2016): 7–17. https://doi.org/10.1386/smt.10.1.7_1.

Vallance, Tom. 'Celeste Holm: Oscar-Winning Actress Best Known for "All About Eve" and "High Society"'. *The Independent* online, 16 July 2012. https://www.independent.co.uk/news/obituaries/celeste-holm-oscarwinning-actress-best-known-for-all-about-eve-and-high-society-7946744.html.

Verstraete, Pieter. 'The Frequency of Imagination: Auditory Distress and Aurality in Contemporary Music Theatre'. Doctoral thesis, University of Amsterdam, 2009.

Voegelin, Salome. *Listening to Noise and Silence: Toward a Philosophy of Sound Art*. London: Bloomsbury, 2010.

Voegelin, Salome. *The Political Possibility of Sound: Fragments of Listening*. New York: Bloomsbury, 2018.

Voegelin, Salome. *Sonic Possible Worlds: Hearing the Continuum of Sound*. London: Bloomsbury, 2014.

Wald, Gayle. '*Passing Strange* and Post-Civil Rights Blackness'. *Humanities Research* 16, no. 1 (2010): 11–33.

Wall, Carey. 'There's No Business like Show Business: A Speculative Reading of the Broadway Musical'. In *Approaches to the American Musical*, edited by Robert Lawson-Peebles, 24–43. Exeter: University of Exeter Press, 1996.

Warfield, Patrick. 'The March as Musical Drama and the Spectacle of John Philip Sousa'. *Journal of the American Musicological Society* 64, no. 2 (2011): 289–318.

Weidman, Amanda. *Brought to Life by the Voice: Playback Singing and Cultural Politics in South India*. Oakland: University of California Press, 2021.

Weinert-Kendt, Rob. 'From Rags to Revolutionary: "Hamilton" Tells a True American Story'. *America* 212, no. 8 (2015).

Wells, Elizabeth A. 'After Anger: The British Musical of the Late-1950s'. In *The Oxford Handbook of the British Musical*, edited by Robert Gordon and Olaf Jubin, 273–90. New York: Oxford University Press, 2016.

Whitfield, Sarah K. 'Disrupting Heteronormative Temporality through Queer Dramaturgies: *Fun Home, Hadestown and A Strange Loop*'. *Arts (MDPI)* 9, no. 2 (2020): 69–82. https://doi.org/10.3390/arts9020069.

Whitfield, Sarah, and Sean Mayes. *An Inconvenient Black History of British Musical Theatre 1900–1950*. London: Methuen, 2021.

Williams, Bert. *Really the Blues?-A Blues History 1893–1959*. CD. Vol. 1. 4 vols. Toronto: West Hill Radio Archives, 2010. 1SS0010415 D1 BD6 WHRA. British Library.

Willson, Meredith. *'But He Doesn't Know the Territory'—The Making of Meredith Willson's 'The Music Man'*. Minneapolis: University of Minnesota Press, 2009.

Wilson, Nia. '*Hadestown*: Nontraditional Casting, Race, and Capitalism'. *TDR: The Drama Review* 65, no. 1 (2021): 188–92.

Winkler, Amanda Eubanks. 'Politics and the Reception of Andrew Lloyd Webber's *The Phantom of the Opera*'. *Cambridge Opera Journal* 26, no. 3 (2014): 271–87.

Wise, Tim. 'How the Yodel Became a Joke: The Vicissitudes of a Musical Sign'. *Popular Music* 31, no. 3 (2012): 461–79.

Wise, Tim. 'Yodel Species: A Typology of Falsetto Effects in Popular Music Vocal Styles'. *Radical Musicology* 2 (2007). http://www.radical-musicology.org.uk/2007/Wise.htm.

Wolf, Stacy. *Changed for Good: A Feminist History of the Broadway Musical*. New York: Oxford University Press, 2011.

Wolf, Stacy. 'Hamilton's Women'. *Studies in Musical Theatre* 12, no. 2 (2018): 167–80.

Wolf, Stacy. 'Introduction'. In *The Oxford Handbook to the American Musical*, edited by Knapp Raymond, Mitchell Morris, and Stacy Wolf, 3–6. New York: Oxford University Press, 2011.

Wolf, Stacy Ellen. 'Keeping Company with Sondheim's Women'. In *The Oxford Handbook of Sondheim Studies*, edited by Robert Gordon, 365–83. New York: Oxford University Press, 2014.

Woll, Allan. *Black Musical Theatre from 'Coontown' to 'Dreamgirls'*. New York: Da Capo, 1991.

Wollman, Elizabeth L. '*Passing Strange* (Review)'. *Theatre Journal* 60, no. 4 (2008): 635–37.

Wollman, Elizabeth L. *The Theater Will Rock: A History of the Rock Musical, from Hair to Hedwig*. Ann Arbor: University of Michigan Press, 2009.

Wollner, Clemens. 'Audience Responses in the Light of Perception-Action Theories of Empathy'. In *Music and Empathy*, edited by Elaine King and Caroline Waddington, 139–56. London: Routledge, 2017.

Woolf, Brandon. 'Negotiating the "Negro Problem": Stew's Passing (Made) Strange'. *Theatre Journal* 62, no. 2 (May 2010): 191–207.

Woolf, Virginia. 'Middlebrow'. In *The Death of the Moth, and Other Essays*, 176–87. London: Hogarth Press, 1942.

Zadan, Craig. *Sondheim & Co.* 2nd ed.. London: Nick Hern Books, 1990.

Zelechow, B. 'The Opera: The Meeting of Popular and Elite Culture in the Nineteenth Century'. *History of European Ideas* 16 (1993): 261–66.

Zipes, Jack. *Breaking the Magic Spell: Radical Theories of Folk and Fairy Tales*. 2nd ed. Lexington: University Press of Kentucky, 2002.

Žižek, Slavoj, and Mladen Dolar. *Opera's Second Death*. New York: Routledge, 2001.

Zuccarini, Carlo. 'The (Un)Pleasure of Song: On the Enjoyment of Listening in Opera.' In *Gestures of Music Theater: The Performativity of Song and Dance*, edited by Dominic Symonds and Millie Taylor, 22–36. New York: Oxford University Press, 2014.

Zuim, Ana Flavia. 'Speech Inflection in American Musical Theatre Compositions.' Florida Atlantic University, 2012.

Index

For the benefit of digital users, indexed terms that span two pages (e.g., 52–53) may, on occasion, appear on only one of those pages.

Figures are indicated by an italic *f* following the page number.

Abbate, Carolyn, 7, 24, 33–34, 51, 53, 212n.5, 213n.21, 215n.79
acousmêtre, 5–6, 71
African vocal styles, 43–44, 205
  call-and-response, 84–85, 89, 120–21, 123
  commodification and appropriation, 14–15
  cries, 80–81, 84–85, 86
  growls, 86, 89–90
  'noise', 86
  'primitive', 86
  rasps, 86, 89–90
  shouts, 86, 89–90
  'unruly', 86
  See also 'Blacksound'; crooning
Alston, Adam, 57–58, 67–68, 79–80, 112, 129–30, 159–60. *See also* decadent appropriation
Altman, Rick, 178
American Dream, The (cultural concept), 11, 80, 137–38, 139–41, 186–87
amplification, 25, 26, 49, 57, 62–63, 65–66, 67, 78, 84–85, 92, 98, 133–34, 200–1, 220n.26. *See also* microphones
Appalachian folk song, 54–55, 68–69, 70, 74, *103*, 221n.42 See also *Floyd Collins,* yodel
appropriation. *See* decadent appropriation
Arcadians, The (1909), 16–17, 100, 112–13, 114–15, 116, 120–21, 130, 137–38, 164, 202–3
  'Arcadians Are We', 101–3, 152–53
  Florence Smithson vocal performance, 108
  'The Joy of Life', 107
  Melancholic vocality of 'My Motter', 109–10
  'The Pipes of Pan', 107
aria(s) (song form), 24, 36, 39, 40–41, 44–45, 64, 65–66, 107–8. *See also* recitative
Asare, Masi, 52–53, 80–81, 126–27
  'twice-heard' performance, 52–53
  See also belt(ing); Schechner, Richard
aural anachronism(s), 179. *See also* bio-musical; ventriloquism
Barthes, Roland, 5–6, 153, 189–90
Baudrillard, Jean, 17, 186, 198, 204. *See also* hyperreal(ity); simulacrum; simulation
Bauman, Zygmunt, 16–17, 115, 118
  liquid modernity, 115–16
  See also chorality
Beautiful: The Carole King Musical (2014), 173, 188–89
Beautiful Noise: The Neil Diamond Musical, A (2022), 171–72, 173, 188–89
belt(ing) voice. *See* voice
bio-musical, 17, 170–71, 200–1, 204–5, 209–41
  trope of concerts in finale, 188–89
  trope of recording studio sessions, 188–89
  vocal imitation, 13, 171–72, 189, 191, 195
  See also simulacrum; simulation; simuloquism
blackface (theatrical practice), 14–15, 42–43, 86–87
Black Crook, The (1866), 45–46, 47–48 See also *Evangeline*
'Blacksound', 14–15, 59, 77, 88–89, 92, 119, 120, 125–26, 160, 205
  as methodology, 14–15
  See also Morrison, Matthew D.
Bloch, Ernst, 9–10, 84. *See also* utopia: 'abstract' utopia
blues music, 42–43, 200–1
Bowman, Laura, 219n.22. *See also* Hampton, Pete
Boym, Svetlana, 17, 169–71, 176, 197, 204. *See* nostalgia
Bradfield, W. Louis, 60–61, 62–63, *77* See also *Florodora*; voice: speak-singing
burlesque (theatrical form), 3, 42–43, 44–48, 49

Bush Jones, John, 112–13, 114. *See also* Jones, John Bush, fragmented musicals
Butler, Judith, 174–75
Byrne, Kevin, 168–69. *See* Fuchs, Emily; jukebox musicals

cakewalk, 43–44, 54, *62* See also *Florodora*
call-and-response, 68–70, 81, 84–85, 89, 120–21, 123, 137–38. *See* African vocal styles
cantorial song, 55–56, 134–35, 143, 200–1
Carlson, Marvin, 170. *See* ghosting
Carter, Tim, 35–36. *See* opera
Castrati, 38, 67. *See also* voice: countertenor (falsetto)
Cavarero, Adriana, 5–6, 7–8, 73, 77, 108, 154
Chase, Malcolm (and Christopher Shaw), 17, 140. *See also* nostalgia
Chavkin, Rachel. See *Hadestown*
Chernow, Ron, *155–56* See also *Hamilton*
Cher Show, The (2018), 189–90, 190*f*
Chion, Michel, 5–6, 175–76. *See also acousmêtre*; lipsynching
chorality, 107, 111, 114–15, 116, 123–24, 128, 149, 164, 202–3, 206
  contingent chorality, 111–12, 115, 116, 118, 121, 122–24, 127–28, 129–30, 136, 137–38, 144, 152, 154–55, 202–3, 247 (*see also* utopian)
  as dystopian, 204
  intentional chorality, 107–9, 111, 115–16, 119, 122–24, 127–28, 129–30, 163, 164, 202–3, 246–47 (see also community)
  liquid chorality, 115–16, 117–18, 119, 121–24, 129–30, 147, 150–51, 167, 202–3, 204
Chorus, 8, 59–61, 66, 84–85, 92–93, 97–100, 101–7, 111, 114, 119, 126–27, 130, 138–39, 202–3
  as spectacle, 202–3
  synchronicity, 97, 101, 102–3, 105, 114, 121–22, 123, 124, 127–28, 152–53, 164
  unison, 97, 101, 105, 106, 121–22, 123, 144, 155
  as utopian 247–48
  vocal blend(ing), 101–2, 104, 105, 107, 114, 115, 121, 123, 124, 137–38, 152–53, 154–55, 163, 164
Chorus Line, A (1975), 110, 203, 205–6
Chude-Sokei, Louis, 88. *See also* Williams, Bert
Clément, Catherine, 7, 38
Comic opera, 44–45. *See also* Gilbert and Sullivan; operetta
community, 16–17, 203. *See also* chorality; Turner, Victor
Company (musical) (1970), 16–17, 120–21, 124–25, 127–28, 130, 133–45, 147, 202–3, 204
  'Another Hundred People', 117–18
    as dystopian utopianism, 117–18
    as vocally empty space, 117–18, 119, 201–2
  'Company' (song), 138n.67, 147–48
  counterpoint and individuality, 137–38
  See also chorality
Connor, Steven, 5–6, 17, 71, 106, 180, 202–3
  ventriloquism, 17
  'Vocalic body', 5–6
  See also chorality
crooning, 244. See also African American vocal styles; Guys and Dolls; McCracken, Allison, 15–16, 54–55, 57, 78, 79, 89, 92, 139
culture
  high(brow) culture, 3–4, 7–8, 16, 25–26, 29–30, 41–42, 43–46, 58–59, 61, 63–64, 65, 74, 75–76, 79, 91–92, 200
  low(brow) culture, 3–4, 16, 25–26, 48–49, 52–53, 58–59, 61–62, 70, 74–75, 81, 83, 91–92, 180
  mass culture, 29
  middlebrow culture, 3–4
  musical theatre as middlebrow, 16, 48–49, 54–55, 56, 57–59, 61, 64
  musical theatre and popular culture, 3, 4–5, 7–8, 13, 14, 18–19, 29, 48–49, 55–56, 88, 112–13, 125–26, 146, 169, 189, 194, 195
  See also Savran, David; Woolf, Virginia

Dear Evan Hansen (2016), 49, 58, 104, 164
decadence. *See* decadent appropriation
decadent appropriation, 58–60, 62–63, 64, 88, 91–93, 157, 197, 200–2, 205
  appropriation, 55–56
  decadence, 57–58
Delphic Oracle (Pythia), 181–82, 184–85. *See also* ventriloquism
Derrida, Jacques, 5–6, 73, 128. *See also* echo
Descartes, Rene, 34–35, 39–40
de Shields, Andre, 129, 131–32. *See also* Muñoz, José Esteban
Die Zauberflote (1791), 39
  Queen of the Night aria, 39
  vocalise, 39
Dolan, Jill, 9–11, 129, 199–200
  'utopian performative', 9–10
Dolar, Mladen, 5–6, 7–8, 39, 40–41, 217n.121

Dyer, Richard, 9–10, 13, 99, 106, 119, 130, 131–32, 199, 220n.31
'Entertainment and Utopia', 9
See also utopia
Dystopia, 11, 13, 62, 87, 104, 106, 107, 111, 115–16, 117–18, 119, 121–22, 123–24, 128, 147, 201–3, 204–5
and dystopian utopianism (Beaumont), 117–18, 167
See also nostalgia; utopia

echo (vocal effect), 70–71
and *acousmêtre*, 87
and 'acoustic relationality', 73, 127–28, 145–46
and coordinates of space, 1, 71–72
digital delay, 70–71, 200–1
Echo-duet in *Rappresentazione di anima e di corpo, 70–71*
fleshness of, 71–73, 97–98
as metaphysical, 70–71, 200–1
as residual material in myth, 70–71, 72–73
utopian properties of, 73, 74, 128
see also *Floyd Collins*; yodel
Edwardes, George, 23, 46–48, 198
Eidsheim, Nina Sun, 14–15
Ensemble, 92–93, 99–100, 102, 105–6, 107, 110, 114–18, 119, 126, 202–3. *See also* chorus; chorality
Evangeline (or, the Belle of Acadia) (1874), 46, 47–48. *See also Black Crook, The*
extravaganzas, 41–42, 45
extra-vocal acts
hum(ming), 120–21
emotional response of, 121
as frustrating utopia, 121
laugh (laughter or laughing), 81–82
as escape, 82
as feminine, 81
as subversion, 82
scream(ing) as demarcation of musical theatre of opera, 65–66, 80, 92, 199
shout(ing), utopian potential of, 153, 154, 187–88
sneezing as disruption, 80, 82–83
See also Connor, Steven; LaBelle, Brandon

Fach system, 38. *See also* voice types
Fleeger, Jennifer, 5–6, 175–76. *See also* voice
Florentine Camerata, 27–28, 29–30
Florodora (1899), 54–55, 59, 63–64, 69, 75–76, 77, 92, 109–10, 219n.22
'Phrenology', 60–61
presence of speech-inflection, 77
'Queen of the Philippine Islands'
Evie Greene (performer), 59–61, 62–63
influence of opera on musical comedy, 59–60
'Tell Me Pretty Maiden', 61
Cf. 'Tell Me Dusky Maiden', 62
influence of cakewalk dance style,.62
Floyd Collins (musical) (1994), 1, 68, 200–1, 205. *See also* echo; yodel
folk music, 3, 42–43, 53, 55–56, 68–69, 70, 74, 120, 142, 200–1
frictive vocalisations, 89–90
Frith, Simon, 6–7
Fuchs, Emily, 168–69, 170–71. *See also* Byrne, Kevin; jukebox musicals

ghosting, 170, 171, 173–74, 181, 188–89, 205
ghosting singing, 173–74, 205–6
Gilbert (W.S.) and Sullivan (Arthur), 23, 44–45, 46–47, 54–55, 101
gospel music, 3–4, 54, 55–56, 84–85, 89, 120–21, 125–27, 200–1
Gramsci, Antonio, 16
and hegemony, 56–57
Guettel, Adam, 68–71 See also *Floyd Collins* (musical)
Guys and Dolls (1950), 54–55, 75, 87, 89, 103–4, 139
'Marry the Man Today', 81–82
aural accommodation, 82
call-and-response, 81
'My Time of Day', 77–79
Queer vocality (Sky Masterson), 79, 200–1
utopian aesthetics of Adelaide's vocal character, 80–81
vocality as cultural resistance, 79–80, 205
as vocal melting pot, 75–76

Hadestown (2019), 16–17, 23, 120, 130, 131, 201, 202–3
A cappella as subversive resistance (Hermes), 129
Call-and-response effect in 'Why We Build the Wall', 123
.dominance of macro-voiceworld, 120–21
Fates as close-harmony trio, 121–23, 124–25, 153–54
Orpheus (vocal analysis), 201, 206
'Road to Hell', 120–21
humming as utopian paradox, 121
influence of African vocal practices 146

Hadestown (2019) (*cont.*)
utopian potential of chorality in 'We Raise Our Cups', 124
See also African vocal styles; chorality; intermediate vocality; List, George
Hamilton (musical) (2015), 1, 13, 155
'Helpless' and separate emotional spaces, 162
compare 'Till There Was You', 141
Plosive intensity in 'My Shot', 157–58
'Satisfied' and masculine space of rap, 161–62
'The Schuyler Sisters' and pop trios, 161
'Who Lives, Who Dies, Who Tells Your Story'
'fabricated' unity, 163
and patriarchy, 164
See also chorality; hip hop; intermediate vocality; List George; rap
Hammerstein II, Oscar, 8, 23, 102
Hampton, Pete. *See* Laura Bowman
Harrison, Rex (as Henry Higgins), 131–32, 133–34, 135–36, 138–39. *See also* intermediate vocality; *My Fair Lady*
hip hop (music), 3, 13, 25, 49, 55–56, 75, 157, 158–59, 160–61, 164, *200–1* See also *Hamilton*
Holm, Celeste, 24–25. *See also* Richard Rodgers
Hughes, Bethany, 16–17, 97, 100
'manifestation of community', 16–17, 97, 100–2, 113, 114, 130, 203
hum(ming). *See* extra-vocal acts
hyperreal(ity), 186–87, 189, 191–96, 197, 204
as characteristic of musical theatre, 187–88
as characteristic of recorded music, 188–89
See also bio-musicals; simulacrum; simulation; simuloquism

intermediate vocality, 133–36, 164, 165–66. *See also* rap; List, George; speech inflection; voice: speak-singing; Sprechstimme
Into the Woods (1987), 99, 147, 158–59, 162–63
flow in the Witch's rap ('Prologue), 150
function of spoken narrator, 149, 152–53
predominance of micro-voiceworld, 150–51
shouting as parallel to singing ('Your Fault'), 154
utopian ambivalence of intermediate vocality, 150–51
utopian imperative of chorality 'Children Will Listen', 154–55
See also chirality; intermediate vocality; List, George
In Town (1892), 46–49

jazz music, 3–4, 42–43, 53, 54, 55–56, 57, 75, 77–78, 82–83, 84–85, 120, 157, 200–1
Jersey Boys (2005), 188, 193–94, 195–96
Jesus Christ Superstar (1971), 51–52, 90, 125. *See also* countertenor (falsetto); vocal cry
Johns, Glynis, 131–32, 133–34, 135–36. *See also* intermediate vocality
Johnston, Ruth, 173–74. *See also* ghost singing
Jones, John Bush, 112–13, 114
'fragmented' musicals (or, concept musicals), 112–13
jukebox (cultural history of), 169
jukebox musical, 3–4, 167–68
and ghosting, 181
and nostalgia, 169–70, 197
types of jukebox musical, 168–69, 170–71
See also bio-musicals, ghosting

King, Carole see *Beautiful*; Mueller, Jessie
Knapp, Raymond, 1–2, 76–77, 139–41, 148–49, 151
Komaniecki, Robert, 157–58
application to *Hamilton,* 159–62
five pitching techniques in rap, 157–59
See also *Hamilton*; intermediate vocality; rap
Kumar, Krishan, 102–3. *See also* utopia
Kun, Josh, 79–80
'Yidditude', 79–80, 103–4

LaBelle, Brandon, 65–66, 81, 154. *See also* Connor, Steven; extra-vocal acts
Lacan, Jacques, 5–6, 40–41
Landau, Tina. See *Floyd Collins*
Langley, Carol. *See* lipsynching
Lapine, James. See *Into the Woods*
Lasch, Christopher
'culture of narcissism', 112, 154
Last Five Years, The (2001), 52–53, 110, 203
laughter, 81. *See also* extra-vocal acts
'Legit' voice (legitimate). *See* voice
Lerner, Alan Jay. See *My Fair Lady*
Les Misérables (1985), 24, 52–53, 92, 102, 164–65, 198, 203, 205–6
lipsynch(ing) (also known as miming, dubbing), 172–74, 175–76, 178, 179–80, 197
mainstream success of, 174
as 'vocal drag', 172–73, 174, 179–80, 187, 188–89, 191–94, 195, 204
See also ghost singing
List, George, 134, 135*f*, 154, 157, 164, 165–66. See also *Hamilton*; intermediate vocality; *Into the Woods*; *Music Man, The*; *Oliver!*
Little Night Music, A (1973), 131, 133–34, 149
'Send in the Clowns' (song), 131, 133

See also intermediate vocality; Johns, Glynis
liturgical music, 3, 134–35, 143–44, 200–1
Loesser, Frank. See *Guys and Dolls*
Loewe, Frederick. See *My Fair Lady*
logocentrism (also *logos*), 5–6
London Road (2011), 8–9, 205–6. *See also* intermediate vocality
Love Never Dies (2010), 1, 6, 199, 200

macro-voiceworld *See* voiceworld(s)
Malawey, Victoria, 77, 223n.90
Martell, Luke, 11–12, 82, 83, 200–1
utopia (as pluralistic), 11–12, 83, 91
McMillin, Scott, 8, 9–10, 24, 99, 102
book time, 8, 24
chorus/ensemble as 'voice of the musical', 97, 101–2
lyric time, 8, 24
and 'space of vulnerability', 9–10, 99–100, 107–8, 110–11, 117–18, 131–32, 154, 163
See also chorality
megamusical, 8–9, 64, 65, 200
melancholy (melancholia), 88, 109–11, 119, 130, 145–46, 203, 205, 206
Freud, Sigmund, 111
vocal melancholy as utopian, 111
melodrama, 3, 41–42, 45, 110, 142
Merman, Ethel, 26, 52–53. *See also* belt(ing)
microphone(s), 25, 49, 51–52, 57, 78, 133–34, 178–79
as visual cue in bio-musicals, 177, 188–89
See also amplification
micro-voiceworld. *See* voiceworld(s)
Mikado, The (1885), 55–56
discussion of adaptations, 54–56
minstrelsy, 3, 41–43, 44–45, 77, 78, 82–83, 86–87, 88. See also *Passing Strange*; Williams, Bert
Miranda, Lin-Manuel. See *Hamilton*
Mitchell, Anaïs. See *Hadestown*
Monckton, Lionel. See *Arcadians, The*
Monteverdi, Claudio, 27–28, 41–42
L'Orfeo (1607), 27–28, 33–34, 41–42
More, Thomas, 10–11. *See also* utopia
Morris, Mitchell, 1–2
Morrison, Matthew D. 14–15, 42–43, 77–78, 160, 232n.10. *See also* 'Blacksound'
Mozart, Wolfgang Amadeus, 37–38, 40–41, 50
Don Giovanni (1788), 37–38
Don Juan (baritone), 37–38, 50–51
Don Pedro (bass), 37–38, 50–51
The Magic Flute (1791), 24
Mueller, Jessie, 172, 173–75, 178, 179–80, 191. See also *Beautiful*; lipsynching
Muñoz, José Esteban, 17, 129–30, 177–78
musical comedy, 16, 25–26, 41–43, 45–48, 49, 56–57, 59–61, 75, 77, 79–80, 87, 100–1, 104, 108–9, 110, 111, 168, 200–1
musical theatre (history of), 23, 41
music hall, 3, 43, 44–45, 46–49, 54–56, 60–61, 77, 142, 143, 146–47, 180
vocal character of music hall, 77, 92, 109–10
Music Man, The (1957), 136, 142–43, 144–45, 154–55, 167–68
emotional distance created by un/voiced plosives ('Seventy-Six Trombones'), 138
Harold Hill as redeemable huckster, 136–37, 201–2
Harold Hill's voice as paradox of utopia, 141–42
Robert Preston (actor) as 'high-class hollerer', 136–37
'Rock Island' as pure dialogue, 136
'Till There Was You' and utopian vocality, 139
'Ya Got Trouble'
as chant, call and, 137–38
contrast with townsfolk chorality, 137–38
See also intermediate vocality; List, George
My Fair Lady (1956), 104, 105–6, 131, 138–39. *See also* Harrison, Rex; intermediate vocality

Nester, Nancy L.
empathy as character of utopia, 108–9, 203, 205
Nixon, Marni. *See* ghost singing
nostalgia, 17, 140–42, 146–47, 169–70, 172–73, 177–78, 179–80, 189, 195–96, 204–5
and Baudrillardian full meaning, 193, 194–95
musical theatre as manufactured nostalgia, 169
rediscovered nostalgia, 185–86, 193, 195–97
reflective nostalgia, 169–70, 172, 176, 179, 182, 184–86, 193–94, 204
restorative nostalgia, 169–70, 172, 176, 177–78, 179, 185–86, 189, 204
See also bio-musical; jukebox musical; utopia as 'counterpart'

Oklahoma! (1943), 24–25, 57, 58, 97, 101, 102, 103–4, 109, 114, 118, 130, 164, 205. *See also* chorality
Oliver! (1960), 142, 155, 167–68
effect of inverse plosives ('Be Back Soon'), 144
'Reviewing the Situation', 144–47
Jewish influence (Fagin's vocality), 144–46, 205

Oliver! (1960) (*cont.*)
Vernacular 'shouty' vocal quality, 142–43
'You've Got to Pick a Pocket or Two', 143–44
unvoiced plosives (cf. Harold Hill), 143–44
See also intermediate vocality; List, George; music hall
opera, 3, 7, 16, 41–43
as fetishizing 'warbling throats', 35–36
as high culture, 16, 30, 31
as 'historically closed', 30
history of form, 27
metaphysical vocality, 16, 32, 46
in musical theatre, 200–1
not musical theatre, 3–4, 24, 25–27
Opera buffa, 23, 38, 45–46
Opéra comique, 23
Opera seria, 23, 35–36
Squillo (in opera), 25–26
use in musical theatre scholarship, 50
See also belt(ing); Mladen Dolar
'operatic voice', 24
as 'desired, worshipped and fetishized', 24, 35–36
problems with term, 212n.3
operetta, 3, 16, 23, 25–26, 44–45, 46–48, 49, 54, 55–57, 59–61, 62–64, 65–66, 67–68, 74, 107, 200–1
Orpheus (character in opera), 33–34, 40–41

Parker, Roger, 24
See Carolyn Abbate
Passing Strange (2008), 54–55, 84, 167, 200–1
'Baptist Fashion Show', 84–86, 120–21
call-and-response as 'genre-specific prosodic marker', 84–85
gospel music, 84–85
jazz phrasing, 84–85
speech-inflection, 84–85
'The Black One', 86–87
'Blacksound', 88
influence from minstrelsy, 86–87
influence of Bert Williams, 88
melisma, 87
mugging, 87
twang, 87
vocal exaggeration, 87
'Church Blues Revelation/Freight Train', 84–86
call-and-response, 84–85
influence of African American popular vocal practices, 85
See also Morrison, Matthew D.; Stoever, Jennifer Lynne
Peri, Jacopo, 23, 27–28, 33, 41–42
L'Euridice, 23, 33, 41–42
Persley, Nicole Hodges, 160, 163, 164, 165–66
Phantom of the Opera, The (musical) (1986), 1, 54–55, 63, 92
Daaé, Christine (character), 1, 9, 51, 199–200
Straight tones 81
voice as inversion of operatic ideals 80–81
Phantom (character), 1, 9, 51, 199–201
countertenor as otherworldly (queer) 81–82
voice as 'subversive resistance', 67–68
Raoul, Vicomte de Chagny (character), 1, 67–68
Vocal parallel to The Phantom, 67
'The Music of the Night', 67
'Think of Me', 65–66
cadenza, 66
sound design 80–81
See also extra-vocal acts
Pharsalia. see ventriloquism
phōnē, 5–6. see also logocentrism (*logos*)
Plato, 10–11, 14, 33
Poizat, Michel, 7, 39, 51
vocal cry, 39–41, 51–52, 53
polyvocality (also polyphonic vocality), 99, 114, 182–84
pop (or popular) music, 3–5, 6–7, 14–15, 25, 42–43, 45, 47–48, 49, 51–52, 53, 55–56, 58, 63–64, 67, 77–78, 80–81, 82–83, 85–88, 111, 120–21, 125–27, 146, 157, 159, 169, 171, 174, 175, 188–89, 200–1. *See also* 'Blacksound'; Frith, Simon, Morrison, Matthew D.
poperetta. *See* megamusical
popular voice (and singing) styles, 16, 47–48, 56–57, 74–78, 82–83, 85, 86–87, 89, 113, 189. See also Simon Frith, Matthew D. Morrison
Potter, John, 16, 56
Theory of vocal style, 16, 56
decadent phase, 57, 60–61
development phase, 56–57
renewal phrase, 57, 68
voice and 'stylistic pluralism', 57
See also Alston, Adam; decadent appropriation; Gramsci, Antonio

rap, 49, 134–35, 150, 157–59, 200–1
association with African American masculinity, 159, 160–61
comparison with recitative, 237n.98

as cultural commentary (or resistance), 160, 165–66
See also *Hamilton*; hip hop; intermediate vocality; Komaniecki, Robert; List, George
recitative, 24, 35, 36, 44–45, 64–65, 133, 134–35
comparison to aria, 24
types of, 32–33
rediscovered nostalgia. *See* nostalgia
Retromania, 169. *See also* bio-musical; jukebox musicals; nostalgia
revue, 45, 110, 168
French revue, 41–42
Reynolds, Simon. *See* Retromania
Ricoeur, Paul, 16, 27, 30
'reaffirmation' (ideology), 27, 29, 30, 41, 45, 51, 53
'rupture' (utopia), 27, 29, 41, 44–49, 200–2
social imaginaire, 27–28, 41, 45, 47–48
rock (and rock and roll) (music), 3, 25, 49, 51–52, 53, 54–56, 75, 86, 89, 125, 126, 137–38, 140–41, 157, 200–1, 204
Rock voice. *See* voice
Rodewald, Heidi. See *Passing Strange*
Rodgers, Richard, 24–25, 77, 155–56. *See also* Hammerstein II, Oscar; *Oklahoma!*
Rothstein, Edward, 10–11, 167, 224n.123
Runyon, Damon. See *Guys and Dolls*

Sargent, Lyman Tower, 11–13, 16–17, 101–2, 104. *See also* utopia
Savran, David, 3
Schechner, Richard, 52–53, 80–81. *See also* Asare, Masi; belt(ing)
scream(ing). *See* extra-vocal acts
Shaw, Christopher (and Malcolm Chase), 13, 140. *See also* nostalgia
shout(ing). *See* extra-vocal acts
Show Boat (1928), 57
'Cotton Blossom' chorus as comment on segregation, 102
Shuker, Roy, 55–56
simulacrum, 17, 187. *See also* simulation
simulation, 172–73, 186–87, 191–94, 195–96, 197, 198, 204. *See also* simulacrum
simuloquism, 195–98, 204–5
bio-musicals, 204–5
definition of, 195
relation to rediscovered nostalgia, 204
Sondheim, Stephen, 16–17, 23, 112–13, 131, 133–34, 147–48
sonority, 7, 10, 14, 17–18, 33, 51, 74, 81, 151, 154–55, 164
Sternfeld, Jessica, 65. *See also* megamusical
Stewart, Mark (Stew). See *Passing Strange*
Stoever, Jennifer Lynn, 14–15
'the listening ear', 15, 87
'the sonic color line', 14–15
Stuart, Leslie. See *Florodora*
Summer: The Donna Summer Musical (2017), 178–79, 182–84, 189
'MacArthur Park': Polyphonic vocality in, 182–84
Symonds, Dominic, 1–2, 53, 67, 220n.26

Talbot, Howard. See *Arcadians, The*
Taylor, Millie, 1–2, 51, 170, 234n.44
Tessitura, 24–25, 37–38, 60–61, 75–76, 77–78
Thomaidis, Konstantinos, 5, 6
'listening across', 13–14, 15–16, 17–18, 199, 205
Thompson, A. M. *See The Arcadians*
Tina: The Tina Turner Musical (2018), 172, 176–77, 180–81, 190–91
Comparison of original and biomusical, 233
'River Deep, Mountain High', 216
Tin Pan Alley, 77, 78, 168
Tomlinson, Gary, 7, 33–34, 37–38, 50–51
Opera voice as metaphysical, 7
Turner, Tina, 171, 172, 180–81, 204. *See also* bio-musicals; Simuloquism; *Tina: The Tina Turner Musical*; Warren, Adrienne
Turner, Victor, 16–17
communitas, 105
See also chorality; community

utopia
'abstract' utopia (Ernst Bloch), 9–10, 199–200
as accommodating, 11–12
as affective not structural, 9–10
as changeable, 11–12, 13
as 'dreaming forward' (Paul Gilroy), 84, 85, 91, 167
dystopia as opposite, 11, 13, 62, 87, 104, 106, 111, 115–16, 118, 123, 128, 147, 167, 185, 201–2, 204–5
and empathy, 109–11, 130, 203, 205
and failure, 135–36, 167, 185
as 'index of the possible', 9–10, 199–200
and melancholy, 109–11, 203, 205
nostalgia as 'counterpart', 17, 140–41, 167–68, 170–71, 204
as paradoxical, 11, 201–2, 205
as political ideal, 10–11, 201–2

utopia (*cont.*)
as 'something better' (Dyer), 9–12, 13, 17, 91–92, 130, 131–32, 141, 142, 152, 154, 164, 169–70, 200, 206
and tyranny, 167
vocal utopia, 9–10, 12–14, 15
see also Dolan, Jill; Dyer, Richard; Kumar, Krishan; Levitas, Ruth; Martell, Luke; Rothstein, Edward; Sargent, Lyman Tower

vaudeville, 41–42, 45, 200
ventriloquism, 17, 179, 187, 189, 193–95, 197, 204, 211–12
as audio filter, 17
'twinning' voices, 180–81, 184
Victorian popular entertainment, 180
as 'vocalic space', 185
vocal plurality, 182
See also bio-musicals; Connor, Steven; Delphic Oracle (Pythia); nostalgia
vibrato, 25, 59–60, 61, 81, 82, 101, 133, 190–91
virtuosity, 24, 35–36, 38, 40–41, 43, 52–53, 108, 109, 133. *See also* Merman, Ethel; *Arcadians, The*: 'The Pipes of Pan'
vocal cry, 39–41, 51–53
or 'money notes', 51
See also belt(ing) voice
vocal drag, 172–73, 174–79, 187, 188–89, 193–94, 195, 204, 233–35. *See also* bio-musicals; lipsyching; nostalgia
'vocal dramaturgy', 97, 100, 103, 145–46, 147, 148–49, 165–66. *See also* chorality; chorus; ensemble
vocalise, 36, 39, 40–41, 69–71, 72–73, 221n.49
Voegelin, Salomé, 9–10, 14, 222n.59
voice
baritone, 37–38, 61, 66–67, 69, 70–71, 75–77, 139
bass, 37–38, 89–90, 101, 122
belt(ing) voice, 26, 52–53, 81, 84–85, 110–11, 122, 161, 204
countertenor (and falsetto), 51–52, 66–68, 69–70, 122, 127–28, 134, 145–46, 162–63, 200–2
discussion of registers, 1–2, 209n.4
as haptic, 97–98, 99–100, 124
as an 'in-between', 6–8, 10, 12–14, 16, 17, 18–19, 49, 70, 75, 78, 88, 90–91, 195
'legit' voice, 25–26, 57, 58, 149, 152, 197, 204, 217n.121, 223n.99
as material, 7, 33, 37–38, 40–41, 71, 73, 127–28, 189–90
as metaphysical, 7, 16, 32, 44–45, 46, 47–49, 50, 51–52, 53, 58–61, 65, 67–68, 69–74, 90, 92, 99, 108–10, 181, 184–85, 200
mezzosoprano (or alto), 38, 50–51, 59–60, 61, 80–81, 82–83, 122
as a 'problem', 5, 18–19
Rock voice, 54, 89–91, 92, 190–91, 197, 200–1, 204
soprano, 38, 39, 50–51, 65–66, 69–70, 75–77, 81, 101, 107–8, 151
speech-inflection, 16–17, 47–48, 57, 60–61, 62–63, 77–80, 81, 84–85, 87–88, 89–90, 92
Sprechstimme (Speak-singing), 92, 109–10, 122–23, 129, 131–32, 133–34, 136, 145–46, 152
tenor, 9, 37–38, 51–52, 64–65, 66–67, 101, 122, 198
voice types (general), 1–2, 37–39, 40–41, 50–51, 53
See also Clément, Catherine; Fleeger, Jennifer; List, George; Malawey, Victoria; Potter, John
voiceworld(s), 58–59, 60–61, 64, 65, 67, 68–69, 74, 80, 88, 92–93, 100–1, 111–12, 117, 118, 119, 120, 129–30, 134–37, 138–39, 142–43, 147, 148–49, 153, 157–58, 160–61, 164, 171, 172–73, 187, 189, 197–98, 199, 200, 202, 205–6
comparison with soundworld, 219n.12
and decadence, 82, 83, 84
as dramaturgical, 97, 226n.12
macro-voiceworld, 97, 99–100, 101–6, 107–8, 113–16, 119, 120–24, 127–28, 130, 137–38, 142, 143–44, 150–51, 152, 154–55, 167, 202–3
micro-voiceworld, 99–100, 107, 109–10, 111, 114, 115–16, 124–29, 130, 150–51, 167–68, 202, 203
as utopian, 74, 92

Warren, Adrienne, 172, 177, 180–81, 204. *See also* bio-musicals; simuloquism; *Tina: The Tina Turner Musical*; Turner, Tina
Webber, Andrew Lloyd, 1, 23, 63–64, 198
Whitfield, Sarah, 43–44, 129–30
Wicked (2003). *See* Wolf, Stacy
Williams, Bert, 42–43, 88. *See also* blackface; minstrelsy; *Passing Strange*: 'The Black One'
Willson, Meredith. See *Music Man, The*
Wimperis, Arthur. See *Arcadians, The*

Wolf, Stacy, 1–2, 3, 4, 50–51, 81, 82, 160–61, 163
analysis of 'For Good' (*Wicked*), 50, 209n.4
Woolf, Virginia, 3–4. *See also* middlebrow

Yiddish comic vocality, 15–16, 79–81, 82–83, 89, 92, 103–4. *See also* Kun, Josh
yodel, 70–71, 72–73, 77, 92
'feathering,' 70
yodeleme, 70, 74

Zipes, Jack, 147–48, 149, 152
Zuim, Ana Flavia, 24–25, 77, 133
musical theatre voice as 'different muscular demand' to opera, 24–25
See also speech-inflection